NORTH OF SMOKEY

A NOVEL BY

DAVID DOUCETTE

CAPE BRETON
UNIVERSITY
·P·R·E·S·S·

Cape Breton University Press recognizes the support of the NOVA SCOTIA Province of Nova Scotia, through the Department of Tourism, Tourism, Culture and Heritage Culture and Heritage. We are pleased to work in partnership with the Culture Division to develop and promote our cultural resources for Nova Scotians. We acknowledge the support of the Canada Council for the Arts for our publishing program.

Canada Council   Conseil des Arts
for the Arts   du Canada

Cover design Cathy MacLean, Pleasant Bay, NS.
Layout by Mike Hunter, Louisbourg, NS.
Printing by Marquis Book Printing, Cap Ste Ignace, QC.
Printed in Canada. Typeset in Caslon and printed on 100% recycled post-consumer fibre, Certified EcoLogo and processed chlorine free, manufactured using biogas energy.

Library and Archives Canada Cataloguing in Publication

Doucette, David, 1966-

    North of Smokey / David Doucette.

ISBN 978-1-897009-23-9

    I. Title.

PS8557.O7858N67 2007   C813'.6   C2007-905592-

Cape Breton University Press
PO Box 5300
Sydney, Nova Scotia
B1P 6L2 Canada

NORTH OF SMOKEY

A NOVEL BY

DAVID DOUCETTE

CAPE BRETON
UNIVERSITY
·P·R·E·S·S·

one

In the precious time he had, Frank Curtis played feverishly. With clear forehead and a clear view, his eye followed the strings along the fingerboard and out the window, to where the wood road rose and where his brothers Clifford and William had climbed. Both by now were up the mountain. Autumn leaves stirred, the moss bank unaffected.

Their father, Adrian was at work in the cellar, pulling nails out of a board. He had to stop, to listen past the lamplight. Who the hell? Not Frank, surely to God. But the other two are up on the mountain. We got visitors? That's it, go now... up the scale. Flow. That's what the good players have bred in them. The little I do know, I hear. Ah, listen. Merciful Christ – one of them has something in him.

Jessie was having a lay-down in the room nearest the road, eyes wide open, moist as she had just been drifting off. She stared at the ceiling. That can't be Frank. But the other two sons are in the woods? He knows he shouldn't be at that violin, Clifford will take a strip out of him if he catches him. But listen now, rhythm. I coached him on the foot, out by the backroom stove that day. Make it lively, get shoulder and wrist into it, I told him. Stomp too, make music there equally. Just you listen, that is some powerful bow hand, I'll tell you that right now! Archie MacDonald from the North Shore was the only one around to tune the instrument, he did so when he came to see Adrian. It always fell out. I don't know how it was music ever got learnt here. The day after Archie left the house I saw Frank pick it up, the end of summer. He tuned it all by himself, by ear. Where'd he learn that? The other boys didn't know; no one in this house did. Clifford... that set him off, his youngest brother showing him up. The violin was supposed to be his interest. When Frank got out half a tune, the older tore it out of his hands. 'That ain't in tune, bai!' But I heard: it was. Adrian hollered when the two started in on each other: 'I'll take the thing outside myself, set it on the chopping block and split her right down the middle! If yous two don't simmer down.... If I don't get some peace around here. How's that? Make an example. And then I'll burn it.' William was looking on, unmusical, the middle child, the politician. Clifford sulked with the inarticulate anger of the region, its spiteful jealously. Grace had waited on the stairs, to see.

But – hear now! A strathspey and, that's right, a reel: the hard, hard stuff you have to have a foot for! Go, Frank, you play on. You play on because there's no one here to stop you and it does a heart good to hear someone in this house with some bit of know-how. As God is my witness you'll get up on stage yet, talent like that. Saint Peter's Parish, the Christmas Concert. Saint Patrick's at the very least. I'll put the word in, needed or not, I'll give you some courage. Oh. But oh no, Clifford – seeing his youngest brother better him, tch, tch, in front of the parish. That won't do. He had put in time on the instrument too. He knew notes, where the fingers fell. Not the foot, tragically. Not like this other one, here.

Frank Curtis studied the wood road, past curtains, sharp eye scanning the banks, tongue bitten. His brothers would return only where they went in, the rest is too steep.

He broke into a fiery reel, the first part major. He dropped all into a minor, the driving melancholic wolf-pack notes that constituted the soul of this stuff. He shuffled these low notes, only barely hearing his father tap and call up the chimney stone.

"You liven her up, bai. You keep on. Drive the hell out of her like there's no tomorrow, I say. I can't take the quiet!"

He heard his mother too, now that she had swung a foot over the bed. Bringing the second foot down, she stood to kick the balls of her feet, snap her heels, her feet moving like fish breaking. Ball. Heel. Thump. The matron stomped, the vibrant wood floor awakened by her sock-footed quality.

Grace called from above:

"What the hell's all the racket! Yas all half retarded?"

Frank caught sight of a red jacket... William's. He saw the pale-blue plaid work-shirt, tail out. He took a gentle step back from the curtains, but the frog caught. He yanked to free it, but snagged the curtain and brought the whole assembly down. Fabric encased struggling arms, it clutched tuning pegs and bound him like an invalid.

The kitchen door came open with a thief's touch. Frank turned. In full frontal, Clifford came marshalling forward, Frank's mouth a circle. The elder hauled off and broadly struck the younger's temple with the fleshy part of a fist. The violin escaped, fell to smack the woodbox, its bridge flicking free with a twang and disappearing under the table where the dog cowered. A bounce, and the instrument lay arrested, face down on the linoleum. A lank Clifford hissed, put his whole arm into a backhand. Brash knuckles hardened by the woods struck Frank, unready to stand his ground. With glistening tears he whipped the bow out for action, positioned its threat near his brother's face. William was at the door, eager, knob in hand, freckles cast to brown. This was coming. He knew this was coming.

"I only want you to," said an intimate Clifford to Frank in vicious half-whisper wholly invitational. "I only want you to."

Half waiting to see what would happen, half hoping her Frank would take a stand, Jessie stood erect at the living room doorway, her mouth opened to speak, ready to call out. She had to step aside though: the hatch was rising at her feet. Adrian's cocked monkey face peered from the black, hand catching poorly above his head, the sharp hatch handle cutting his flesh.

"Hear... what's going on up here! You two, is it? At each other's throats again. Well, the pair of you, I say.... So help my God, I'll get a switch of some sort and settle this score myself. Make an example out of yas. He can play it, mister! He's got a right to it as well as any. It's mine to begin with! So you ease off."

"I'll ease off, soon as this little prick learns his place around here. Just look now what he done to the violin!"

"I didn't do it! He made it go flying! He hit me in the face!"

"Which I intend to again soon as they aren't around. Don't sleep tonight."

Frank took his ear and broke burly into the backroom slamming the door with all his might. He climbed the bunks, lay back, cried into a pillow. Thirteen, in February. And every day growing. He won't be able to dish it out soon because I'll not have to take it. Time, only time. Wait and see what's in store for you. Wait and see if what's right doesn't win out.

The porch door slammed. Boots paused by the woodstove. Grace had entirely descended from upstairs, now looking boldly at William, her face closing in: "What happened?" William wove expansively, a full hand – as if he alone were the most insulted here today.

"I don't know how to put up with it any longer, the rambunctiousness. It's plaguing the soul right out of me." Jessie adjusted weight at the oven door, checked bread, frowned in the soaring heat. The bread had not fallen. Adrian spoke from the hatch:

"And you. You control your kids, you. You're up here. And I'm calling for outright control, for once!" The hatch sealed easily, in the bitter humour.

Frank blew, looked along his pillow. Past the glass, autumn leaves twirled on the property border. But Clifford achingly walked into sight for the woods, the menace of his shirttails accenting his sliminess, twelve-gauge slung over a forearm. The elder turned, looked back for the house, looked for the backroom window. Frank averted his hot cheeks, felt the cold tears on the lumpy pillow.

But within minutes, the boy again contemplated the crispy red in the grey maples. He turned for the beech, that particular leaf slowest to yield: tough, not ready like the others. Its harsh foliage, a dead copper. The beech leaf could twirl the whole winter through and not let go; it might not let go and twirl through the next. Frank had really played the violin. This was the affront, the tragedy. He knew in his heart he could get better. His mother Jessie said that when he was a baby he only ever stopped crying when the radio came on; turn it off and he'd scream blue murder. The batteries died; the radio itself was no more; and no one knew what became of it.

Frank Curtis had no cunning. He had perseverance. Patience. He could emerge from this shadow, from any dark spot. This is what it was to grow up after all. And it was true… one day he would get big. And most definitely, one day, right does become the thing to win out.

two

The ocean froze. The floe could be reached.

During the night, when high northern drift arrived to isolate the water of Ingonish Beach, it occurred. The blockade ended surface movement and deep solidification took place, enough to allow walking on saltwater. Temperature played its role. At three a.m. the mercury had dropped to minus fifty-one.

It was February 19 and this coming Friday, Frank Curtis would turn fourteen. It had been more than a year since the violin incident. Now, at five-foot-six, shoulders broad and neck thick, Frank was big for his age. He was the dead spit of his grandfather Joel Robertson. Jessie had said Frank had the Robertson blood, and from this stock came the strongest men ever to live North of Smokey.

Frank's green eyes were on the wiry grey Mililica. He wanted to see her reaction in the frost out here, down off the beach, her four paws on a frozen flat world neither had ever known. The destination was past the cropping floe, to open water where the ducks waited.

The flattest breadth ever, this crunching white sea. Each looked behind at the hundred feet or so back to shore as iron skies bore down to give the feeling all was an impressive game, boy and dog merely game pieces come to life, set free on this expansive board. Latent seals barked.

Frank exhaled, tasting ice at his cracked lip. The air held at minus forty. The night before, mercury dye had deepened to marrow red, to a speck registering minus forty-four at bedtime. A wax stub on the living room sill lit the reading of it. He expected the cold to put the stub out.

Sound travelled from a long way off out here; unburdened by moisture, the Arctic air mass could only yield. Every event in nature seemed at arm's-length. Far off, ice cracked like a whip at the ear, a distant batch groaned, as if at hand. Sound came crystalline. An eagle whooshed, single crows flapped. Kelp trimmed beached ice, its sniff-worthy rot also covering distance. Yet, dead, lead calm.

Frank's thumb drew aside the locking clasp and with a hard flick he broke open the shotgun. He spied down the chamber to see light. His tanned leather mittened right hand comfortably cupped the weapon at the break, the other adjusted the coiled rope at his shoulder.

He hoped for open water at the promontory head. Yesterday, travelling the greater promontory, he had spotted ducks floating on a swollen current. The water appeared to support the flock, giving it a place to land and fish, to hide it blackly from predators. Frank carried no gun yesterday. He was allowed none. This discovery of game, this discovery on his own, prompted this particular disobedience.

Frank and Mililica climbed onto the floe, only to make worse time. Frank used a flat mitten; upper arms and shoulder balanced him where footing was improper.

"Out of my way I said. Now I don't want you to be in my way, now."

The dog bent its ears. Frank spied emerald pools, imagined incredible depths under black bottoms.

Mililica halted: they had arrived at open water.

Choppy frigid sea arrested their eyes as they blinked out the Arctic gust, whipping around the headland, entering Frank's hood, tugging the grain of the dog's fur.

The ducks were under the pink granite cliffs where ocean waters pounded and sloshed. In cascading crystals, salt spray was thrown to heights enough for their spillage to coat slate croppings.

And yet ricocheting waters defended these cliffs, working constantly to hold off the insistent floe. Shooting a duck in ricocheting waters meant the kill came on its own out to the floe, drifting to where they could walk over and fish it out with rope and iron hook.

Mililica shifted her paws, backing up.

"Nervous, dog? Don't be, girl. Wait. Then you be nervous."

Frank had considered having Millie go in after shot game; that consideration had come the night before, in a warm bed. He saw now she could never do it. Water this cold, current this strong would freeze her instantly. It would pull her under and sweep her out to sea without the least resistance. She might be good company, but of little value in the hunt.

"You good company, girl?"

Frank had only recently stopped abusing her, particularly his pelting her with snowballs to drive her home whenever he was about to set foot off the property. But here she was, good, out here. He never believed she could be this obedient. Instincts had taken over – was that it? She feared being far away from her home and so stayed close. She pissed frequently as strategy to find her own way back, should need arise. She had pressed up against his leg at the beach, not wanting to come out. It was the border collie in her. Devotion, is what Frank's father had to say. On returning to the house after walks in the snow, Frank saw this devotion. He saw it relinquished, once inside the house, as she got on her belly and cowered under the low-rung chair between the woodstove and the window. She stayed there till someone carried a plate of food to the table; till she saw one of the other boys suit up to go out; an offhand mood could mean permission to go along. Mutt. Fear her the helm, not devotion.

Holding the gun in the small of his arm Frank pulled at his jacket zipper. He wanted to expose his chin, his throat; to breathe, to look. He wanted the zipper contraption down, but it wouldn't come. Moisture from exhalation created metallic frost in the track. Hands in mittens did no good, especially with gun between elbow and hip. The job needed the dexterity and grip of bare hands.

"Ah! To hell with it."

With limited vision, Frank peered for the brutal frozen world.

Pink cliffs had lost the appeal they had from the beach. Out here, they loomed. Nor did the granite, nor slate facets have the attractive footholds he had imagined. These dizzy heights were not places to climb on the sunniest days of high summer, in the right gear. In periscope fashion Frank turned and leaned. He saw the iron sky ever lowering to the rigid, wasted expanse.

He walked on, his tinkling boot buckle the uncommon reminder that his feet were dry, which, he had learned, was the only real concern out-of-doors: in dry feet you had no reason to be cold. A knot in one of the three sock layers bothered his left foot. His right gave no trouble, socks there stretched evenly and the foot fell flatly. The second layer, least easy to reach; that was the problem. There had been a hole in the big toe. Was the problem the hole in the big toe? Relief could be gotten by taking off the boot, but it was too bitterly cold for that. Up on the bank he could get it off. Up under the black dwarf spruce where generous boughs covered solid land.

The tinkling ended.

Constrained, Frank adjusted the coiled rope on his left shoulder, its fastened iron hook digging into his armpit. This hook was the working end of a fishing gaff, the same rusted instrument that had lain on the windowsill in the porch for how many years, he didn't know. When Frank spotted it two days prior he had made the mistake of reaching for it with an uncovered hand. Super-dry metal, wanting the moisture, stripped his skin. Frank's violent reaction of flicking the caught hand sent the heavy metal across the work counter, taking with it sizeable chunks of flesh from thumb and finger. The pain was excruciating and the red of the blood produced a fear that haunted him. The shock of having outwardly harmed one's body through private stupidity was deeply troubling. That night he lay with digits wrapped tightly in toilet paper. He didn't tell a soul, said he was in here reading, when questions came. But young flesh seals and pain falls off. He knew he could use the hand to get a shot off. He told himself so, though he had never fired a gun.

The rope and hook were means to retrieve blasted game, provided current did not wholly effect a dead duck's coming to the floe. He would toss in the weighty hook and ensnare a bobbing bird. No, no shot bird in this water could be snagged – he saw that now. It would freeze, it would sink. His bright idea for all this had come during a night of anticipating this out-of-doors adventure, coming to him where the best conditions for the physical world exist: in warm sheets under a dry roof, far below stars that shone icily in a benign night sky. A target this small, slippery, bobbing, frozen; what would be more impossible to ensnare? To extract from a winter sea? Unless a wing were gaffed. Ricocheting water: was his best bet. Feathers – they have pockets of air. Birds don't sink.

He inserted a shell into the chamber and flicked the neck up for its closing snap. His mitten caught. He tried again, using his left on the wood of the forward stock for leverage.

An excellent calibre for duck, the single-barrel twelve-gauge was longer than most, and basic, no artistry in the wood or near the lonely black metal housing the trigger. Much of the veneer had worn clear, from carriage.

The slim red-plastic shell now in its barrel base held beads of lead. Three nights ago Frank opened such a bullet. He had used a hunting knife for his investigation, pouring beads onto a flat palm. When the weighty slew came all at once, some dropping onto the workbench, some onto the floor, he turned briskly. No one was there to witness.

The key was to shoot just above the target. Both brothers had said so and their father's prompt agreement came. Lead shot drops when exiting a barrel, gravity the constant. Also, you did not want too much lead in the animal. Just the bare minimum so that life was removed. If you erred, you struck the target dead on, you filled the carcass full of lead and you spit shot onto your dinner plate. Frank knew he would not care when it came to pulling the trigger whether high or low. Such technical points were meaningless on the first expedition. Finer points were for subsequent trips. The first kill meant only that:

the kill. Effort to effect success. To carry a dead animal home and into the house, is to reign supreme. He would dig beads out later by himself when standing over the sink with the tip of the hunting knife working, one hand grasping with surety an elongated wing.

The twelve-gauge was his father's, though Clifford had laid claim.

Clifford. Family hunter. "I saw what you did to that bullet you maligning little prick. Wasting a good shell like that. What I should do is beat the face off you right now."

Clifford had come to Frank's pillow to say this, a fist pre-formed.

"Once more, and I'll take you out in the woods and waste one on you. How'd that be? See how you like the destruction of people's property. You listening to me, bai? Lay one hand on that gun. Even think of taking it into the woods and I'll murder you where you sleep. Make those your last thoughts before dreamland."

Clifford carried the gun year round. He used slugs to buckle big game. He shot moose. He shot deer. Slugs are not the fragments, but single units of lead. You had to be an excellent shot to make full use of them as your choice of shell. Fat, grey – a slug was the used-up grey crayon with paper peeled back. Apparently there were times when Clifford, creeping close enough, could get off a shell and drop a deer instantly. He aimed for the shoulder blade and the animal never knew what hit it. No leg kick, no whimper. Stark, pure death in a dark woods.

It was no good chumming up to Clifford. He was a loner through and through. Never would he think of passing over the gun. But, gun or no gun, when you happened upon him in the woods he wanted you silent right away, his hands wove you down. For him there was always game just up ahead, left, right or behind.

Frank knew why his brother wanted silence. He knew now the securing of place, the tactile stealth, to be ready. Hunting wanted silence. Travelling with a gun wanted silence. Observation became key when you knew you could kill and that was your objective. It's what it is to be older – the hunt always on.

Frank had seen Clifford come home well after dark, but in the fall, when light was put to bed early in these parts. His brother's face would have aged in a single day to make skin handsome, a beard blue black. Taller, straighter, trim features altogether; a sharper ebony eye shifted allure, with an anticipatory gleam. Clifford would have been tracking a cougar since daybreak and now in the kitchen, at the table, their father looked up from a second evening meal of eggs. Wearing the bifocals to see his food, eyewear used for the fine cuts with his handsaw, the patron would ask: "Shoot anything, Cliff?" Both waited. Father saw his eldest boy. He saw this reaching behind the back, felt bliss at the weighing down of the kitchen table. Roar! Life from the wild, blood frozen, fur matted, rigid. Yes, cold savage bone and flesh appearing for the first time in a heated house. An account followed of how it was taken. One that satisfied Adrian to no end. Jessie too. Working grates, poking rising bread; she squawked at the sight of the cougar, protested grandly. "We can't eat that! Not a cat!" She'd listen to the recounting that lasted half the night, till all had to get set for bed. None worried about Clifford, when Clifford was out.

Today the great hunter cut firewood on the mountain with William.

William. Fiery hair, freckled nose, pooling brown eyes. William was as tall as Clifford, but lighter-footed in timidity. He had a foul mouth when outside, swore as if speaking life was mainly this. One could never get off as many fucks as what was required.

Cold snaps like this allowed their crosscut passage through the yellow birch and the knotty beech they sought. The night before last, while both stood at the woodstove, William the woodsman had expounded for bifocalled Adrian the principle role cold plays in cutting firewood. William used a language remarkably purged, as if now it were time to impart the little he was sure about. He himself needed the contrast. "You don't have to work through the wet, you see. Greenness is done with, in real cold. So dry, see. A tree will split her trunk just standing there in the real cold. Kind of shits its pants. You hear them splitting back there, like someone spoke your name. You turn, you look. You can't spot where it came from. Bark covers everything, and each tree looks guilty. Me son, I will say the sound is some spooky back there. Like this hidden orchestra tuning up. Then, snap-oh!"

Adrian listened to his middle son, both hands on the kettle handle. Frank approached, and the three watched as William spit on a stove grate and silver beads bounced, collected, spun, split into smaller pellets that shot off tangentially to influence oddly the smell of the yeast working in the bread.

"Also, easier to haul the wood over solid crust."

"How solid?"

"Solid enough to walk on. Crust stiff like the half quart of molasses needed to loosen up the old lady's bread?"

"Shut up, you!"

William knew names of trees, leaf patterns, needle numbers. Trees were everything. He loved their destruction as a boy. The calling of "Timber"; the smile at their groaning, aching descents, their swoosh. "I enjoy a clearing in the woods," he said. "It civilises a place, allows the light in." High stumps from his winter cuts marked open areas. You happened across him stacking lopped limbs; jumping on fires to get them going. Before the two left at daybreak, Clifford had made a second trip to Frank's pillow, chest level with the bunk.

"So, you heard me, bai. About the gun. And don't be pretending you're asleep. I see the shallow breathing. Remember. One hand on it and you're getting your death."

Frank coughed; vapour smoked. He blew sharply from his nose, then turned to see the slinking family pet. "Better get that duck dog. You and me. Hear me, now?"

three

*F*rost was on the barrel. It had come from the mitten that touched the floe, the mitten guiding Frank forward. He stopped, snorted ice to clear his nose, broke open the gun to check the shell. *12 calibre*, the inscription circled the brass. He called the dog, remembering suddenly to break open the gun again and remove the shell, he had to be careful. He touched the safety catch, which came too easily.

The two walked for the peninsula. Frank studied the colouration of the ice while stepping past slabs of pack ice, carefully placing his irksome left foot. Wind came from the northwest. Both faced out of it when chance arose, travelling obliquely in it, always looking down.

*A*fter the older boys left the house that morning, Frank had dressed. He poured canned milk and water onto his porridge and told his mother he was taking Mililica out on the harbour.

"You're not to take the gun, hear? Your brother is adamant ever since he caught you with it out behind the house. And I don't want you to, either," she said.

Jessie was a slim-legged woman. Broad shouldered, tall and husky, possibly too much so for her slim legs. Her comely raven hair had two prominent grey strips starting at each temple. Swept back tight, these strips delineated the shape of her skull. She was forty-four, with coal-black sparrow eyes and slick pitch eyebrows, ate just as much as the rest, was just as vocal, with a reserve she never drew on, could never articulate, but held as precious. She waited, expectant for some pouncing travesty that would one day cut the family down, but hopefully find her prepared. She would have to draw on every ounce of this reserve to deal with what was coming. What, she didn't know. Only that it was on its way and the bottom of her soul was touched by it. "You heard me now, Frank Joseph. I said, you're not to take it."

"For Christ sake. I heard you, I heard you."

Frank was at the kitchen window. He saw the priest, Father Alvin MacIntyre coming up the road on foot. Nearly at the top of the hill, the priest could only be coming for a social call. Frank hurried outside in time to catch sight of his father disappear down over the hill to the well house. Adrian wore his heavy curmudgeon coat, coniferous green. It was blustery, Frank caught up, working thighs to muscle a new path through the snow.

They got behind the well house where the firewood was bucked, but not yet split. Snow had built between woodpile and well house, a drift so deep the door no longer came open enough even to squeeze through sideways. "Find the axe. You know where it is? The other two take it?"

Jessie came out, appearing from behind the frozen clothes on the line. In a frosty high-rising breath, just above a whisper that arrived clearly, she hissed in appeal:

"Hear. Yas're not leaving me alone with him now are yas?"

"What the hell's he doing here?" whispered Adrian. "That I'd like to know. This hour. This place. In this miserable pock-eating frost."

Adrian stood bitterly at the side of the well house, arms akimbo, but also with elbows partially drawn in. He was frozen. He turned swiftly when he saw the cherubic cleric emerge from the spruce trees at the road. Then with his back to the scene of road and house, he cleared his throat and freed the discovered axe from where it leant against the wall, three-quarters buried under the drift. His wife had turned for the house, hair rising in snowy gusts.

"We haven't got enough to do around here?" Adrain asked. "Just to stay warm, alive without him having to come and make his rounds. Likes his gossip, that fellow. Got to be right in with the women."

"Must be the woman in him," said Frank. His father looked.

"What are you looking at me for?" said Frank. "I said, I know. I'm agreeing with you. He pokes his nose in other people's business where it don't belong, that not right?"

"That's right."

"All the church is good for?"

"That, and making you feel you're a product of hell at every turn you take. For doing the least little thing that might bring you a sense of joy. I didn't know you were taking notes on the subject. Is it right for a fellow your age to be so opinionated? Bad talk, Frank, from someone young as you. Impressionable. Just let him come down here, see what he gets.... Come on, Father, bring that white collar down over the bank so I can take this axe and chase you down the road with it, clickitty clank all the way back to the Glebe. Lord. I'm the one who needs the strength."

"He won't come down here."

"Don't I know it. Not where there's any sort of work being done. Look. There. He's on the porch. Wave, bai; wave to him quick."

"After what you just said? You want a wave now?"

"You said something, too. Raise your hand, bai. She brought him out to have a look at us. To get back at us. Ah my... strength. Wave, bai, wave."

"I am, for Christ sake!"

"Yes, that's right now. You go back inside now where you like it. Where there's tea, scones and gab. The latest dirt. Learn all you can about the goings on."

Frank kept hands jammed in his pockets despite dry mittens.

"Nice frost, I know that."

"Frost, me son – that what you call it? This ain't frost. We passed frost twenty degrees ago. This here is the backside of Pluto. Ah, bai.

To tell you the truth, it's getting me down. Right down. And a father has to tell his son that."

"What is, the cold?"

"Yes, the cold. Yes, the cold. I had two pairs of woollen worksocks on me last night. They worked all right, worked down past my ankles to get all scrunched up in me toes. I took them off, lost them then. That wasn't bad enough. She kept hogging the blankets and I had to get up and search for a wool hat for my head. I couldn't find a damn thing in the dark and I so go and goddamn-well smack my kneecap, plus big toe, on the chipped corner of the woodbox. I pretty well ruint myself. Right where one of you fellows dug it with an axe too, chipping it for the joy of it. That's where I brought up against. Solid. What a wallop, I wanted to rip the house apart board by board and, would have."

"I heard your cursing. Woke up everyone in the house."

"That's how she goes sometimes."

Adrian looked down at the same stocking-hat he had slept in, the same he had eaten breakfast wearing. In his hands he unrolled then rolled it to maximize material at the ears. His large-sized sheet metal work gloves with their threadbare index fingers and broke-through thumbs turned the procedure into a hell of a job.

At the chopping block, Frank waited. Vertically he steadied with both hands a chunk of birch whose ends were snowy. Adrian raised the axe above his son's head then smacked the wood dead centre, bursting the chunk from Frank much too quickly, a loud ping entering the morning cold.

"Jesus, Dad! Easy! Easy I say, I had my hands out there! You almost took me off at the wrist."

"I meant to go easy, Frank. But she passed through like butter! Sorry about that, son, I'll go easy on the next. But no, she wasn't held together all that well, was she, that chunk? I thought it'd be more solid than what it was. The ping, hear that? The real cold, what William was going on about. Easier to work wood in the cold. ...The blood in your heart don't congeal first."

On the next swing the axe bit flew off while Frank held the chunk. He ducked, violently pulled both hands back and used them to cover his head.

"Trying to take the head off me now!"

"No, I'm not, Frank – the wood in the bit must have shrunk! Good thing that didn't strike you."

"I'll say, good thing!"

Frank retrieved the bit from the snow. Easily they got it on the handle, but then they could get no chunks from the woodpile because their ends had fused in the frost. Like spot-welded steel, all.

"Ah, hell. And I just put a hole in my boot, from this one with the branch not limbed properly."

With both arms, in mighty swinging anger, Adrian smacked the axe against the well house broadside, splitting shingles. Something deep inside the building, a hubcap perhaps, dropped off and clanged to a spacious floor.

"I got two words for this situation. Fuck. This."

He looked at his son, looked through him then turned away. "...Like a rock, the whole goddamn world frozen like a big goddamn rock. How do they expect a person not to perish altogether, living down here? Up to the cellar is where I'm headed. Where I can find some peace, get out of this wind and wait for old Father Tea to vacate. Their feet above will tell me all I need to know about how the show goes up there. I got to keep an eye on the water jugs anyway. Take their caps off so they can swell free if frozen."

"I know what caps you'll be taking off," said Frank.

His father paid no attention; they were all saucy-mouthed now, his boys. He walked instead up under the clothesline, where three pairs of iced longjohns and two stiff long-sleeved work shirts hung like corrugated metal. A big pair of blue drawers sat three days now, out halfway across the field. A crow had taken them. The drawers became the trap for copper and green spruce cones rolling over crusted snow.

On a ledge of the foundation frost wall, in the hard dirt below the floor, sat Adrian's supply. He waited. His supply was wrapped in seaweed collected in the fall when he was insulating the house. He had learned of seaweed being a good insulator from French fishermen mooring at the sandbar. Adrian, alone, had taken up the project to warm up the house. The boys had no interest in helping him. He went at it one room at a time till the snow came. He said he was glad to see the snow because the careful removal of the wallboards with their rusted nails – jabbing with a stick to get seaweed into places he didn't know he was reaching – was hellish work, altogether.

He blew, listened for steps above.

Frank was still at the well house. He used the axe to beat free a chunk, scraped an end off and, split it. He considered his father and his cellar retreat. Frank had counted eight bottles of the old man's stash when coming down into the cellar for a scuttle of coal the previous day. On his fourth run, the late evening, he was confronted by a long accusative finger. Half-cut, Adrian had remarked: "You touch any of these quart bottles over here, bai? Because I had eleven and now there's only eight! I suppose they all just disappeared. I asked you a question, so answer me. Did you? No, it wasn't you, how could it be you? You got too much of her in you for that. The saint. Them mealy other two, that's who it was. They're up there now with their bellies full of deer meat. Wait till I get them clear of her. And let me find one more bottle missing, I swear to Jesus I'll clean the clocks of the whole lot."

Frank did not take the three bottles. He took one. And only after discovering his older brothers drinking theirs in the attic of the backroom, above the bunk, feet dangling in woollen worksocks. Frank heard when a bottle was set on a rafter, its spilling, the mumbled cursing. Frank drank his outside, out in the barn, alongside the horse. Then, three-quarters drunk, he had to go down into the spruce trees to sober up. He followed the untried path all the way to the shore. On the way back he saw his sister Grace go up to the road and he waved at her. She looked at him strangely.

The old man was about to be surprised again. Frank saw him come out from under the clothesline and relieve himself against the cabin. Steam rose from shingles. He can't have made the discovery, thought Frank. The temperatures, dropping as low as they had in the night, had forced even the fire out. Shards of glass, once his precious bottles, were all that was left. Frank saw the breakage in the early morning, when coming for the scuttle of coal. Clifford and William must have learned what happened too, and why they went hauling wood at so early an hour – so as not to be around when the old man learned the fate of the quarts. The malcontent would silently go berserk, be hard to deal with the whole day. He would give everyone the hardest time, same as if each had actually had something to do with it. Archie MacDonald from the North Shore, the redheaded violin-tuner, had secretly given Adrian the case of beer made from spruce needles. Adrian had served in the war with Archie MacDonald, had apparently saved the redhead's life in a drunken brawl. Archie Mac-Donald made it a tradition to bring a spruce dozen, every winter.

Adrian had to watch it. This priest had voted Ingonish dry. Alcohol was not illegal in the parish, but it was banned. And here was the priest, trolling the floor boards above the stash. To top that all off, Adrian's brother Leo was now appointed acting sheriff. With the ban on, home-made liquor flourished. Home-made liquor was naturally illegal. Brother Leo, Sheriff, took his job seriously. Too seriously. In a way, the seriousness was responsible for his being at present a mucky-muck in the community.

Ice groaned. Then, from one end of the bay to the other, there charged a resounding crack. Frank stood poised as if for action, studied surroundings, felt safer then amongst the floe. The crack had come behind, in on the flat ice. The rising tides did that. Strain, violence. This ice could hold a fortress. He had his arms out, though, ready to go down.

He saw the houses of Ingonish, especially the linear settlement along the sandbar. The white shingled lighthouse with its red apex, punctured the boundary's end on the shore side of the gut, stolidly holding ground. It denoted a narrow harbour entrance, sitting jammed, deserted. No light flashed on this dim day. No vessel could get within a hundred eyeshots. Adjacent houses looked equally sequestered. Winter did that, though many families vacated their sea homes for inland dwellings. They wintered in places such as the Clyburn Valley at Ingonish Centre. Log cabins there were built in against steep valley mountains, some under forested scree. Adrian had cautiously pointed out the residences to the boys on a summer walk. Other winter lodges were at MacGean's Interval, this side of Ingonish, south. The structures here sat perfectly sheltered from the harsh stripping of open terrain. In both bold spots, rivers running below ice provided drinking water. Hardwood could be taken easily from mountain slides and the heavy stuff, once as high as the waist, could be carried down promptly for burning. They shot deer. Ate potatoes.

Frank studied the sun's position. Too soon, the deficient orb had crept over Smokey Mountain. Far below, on a mere tuft of land, sat Jerome Robertson's house. The hermit's ocean-facing window and door were in the lee of any early-year northwest. Not one ray of sun had touched the roof for months, its hand-cut shakes all but forgetting what thaw was. Wavering plumes lowered from a working flue. Mountain draft at times forced the smoke to veil the house's outline. The property looked bare and wanting, its surrounding trees having been cut for firewood. The old fellow could not have anticipated the loss of sunlight in winter when selecting location. His decision must have come in high summer. Here, like many, was a dreamer. Characteristic of the house, on its mountain base tuft just wide enough to hold a dwelling, was the fight for solitude. No one had better come around. As a member of an isolated northern community Frank understood this sense. What started vaguely with loneliness found trust in peace. The house, the man; they occupied land. "Which is what we are all doing," Adrian had said. "Hanging on to what's here so no one else will take it. Why, I'll never know."

A stiff breeze struck Frank's nape and, though jacketed and hooded, travelled the bones of his spine. Hiking up the gun, he spoke to the greyness of Mililica down past his hood. No straying now. Not so much as a yard. They continued, all the time farther and farther from home, over this irregular, cropping, bracing Atlantic floe.

Facing open water, he had found a spot where the shooting could take place. Within yards of the chop he adjusted his footing on the caked seawater forming a slippery perimeter under a dusting of kernel snow.

"Shush now, shush. You see too, Mallards."

The flock rose in chop and slid down wavelets. A sword of sun fell, freshening the scene, lighting the armada, glorifying its presence and colouring all to that of bear fur.

Frank bit his mitt. With cupping fingers he handled the pocketed shell, sliding the slim graceful volley back into the gun chamber. He brushed back the fur of his hood, then aggressively doffed it, only to choke his windpipe. He eased the gun barrel shut and raised it to bring it level with his head. He closed one eye to make a squint of the other. Easing back the hammer with hurt thumb, he heard the magnificent click.

Aiming was not possible. Not in this wind. The salt was stinging his eyes. Sea chop and an ascending breeze hurling ice pellets spoiled any target sighting. A due north wind filled the ear. When did this rise? His heart broke as he lowered the rifle. The distance was too far for any rifleman. His best bet would be to clamber to shore, to perch up on one of the pink cliff ledges and take sheltered aim. He did well not to pull the trigger.

The flotilla paddled under the cliffs.

He would have this floe to return to – to retrieve what he shot – it was going nowhere.

"Come on."

Mililica looked up inquisitively, as would a luckless human lost between attention and obedience.

"Come, I said."

Frank's frozen ear, his harassed neck and cheek caused him to pinch on his hood again.

They made shore leaping tidal seepage – the yellow ribbon fault line denoted the accommodation of tide at shore, which the frigid air froze and the bobbing sea broke. Brine rose. Millie snorted pellets.

The two walked on bevelled ice, but soon entered soft drift when they came to a windless bank. Above was a prominent boulder, stripped of weather, one with bare climbing ledges.

Frank raised his left arm, carefully placing the rope and hook on the first ledge. He brushed the dangling rope loop with his mitten, pushing it, to raise it all. He got on tiptoe, dug in a knee. He had his left arm fully extended grabbing stone, when his right, stationed at the trigger area and responsible for it, became confused. The gun got free, sliding only a tiny distance, but neatly allowing the exposed twist of trigger to catch his sleeve's cuff. The cocked hammer sprang and there was a powerful discharge.

$\mathcal{A}$ resounding bang disturbed an entire bay. The gun clanked against rocks.

Stunned by the report, Frank clutched his chest, which swelled most unnaturally, pushing material of his jacket grotesquely upward. Echo.

The torment filled all ice nooks and frozen clefts of the desolate region. The ducks, slow to take off, now flew the air. Hidden crows took whooshing flight. Seals rustled flippers. Then... nothing; only Mililica staring upward, gravely, the sole representative of all lower life forms in the ice-locked bay.

Dull mental process glimpsed the troubled dog, a process that replaced forlornness that lingered. Frank's slow physical response arrived, but with this: truth unwelcome.

The moment prohibited his catching his breath. That was the thing. To come to terms with what had occurred needed some measure of controlled breathing. Pain, yes. There appeared the weapon at his feet. And yes, ah yes. Hammer. Needs replacing after taking aim, a shell inside. But the shot... how fast and mercilessly complete. Salt was on his lip as there came with precision the smell of his mother's uncapped iodine bottle, down from its top shelf in the kitchen to treat some wound. His dry lip was minutely bleeding. Iodine, its association with blood. Blood that now speckled snow. Blood not from the dry lip. He blew out, twice, gripping reality.

Frank Curtis had shot himself.

four

Ache came from his left side. There was coping, provided movement was minimal, animal. The first order was to slow the heart. Jacket material on the upper arm had been torn asunder, insulating feature spoilt. A late wisp floated now upward, got carried off. The blast had caught the upper left bicep, the indenture beginning at the deltoids. Frank could feel its harsh sting while fully cognisant of a larger reserve of pain wishing to manifest. Much of the blast had passed through the clothing.

Please be so, please. There cannot be this much this quick in early life. The situation could be innocent, yet. That he could not see where he had been hit wholly worsened the plight.

Erroneously, he allowed the lowered arm sway when searing hurt unlike any he had known paralysed him. His heart rippled while, inconsistently, fear arose of whether or not sheared jacket material might infect torn flesh; the fear vied, became foremost in his mind.

He redirected hooded vision, bent for the gun and got it. He let it slide down his thigh to rest on his leg before wilfully kneeing and kicking it from him. He removed himself from the bank, got to the bevelled rim ice where in better light he saw blood had soaked through the outer jacket. From his left cuff came the first falling crimson, drips thinly alighting at his feet to gather on the green ice. Some caught in escort, twisted to land on white snow. He let it bleed. He looked toward the houses, glanced the tragic emptiness of the bay. No witness in this bleak world. This was fortune.

Mililica came, sniffed a boot and he drove her off. The fresh blood roused the bitch, making her whine to communicate distress. She hushed up then, to sniff more. Frank turned like a periscope for the lighthouse, peered there in hooded prayer wishing he had not come out today. Any point from the promontory of Middle Head stood four perpendicular miles to his door.

He moved along the shore. He had gun and rope, but dropped these in favour of removing the aggravating hood. He worked the zipper with his bare hand whose mitten he bit off and spat in the snow. The zipper drew, then snagged at the throat where escaping heat and nasal drool produced frost in the track. He fought the device, to no end. His right hand by itself was useless. He breathed through his nose, bit on trimming fur for purchase. He employed combinations of patience and force till the right moment came when improved balance brought a general loosening, then success. The zipper audibly passed down the track, snagging mid-sternum. But the hood was off. He could see, feel, hear, breathe, wriggle the good shoulder.

Reaching in past precious body heat, he played fingers lightly on his upper arm, unable to entice himself to go directly to the portion of skin sheared. Mystery harassed him while blood soaked fabric, its slick heat deceptive: sinister in that it provided some maddening reassurance. He felt around the chest, illogically, following the silken indentations of his rib cage. There was no damage to any substantial region. But then, footing went. He struck the ice profoundly and cried out in great anguish. The dog whined mournfully. Barked as Frank got to his knees.

He had tried to flex the arm; a mistake, the pain hitting him as alien, one travelling ocean miles to come and now stay. He wouldn't do it again. But another assault, like receiving a falling crate, broke down his left side, in plugged pulse determined to drive him down again, to keep him on the ice.

"God, please. God, ah."

On his knees, open mouthed, saliva filling corners, he waited – squinting at the sharpness not receding, not cowering. He uttered nothing, merely stayed on his knees, breathed. The arm, pitched forward, was all-controlling. Spasms cut short his breath.

Then, all eased. He waited, refusing guile. Intimate with the wound, learning and relearning its power over him, he willed no attempt to flex again. The dog barked and barked. It bounded on its forepaws as if prompted to fetch a stick; the tail wagged. Frank rose to his feet, ignoring the instinct plaguing him: to pull the arm clear of its sleeve, to see in plain light what faced him. Imagined suffering obliterated the idea.

Smokey Mountain, its long range ridge, its vague sun. But where exactly? There. The arrested sun waited at the hump, the point where its orange face swiftly ended afternoons during interminable winter. Light gone, four horrifying miles to the door.

True, Frank had function of his right hand, but how dreadfully the pair had always been bound in the simplest of operations. He must instruct the right to act with autonomy. With gun and rope he began the homeward walk. The ducks had returned, were close now; shared his company.

He eased across the floe using hip and shoulder and where he need not circumnavigate he took the quickest route to the raft ice. Moving, sundry crimson drops did not come fast off the cuff, but rather came as they did from any shot animal whose freedoms were impaired with finality – whose passing now over increasingly bleak terrain left the savage waltz, scored in red.

Frank followed Mililica, hastily got in front, kicked her lithe back paws away. She ran, resuming lead, turned back to survey progress. But she stopped, spooked entirely when the moment came for the ice's evening habit: to protest, to groan, to be forced to usher the large rippling evening cracks of the bay.

They had reached the exposed flat ice, the tide falling. Halfway across now. Still far from all.

The distant yellow-cleft shoreline produced visible seawater squeezed from below to form blue ponds. Water on the move, there. One that refused freezing because of its salt content, because of its temporary status. Why did it arrive, if tide was falling? To necessitate an ice field on the move, a bevelled shore-ice declining. The dropping tide was a force large enough to pull the entire floe back out to sea within an hour. A force misunderstood, in that it did not necessarily coincide with the coming of night, but only seemed to. Could it wait a little longer?

The wind blew over the bay. In it, the finest of sleek ice bits. Frank kept his eye on Smokey's ridge where the sunken sun sped to remove light and the lost land rose to erase it. Twilight. That which silently heralds the black hours, then takes its leave – it had arrived, expertly guiding itself across a dangerous bay. The tide was on its fast point of dropping; between the slow high-state and the slow low-state. It made this frozen beach yawn and made visible a large blue-black channel of now opening water between Frank and shore.

The ice was moving off.

Frank had considered this before leaving, that his ice would go. His plan had been to come back over land, in over the Middle Head trail. Not the shortest route, it required scaling banks, but did win solid ground. He could scale no banks. That recourse had dissipated like remembered fog. Heavy snow collected there amongst the trees, and the skirting... should he get up, the crossing of windfalls... that alone would make trail return impossible. Yesterday had been a challenge. Yesterday, he carried nothing. He was sound. Crust you could walk on had been in open areas where Europe's wind climbed cliffs, its breath polished points exposed. No one used the trail this time of year. Out here, someone could see him. No black spruce branch whipping back to catch the arm, out here. Once up on the beach, the Beach Road, someone could find him. A small likelihood, but Chance showed her face in small likelihood. It was law. What gave meaning to prayer.

The seals were gone. The crows. The eagle. All nature fixed on the mute hour between the dog and the wolf. Mililica was silent. The pressing floe behind had frightened them both into silence. Groaning, yawning, lazing ice roused the necessity to adjust its posture: night currents had begun. Mountain dominated sun. Temperature dropped like a curtain.

They moved on, made time.

Frank paused well beyond the summer swimming point. Where inside buoyed ropes no more delineated a playful sea swim, squid-ink black open water interred him. And he discerned no freak ice crossing as he presently walked to where ice stepped out farthest. One hundred feet of salt water between him and sheltering mammoth pans, beached on waiting sand. He had options: to follow the main floe south to the sandstone cliffs of Smokey Mountain, passing the gut, the lighthouse. Conversely he could go north. To the base of the commencement of the Middle Head promontory where sheer crust fields covered flanking bay cliffs. He could kick in the toe of a boot, climb the ice crust like a ladder. If he got ashore.

The ice moved as he stood; he felt it sail. He turned for the black sea, the tracings of his crossing steps already dusted free. Mililica whined, her face sharp, anticipatory, sniffing a seaward kelp breeze and waiting on word. Frank turned once more to a blank ocean where no moon climbed; tonight only, black blunt banks of Middle Head darkly squatted miles away. The frozen topographical finger made its icy breadth known. Bent in the night, the promontory finger waited with clear answer to the problem. Go there, it pointed. Skirt, to the heights of Smokey Mountain where beyond is civilisation. Always there had been this solution for woe. A full flash of the lighthouse broke suddenly; floe-jammed stalagmites appeared in its wan illumination. The keeper had lit his torch. Too far. Same problem of scaling, getting ashore. The chance was this and merely this, open water. Beyond which lay the hard Beach Road, sleigh-runner compacted, horse-hoof trampled.

Mililica became impatient. She snorted ice pellets, braced on her slim forepaws, abhorring delay. She pranced, unintentionally comical, just then to show how the ice and the sea at night were new to her too, and just as distasteful. All was a nasty, exposed understanding, therefore they must be moving on always to close the distance between this and the flat, dry kitchen floor. That's what padded paws and worn nails knew. The animal paced in border collie parade, jaw-bones tight. It took three breathy pants; backed from the edge now, backed to where a thin layer of snow momentarily hid paws, whining, whining.

"Shut up, shut up, shut up! No, no. Come here, girl."

With shrewd ears the animal knew awful risk was wanted of it. She held her ground.

"Stay then, stay the fuck here, then."

The dog twisted, howled, but she stopped as coyotes stationed in mountain fissures returned her plaintive wail.

Frank knelt at the frozen edge. He had got the shotgun down through his belt and, sitting, swung out his boots, to pause a moment, straining hamstrings above the ebony pond. He submerged too-buoy-ant soles till water came over their felt tops. He faced shore, craftily dropped to his waist, his good arm carrying strain at the wrist, his good forearm taking full weight as he lowered in the injured arm and pushed off the floe.

Water spilt between buttocks and came in over his neck. Out from the ice ledge it came, through a heavily-clothed front, finding easy pathways through sleeves, down his throat, washing past his naval. Hyper-respiration cornered lungs in this brilliant, stabbing cold of overall soaking; internal bursting bleeding was the sense and, "ah, ah!" he panted, as a thousand ice knives twisted and tore breast-bone, as freezing mail-plated vices clamped the small of the back and barbed-wire frosts ravaged shoulder blades. Open-eyed, Frank saw nothing.

The twelve-gauge was under water – its breech caught fast to his belt. He threw the good arm out while worry of the gun's rusting conferred the general dissonance of being in the water. His brother's anger had made it easily into the provocation for this swim. Frank had not broken open the gun after the shot, an empty bullet jacket lay inside, it will corrode; rust will seal the rifle shut and ruin it, forever.

He choked, spat frigid brine. He was buoyant, could not see, the hood in his way. He swept it back with forearm but it floated at face level, the lining forming clinking riddles, icicle shoots. He had to remember to kick at the sea with felt-lined boots, hating every moment the puff at the jacket's back: there, by the covetous air space he felt, where a hump rose out of the water to ridicule him further.

He gained several feet in the black depths, his good arm lunging, smacking once again the terrible surface. The pliability of his fingers ended, their sense as members of a hand went. His mind alone was now responsible. He had taken off the mitten before getting in the water, had put it in his pocket. A cupped hand gathers water. A cup, that holds, that is. When the good arm broke again to swing ahead, he tried to see.

The dog filled the bay with its suffering. Over and over the creature howled its fate at being abandoned on the moving ice – whimpering, whining, panting, pacing its misgivings. Frank paid no attention; ice and trapped dog were behind him, forever too. All was the intimate struggle of a desperate body fighting savage conditions. He made way, fought as never before, as he never wanted to learn.

The shore loomed. Then it was near. No waves called. The difficult decision became when to drop legs to procure bottom, a move that would end precious momentum. But there were the playful peaks and troughs, then – shore wavelets, implying a beach floor rising. It was winter; what Frank knew of a summer bottom had to have changed as much sand was hauled out to sea yearly. But did it mean shallow falling away from shore? He would not be able to get re-started, dropping legs to nothing, not now.

Wavelets played with his hood, sloshed about his cheeks.

Here was his greatest suffering. Indecision always held it. He dropped one leg but the other came with it. Nothing. Then the rifle dug in. Hatefully the sense of his legs moving, a toe touching even, but too, too long coming. He struggled for his life now, lurched, choked, went under, tried desperately to touch something. He pulled at the gun, somewhat, swallowing salt sea. Were the feet touching? Yes. Tiptoeing up a drop-off, his cold neck straining. Rushing of the sea left his ears. Rushing sea left his coat, his waist now, then from powerfully unknown legs its spilled down feelingless thighs.

Shivering, pushing through Arctic night air, Frank stepped out of the surf, staggering in a tangling ankle-height ocean. Amid tall sanded ice pans then, in a miserable mechanical motion with sluggish brain motor response he removed gun from belt; his blue shivering and coughing impacting with greatest violence at his scrotum. Labouring with binding breath, he took a shaking sopping mitten from his pocket. He bit the shimmering wrist material, gnashed teeth to get it snug on his good hand. Along his left forearm, down to his frozen left side he investigated with a patting, the force of which he was heartbreakingly uncertain. All was numb. He balled up the hand of the bad arm and, tenderly as he could, put its fist inside a pocket while seawater yet drained from him like a cold-water faucet easing to close. The arm was dead, deadweight. Yet he had to immobilise it for the walk. He undid his belt.

"Millie... come."

No sound. Coyotes also had desisted making themselves known. Shifting snow and ice was underfoot, crunching. Waves played upon the shore. Dripping seawater yet spoke loudly to Frank: marshal forward, leave beach, get on the road. The distant floe was menacingly silent, far more so than the landscape. "Millie. Come now." Shivering buckling legs, Frank heard something. Far off yelp? Seal? Ice talk? Where? Direction keeps leaving. All right, dog, last on your own. Curl up, you'll have to wait for tide. You're not meant for it, I know you aren't; you have rope and gaff hook on the ice with you to mark the spot, if anyone gets back out, if no snow falls.

𝐹rank climbed between pans on feet of stumps. He ascended the beach and walked onto hard-packed snow. A patch of stars twinkled through broken cloud, small and far off, piercing the black sky like dart holes, further darkening the true dome by their contrasting insignificance. The barrel tip of the gun was in his right hand, the neck still unbroken. He wanted to eject the shell, but had no courage to dally for its removal. The heavy gun impeded pace; the heavy gun could mean the difference between making it or not. He kept it, though, dropping the stock on its butt. The weapon struck firm snow to support walking, but having to lift it, to swing it forward, taxed. The sighting bead passed through the worn mitten to frozen skin, producing a far-off sensation. Tonight would be his first night to come home after dark. There would be hell to pay, with his mother, the same hell as there had been to pay when the other boys had their first time out after dark. He concentrated on the sighting bead as it dully made contact with his frozen flesh. The gun went ahead; he waited for the sighting bead to come back.

"I'm shot," he said, crying, his chest heaving.

No, no, no, smarten up. Just get home. Home, home.

The road was marked with spruce saplings jabbed where land fell off and bog began. The openness, denoted best by tall sporadic perimeter marsh reeds, was evident ever more in the luminosity of the snow. A forlorn sense spread over him, particularly here, one that drew strength from his midsection and made Frank avert his face from the enemy ahead. He remembered catching frogs in the heat of summer here, the Nook. He kept his eyes down, making sure his feet brought up solid with each step.

Passing the Nook, meant the hill.

The hill was steep and icy, but the only great obstacle between him and home. He would not think about it. Moreover, there were the two houses to pass: the Hawleys and the Donovans. This constituted an emergency. He could go into any one and ask for help, but upbringing interfered to make fleet of the notion. He had been raised to take nothing from no one. Adrian was a proud man; Jessie a proud woman. Pride, pride. Villagers drank the trait. The trait became a grand conceit and, long hardened by isolated living, deeply possessed. It stymied much opportunity in life. Its paradox unbreakable.

He saw both houses. He saw their long paths down to their latched doors. Poorly trod paths with high banks and hidden ice. He would never make it down should he try. He would fall, be found in the spring. Supper hour, definitely no hour to enter a person's house. To see how the village ate was taboo. Close friends, relatives embraced this as law. As well, the seeing of Frank at the door in his state ... how horrified any would be. Frank's family would be marked for good, the largest of millstones to hang on Adrian and Jessie Curtis. It would be the talk from this generation to the next, should any get a firsthand glimpse. No, his own family would receive him. They only. He continued the hill.

A lonesome figure approached on the road. Ranald Shea. The old man had come out for his nightly stroll, for his open-air pipe. Frank adjusted the grip of the gun. It could be a walking stick, in the dark. As Ranald descended, characteristically bent, hands behind his back for support, the distance closed as the crunch underfoot increased. In summer, the old man searched the ditches for bottles he could sell at Fairway Market. He had to be ninety. The elder switched to the other side of the road, a move to show preferred avoidance of young people. Frank had himself been planning such a switch.

"Evening, Ranald."

"Good day there, skipper," said Ranald Shea, all body, peering into the dark, stopping. "That one of Adrian's?"

"Yes. Adrian's boy. Frank."

"Nothing wrong, is there? It looks the hell like there is?"

"Nothing wrong here. Good night now, Ranald."

Frank stepped onward, smelled pipe tobacco yet saw no pipe. Eyes stayed on him, he knew. So drawing a shoulder back, he pronounced upward his chin. Ranald Shea was supposed to see ghosts. He favoured certain ditches along the road and would travel down in them only, because of spirits above. Witches, he saw all the time. This has to spook him, and he'll have no trouble telling anyone of it, but he will have a hard time getting someone to believe him.

Ranald Shea was stopped, turned, studying the defiant silhouette: that young fellow has a rifle he's passing off as a stick. He shoot something perhaps, and doesn't want anyone to know? At the beach – there's no game at the beach! Adrian Curtis's young fellow. He's big. Something the hell is wrong with him. I know it by looking, using his rifle to keep from falling.

"I say there! You sure you're all right up there, young fellow? Answer me now. Because I can get someone."

"I'm all right, Ranald. Night now."

Frank neared the top of the hill. He could feel only his inner core.

He saw the porch lamp. He saw the path, the sleigh track made slick by the sleigh's heavy wood recently hauled over. His whole left side was stiff as iron, yet he didn't sing out. He took the path at the centre, avoiding the track. He coughed, becoming massively awash in tears he had been saving. At the corner of the house he stopped to wipe his eyes. A stack of twisted maple tied down with slim fishing rope was on the sleigh, the load his brothers had brought home. The load had shifted. It glistened in the illumination of the porch lamp, the burning oil set to shine for him; what his mother had hung, Jessie. Frank's tears eased. He swallowed, feeling her worry enter his chest. This lamp triggered this. His mother, a superb worrier would at last have something to worry about; he felt better that his suffering was to be picked up. He wanted her involvement now in a suffering just beginning in so many respects. The event would separate him from the others. Would he get a beating for arriving after dark? Possibly the worst because of having bulked up in the summer and fall. She must now work to hurt him. No, no beating. He would get nothing for this. He would get nothing ever again.

At the door, gun leant against shingles, Frank fumbled with the simple but poor-working latch. Something was at his feet, creating an obstacle. A thing living, a thing that had been following him all along, but chose now to make itself known, to move into the light. He stepped back. The light shone.

She sat still as a crusted field. Her limbs frozen. She shivered and her eyes closed meditatively. The broken spirit told everything of her ordeal. Yet she twisted, got better into the light of the step as if this miracle alone might warm her. So desperately cold and ragged, she looked not long for this world. The icy step did not please her. Yet her resigned paws could not fight that which did not please her. So patience and tenderness came. "Come here." She had travelled the floe, past the sandbar, past the gut, past the lighthouse. She had come ashore where swim was shortest. Her frozen limp tail told it, bent useless as an artist paintbrush. "In the water? You too? No energy to shake the ice? Get back." Frank took his bitterly cold hand off the latch, got it back in the mitten, touched the gun with the back of his mitten: got it better situated against the wall.

With open hand he drew back and struck the window, rattling hellishly its four panes.

five

"Where the hell were you! I was worried sick, you!"

Jessie hauled off and struck her son. She hurt her hand. Frank drew back uttering a muffled animal sound, a cutting anguish that Jessie had not heard before and one that stopped her dead in her tracks. Frank could not answer her. And when she saw how he moved after the striking, how he favoured an arm stiff with frosted black blood from sleeve to mitt she said, "Oh, my God."

She brought him through the second porch door, into the light of the kitchen. She called out for Adrian who stood in the front room with his backside to the wood stove. He straightened respectfully, re-linquishing his meditative stare at a votive candle with drowning flame. The candle was on a shelf at face level so his eyes were screwy; he had to collect himself having drunk on an empty stomach the four stub-necks he had wrapped in seaweed and buried deep in the cellar soil.

Clifford and William were in the backroom with their own fire going in the potbelly stove when they heard the commotion. They had been back from the woods for three hours. After supper they had slumped in the chairs in the kitchen, with feet on the table, till Jessie drove them off in order to bake her bread. Clifford stepped from the potbelly, raised his hand, hushing the other.

Adrian entered the kitchen as Jessie twisted her spine to set her youngest on a chair Grace had recently vacated. "Help, I say!" she called with ashen face and sweeping chin – a gesture to indicate the blood on the sleeve.

"Happy, you? One of them is finally hurt."

"Am I happy?" said Adrian who had just got his glasses down from the cupboard and was opening their ends. "What happened, Frank? You tell us now?"

Frank searched his father's face, a face turned horrid, deathly pale; past untrimmed nose hair the father blew forcefully. Frank wanted to cry openly in the comfort of his home and though the rawest moment had arrived in the face of his parents, nothing came. A constricted throat made speech and tears impossible.

"Get the jacket off – ah, this goddamn zipper contraption. I swear, to Jesus, Jessie; I never liked it and wherever you got it I wish you'd left it! Get me something. Cut it!"

The other two had fully emerged from the backroom, heat trailing. Both had eaten three plates of salt-cod, turnips, potatoes in jackets. They had shared a can of beans and so smelled. Wonderfully they were tired, but dreamy eyes dimmed and pupils focused. They had offered to search for him, after their food had digested. In turn, their parents had said no. Frank would come home on his own at any moment. With boys you got to expect this first night when the next would come home after dark. It was a rite of passage and then there was no stopping them: how long they went out, or where. But Frank. The baby.

Clifford and Will maintained the table between them and the spectacle. "What happened to him?" asked William as Clifford shifted aloft to study the doorknob. Clifford knew the gun was involved; he sniffed spent powder.

Jessie and Adrian directed Frank toward the better chair, pulled the one with no arms out from between wood stove and window.

"Here, Jessie. In the light, till I have a better look."

They faced Frank for the dinner table but in the move struck his elbow badly on the windowsill. He spoke articulately, with candour in delirium.

"No one touch me. No one move me. Please, can I have that?"

The boys looked at each other. They watched the head take support from the wall. The radiant kitchen heat made their brother sway in and out of consciousness.

Grace came down from upstairs, stood in men's slippers at the living room threshold.

"Get him some water, one of you!" said Adrian. "Jesus Christ. Tonight of all nights. Why?"

The dog was at Frank's feet, on its way to its spot below the removed chair, at the wood stove. With a brisk side-foot Adrian drove the cur the hell out of the way, but then saw it stumble. This scared him. The dog got under the table, where it swished no tail. Adrian got his son's jacket open, off him.

"Christ Almighty, will you look? The boy shot his goddamn arm off!"

"Merciful God, how? Shush. Just shush now."

"Don't shush me!"

"I'm not shushing you. I'm telling him to shush."

Adrian held out the bloody jacket, pinched it with both hands. Jessie, behind with both arms straight down, took it. She turned to her standing sons to see them healthy and tall. To see them receive her mute correspondence at last of how they needed to be careful in these woods, along these shores, on these mountains. Them with their cursed-eyed axes, saws, guns and the like.

The shot had torn away material in Frank's blue flannel shirt, an old shirt of Clifford's. It ripped the white cotton undershirt of William's. And Adrian's longjohns, those it shredded easily. A fleshy hole was a blue brutish grey, the rim a kidney red of marrow blood.

"Get them fellows out," said Adrian. "And tell your daughter Grace there not to enter further. To get back up to her room, this is no place for any of yas! Go. Now. Go!"

"Adrian stop with the hurrying. Stop with the noise, can you?"

He looked at her.

William and Clifford marshalled single file, but past, out into the front room, gaining speed after a commanding sweep, nod and twist of their mother's head. Grace had retreated moreover. All guiltily.

Adrian and Jessie expertly got Frank to his feet, guided him into the backroom where the boys slept. They got him down onto William's bunk, stationing his feet at the head. The arm could be outside in this case, where they could work on it. Frank felt the heat, he experienced the washed light and near silence of his home. There was clicking.

"Jesus Adrian," said Jessie aside. "I struck him when he came in, with my fist."

"You didn't know. How were you supposed to know?"

"I wanted to knock some sense into him. They're always out there somewhere making my heart sick with worry. And now look. I'm telling you it's too much for a soul to bear."

"Not the time, Jessie. Just get the pants off him. Strip him of his longjohns, make him comfortable. That's primary."

"He's frozen, too. I never saw this before."

"They've been frozen. They've been hurt too, hear? So calm it down. I need someone stable. William! Clifford! Get the hell out here with some wood! Dry stuff, from in around the kitchen stove – hurry, I say!"

William entered with an armload of kindling which he set near the potbelly.

"Poke it good first, before adding. Get the heat cracking."

Clifford entered with a bundle of birch bark, pushed William aside and got the crackle and spit. Clifford hissed, showed a backhand when William raised a stick of kindling to add. "Just go get me more wood from the kitchen," he said through clenched teeth. But William refused his brother and got his wrist powerfully slapped when he tried again adding kindling on his own.

"Leave it both of you! I have to do that myself, too! Get the hell out," Adrian stood with fist formed and ready at his side. "Out in the other room, now! And stay put out there till I say different."

The backroom was twelve feet across, nine long, with a seven-foot ceiling. It was lit by a red hurricane lamp. A bark fire roared, an east wind was in the flue; only an east climbed the pitch roof like that. Bricks stayed heated in an Easterly. Green wood burned. A family grew to depend on an Easterly.

"Get a sheet, Jessie. A clean sheet of some sort. White."

"It has to be white?"

"Has to be white. Keeps infection down. So go."

Adrian looked to see the door was closed. He saw pokes in panelling where two had fought one occasion with a broom. The broom had not passed through. He stood over his son's midsection, but blocked the light of the lamp. Blood had swollen underclothing to a gore that stuck sloppily to the boy's sides. With pillowcase, then a curtain, Adrian sopped it up. These fabrics filled and he tossed them in the corner laundry pile. He extended his chest, sighed, looked toward the door. She was just not coming. Lamplight made another screech for her unjust. He pulled out his own tucked-in shirt above the belt and undid lower buttons then tore his pocketknife into the plaid, ripping outward. He soaked up more blood with this rag then threw it in the corner. He cut again, this time getting a long strip he tied at Frank's shoulder.

"Dad, ow, Dad, ow!"

"To stop it Frank, I have to."

"The ice moved off. I had to swim for it."

"That cursed Middle Head. Not another word now. No one's angry here."

Adrian found the artery and tucked the knot over it. He felt for diminished flow. Thankfully no lead had pierced this. The area hit was inside, beginning at the shoulder. Tendon lay dreadfully exposed. It was too clear how human anatomy relates to the skinned animal. Adrian could never expect lead shot to do so fine a job. The blast had to have come at close range. Possibly exiting barrel tip only. It looked direct, the work of a slug. Maybe it was a slug. Where did they get slugs? A man could come out of this, not every man, but a man could. A boy was a far different matter. Spirit would be tested. His. Mine.

All of ours. He had spirit this one, not like the other two. Adrian became swept up in sadness then – and in pride. How far had his son walked, over ice, in this state? That cursed drift ice. The lure for a boy. What's it doing here, mid-winter? Climbed the Middle Head rocks, eh, had to get in the water in this frost? I could never have made it. A creamy ligament visible against its red backdrop tore at Adrian's heart. Partridge parts held muscle like this. Cleaning them I played with them. He turned, stood boldly to address the door.

"You coming back out here or are you not!"

Jessie stepped through.

"I need flour. I need cornmeal. Sugar and salt."

"Shouldn't we warm him up first?"

"No not first. The infection is to be stopped, first. It likes sugar, eats it, stays away from the core then. He's warm. The wet is taken off him. I could use some water, scalding. I can get the bleeding controlled, but I need to clean it before I make the poultice."

"The what?"

"Get what I said, Jessie, please. And bring it here, please. Bring salt!"

Adrian took the flannel sheets she had cut into strips for bandaging. Flour does bring down inflammation, he thought; it builds up healing tissue. He would tell his family just this when they questioned him. Field dressings, overseas in the war, they were poultices. Adrian had never been involved in any direct or dire conflict where the dressings were applied. He had seen field care, naturally, after the fact. He should have paid attention. He had heard, believed he had heard, that flour, sugar and salt was the way to go. Even porridge. He could have learned it here in Ingonish, a treatment the old-timers used, maybe one the Indians up the Clyburn gold mines used.

He brought the hurricane lamp forward, hung it on the iron bunk frame, but in such a way as to cast aside shadow. He spotted lead embedded deep in the boy's arm. Those bits will have to come out, but there's no tool for that. A hunting knife generally digs pellets from rabbit, from small game. But how could we secure an arm well enough to go to work on it like that? Get someone. Jessie couldn't bear the strain. She can't bear this, her. His brother Leo had needle-nose pliers. Nope. They would handle this on their own, as a family.

He felt wretched looking at the horror of the wound, its wastage on a young limb. He tried all he could not to think of the misery his son now faced, in life. Of course blame began in his mind, the finger got pointed at everyone in the house. The community itself had played its role. Because, who in their right mind would choose this geography to settle in? Had they all been that poverised elsewhere to have to come here and make a go of it? Cut off from any real care, cut off from the civilised world. In Europe, I should have kept on going. There were girls there to wed. I should have got goo in a foreigner. Or at least waved toward shore when the Queen Mary drifted from Halifax, waved a good goodbye. It would have been better for all their sakes, as well as my own. A scowl came at the thought of the other two, warming their arses by the fire in the front room. Why couldn't they have included Frank in their woodcutting? In any of the projects they had going? They were all brothers. The youngest always had it tough. I know. I was the youngest of a brood. Clifford. He was the instigator. William's the pup that follows the lead. Clifford won't have anything to do with Frank because the eldest always has it in for the youngest. Jealousness. The first and last end up adversaries. Frank, you tough? You will be, bai. Will have to be. Maybe that's the real reason for Clifford turning his back, he knew the day was coming when Frank would put a pounding on him. You two fellows already are the same height. Power struggles. The community was chock full, locked in them, and they didn't end as a person got older, no matter what anyone says. Was I to blame? I could have kept working on the woodpile with him in the morning when the priest arrived. Now, now, there. There's the source of it, that goddamn priest! That should get its teeth to drink, that.

Jessie entered with a basin of flour and cornmeal in a cup.

But Adrian passed her in the doorway.

"I'm coming back. You bring scissors? I cut some of the underclothes off him with my knife. I'll be back to put on the poultice. I put on a temporary bind to stop what flow I could so don't touch it. Where I have it tight now, you leave it."

"Where you going, Adrian?"

"Out here. Don't ask me where, I'll be right back."

The door eased shut and Jessie could only think: fools and cowards, as she turned for her son. "Your mother's coming, Frank."

Adrian returned, carrying a chair. He smelled of liquor, but didn't try to hide the fact he had gone to the cellar to drink the last of his secret stash. No freezing down four feet. In three swallows he had drained what was left of a thick glass medicine bottle of 'shine. They wouldn't understand. He had to stop the shaking. The boy couldn't use 'shine. Too powerful, and they didn't understand that it was I who needed it. And how long it has been down there, I don't know. Might not be safe. I laid down his glasses somewhere in the quick trip and still didn't know where. That slowed him.

Jessie had heard the crafty rising of the cellar hatch in the front room, the open communicating of pretence to the boys and Grace. She had heard his digging at the medicine cabinet in the kitchen, pulling everything off the shelf. This, while she waited, studying a sloppy tourniquet and temporary dressing. To hell with him and his nature.

"We're cleaning you up yet, Frank." "Be still. He's back now."

Jessie stood, fist patting her breast. She had cried getting Frank into the lower section of dry longjohns. She had pulled good wool socks on him while one clean towel covered his midsection and another caught seepage under the arm. Frank lay still through the work, followed instructions. He listened to how the wild wind struck the roof.

"We getting a storm, Mom?" He spoke that with more of that same frustrating clarity.

"Shush, shush now, hear me."

"Could you go out there and find me my glasses?" said Adrian, a second chair in his arms. Jessie sniffed the air when faces were level.

"Here. In your pocket."

"Ahh, cursed be to hell. Close that door will you. We got to keep the heat built up in here." Adrian placed the second chair alongside the bunk and on it set basin, cup of cornmeal, jar of sugar, salt and a kettle with vapours. He tasted the salt to check whether it was salt then set a huge spool of green fishing twine on the chair.

The bleeding had continued. It had soaked through to the mattress. "We got to get pressure on this better, Frank. We'll be out of the woods then, when we do." Clear-headed, the father touched the arm his wife had sense to keep outside the towel. He drew the wool blanket up to his son's midsection, keeping its roughness off the exposed naval. He undid his first bandage and neatly dabbed the wound's edges with it. He tilted the kettle spout and dampened a strip of bed sheet; applied cornmeal, flour, sugar then salt. Plenty. He used fishing twine to keep the new bandage spread tight. From his shirt pocket he carefully took his carpenter's pencil next, inserted it in the tourniquet knot. He twisted. Frank jarred his heels.

"Please no Dad, please, please, I wish you wouldn't."

"Jessie, Jessie! She'll hold you, Frank. You hold him. He's yours. Till I get the pressure I need."

Jessie knelt, was beside herself with dumb complaint. Each instant plagued her soul. It was all she could do to act when beckoned. She didn't like Adrian contradicting himself, applying this dressing, then that. He was in the war. He had seen it. Yet a hopeless night was now in store for the lot. Her mother could not have desisted? Allowing her to marry at sixteen? To get hauled into this man's world, a mere child? To enter his predicaments, be on hand for his mess-ups? Childbearing, childrearing. Dirty diapers, petrified screeching, dishes piled, boots! Everyone with a concern. Baking and baking. She could smell the bread. If she had spent just one more year on her own she might have developed a sense for it. Second-guessing was worst. Ah, Frank, not favoured. And it was you who had my encouragement.

"Fine, Jessie, stand back now."

She retreated and picked up the bloody rags. A curtain, pillow-case, piece of shirt, even. All thrown in the corner empty of regard. With hot tears in her eyes she started a neat pile at the woodbox.

"Ah, no," said Adrian. "I won't have it. You can't see I need some heart here? You can't save that for later? The boy shouldn't have to see his mother like this. Try to pull yourself together! All right then. Go out in the kitchen if you have to. Take that bread out, best to busy yourself."

*A*drian Curtis. He had taken no action. Disciplining was hers. She doled out the slappings. Each day the bare minimum was required for something or other, for general edification. He stepped around the corner of the house when it began. He liked it as much as he did socialising.

Frank lay lucid and curious. He studied his father's eye, this skill, concentration, gentle touch. And communication too, of what had to come next. "You're my youngest, Frank. Don't you forget it." The image was soon hard to lock onto because the room spun as a spring flood rushed in to float all items from floor up, make level all with the bunk. Walls bent. Seaweed sloshed. Laundry sloshed. Clifford's single bed across the way shook, let go. Frank fought for consciousness. He focused on his father's work, tried to hear the voice; maintaining a sense of the man's narrow displacement at bedside. His father sat in the spot his mother had, halfway down. Frank's first room had been the cold room, opposite his parents'. His mother sat in with him at night when the serious illnesses of childhood hit. "I see the moon, the moon sees me. I see the moon in a great big tree." Outside the cold room she never sang, never hummed. Frank had been in the backroom these past two years.

"Mom…?"

"She's here Frank."

Adrian turned for the door. Jessie approached.

She stood alongside, set down iodine.

"He's asking for you."

"And I'm here."

Adrian dabbed the dressing ends with hot salt water. He asked for scissors to trim his work. Jessie produced them from her pocket.

Grace stood with the older boys at the kitchen stove. Golden bread was on the table. Clifford had poked his face through the backroom door at one point to get a peek, to learn the direction his anger would take. He closed the door: "this was plenty." He brought the gun in from the cold, but stood in the porch light to break open the barrel. With his knife he dug the spent shell. "Save it?" said William, over his shoulder, receiving an elbowing – the brown-eyed redhead reaching to touch the safety catch.

"That what you filed?"

"What're you talking about?"

"You said so, in the woods."

Grace's face was at the window to the porch. She looked on cautiously, her raven hair fanning while the greying Clifford peered headlong at the glass. She dispersed completely.

six

"What are we to do?"

Jessie spoke in a faraway voice. Adrian looked at her. She had hands folded at her midsection, on the hump left after giving the first birth. Her jaws tensed. There is never only one victim.

"We're going to help him, do what comes natural. What we are doing. We followed procedure, cleaned him up. Just good thing nothing major was hit."

"Did it pass through?"

"It passed."

"But they have pellets, some of them. Did this one have pellets?"

"You saw that it did. It was close range, the shot cleared."

"The majority cleared."

"Ah, Jessie, I'm no doctor, am I? We're doing what we can. What we should. I'll tell you one thing. That boy is as tough as nails. No one I know could suffer through what he did and live to talk about it."

Jessie turned, agreed, felt she had this to hold.

The bleeding continued. Frank dug his heels in the mattress, bit down on molars and exhaled what he could when his father twisted the pencil tourniquet, ending flow again. "Did I say you were a soldier? Brass, you hear? And don't you forget it."

With salt water Adrian wiped to the wrist and dabbed each fingernail. The kerosene was low, the lantern now flat on the bureau above the sock box to catch its fuel. He had been having trouble seeing and was about to ask Jessie to clean the shade. "No, bring it forward, will you?" She got up from Clifford's bed and crossed the room. "Dim it some. Set it here on the second chair. You've been one great help. We'll be all right here. Wait, what's this? Jessie, you didn't remove his other mitt? I didn't notice till now, under the blanket. Why?"

"I didn't have the heart. It was soaked, frozen. I thought it was stuck to the skin."

"He's your son. Realise that he is. You got to do things when they slip up, when it's called for. Frank? Asleep yet? Can you wait till we get a second clean sheet under you? Someone's bringing you something hot."

Blood flowed.

"Cursed hell, this needs to be redone."

"No, Adrian, seepage. All wounds seep some. In the morning, change it. Please not now, I say."

He looked at her. It seemed a point of particular concern.

"You're right. You're right. Don't mind me, my nerves are shot. He needs to be still. Been a long night for all involved. I'll stay in the chair if you want to go and get some rest. Tell Clifford to go in the living room and bring in here another armload of wood. Tell him to go outside if he has to. And tell that Grace to bring in the soup and bread she was supposed to. Also, could you get one of them to go up to the road and tie something red to a tree."

"Something red, what on earth for?"

"We got an emergency here."

"The doctor passed through the week before last."

"He did?"

"I told you he did."

"Ah, cursed old hell, what next?"

"He won't be by for a month, Adrian. And the weather."

"Do as I say. I still want something up. Someone will see it, can you see to it that that girl is in here with the soup?"

*F*rank tried to be conscious for all, and he was, till the darkest hours, till the house lost the clicking. His father's reassurances and the painful action taken, this cleaning and redressing of the wound – all quietened, and so, he hoped, all must be ending. A body heals. No injustice lasts when it comes to a young body healing. Under the sheets, sweat soaked him from foot to neck. He wanted to say one last thing to his father.

"Arm, Dad."

"What about it? Go ahead."

"It's cold. I'm frightened to say so."

"Don't be frightened of anything, hear. Of no thing or no one here on in."

"I won't."

"Here. I'll just put this towel over and if it's still cold you tell me. I'll put my jacket on it. Still cold then, a mattress. I'm right here. You're a smart lad. The best I got."

Jessie came in with pea soup and bread. She handed Adrian his eyeglasses he had set on the bureau where they got lost under slacks. He nodded thanks. His eyes enlarged, peered past a sharp nose to check his work. The wind shook mercilessly this part of the house, the direction having swung around to the northwest where it blew from as many cruel points as it wished; it was hard to keep a good fire lit in a Northwest.

"Dad?"

"Right here?"

"Suppose you could bring in Millie?"

"Say again."

"Millie? Could you set her in the backroom with us?"

Adrian couldn't meet his son's request, all was mumbling.

"The dog, Dad, the dog!" said Clifford, his long back to the bunks. With an axe he broke apart, gently as he could, kindling on the floor.

*F*rank woke in a clammy sweat that covered him to his socks. He discovered this had been no dream. Turning his head, his right knee bracing the wall, he saw deep night not ending. The arm was stiff, heavy. The lantern wick spat, she was on her last hour.

"Dad? Could I have water, Dad?"

"Have whatever you want, Frank."

Adrian stood, and the light of the woodstove flickered on his front. He wore his green workpants which were darkly scorched from cuffs to knee. The scorches came from burning cut limbs and lopped off black spruce crowns down at the Rock two days prior. He had climbed the smoking stack down at the Rock, jumped on it to get oxygen into boughs below. Frank had been with him the whole day and laughed to see his father juvenile, bouncing like an excited child in the centre of his high green pile. It wasn't cutting cold, though the snow in the woods was deep. Thick smoke spun from below Adrian's feet, it rose to gag him. He beat it away with his hunter's cap using his second arm to hide eyes in the crevice of an elbow. He kept up the bouncing while Mililica ran around the perimeter barking her head off, getting herself more and more worked up. "'Got to get the air to her, me son – by the old dying frig, I'll be choked yet!" Adrian suffocated but kept on, till a foot dropped out of sight and the whole leg was ensnared in limbs. He straightaway pitched forward, rolling free to escape the stack's flames. The boot pulled off, disappeared at the stack edge, but when turning for it a yellow flame shot out to singe Adrian's forehead, frightening the life out of him. He rolled twice more, stopping to wrestle Mililica. "Come here till I get a hold of ya!" The boughs caught fully and smoke billowed into a blue sky. They were unable to retrieve the boot. Adrian stood with a foot on a bough; he had to hop, with Frank's help, up to the house. Frank came back on his own to watch the pile go heavenward, roar like ignited gasoline, shoot sky-high.

"I said, do you want your mother? She's in the other room."

"Is she?"

"I'll get her."

"I don't want her."

Adrian inserted a stick of birch into the fire. This was the good wood he kept for social purposes, what was stacked against the storm door in the front room, the door no one used. Flames crept over the white wood to make it crack and burst. Frank could not see directly into the tiny woodstove window, but he heard swirling wind in the flue, its howling and coaxing of burning flame from this tempered wood. Outside, across the field, trees rocked. This was visible from where Frank lay, though there was no moon tonight. The branches dipped in whooshes then sprang when wind tore off hither. With keen ears he heard his parents. They stood a pair, now in the kitchen.

"He's running a fever yet. In the morning I'll change the dressing, what's coming out is hardly even red. Type of pus. The mixture has to be taking effect."

"There's no one to come? Those pellets have to come out, you know that they have arsenic in them."

"I know. I know they need to. No, no one can come, not tonight they can't. This is not Montreal, Toronto. I'm the only one with training in Ingonish, the sole one to come back from the few who left. I watched what was done over there. Don't worry. The *Aspy* isn't sailing, with this drift ice in... she sure as hell isn't. Otherwise we could get word up that way, to North Sydney. And the private guys with their boats don't sail this time of year. The ocean is clear solid, has us locked in like an embargo. The doctor will pass, how long you say? Heavens. Well. We'll hold out. Did you get one of the young fellows to go up to the road, hang out the red material like I asked?"

"William went over the crust without a jacket and wearing only boot felts. Do you hear me when I tell you the doctor won't be here for weeks? That's too long Adrian. We have to get word out, not a red shirt."

"Tell William to go back out in the morning and pull down whatever he put up then."

"What? Why? Why when you had him go out and put it up? It's not good to have up?"

"No, on consideration. And because I said so is why. Stop contradicting me. I thought on it and decided we don't need all those fools in here that will come around snooping, giving advice and opinion not called for. I don't know what I hate worse. First your people, then mine. The priest will get wind. Oh, all I need, that. I tell you the boy can't take it, Jessie... any of it. It'll rattle him."

"How will the doctor even know someone needs him here if now you're saying we're going to go with no sign? He'll ride right past if and when he does set foot in these parts."

"You're not hearing, are you, because you won't be patient long enough to listen. No one said we're going to wait on it. First light, I'm sending Clifford with word."

"Where? Not to North Sydney! By the old Joe Frig. For the love of God where is your head, Adrian?"

"Why? And yes, to North Sydney! His brother can go along. Let them sleep for now."

"–I ain't going, it's freezing out. I'm froze here."

The parents turned as one to the living room.

"Who's that? William Thomas, that you awake out there?'

"Half."

"Listen, your mother and I are having a private discussion so go the hell back to sleep, mister. We need a peaceful house tonight."

"Sleep? How can a person manage the likes of that when the couch's arm is like lying your head down onto rock?"

"You'll get rock. Listen, bai. I said your mother and I are talking so shut them eyes this very instant!"

"Adrian," said Jessie, stepping toward the kitchen window. "The trip is seventy miles. Many in the community have never even been there before. Our boys haven't."

"What? North Sydney? It's not seventy, it's hardly sixty-five. That ain't far, they'll make that. There's a trail, and who's any more used to travelling the woods and shores than those two. They can do an agile thirty mile a day, easy. They'll make up the extra ten, in change."

"I don't know. Look out the window. It's a hellish night. A storm's brewing. You can tell."

"Storm? It's been storming here for six months! Can't let a storm stop us. It's the hour, Jessie. It's dark and grim always at this hour."

Adrian flattened hands on the glass, peered out alongside his wife. The field was drifted, blustery and wanting. Jessie drew back and he flattened his forehead on the pane to do some thinking. The skull felt perfect on the hardness of the cool moist window.

"I say this is no storm. Thing is, I walked it. Me and Brian Hawley right after the war. Poor Brian had to walk it both ways, up and back. He had come up to greet his brother Patrick at the train station. I told you this. It was some awful moment. Him there on the platform, waiting. Fingers like sausages, that boy. I don't know if he was fifteen yet. Then to have to tell him his brother wasn't with me. They always travelled together them two. Heavens, how I hated having to tell him. It was winter, just like this. I had on me my uniform only, low-cut lace boot, army issue."

"It wasn't winter. You always said it was spring."

"Month-wise, perhaps. Cold as the dickens. Like this. I know that. No – worse!"

"William has to go along, if Clifford does go."

"I promised you he would."

"–But I ain't."

"You still awake? Listen mister for the last time, close them eyes or I'll close them for you!"

"Yalp… right worried."

"You will be worried. This is your father speaking. So, so help me, get to sleep!"

There was a rustle on the couch, the chesterfield opposite remained mute.

"It would be good to have one of them to help out here, but we can manage things. We got Leo to turn to if things take a turn for the worse. They won't."

"He's fourteen, on Friday."

"I know his age, Jessie."

"Will they take the horse?"

"The horse? That couldn't make it up the head of the salt lake."

Each parent made sounds of shifting weight on the floor, while in the backroom Frank felt himself begin to go haywire. His balance, though supine, rushed from him as if he were on a black staircase ascending that final step he only thought was there. His body jolted, and jolted again. Moreover, the room shifted its furnishings, the wall construction buckled. The heat of the fire. It was too much. Frank experienced his mother's cool hands on him, his head being lifted.

"Drink from the bowl this time, the cup went all down your neck remember."

Jessie touched his forehead flatly and how Frank hated that she was so silent, that the hand was as waxen as one from a casket. There would be no sleep, not till he wore himself out.

Adrian stood behind.

"Hang on," he called. "I know it's bad, but we're getting some help, hear?"

Frank said that he'd stay calm, but then cried out mortally for his mother. They both took him in their hands, then Adrian looked to his wife and he let her have him all. She adjusted weight on the bunk frame.

"I'm here so you shush now."

"Mililica make it back, Mom? She was half froze. She got in the water too."

"She made it back. She made it back with you, you don't remember? She's curled up at the foot of the stove in the other room, they gave her a slice of boloney."

"Can you bring her in? Let her by this stove?"

"We'll bring her in, but you just try to sleep for now. Can you do that?"

"Could I have one more aspirin? Dad? He stop… get it stopped?"

"Yes. That's enough for now. Sleep, I said. We're getting help in."

The glass lantern, half-filled again with pine-scented kerosene, sat on the chair. With wick raised it lit the steel laths and steel coiled fastenings of the overhead bunk. Deep urine stains of the flipped-over mattress were traceable, the laths extra sharp between taut shadowed coils. Frank turned his head and saw that the boys did not sleep in the backroom tonight. They slept at the big drafty fire in the front room. Who had the chesterfield by the fire? Who had the short couch by the window? William had the couch. It's where he falls in line. Frank then remembered what his mother asked of him. He closed his eyes.

seven

$\mathcal{N}$ear dawn, ending this first night, after the wind had shifted fully west and the temperature climbed to minus twenty-four, Adrian spoke softly from the kitchen out to his two sons. He asked in an unadjusted voice for them to rise off their couches.

The smell of fried bologna and eggs filled the air. Smoke lifted in plumes from the frying pan and curled among wooden rungs of the ceiling's clothes drying rack. Too much heat cooked the food; Adrian added a second scoop of lard to lower its temperature. The pan sizzled as burning food got momentary respite. William watched from the couch his father's squinting into the cooking. He could not see wholly, as the wool blanket caught by two nails and draping the doorway to hold heat in the kitchen, obscured vision. When courage came to face the frost William swung out his legs. He quickly pulled on a cotton shirt then a sweater. Shivering, he reached inside his longjohns for a fast scratch at an armpit. There was water on the floor, a heel went in it. "By the old fuck," he muttered bending and drawing wide the laces of his boot; his felts had spent the night drying by the fire, a fire long gone out. He walked in unlined boots to the woodstove. He checked the felt heels then the toes for dampness. His complexion, his red freckles came to mind while working the felts inside. His freckles were duller these winter mornings but also, age was a factor. Age was erasing the distinctive markings from his face, much to his relief. Freckles were funny, yes, but as a childhood feature. No one took him seriously. The mirror was at the sink in the kitchen, an area colder yet, near jugs of water whose surfaces you had to jab with a bread knife to break. William spoke, working in the second felt, an exposed foot stationed on the cool damp boot below:

"Dad. You never cooked."

"I did, sure. When your mother was busy having yas I cooked."

William drew the laces taut and when the tongues were even he tied double knots. He saw how Clifford was lying on the chesterfield, eyes shut, head upright atop the wood arm, his nose indicating the ceiling. Cushion with sections gone supported the rigid neck. Clifford now had silken sideburns and moustache, both black as the ace of spades. But everything about that prick was black, including his heart. In his hair was the handsome silver streak, the premature greying. He cut a striking figure overall with this marking, in the low visibility of the front room.

Clifford's eyes opened, studied the ceiling, turned for his brother.

"What the hell you staring at?"

"Not much."

The elder's eyes soured and the head turned back to contemplate the ceiling's drywall tape. William bent to the creaking hinges of the woodstove door, and saw Clifford lick his moustache. He remembered hearing licking was the way to grow it.

"Don't add much to that fire," said Clifford. "We're going out."

"To what fire? The thing's been dead since midnight."

"There's coals."

"Coals, yalp, maybe one. Cold, more like. Stone cold."

For the longest time, while Clifford's moustache was coming in, Jessie had asked him to shave it. "You'll look better. Feel better." He told her to stop telling him this. And she did, the feeling coming that this would be the last thing she'd ask him. Clifford coughed. He needed a smoke but he was out of tobacco.

Pushing the blanket partition aside, William entered to the kitchen.

"Jesus. Dad. The house is like a barn!"

"Watch your mouth you. What did your mother tell you about cursing?"

"I'll stop. Today. That wind is barrelling straight down the chimney, and there's no getting that other stove on this morning. Not with what wood is out there. The stuff down below is wet."

"Then get the hell down in the cellar for a scuttle of coal to perk it up."

"Why is it me who has to?"

"Because you're up. You're standing and asking."

"Fine way to wake, this is."

From the Chesterfield, arms under an army blanket, Clifford said: "Dad."

"What?"

"He come through the night?"

"He came through. But get up and out of there now. There's a thing I want you two to do."

"Here we go," said William, to the grates, to the frying pan while leaning over it, arms crossed, elbows in.

But Adrian left the kitchen to go stand above Clifford. He clutched the bread knife that he used to cut the bologna. Bits of wax from the wrap were on the blade. He followed his eldest son's eyes to the bits, wiped the blade in the second shirt out over his belt, at the hip. He had come to show Clifford the chops from the pig, what he had kept in the porch tied to a spike in the ceiling, up out of the reach of the dog.

"I'm giving you one of these, each. And your mother has got a good lunch prepared."

"For the jaunt?"

"That's right. I need both you two to head up the North Shore, then on into North Sydney. We got to get someone in to see him. The situation is grave. Beyond what any family could muster."

"North Sydney? Nice piece!" said William, passing the two on the way down the hatch for a scuttle of coal. "How we supposed to manage that? The horse will never make it. We wouldn't get to the top of Smokey before she'd be coyote meat. Cold crow leftovers."

"You're not to take the horse, hear. And you'll be coyote meat. You're to go on foot as I did. As I'd do now if it wasn't that I got to stay here with your mother, case he takes a turn. We've got to get a doctor in, proper attention. And there's no two ways about it so up Clifford, I say; no time to be dragging your arse. Eat what I got together for you, then get going."

William showed his head at the hatch. He handed up a scuttle of coal to his father. Clifford put his feet to the floor.

The boys in turn stepped into the porch, in boots and tight longjohns. They eased open the heavy outer door that wanted the wind then pissed with good force to take it beyond the step which, newly covered in snow, hid most activity of the previous night. Blood was on the porch floor. Each had stepped clear of that. None was in the kitchen. Spruce drew back, as if to strike across a disappearing field. Showering crowns snowed in rustling rushing wind while swirls of free flakes swept near expanses before tearing obliquely down over the woods. But eddies there gathered in the trees, moved brown cones and copper needles till a consensus developed for the long dark downhill dash for the shore. From the porch, at this hour, it looked as if the whole country had bargained away the feature of light to meaningless other lands.

At the kitchen table, at the sock box carried in the night before from the backroom, the boys slid bare feet into dress socks. They pulled on the two pairs each of warmed woollen worksocks their father had set during the night over the drying rack. "They'd better be dry. I had them in the oven first going off, till smoke forced me to crack the door a bit. Here. Put on these dried longjohns over what you got on, your mother's people sent them up the road last Christmas. Each of you. Here I say."

The boys drew on the green-knit army longjohns. Their mother had set pants aside, too. Two pairs of black wool were splayed out over William's couch end. Two long-sleeved flannel shirts hung from her bedroom doorknob. They returned to the kitchen, buttoning plaid long-sleeves shirts over underwear tops and cotton tee shirts. She had set out sweaters at the back of the kitchen table where the boys now sat.

"Where're yas going," said Adrian. "The North Pole? That's too much you got on there. Be reasonable."

"Be what?" said William. "You step outside today? You have a look at what's blowing? The North Pole is exactly where we're headed."

"Do as you like. But you'll find those sweaters too much. They'll get bound up and heat won't circulate."

The boys waited at the table.

Adrian handed his own good mittens to William, who set them under an elbow. Clifford would wear the gloves he got from Claire Dunphy. He and Claire were going out now. Now since the gloves. Clifford never spoke of Claire. The topic lay in a tomb where everything else with him was pent. Adrian passed plates of breakfast food. Bologna, eggs, two helpings of salt-cod cakes, along with the crispy pork chops.

The boys stopped their munching to look up.

Grace had descended.

Grace hesitated on the first step to the upstairs, in the near dark. She had reached the age when a girl cut a moody figure in the morning. She set a socked foot down and crossed the kitchen floor without a word.

"You're not going to ask about your brother?" said Adrian.

"I am. How is he?"

"Still. And that's the way we'll keep him, still."

Grace's curly black hair was a tangled bush, her pasty face lined from a crinkled pillowcase on which she had heavily slept. She was never on deck at this hour so the strain of it made her look like a Jezebel. At the sink she lifted a heavy water jug to fill the white basin, ice bits came. She dipped fingers into the icy pool, rinsing her face with a cupped hand.

"You go easy on that," said Adrian. "I don't know how far down the ice is in the well and we'll need all we got today. Snow is out – that takes forever to melt that, so, easy I say."

"I heard you the first time," said Grace, drying with a towel on which traces of caked bread dough formed sharp pricks. She was not conscious of the pricks, only discovering them after cutting her face.

"Not bad enough I'm froze to death in this barn, but you got to have towels like this laid out." The boys raised their chins and grinned. Grace put on her fashionable red coat, drew its belt across as her black eyes flashed in scorn. This coat was identical to Jessie's, with its wood buttons and rope clasping-loops. A black horizontal strip set off the fashion aspect. Grace flipped up the oversized hood and let its drawstring dangle. At the door, she stepped into a pair of Adrian's boots. She crossed the porch and at the table the boys listened for the outer door to blow from her, its wide swing smacking fully the side of the house. The outhouse was beyond the cabin and the horse, past the chicken coop. Grace had to go here. When she returned the boys had on their jackets and wool hats. They sat in chairs pushed out from the table to blow on tea.

"What kind of wild morning it is anyway, I near blew away! And, Dad. Could you tell your two pigs here to take their leaks away from the step to a spot where none has to cross it. Frig sakes. Frigging slobs."

The boys burst into laughter and Adrian said, "All right, you two. Respect your sister. And keep it down."

Grace's hair was all about her head making her at present a witch blown off course. Her young skin had come fresh and consistent in the raw early morning, its frigid bluster. She lifted tangles from her black eyes.

"He any better?"

"Who?"

"Who!" She tightened jaws, in tradition. "He, who."

"Not a whole lot. The boys are going for a doctor."

"There one near?"

"You know that there's none near, and does it look like these two are dressed for any travel that's near?"

"The *Aspy* isn't sailing. How can they travel?"

"Grace. Don't have me explain it to you, too. There's no boat of any sort sailing, the ocean is frozen clear across to Europe. They're heading in to North Sydney, on foot. That satisfy you?"

"Jesus. I was just asking."

"Well, no wonder. I'm after going over it again with your mother, these two, now you. My nerves will be wrecked altogether yet."

Clifford stood. William stood, flicked drops from his plastic Thermos teacup on to the dog's back. He screwed on the cup, his freckles a livid orange in the heat of his clothes, at the fire of the kitchen.

"You put in more tea, bai?" said Clifford to William. "You fill it right up? With the hot water and the canned milk, because I told you to put in more tea yesterday and you didn't. I ain't frigging drinking it weak out there. Let me tell you that right now."

"It won't be weak, bai. I put a handful in so shut up about it."

"Don't tell me to shut up because you're dead if we get out there and it's weak like yesterday."

"That wasn't my fault. Those were reused. Today's are fresh. So, just go home."

"Who you telling to go home you freckle-faced rat."

"Enough!" said Adrian. "Or I'll brain the pair of yas. A big job is required of yous two today so pull yourselves together and get along, hear?"

Clifford stepped into the porch and set his army-issue backpack down on the sawhorse. He checked for matches. He touched his compass, rope and his sharp knife. He thought of the good hunting territory they would soon cross, when William entered the porch with Adrian, who handed over the lunches their mother had prepared.

"Mom not getting up to say good bye?"

"Leave her where she's at," said Adrian.

Clifford stuffed the lunches into the backpack and the three stood under the wall mount of deer antlers. William looked his father in the eye.

"I guess you'll have to take care of the horse and the other animals."

"Other animals? No chickens survived the cold snap?"

"One did. I saw it hiding when I brought hay down from the loft before bed last night."

"That's good, then."

"And the wood," said William. "Can you handle that?"

" I guess I can handle it. Don't you worry about here, it's high time you two shoved off."

Adrian took Clifford aside.

"Listen, you're in charge. If it gets real bad I want you to turn around." Adrian had not hushed his words but had in fact included William in their saying. William appreciated this. Adrian nodded, focused a naked eye, communicating clearly that this latter part was no real option, but that he had said it only customarily. "It isn't as far as you think. Draw your hoods tight. You fellows have twice the strength I ever had, and these legs made it. Thanks to your grandfather's people you have a thing called stamina."

"What's that, a disease?"

"I'm hoping you'll find someone on a sleigh along the way. Someone going into town for one particular purpose or other. Tell them the situation. If you must. Get them to give you a ride. Which they can't refuse. You can overnight at one of the Scotsmen's places on the North Shore if you're stuck, that folk will take you in. Here. A dollar."

Clifford took the money. With nothing further the boys set out.

From the crack in the open porch door Adrian, then Grace, watched their breaking the snow, their making the road. The porch was covered in a hoarfrost. The two went inside, came to the front window and saw Clifford face the road wind, carrying the pack, leading. William carried a sheathed knife at his left hip. "They'll be all right," said Adrian, letting loose the curtain, turning to see Jessie, standing in her night coat.

*O*ut on the road where the trees were missing from the bad turn the wind howled in sixty-knot pushes. William hollered overhead to Clifford:

"The end of our lives, here!"

"What!"

Clifford had to wait for William.

"I got snow in my boot!" said William

"You would, you disgrace. Here, take this pack!"

"I'm not taking it. You carry it. It's yours. I'll take it after it's lighter."

"Take it or I'll slap the face off you."

"This'll be our end. You do know that."

"It'll be yours, you don't keep up. Ahead in the turns she'll slacken off."

But the forward sheltering turns ended quickly and the boys were suddenly faced with the straight stretch of the clam-flats, geography that began the head of the harbour. The wind here bore flat-out northwest, funnelling from mountains, gathering in gusts, slinging from the tower-flanked now-frozen valleys at the head of Ingonish Harbour.

They saw the gusts. Saw how their merciless rips from the hills tore down the harbour ice, only worsening there, creating fierce blasts that roared hell-bent for an open sea.

The boys turned for the bank when properties barring social access to the harbour had ended. Descent was west now, down past the Piper's property, Simon Donovan's gang with his seven boys straight. No sign of life came from the single-story dwelling only a wildly swirling wood smoke at its roof peak. No flue was visible. Just the smoke, pouring talons over the roof's ridge.

They faced the unbridled winds then, here and there hanging onto crinkling alders for balance.

"Get your hood up, good! We're heading across!"

The boys stepped out onto the ice. Clifford chose the exposed route of the flats to cross because it cut down on distance. This section of the harbour ice sat heavily on the clam-flats. Beneath the ice, in parts, water was in three channels, the delta extending from Ingonish River. They marched outward but quickly lost visibility, progress becoming less certain. Granular wind got in to sting the right side of their faces and in some blows they were forced to cower as ice grains pelted their deeply shut eyes. They hurried then. William attempting to put his feet where his brother had.

"This frost!"

"What?"

"Keep on, keep on!"

They passed over the channels unknowingly and reached the banks of Hawley's Point. Here they got under the pine trees and pounded leather mittens as the shelter brought profound order to a wild world. They lowered their hoods, to resume with a lightened step under tall swaying brutes whose crowns howled with wind.

"Feels like a big house we're in all of a sudden," said William.

Above the noise of the wind they heard their bootfalls, successive breaks through hard crust as they meanwhile looked warily toward the savage harbour. They followed banks at the base of Robertson Mountain, their objective here to stay within sight of the frozen shoreline. They saw their house at one wintry pass, across a deep water section of the harbour. Scrub spruce limbs swayed in and out of the delicate scene. They left the cover of trees then to walk the ice, to bypass the hermit's, entering cover again only to arrive with finality at the foot of Smokey Mountain, their largest obstacle in the journey to come.

The mountain base was barren, a land whipped forever by rising wind torments striking northwest out of the harbour. The first settlers had cut trees here to access fields for their animals. The boys studied dropping snow showers from lofty crowns, and white-wedding eddies below, as tall as they. A mature stand of hemlock bordered the fields, but further up: in the direction they would take. The two began, staying close to these hemlock, and soon they traced a forest with their path. The drifting snow was not packed hard here as it had been in the quieter pine forest at the head of the harbour. A softer snow slowed the going as it rose consistently to the tender shin. Kneecaps worked. In forward motion, laced leather dug toes into steep terrain to strike a deeper crust, keeping the circulation up. Crusty footing was the result of weather two weeks prior, days of uncanny wet rain that had settled fully over the region. A silver thaw coated the mountainside making, for one day, all things pretty. Lustrous, its underlay now helped the ascent. The concern was not of physical requirements, but of a day that remained bleak. Powerful weather systems tormented the higher sky, ones which could well manifest into heavy snowfall. The boys did not speak of it. The going was tough. They concentrated on climbing. Once up Smokey they would feel better.

$\mathcal{F}$rank slept. Adrian looked out the backroom window, his face positioned above the oblique rising rime of ice on the pane. This undulating pattern on the pane was what the four loved to play with as children; its green scum likening it to a mountain ridge whose tops they broke off and let ease down the glass. He saw Smokey Mountain rise, above the flat frosted sea, above the sea's teeming vapours. He could pinpoint their trail, just above the harbour ice. His eye judged distance yet. He could mark where the two dark figures had begun their assault, rejoicing when their path broke free of the hemlock and pushed straight upward. The two chose the rockslide to continue! The scree! The shortest route, always, how he taught them how to travel.

"Mmm, uh, huh!"

Adrian whipped around. Christ. Christ. Hang on, me son.

"Shush now," he urged across the room.

"Come over here, Grace," said Arian in gushing whisper. "You look for me, will you? That's them, isn't it? Out of the trees? Well, they made it that far so they can do the rest but Jesus, wind, will you let up and choose another day! Blow then, for all you're worth. What makes the going hard is the wind. Once they hit the top of Smokey, though, the North Shore, it'll sort itself out. A whole other world is up there, on the other side. They're liable to hit sun."

Grace retreated. She went to her mother. Adrian let go his grasp of the curtain, its crinkled material fell somewhat back into place. He brushed hair from his forehead, stood, and could still see out the window. Me? No blessed way on this earth I could have made the trek. I'm here for good now, I guess. How fast a man falls into the place he won't soon get out. Realise then, what he can and what he can't.

Smelling a change in the wood fire, Adrian turned and crossed the floor. He removed a grate with the lifter while Jessie watched him. She sat with black prayer beads out on her lap, their crucifix in her fingers. It was her turn to turn to glimpse the forlorn window whose curtain shifted softly in a draft of neat air entering, enjoying the little crack it had found.

eight

At mid-morning the moaning started. Adrian could soon take no more and left the room. He walked into the kitchen, and, assisted by an indicative thumb, said to Grace, "Go back out there see if she needs anything. And get an armload of wood from the cabin when you're finished. I'm stepping out for an hour." Jessie opened the door to the backroom, hearing this, showing herself fully.

"Where you going? You're not going anywhere."

"I'm not, am I?"

"No and don't have me plead. Where are you going, Adrian? We got a boy who needs us, here."

"Which is where I'm going. To see if I can find someone. We can't manage this on our own. Not now, not anymore."

"Will you listen to that – that's what I've been trying to tell you."

"Yeah. Well."

Jessie kept her eye on Adrian whose ears were red and jaw loose. He inserted a dried-out felt into a snowshoe boot while offering only profile. Jessie knew the wrong word here would set off a tongue-lashing, from both directions.

"Adrian. You're not going for liquor. Tell me you're not. Not now you're not."

"I'm not going for liquor, Jessie. I said I was going out to see if I could find someone. So don't give me any debate on it. You tell me what I'm supposed to do, eh! Keep my hands in my pocket? Sit here doing nothing, listening to that, waiting for someone? For some thing! Not as man of the house, I can't. The wailing alone, you hear him out there."

"I hear him. Better than any. The boys will bring someone. That wasn't your purpose in sending them? Ah, you don't fool me, mister, where you're going, what you're up to. You don't fool anyone. Just get the hell out then, go hide in some bottle. Man of the house, man my eye. Pfft, you're no more man than that broom leant against the wall. Go on, go on! It's all you're damn-well good for."

"Hear! I don't need to hear from you all I'm damn-well good for. Not enough that I work to feed everyone."

There's a laugh. When do you work? When the sun's high and the daisies are up, is when, the only time you'll set foot out the door to earn a dollar. And don't you forget, mister, it's me who manages the household things and budgets to keep us above water. We'd be in the poorhouse without my efforts. January alone would finish us."

"I'll return when I return and I'll say no more on it."

Adrian forcefully grabbed the arm of his jacket which was on a card table buried deep under blankets and heavy coats. The pile tumbled, he bent.

"I'll be back. I'll stay put. You'll see. I won't go out afterwards."

He struggled with the doorknob, having to shake and twist it free of its clasp. The handle was badly set and, depending on the season, exit and entry were made difficult. Wood swelled to make its functions act up, but the house also settled onto the doorjamb. Both doors, inside and out, were bad and every single time Adrian got caught up passing through he meant to take the planer and shave both bottoms and tops.

The second door in the porch was caught by snow. This he managed to squeeze through and once outside drew a long breath, harsh wind entering his throat. He bit a glove to get it on, a pair his daughter or wife wore to Mass. With a bare hand he struck a wooden match for a homemade cigarette once behind the corner of the house. The glue of the rolled paper came apart, tobacco threads blew into his eyelashes. He swore mightily, threw and spat away what he could, brushed his front where strands stuck. He took a chew of tobacco from a piece in foil wrap in his front pants pocket then got on his glove, balled up both hands and shoved them deep into his pockets. He started for the road, feeling ice pellets through his leather boot bottoms.

Out on the road he saw Claire Dunphy make her way toward his house, her right side braced to the squealing wind, her long curled tips of hair rising past exposed cheeks and a secure toque. Her hands were firmly in her pockets, as well, her forearms likewise locked to her sides.

"Cold enough for you, Adrian?"

"Young Claire, ho. You better believe it."

"I couldn't see coming up the road."

"I don't doubt that."

Claire Dunphy was the prettiest girl North of Smokey. Moreso since the shapely curves started the summer before last. She wore a red Christmas scarf high on her chin which she pinched with the thumb of a mitten to speak, but material rose on its own and she had trouble keeping cotton from her mouth. Above the scarf her cheeks burned a precious hue. She had started hanging around Grace when interest in Clifford had developed. Adrian first wondered why this beauty had come around the house to see Grace. Grace had not the looks near hers. They were the same age; that was enough, around here. Claire's people fished along the Sandbar in summer, as barren and exposed an expanse as ever to know. They wintered up at MacGean's Interval, the best valley for sheltering out the heavy weather. Their cabin, as it sat amongst the flanks, gave the chance walker coming upon it the feeling that this family is hiding from the world the gravest of secrets.

Claire's mother Jeanette was a Frenchwoman from further down the east side of the island. Her people had special dark features, a degree or two shy of sinister. Full, pouting lips, lips people here never knew to exist here, beyond being something equatorial. Claire's brilliant coal-black eyes came straight from Jeanette. Her hair though, the real treat – that was all Dunphy. Poor beauty – even in stark winter, torch red locks.

"Listen, ah, Claire! Grace is home, but we got a little trouble back at the place. Young Frank suffered an accident while out yesterday."

"Jesus. Then he did, did he, is it serious?"

"Pretty serious, why, what did you hear?"

"Wilfred Gillis was up the house last night for cards and told us Ronald Shea saw one of your young fellows out, coming back from the Beach Road, with a rifle. The old fellow thought something was up but didn't know what. What a sin. I like Frankie. I hope he's all right."

"We're doing what we can. Still, the house is in a bit of an uproar I want to tell you. But here is no place to ruminate on it so you go on. Claire? Tell Grace to get a blanket on the horse? Our chickens froze. Some job cleaning them."

"I imagine."

"Like a rock. All five rock hard. See you later then. I'm heading down the Crick a minute."

As Adrian made his way down the road he thought right away of how this young Claire was related to the man he was about to see: Captain Daniel Dunphy. Her uncle by blood, half-blood. His half-brother Charles was Claire's father. The Captain married Claire's mother's sister, another Frenchwoman. Both fellows had good-looking children by these women, all right. Real good features must come from marrying outside your own. The half-brothers had mixed in with the Frenchwomen while dealing in boats. Daniel and Charles built schooners from pine logs cut at the other Interval, MacKinnon's, the valley south and out of which much of Ingonish River flowed. The men floated boat timber on spring freshets. The passing French of Isle Madame liked the pine boats they saw, and as soon as the Dunphy half-brothers sold one, straightaway there came orders for others. After embarking on the enterprise, however, Daniel and Charles had a falling out over equipment purchases which ended in a brutal fist fight.

Daniel walked away with a nose misaligned for life. Charles, when he awoke under Molly Mickie's apple tree, sported an open lip and eyebrow gashes. Scars for life. The boat-building venture was done; the two men never spoke again, although they were family and beyond that shared a small community, making it impossible for them not to run into each other somewhere along the way. Yet they kept their distance. Daniel continued entrepreneurial efforts, his contact with Isle Madame proving profitable. He soon fell in with a rough crowd of French and learned from them one skill that would come to mark him. He got his sailing papers, all right, but he also became a cook of sorts, learning but one recipe: for moonshine. Captain Dunphy, long time acquaintance of Adrian's, was the village bootlegger.

They had been friends as boys, crossing paths on their way to school when it was down at the beach. Neither had stayed more than a year as there was much to do around the shores then. In the colder months when one could return to studies there were the tasks around the households. Fires to be kept on, animals to be tended. They saw each other only as older boys then, around the wharves. They spoke in the rough vernacular they had come to enjoy, swearing being its underpinning. They found wives, had children. Then, Adrian's brother Leo became acting sheriff of Ingonish, and that stymied their relationship. By the time of Leo's appointment, Daniel had established a firm footing – on the other side of the law. He had a still with which he made a renowned gin, its fame extending all the way to North Sydney. He mainly sold at various points along the North Shore, but had arranged to get his alcohol on the tables of lawyers and politicians all the way over in Sydney. His product was secure and profitable in the local market; it earned him top dollar. Reputation deserved investment.

People had always enjoyed homemade liquor. Mystique was involved. Where had it originated? How did it get past the authorities? The dodging of government tax forever brought a twinkle to the eye. Prohibition was law in the United States. Strangely, because it was so, there came the notion that homemade was better, had a proper kick to it. Homemade was all the rage. The Captain used what means he could to deliver; boat the primary mode. Merchandise was set down at discreet beaches, hauled by block and tackle up ravines where horses met it. Daniel did not like people to come to his place, and people knew it. His wife had a church profile, and he had earned the privilege of selecting patrons and where to deal with them.

A slick character, Dunphy operated by night. Local lore had his illegal still aboard his boat. In truth, it was hidden in the mountains on land purchased adjacent to McKinnon's Interval near where he had once cut pine for his boats. The law could pin nothing on him and Leo Curtis had little means by which to catch him. There was no boat provided a sheriff's post. Authority was therefore limited to land. Leo Curtis did get a small allowance to keep a horse, a lame Breton. His metal star was ever present, pinned conspicuously. He carried a six-bullet revolver, proudly. Sheriff Curtis had this past year been up and down the mountains how many times he didn't know in search of a still. He kept an eye on the Crick Road, but was never able to spot the Captain's moves. Dunphy was the respectable fisherman, his prim wife the church devotee, their son a clean-cut mannerly lad. What you call pillars. Leo Curtis heard of the exploits, but always after the fact. He wore his gun tightly in its holster, his sole ambition in life being to catch up with Daniel Dunphy.

The Sheriff had something else against the Captain; it went beyond the moonshine trade. It came from long before the outlaw's activities were public record. Leo knew Daniel stole the chickens from his mother's henhouse. The previous sheriff, Jack Jackson, a friend of Leo's, had told him so. Before Leo was deputised he had partnered with Jack one night; unlawfully, perhaps illegally, the two apprehended at gunpoint the young Daniel Dunphy. Finding no chickens, they did manage to have the suspect locked up for two weeks in Baddeck County, on account of a size 12 boot print found at the scene. But with no real hard evidence, a vociferous Daniel, behind bars, swore openly into the courthouse hallways how he would not soon forget this. He wouldn't shut up. They had to let him go. But neither man would soon forget, especially Leo who later found a pocketknife in the henhouse, bearing the initials DD.

Daniel Dunphy became wiser after his run-in and time served. He began a life of keeping one step ahead of Leo Curtis who, now invested with proper authority, was just waiting for the slip up.

Adrian looked at the boathouse away from the Dunphy house proper. He compared buildings. House owners in the village enjoyed detailing rooflines in a bright trim, but these Dunphy buildings included trim on exterior corner boards. The barn and shed got it. The outhouse got it. The corner boards were painted a lime green. The whole property made a fairytale of winter. French influence, thought Adrian. Hers. French like to massacre detail, to make an excess of all. What a mask for this fellow, living in so pretty a place. Adrian shook his head. The Mean grew bright flowers. The Virtuous built tarpaper shacks.

Smoke belly-danced from the boathouse.

Adrian spat tobacco juice, then the chew, near a covered stack of boards. He saw a tarp-covered bulldozer; another tarp outlined a truck.

In colder seasons, men of the village spent whole days in their places away from the main, especially as they grew older. There was better light in a little building outside, and a man could haul in from the wild or off the shore whatever his heart desired. Drag it into a little building with no fuss. No worry. Mud on the boots. Have a few. A man cut a solitary figure in the end. He knew he harmed none, when on his own.

Adrian approached, took off a glove, rapped on the door.

"Who's there?"

"Me."

"Me who?"

"Adrian Curtis. I'm in a bind, Dan. Could you open up?"

The door came a fraction. A large man peered from above.

"Ha, you, of all."

The door was left for Adrian, who mounted a step.

Heat was immediate. But Daniel Dunphy, how he had put on the weight! He looked great! He wore a silver moustache and gold-rimmed eyeglasses. He was steady-handed in a pair of ironmonger overalls and fur-lined jacket open at the throat.

"Shut the door, bai! I ain't heating Ingonish!"

Adrian folded his hat, half bowed, let go of the well-set knob.

By contrast, this larger man stood in self-possession, the tallest of the village residents. Daniel reached up to scratch the mole at his cheek while eyeing Adrian, who remembered this habit, one born not out of nervousness, but tradition, as juxtaposition between a larger life's varied moments.

Daniel held a copper pipe in bare hands, his thick fingers with fleshy tips creating insignificance in their fingernails. Those fingers came from a life of manual work. Adrian's own approached these. Fat, meaty, bloodless. Ingonish fingers.

"What of it, man? Speak. A Curtis needs some favour from the likes of me. Ho, I thought you people were too good for favours. Right in, I say, come right in."

Adrian hesitantly followed past floor-to-ceiling shelves of planking. He smelled birch, mahogany, spruce and pine. He had entered a well-built, well-heated building with pleasant-smelling wood shavings and the remotest scent of uncapped turpentine.

"Excuse me, have to close that door again, Adrian. Make it tight."

"Go. Yes, she's some awful frost."

Daniel touched the curtain, peered out. Adrian turned to a coal fire burning in an oil drum modified to act as a heat source. Mending instruments were on a counter below a neat wall of tool families shelved or arranged according to size and function. He saw a falling family of chisels, a rising family of wrenches. An orange fishing net was splayed in large part over the work counter, the mending of its holes taking place. Lead sinkers sat free. Although Daniel Dunphy had been involved in the life of a reprobate it in no way implied that here was an idle man, nor one garnering merely a few skills to turn an honest living. On the contrary. His duplicity evidenced industry enough for two men. No minute went idle. How could it? All was work and work was the dollar. Yet the Captain was magnanimous. He took the moment to speak to you. All he had, yet he never seemed rushed? To take time out for the common man was how he derived leisure. Adrian had heard him say it once. But what it meant, Adrian had never learned.

Daniel had a fish trap, the biggest North of Smokey. He also had the best boat. A sixty-two-foot double-masted schooner called the *Soap and Suds*. Everyone knew her. She contained excellent rigging, block and tackle, a powerful diesel engine and mechanised hauler. Three Lunenburg dories operated alongside the *Soap and Suds*. They set nets, raised oars to communicate with the mother boat, got confirmation, then prepared for their hauling. The Captain's operation employed six men, each of whom had families of ten or fifteen children. Spring, summer, fall, winter, these families survived as a result of Daniel's enterprise. Its ultimate success furnished him with a philosophical quip: "Dire surrounding. Treasure abounding!" This he had painted on his dories, which men broke backs to row. A village stuck out in the North Atlantic. A salt hamlet. A place that sent shudders up the spine of any other business-headed fellow at the mere thought of making a go of things here. It spelt opportunity for Daniel Dunphy. Especially in that few others would attempt commercial ways. Leadership was required. Leadership foremost. Have that and you can do pretty much what you want with people, and one place was as good as any. You just need some version of straggling life around you. As for law, it had its place. Others subscribe. You inscribe! Law was a thing to work around, till ends were met. Which were. And what legitimacy more does one strive for? "His own survive who himself is first helped." Law: what kept order among men. That which he'd be half the man without.

"What can I do for you then? I don't receive here."

"I need a bottle."

"Milk, medicine, marmalade? Where am I going to get a bottle?"

"Not milk."

"Got any cash?"

"No."

"Tell me then, what do you suppose a fellow who, let's say, might have what you seek *in* a bottle do in that case?"

"I'll pay."

"You here on your own accord? You usually have someone else come. Enlighten me on the occasion."

Daniel picked up a bit of steel wool, twisted it into the end of his pipe, made sheer by a recent cut. He cleaned the cut which quickly shone. Adrian saw no a hacksaw near. The hacksaw he saw was hanging mute on the wall.

"I cut this for the fire, this pipe. This part here is for the mouth, see, to blow on. You perk up a fire by blowing, the other end is set just in under the coals. My young fellow Edward took the other one I cut out and lost it in the snow. Fired it at a coyote disturbing the hens. 'Get a gun,' I told him. 'Works better than a pipe.' He's not partial to firearms. I didn't realise how handy that other pipe was till she was gone. I'm thinking of making a few to sell. Think they'll sell, Adrian?"

"Not a bad idea. They should."

Daniel winked at Adrian whose gloved fingers were knit.

Daniel laid the pipe on the counter then drew his shoulders back, vaguely. He bent forward, his face aimed at the window of the oil drum. He drew back large shoulders and turned to study the doorway, back through wood planking. He got up and stepped around to a tarp tied over one of his Lunenburg dories, throwing aside high, long lashings.

"Come ahead here, Curtis. Step up on that yourself and reach in. Take whatever you find."

Adrian came ahead as if having gone through the practice one thousand times.

"These are forties, Dan. Quart will do me. You got any quarts?"

"Oh, you're one of those."

"One of what?"

"A sometimes-man. One bent on figuring there will only be this patch to get through, one who denies the larger picture. Stock up, me son! You're at the bow. Go aft, if you want a quart."

Adrian undid the stern lashes on his own. He satisfied himself with a dark brown quart which he inserted into his jacket front, passing it neck-down through his belt buckle, in along the soft skin of his crotch. He refused to look down in respect for decency; in fact he decided to give no more knowledge of the attainment than a black comb lost in a hip pocket. Yet how the cold neck went down neatly, the feeling of its concealment immediately and wholly appealing. He wished he had spent more of his life doing these very things. Procedure included pleasure most profound.

"Adrian?"

"Right here, Dan. What?"

"You want to tell me what happened?"

nine

"*F*irst chance I get Dan I promise I'll pay."

"First chance you get? Aren't those terms splendid. Sure Adrian, provided first chance is before month's end. I serve like the rest. I got books to balance."

"It still fifty cents?'

"Yes, bai, my prices don't waver. Now, one of your boys get hurt or what?"

"Who told you?"

"I heard. You're here. I'm guessing that's not for him or is it?"

"If he'll take it, it is. Frank, the youngest. He was crawling up over the Jesus rocks at Middle Head when the gun he had went off. He nicked his upper left arm, here."

"Nicked or shot?"

"Shot I guess. I put a poultice on it."

"Poul-what?"

"Poultice. Field dressing. What we used overseas. Flour, scalding water. Sugar inside a good bandage. Infection goes straight for it."

"Ah, me son, you don't mean to tell me you mixed un-sterile flour into a festering gunshot wound?"

"I did. How? It's what's done."

"What's done is it? Well I never heard tell of it done. Not of someone actually attempting it. It sound clean to you? You need proper care, a doctor with branded instruments to look at something like that. The lead pass through? A slug?"

"No, shot. I wish to hell it had been a slug. I can see two beads in under a ligament. Just a couple. But a body can go on a long while with bits in it. I had a piece of tin in my knuckle for two years till I got a notion to cut it out. That hurt nothing."

"Adrian? Look at me when I talk. Adrian? Lead is not tin, a knuckle ain't an arm."

"I know it ain't an arm."

"Do you? Do you know that lead's as poisonous a material as ever there was? It's arsenic. Land sakes, man. Two whole Mondays will pass before the circuit doctor comes through."

"I know. Do I ever know. And I'm in a tight spot because of it. I sent word by the two older boys. They went into town to get someone."

"Now, I don't want to hear it was on foot."

"I sent them on foot, why? It's not all that far."

Daniel Dunphy looked at the grave cheeks of the diminutive man. He noted age and noted generation: his own. He noted dress and posture. Here was a downcast, a submerged deadhead, but so many leagues below he could hardly make it out as a man. Adrian Curtis. He who worked a lifetime of odd jobs. On hand to carry out the bidding of others, to advance others. Labourer, rock picker, ice cutter, trap baiter. He who made the same mistakes consistently till there was no point in trying to sort it out any longer. Widget, impressionable – a fellow who went out in public with tobacco juice at mouth corners and nose whiskers untrimmed. He had kids to feed yet was generously dumb-headed enough to go living year in, year out, this hand-to-mouth existence.

"I almost feel sorry for you, Adrian. No, I do."

"I am in a bind all right."

Daniel opened the curved door of the oil barrel stove. The orange glow of burning graded coal intensified with this greeting of fresh oxygen; the smell of the lively gases reached both men. Daniel squinted. He dug sleep out of an eye. He jabbed the fire with his pipe till he found a suitable spot to blow. Flames leaned as condensed carbon dioxide charged a balanced bed of coals and summoned the fire's not uncommon roar. Instant satisfaction, well-being, normally follows such a sound but here they were denied both men. Daniel spat lightly, copper dust and iron filings into the stove. He closed the door and took a folded handkerchief out of an ironed pocket with which he wiped his mouth very well.

"Adrian Curtis. Tell me. You think this weather will let up?"

"Will it let up?"

"I mean for an on-foot subzero journey, over hill, dale, plain and hollow to be carried out till completion?"

"I'm hoping the hell it does, although she don't look it out there."

Appeal in Adrian's voice had sunk to its lowest since leaving home, since his arrival here. He knew this, but felt appeal could sink to where it wanted now that the subject had been broached. He had the company of a man he had grown up with; not to mention the swelling of a bottle in his jacket front. Beyond a trusting ear, a hard bottle, what more was there? He had done for Frank what he could. It was the waiting game now. Understanding was before him in Daniel, a chance to catch his breath. He blinked. He fixed eyes on the oil barrel door and stared generally. Flames of ignited coal were lost to the door backing.

"Bad weather you're thinking? That can make it auspicious. A person can run an errand."

Adrian turned, his square mouth Irish, hopeful.

"A person who *likes* to run errands, in inclement weather, that is. You catch people at home in inclemency. And how welcoming the faces that see you come, too. Ho, hoar-frosted folks shaken out of being holed up the day, the week, the month, what have you. These nights come furnished with dark cover. Make it perfect for unharassed travel. The ocean being frozen like a frying pan – now, there's terrain to cross. See it for yourself. Look there. All the way out to Ingonish Island she's bound, like iron. If it's the same up the North Shore, which it only got to be, a person like me can make time."

"North Shore? You heading up over Smokey, Dan?"

"I'm sitting here. I'm thinking on it."

"You can pick my fellows up? Get help?"

Adrian kept his eye on Daniel Dunphy, on the handsome whiskered face of his brother's lifelong foe, the same who stole chickens from *his* mother, too. It was the face of urgency, of promise – of God. Daniel Dunphy. Owner of the best team in a village where none had seen a horse, other than nags, not till his team came over Smokey. Elegant Thoroughbreds from Ontario. Adrian moreover stared at the sole owner of the majestic *Soap and Suds*, the sixty-two-foot double-masted schooner with its three Lunenburg dories, one of which here housed his precious wares. Oh, this fellow had it. Fish trap, property, bearing. He lorded over an empire, built and operated single-handedly when all other men could only hope for was to build and operate half-broken, worn, borrowed tools – rowboats that had to be bailed the entire time at sea. Here was the title owner of the hand-manufactured Firebrand horse carriage. Not to mention a top-of-the-line Milburn horse sleigh. Both vehicles were equipped with iron spring suspension and leather seating – the latest in innovation, but among some distant fashion set. The sleigh, the grandest and newest purchase was branded in brass by its Montreal firm. Brass, mind you. It was the current envy of all Ingonish. Its reinforced steel runners meant everything to a savage climate. Any given Sunday morning the whole year through, one of these rigs, carriage or sleigh, set off by its elegant Thoroughbred team, could be viewed entirely in the churchyard parking.

"I'll pick them up," said Daniel. "I'm not guaranteeing you anything. If the ice hasn't pulled off the North Shore we should be able to – and with luck I say have the doctor here early tomorrow. There's someone in North Sydney owing me a favour yet."

"Jesus, Daniel. No?" said Adrian. "Merciful Christ. Look, you'd be helping a man and his family out here. I won't soon forget it either, hear? Take a drink with me then? Come on, bai."

Adrian's gloved hands produced the bottle, both gripping, one tightening the cork. But word was not coming.

"Me? You keep that for yourself, Adrian. I've got to get ready if I'm to go at all."

"Want me along?"

"Stay here with the boy. I travel best alone. You shouldn't be away from your wife, as it is. This being here, even. Not with all that's going on."

"I'm headed right home where I won't stir."

"Go it then. The weather could turn. If I needed anyone I'd take my young fellow Edward, but there's your two to pick up. There's the doctor to carry."

"Here. Take my hand on it, the very least."

Adrian held out an ungloved paw for the big man. Daniel was humoured then grew respectful with memory provoked. He participated in the unexpected rite.

"I said I won't forget what you're doing and I won't. No man in his right mind would. We'll be waiting at home. So I'll leave you to it."

*O*utside, Adrian poked hard at the channels of his gloves. He blinked, inhaled then stepped out of the lee supplied by the outer building: back out in the cold. On the wasted Crick Road, his back to the Woody Shore houses, he twisted off the cork and finished a cold swallow. He parried with a second lifting, the bottle going higher. His teeth clicked glass. Ease of heart came as he replaced the cork – but tightly. It was his first drink of the day, therefore supreme. And this, proper liquor, with its juniper pep, left him with what he marked altogether as spruce needles on his tongue. Oh, did that fellow have wares, what! Ha! The notion, of how people swore him off and that here was nothing but a renegade. Crime Itself. More underhanded than the day is long! To hell with them. I have just bargained with Crime Itself. Only, I feel great about it. He'll want something one day. And he'll get it, too. Ha! That we should shun Fortune where we find her. Power, too. The ticket: his proven record. Look to that. Daniel Dunphy knew things beyond what it was to have children, because not every man knows even that. He knew what it was to send a child out into the world, after teaching it to fend – how it breaks a heart smack open when they do well by you, when they bring home the first deer. The sheer sadness of that alone can upset the balance. Daniel knew what it was to grow up around here, yes, by the old dying. To stagger foggy shores, plod leaf-soaked mountains. Live by the cod jig, by the rabbit snare. Daniel's own people had had it tough: Adrian knew this for a fact. They had survived like the others. To survive is what all knew.

Adrian continued, when it struck him that he had never known himself to be so happy. Happiness rode on the wings of showering snow, arrived on the blusteriest of blows. It forced him to stop. Limber he stood, taking with full acceptance what seized him, the land. He swung about. There, wintered Smokey Mountain in the climbing distance above frozen crowns of swaying spruce and backward borne branches of twisted pine. Snow-covered, it moves in and out of sight depending on how full the retreat of these crowns and these branches. But all-powerful, collected harbour winds deep below advanced to erase the lower scene there. Look! White swirls, ten yards deep, forty feet high. Amassed power made visible. Adrian had help! Real help, this time! The tragic circumstance had made him deserving. But help had always come, in one form or another. He had been his entire life a lucky man. And he had told no one of what had occurred yesterday. He had kept his resolve. Oh, primary, that! To have handled the situation his way. Merely he had to wait it through now. He uncorked his bottle, swallowed more of the drink that was always there for him. Not for everyone but for him. Not everyone appreciated it. And he only ever needed to search to procure it. That's Fortune. Daniel Dunphy can be, regarded as genius, he can! No, no – it was the truth of the matter! I admire him – which becomes my purpose. To get all he had was genius. And Adrian, yes he *should* stock up, so that he could always be ready to be peacified. It sometimes was the most unforgiving of worlds. He wasn't drinking enough. Self-possession suffered.

He moved on, but not before promising that at the next high, well-formed snowdrift he would just drop down into it. Settle in among the howling gusts that rained snowflakes atop his head. Just for a bit. In the wall. Put up the hood. He replaced the cork, but tightly. He stopped to check that he had. His gloves gave maximum strength in their tightening friction, their loosening friction. He plodded forward, happily on the lookout for his drift. No better feeling in the world, this. How could there be, beyond the appreciation of stark beauty? When a person thought it out, the world could never let you down – provided you chose to go out and meet it. The calm, peace to be got. Rest! But you had to go out and meet it, every time. Rest through action. The God-awful pitiful shame, that more of life had not been lived in this supreme knowledge.

He huffed. He puffed. He blinked at forlorn vistas while adjacent wind-crafted crust balls became adornments to forever tinkle in his ear; they bounced on spruce boughs, held themselves together at eye level. The money the doctor would require? Do they require it? No. Even that will not lay a finger here in Joy Beheld. He looked around, eagerly squinting – for the hopeful moment, but newly lost. No, not already? No! I resist! The land born into, the place he mastered. He should partake in more of it. Wind drove him on, lifting and swelling, in its back-bracing unending gusts skyward. "Thank you, then, Lord Jesus. Thank you for this. Thank you. I love you. And you'll see a new man before you from here on in." He coughed. Of little taper, a hemlock swayed. Frank will pull through, then the best of life is to be got. Action taken. Chance played zero part here.

Adrian encountered no other soul on his walk home. He cut through blasted trees and took new shortcuts through snow tumbling from lower limbs to shower his nape. He stopped, raised his jacket collar under a doffed hood. There were people he had not dropped in on for quite some time. Their houses were just there. He would not mind seeing those people. They had warm places, and how they loved his wit. They would like to hear what happened and were no doubt deeply worried. I should share more, with people. No – this once, hurry home to wife and family. To Frank. Because, honestly, to hell with those never present morning, noon or night – to hell, and in a hand basket.

Within sight of his property, standing before a magnificent unbroken drift, a flat glove stationed on a tree, twice more he raised his bottle. He rinsed his mouth with snow and chewed spruce gum. He noted fresh footprints to the outhouse.

Jessie met him at the door, but did not step aside. He took what berth he could, then gave far too grand a show of brushing his toque before her, the headgear of the man who had been out in the elements and was now frozen. He promptly let her into his confidence, explaining what had befallen him while out. He did so before taking off his jacket, before being deep inside the home. "Look. I may have needed something but don't ever think of me as someone who shirks his duty. All right? I came back." He did not produce the thing he said he needed. Jessie searched his midsection. "And don't be concerned about me getting out of control, Jessie. My nerves, you know how shot my nerves are better than any. Here it is, then. We got help."

"From who?"

"Well now, you take it easy. From Daniel Dunphy."

"Oh, for Christ's sake. That rat?"

"Rat is true. But he's going after the boys, Jessie. In his store-bought Montreal sleigh."

"You had to. You had to. Get help from that piece-of-work, from Daniel Dunphy."

"Jessie, don't force an appeal. There's no one else in Ingonish with the horses he's got. No one! A motoring boat would never make it faster. Those animals fly like the wind."

"I'd like to see you fly like the wind. Fly and not return. You make a soul sick, Adrian Curtis."

Jessie turned to think. Ah, how much more was the heart asked. How so little left, to answer! But her husband was right. This fellow did have the horses. He had the sleigh. Poised on the oilcloth, Jessie became swept up by the uncanny universal respect for criminals in emergencies. The reprobate does live his life in a state of alarm; someone is always coming for them, day or night. None knew danger better. None, recourse. Manoeuvring. Still, the news came with only a show of security. Any half-sensible person in this part of the country was well-versed in the antics of Daniel Dunphy. She recalled on the spot histories of other such men. Yes, it was true there existed that line of integrity they held, where they were wont to behave heroically. She knew first-hand the rigs this man rode. Everything he owned encouraged him to be the robust man he was. She saw the drop-off, his French wife, at church on Sunday. Everyone saw that. She saw him step down from the rig, yank his belt end, nose it. Go into the graveyard next to wait for Eloise, back and broad shoulder to the concrete church. Another survey of the headstones. Jessie Curtis coveted the rigs he rode and therefore experienced a swell and ease of pride in her breast at help coming in this form: one of his rigs, the Montreal sleigh, the best money could buy, they said. The family was helped. In the heat of things, right and wrong could take a back seat. Right and wrong could get out and walk.

Adrian had stopped looking. She was mute. Feet passed upstairs. But how she was taking it, he wanted to know. Why she was taking so long to answer? Time parameters were infused with the high feeling from the gin. The kitchen was too damn hot. He knew that. He couldn't breathe. He walked off with his swollen jacket rear, and stepped into the backroom. Beneath the higher bunk he bent, got on one knee at where Frank lay. "Your father's back." But Frank slept fitfully, worn out from the battles put up during the night. Adrian pinched the sheet at the boy's hot neck. He tucked it in. The arm was swollen and grey. He sniffed struggle.

Adrian stood at the window facing Smokey. Gently he raised his elbow to rest on the sill, but missed. He carefully took the material of the curtain into his hand, balled it then drew it backward.

"Come, Jessie will you? There's something I want you to see."

His wife instantly drew up behind.

"Merciful God, you that close? You frightened the life out of me! I didn't know you were that close."

"Can you keep it quiet for Christ sake. For *his* sake."

"I am. I will. Look though. Look out there. In little over the time it took me to come back from his place he's already damn-well near across the harbour. That's him. Those big damn black brutes pulling for all they're worth, they're his. He'll be up that mountain in no time flat. Look, just look."

"Hell. Shush! I am."

"He won no medals in our lifetime. Jessie, that's our help going."

"I know it is."

"And to tell the God's honest truth I don't give a damn about what Leo or his Sheriff star would say. At this moment I don't. That man out there on the ice is off to help a family in dire need. The thing is, he wouldn't be out there doing it if he had played his cards straight. Like the rest of us fools. Maybe that is the way to go, Jessie. I just don't know. Late now, for me. Frank? We got help coming. Tell him, Jessie. You tell him soon as he wakes, tell him. Frank? You just lie there fellow. Sleep through all this, sleep it away like there's no tomorrow, cause a doctor from town is coming to swab that up like it was a scratch on the knee."

Jessie sniffed acetone juniper. It sickened her. She stepped back to let her husband study the dim window on his own. She would not deny him his reporting of what he saw, though would rein him in three or four times, to have him simmer down at least. She neglected to mention Frank was getting weaker, that he only answered her on the third call when she asked whether he needed to use the white basin an hour ago. A flat calm momentarily possessed her. Why it did in the face of all this, precisely now, she didn't know. Was it that real action was being taken? She wished the community knew. A man doesn't see the importance of a general pulling together. They knew of no value that a people binding brings. A man was community-less. This one did, however, strike up the best bargain. He was sloppy. There was no sense trying to communicate with him on any level. Not now. Minds soaked of alcohol can't mesh with the order of the day, no matter the circumstance. Stay where you are then. Stay sunk in that dirt world where there is no calling down to, lost and buried in the hole you're in. At least long enough for a woman to think, uninterrupted.

The curtain hung free. Another of the early nights had come to cap the expansive region. To close views of road and trees, scribed harbour ice and trace mountain ridges. Distance faded to nothing. Intimate proximity became the experience. Grace took her father's elbow. He did not want it taken. He did not want her to remove him from the big chair he had hauled in here to sit at by the window. She looked toward her mother for signal in how to deal with the disregard. Her mother grandly wove a hand: leave him where he's at. Grace returned to the kitchen to spend another half-hour with her friend Claire Dunphy. They had eaten rabbit soup and fresh bread with molasses. They now were finishing warm tea and the quiet game of checkers. Claire had spent the day with Grace. The two had taken grain to the one chicken, hay to the cow and hay to the horse. Claire was trying to leave. Solid night had come; the wind just had not finished dying.

With her back to her husband, a seated Jessie drew shoulders outward to prop elbows on armrests. She sat alongside her son with prayer beads splayed on her lap. In the late morning she had taken up the black beads and tiny crucifix, kept all in her apron pocket the whole day through. She had fondled them when she met Adrian at the door. She prayed now, but also worried because she had forgotten prayer at the onset of the mishap. She feared faith being lost. If she were to pray, does she even deserve strength to come? She listened to the dog whine. She had let the cursed thing out and now it pawed the porch door. She hoped Grace would have the sense to let it in.

Frank slept with the slightest of furrowed brows. Jessie noted her people there. She could note how the face would look when it got to be a man. But that cursed dog, how it whined! She sighed and apologised, to God. Send strength for this, and any nights after. The matron rose.

ten

In his rabbit-fur Mongolian snow-hat, earflaps half-cocked, Daniel Dunphy kept a taut rein on his stallions, especially when leaving the harbour. He had not had them out in four days and knew animals like these had to be properly warmed before asking heavy work of them. Coming wide inside the ice-sealed Gut, he saw first-hand how the salt water had frozen. The scene put him in mind of those many winters long past when family would go out onto the ocean to fetch the pine logs and hemlock tossed from atop Smokey. He knew frost.

The sleigh runners left the thick harbour ice to pass upward and meet the road. They burst aeolian drifts to buck through its many ridges. The horses increased their efforts in order to climb. Combined lusty tugs indicated zeal at being out-of-doors. The pair snorted. They shook heads freely as if openly denying whimsical thoughts. They broke to hard road and with no provocation increased pace. Daniel adjusted position on the leather seat keeping reins between loose and taut, maintaining the art of allowing for movement in beasts while getting a sleigh to pass exactly where he wished. These horses know this man who drives them, he thought. He who has never used physical force or sworn to berate you, both. Treatment toward man might be otherwise. Patience was the game for man, not necessarily beast. Horses knew because they were intuitive creatures. Men knew language, which was useful in order to get them to act, rise from sitting across the room in a chair. People understood what they saw. A village fears the man who goes his own way, who never cows. He flicked leather. Jesus, that he didn't cow, that made the stir. Where were the snowy mountains for that Oriental? Show me camels and mustard seeds out here, yes. See how the prophet fares out here. Daniel had won his Nazareth. None in the community contested him. He effected a general submission. A bully got things done. Not a bully, authority. Daniel hadn't walked in with authority. He gained it, then became it. He established what he had, setting out as a young man. None is born to it around here. Fear, respect, envy. All hard won.

All easily lost. I am forty-seven. The number that presents itself too often these days, each time bringing a dumb moment of heavy introspection. All feels the eleventh hour. So little time to get things right. And death, not the distant star it once was. Looking ahead has ended. Looking behind the occupation, the worrisome view of things gone awry. And repentance was apt to lay itself across his path lately. He could rectify a thing or two yet. How contrary the mind? He had fought any greater good all his life. The fight had given meaning. When had it become hard to dispute? He recalled no debate. This is what the end becomes? Was it a matter of living long enough for truth to come to any life? Sweeping through the most dissolute of camps, spoiling the most irascible of characters as its will gets imposed? Self-serving, replaced by self-sacrifice. "Help the next man." Could he paint this on the dories in spring? The village owed him. Nothing new. Paying up was never a concern. Till lately. Till the thought came that perhaps he should release a representative number. Debt's a nasty circumstance. Any dollar feeds families, closes mouths. And one example was there, in the boat shed.

Daniel knew the rough element. Those along the North Shore; in town. They admired him. They get wind of benevolence: oh! their frames of mind will not support it. Such seeds never quite take in such fallow fields. Level of intelligence was required for benevolence.

Appearing weak was the fear. Yet he had done it, he had released a few. None officiously, but he had. Never officiously. The portrait the village had painted of him must in measure remain. He must remain – the sense of who he was must remain. An odd good turn done furtively could be gotten away with. What do I care, I make the rules. Ah, but coming to the fore, this Adrian Curtis. A whole new landscape, public breech. This very thing might have come along to frig everything else up, garner attention – as it has no doubt done already. All houses face the harbour. Noses poke at window glass most especially on stormy days. To see the big man's sleigh light across the winter expanse, at dark; that has to get tongues wagging.

Daniel lowered his head as his horses climbed. Blew. How would he play it from here? A Curtis was a natural mute, young or old. And the misanthropic ways of Adrian would be enough to keep a lid on much of Daniel's role, till he got back. The family must be told explicitly, that what gets done here is to be hushed. The beauty of it was none in the world expects my involvement. Widespread denial has to result.

He snapped the reins on rising croups, then struck at the animals lightly, seeing how they had worked to gain the first part of Smokey's steepness. He saw in the deeper border snow the tracks of the Curtis boys, and felt instantly bad to see how at points steps had come off the trail most probably because of gusting wind. They had entered a snow too deep for them. Imprints were kneecaps, were groins. Packed drifts contained holes where sorry-clad feet fell out of sight. One had to retreat, there, deepening further and further his footholds in order to extricate the other.

The load lurched, clinked. Daniel's mouth made an O. The horses sank. There was more snow the higher they climbed. With eight long powerful legs, two fourteen-foot tempered-steel runners, the stark situation the boys faced was not his. Never would be. These horses were not bred for this work nor for this region. That was a matter of perspective. Daniel had their birth certificates on his living room wall. Framed English crests printed on gold foil. Thoroughbreds. Stallions. The horse dealer in Ontario had explained these were racehorses, show horses, jumpers. Hardly a breed for mountains and shorelines. They had to be fed good hay, dry or fresh alfalfa, corn, oats, a high quality grass. Daniel mentioned to the dealer where he was from only at the point of sale. He listened to nothing of an explanation concerning what one horse was and what another was not. A horse was a horse, one did the job of any. Yet he had to have the Thoroughbred pair. They were the best money could buy. Only when back home did he realise that though handsome as the devil, they were temperamental. Purity was. He was patient. That wasn't it. He learned intuition. They came around. And true value is appreciated only with time. The creatures towered beautifully over their scrawny field counterparts, the mishmash Breton that people barely kept fed here: that which stood so shamefully lust free alongside his own. There it was – horses! I never thought, but the crux – the village to himself was really a comparison of their animals. Possessions are extensions of oneself after all. No vanity here, my son. We're beyond that. "Right? My babies? Beyond?"

Mounting the first levelling Daniel saw that light had firmly begun to leave day. A sky open to the translucent north, the west and east showed themselves to be clearing. Which means glorious night travel. The wind has swung east, falling to a ten-knot hush. But even this breeze will soon leave off its work and when done there will be only the moon to provide company. Its rising will be late, but out of the barred ocean-scape along the island's frozen North Shore. That will be something, provided Smokey's top is gained before she breaks. He flicked reins. A yellow moon shines silver on a snapped Arctic, on a corralled floe six miles to the offshore. The floe has waited nights in irregularity, in its jammed stalagmites. There can be tonight what few got ever to see: a solid ocean world viewed icily from atop the most barren of bulky mountains. Full moon atop Smokey after a day of storming, over drift ice, watch how it makes nothing of your burning bulbs of Sydney.

Daniel was at pains to comprehend the sudden metamorphosis taking place in the woods. He had just started up, when out of squat coniferous a powerful little form became solid in the prominent way the moose becomes, by pulling all landscape around it into it, going from the dim of dead branches to the whole emergence as the least harassed beast of these woods. This was no moose. The stoop of a Breton horse stood the road.

It had come from an angular swath cut through thickets. It drew behind it a homemade sleigh weighted low with misshapen logs whose lopped-off jagged branch ends can only have been limbed with a dull axe. Daniel squinted. Who in their right mind would be out on the mountain this hour? The driver had full advantage. He had watched as Daniel had stopped to rest. In brute struggle with his load, silently he had advanced horse and sleigh onto the main road, sharp ears and woodsy sense provoked. Here, a woodcutter? The face was absent of surprise: a face fisted and bland hardly by the mere struggle of the day, but by life lived. The form waited still as a stalked partridge offering but profile, as the lesser animal is apt. Daniel looked into the hard weathered skin. He met the eyes of Leo Curtis. The Sheriff.

Leo had come for a load of wood having been certain that with today's bluster none would be out. He cut on crown land, where people with little or no means, no woodland of their own cut (provided their government-authorised certificate had been procured). Scant wood roads, singularly blazed to crown land were found where access could be got. Stands of poor quality were knocked. Gnarly softwoods, dowdy hardwood, spiky windfalls – wood mercilessly difficult to get home because of the difficulty in getting it. Yet; all wood burned, and the only cost of its attainment was labour. Labour meant nothing. Never did. A little toil spent to take a British king's trees for free was a good thing. Until the return trip, that is. The snow had slowed Leo getting his load back. And the load had upset once. But the plain truth was that Leo had been purposely slow to come to the woods today. He was not partial to people seeing him cut on crown land. Thus the return after dark. A sheriff of a community should be a little more law-abiding than the man who cuts wood on crown land (someone who would have a certificate, if others didn't have to be present to see him applying, proving his lack).

On braced buried feet, Leo clapped reins to forward his Breton. He struck at the hindquarters with a slap. Gaining no satisfaction, he jumped forward and struck the beast's front quarter to advance it across the main and head off his interloper. Daniel did have opportunity. The manoeuvre to thwart him in fact was embarrassing. He could put up chase easily. But, that was not how he operated.

"And will you look? Just look at how the twain shall meet," said Leo. "Oh my, oh my. A world laid away. Dull to man, woman and child. But who do I catch sight of, on the black road? My fellow villager. Hallowed-be, I say to that."

Leo was out of breath, but quickly regained it. A groomed individual with the dark features of the Curtis line, Leo kept himself tidier in dress and in aspect. He was the cleaner, the better spoken, the better stood; and sober. The brothers were similar in that neither was what one would call *big people*. Sheriff Leo kept himself in peak physical condition and for thirteen years straight had won the regional snowshoe competition. He was the fastest man alive in the North Highlands of Cape Breton, out-stripping Mi'kmaq hunters whatever the terrain. His specialty was to blaze up timber precipices, employing north-facing trees and their scant limbs as support appendages. Most probably, agility in such terrain had come as he lived on a mountain base. He kept a family in a saltbox at the foot of Robertson, Smokey inward, where no sun struck fall, winter or spring. Choosing to make home on a north-facing slope was what gave him endurance – endurance of mind in particular. He lived on a tuft where the view was the harbour east, but a tuft not exactly prominent enough to be within sight of the Gut. Daniel had crossed the harbour ice bearing this in mind – to which he could not confess, were he questioned. But a Gut crossing had indeed kept him well out of sight of Leo's home and property.

Daniel saw a bucksaw. He saw an axe, both caught in rope tying Leo's load to his sleigh. He saw no rifle. But below the buried braced feet were the snowshoes, secured in their frozen leather bridles.

A horse of Daniel's experimented with front footing. Not fond of the sudden stop, half-slipping, it lurched bringing the other massively broadside. The second took the stirring to mean it was time to perk it up.

"Hold your horses, Dunphy! You're going nowhere! Not till I get a good old fashion look at what you got on board. You don't know how long a man has been waiting for this. Hold up, I say!"

Daniel knew the sheriff had a revolver but did not expect him to carry it up here where he could lose it working the day long in the woods. He was mistaken. Leo unbuttoned his coat to show what he had. Precious metal suspended blackly, in a holster tight at the ribs.

Leo bit a mitt. With bare hand he unsnapped the holster and placed the warmed weapon onto his other mitten. The firearm here took on a pathetic charm. Leo left the coat unbuttoned as if displaying how men like him never felt cold, further, that they could go along like this for the rest of their natural born days, need be. Leo stepped away from his horse and sleigh. His creature could only move backwards now, which it would never do having worked the load through the tangled brush it had.

Leo walked to the back of Daniel's sleigh. He felt with bare hand the good covering, the canvas tarp fastened by constricted rope work. He jabbed his pistol into material at a point behind the seat where the load was best secured. The perfect ping then, of one bottle striking a second.

"Hear that? Only one thing in the whole wide world makes that sound. I'd take it over a nightingale."

The mountain's winter twilight marked poignantly capture and loss. How success and spoils were now another's. Leo peered in where the canvas formed an arc at a roping juncture. He saw the dark of a pit, but subsequently reached in and hauled out a single quart bottle.

"Some smooth glass, that."

"Listen, ah, Leo," said Daniel half turned and speaking for the better part to the aching forest. "Leo? You listening?"

"I suppose I got to. Some."

"Your brother's boy shot himself last night. How bad no one knows. But I'm going for a doctor. Take from me what you found, but you got to let me pass. Time is dear, and I'm in no mood."

"No mood, eh? I see. Time dear, is it? Well you listen to me, mister – I don't give a good goddamn about moods or what time is. I do know one thing. Yours is up! You're in possession of contraband, sir, therefore you're coming with me. The parish voted itself dry, but that's only the half. Moonshine liquor is against the law. And that's what I found on you. That's the charge that sticks. But you know *the law* better than any. What you feel you're above, right? The law? Someone of your kind can do whatever he damn well pleases, ain't it so? Not tonight he can't. Not tonight he don't. Or won't, anymore. I'll see to that. I got you fair and square in the act and with the evidence, Dunphy. Not much cleaner than that."

"I said the young fellow is shot, Leo. Your nephew. Adrian himself came to see me and asked me to go, having sent out his two older earlier this morning, on foot. Over there's their tracks. I'm to pick them up. They're liable to be froze by now."

"Oh, how it grows. I'll tell you what you're picking up – speed. But not in that direction. That! You're to turn this sleigh and those horses around because I'm arresting you for possession of illegal liquor. I don't believe a word leaving your mouth, never did. Not a mouth housing a snake's tongue forked well enough to rid a field of its hay.

"Of course you have some story, a dilly. Stories come to you fellows naturally as breathing does to the rest. You think them up beforehand, I figure, long before you're ever caught. To be prepared. I heard them, hear? Let you go on – yes, yes now. You leave the booze with me, it becomes your word against mine. What kind of fool do you take me for to fall for that, again? I won't enter into no second situation where it's your word against mine. The judge gave you little more than a slap on the wrist last time, making you only the wiser to the system.

"Judges become afraid to lay their hands on fish like you, later, when they're bigger, slimier, hauled in before them. Here's one judge who isn't. Some belly laugh you'd have over me letting you go. Go home! Supposing a redheaded hoard of Vikings is laying waste to greater Ingonish you're not passing here tonight, Dunphy, got it?"

Daniel sized up Leo Curtis. He saw before him a man whose life had reached its zenith. Now came the denouement. Here was a life embracing worth and meaning on the ragged hillside in the snow, in the dark of night. Sheriff catches Bootlegger. Daniel sighed. Poor soul. To dream only that? In his hands the culprit of culprits, the one nugget, having staked the vast tracks, the worthless claims. Having squelched bog and forded river, pan and pick, to squat and shake. All the world for this one nugget. Hurry back now, process its value. You'll soon find gold is never clean, but embedded. That its cleansing quicksilver rips hands apart.

"Have it your way," said Daniel. "I said what I said."

"You said what you said and I said what I said. Turn around. I'll follow. Bear one thing in mind. You make a break for it, when we hit open harbour ice, I'll put up no chase. No, zero. There'll be no contest whatsoever in all that openness, these proud horses pulling for all they're worth. But how splendid a target the open makes. Do you know the shot a man gets to be, living in these woods? I suppose you do. But a man with a badge, imagine that part. It never does get quite that dark out there, on the ice, do it Dan? I'll first go for your pretty horses. Him with the nostrils here, then this big fellow. My ears alone provide me with information enough to drop anything within half a mile. And my little gun. Let's see. That's right. Six misses."

eleven

The moon rose as Sheriff and Accused made their way down Smokey. At the base they turned to take the north bank of the harbour where before long they would skirt Leo's house. They saw a light on at the hermit's. The Mountie station was in a private residence around the harbour, the home of the magistrate. Leo had to mark evidence before having the magistrate officially witness who was brought in and for what? There was proper documentation with signatures to be entered; there were seals and copies. The cell was built in a back room ten by twelve. The real reward would come with the sound of bars sliding across and the key going into the lock.

Leo had them stop at the road under his house, to unburden his horse of its loaded sleigh. Looking up the path, he hoped to spot one of his boys. No one was out in the starshine. He decided in favour of taking his own horse around the harbour as he would need a way to get home. Daniel's rig and horses would be impounded, naturally. But they would take it slow. A good distance was to be covered yet for a creature already showing fatigue, lameness becoming apparent. The unhitched wood lay an obstacle.

They crossed at the head of the harbour passing the iced-over clam-flats. It was a crystal night, no wind. A single dog barked and its echoes spiralled about the icy mountain extremities. When drawing up again to the main road, nearing Adrian's, it was then that Daniel Dunphy drew reins back to his shoulder. "I'll go no further. Down there is your brother's. Do me this. Go and check what I say against what you think is the truth and I'll come along with you, bound and gagged if you want it. We'll tie your horse and mine to the hitching tree. When the visit is satisfied call me all the liar you want. Lock me up, throw the key in the salt lake. But do yourself this one service."

Leo did not like this one bit. He had been apprehensive since taking Daniel into custody, the criminal's story insidiously working into his heart, mind and soul to plague him these five miles around the harbour. Something was up. Someone had told his wife Gloria they had seen one of Adrian's out the night before, walking the Beach Road alone, moving in a queer gait. All Adrian's kids moved in a queer gait. They slunk through life as half-starved coyotes – taking after him. The family was bashful to the point of frightening any who came upon it. This walk of their young fellow had been merely an expression of his and their ways. But if it were true? My God! That one took a bullet, and here was his uncle beleaguering help. That would be it for him in the community. He could never live something like this down. He could well lose his appointment over it. Wouldn't Daniel Dunphy love that? Winning with a full hand? Leo was just doing his job out here, bringing in a criminal caught in the act. And this fellow before him wasn't just any, he was none but the biggest blackest spot ever to be placed on a community. Master scourge, who knew all the tricks. Had stolen from a helpless old woman! Her food! Up in her seventies then, living alone. No, by God, as she lay in the cold earth tonight with permafrost, frozen sod and snow above, the deed in the waking world was ready to be answered for and properly this time.

"Well what say you, Leo? Come on. I won't run. How can I?"

"You'll go down first," said Leo, rigid atop his beast, slowly raising one leg across, pushing himself free in dismount. He removed his mittens and smacked them. He touched his revolver butt to his star, kissed the bullet chamber and then, with the weapon in his pocket, tied the horses to the hitching tree. He patted his creature, feeling its chest and with both hands, down its tender limb. Stepping in file, the men walked below the high fortress banks for the door. Woodsmoke flew from the stovepipe tonight, straight up and missing only narrowly the moon's fat face. It coursed on a neat trail to a bluish starpoked sky.

In the porch there came the striking sense of held-over grimness. And in the kitchen, a cooling fire consumed green wood – chunks of tree living on the mountain only the day before. The greenness scented the home sweetly. Split pieces, between kindling and chunk, dried evenly in freshly stacked piles on the less hot stovetop grates. In behind the stove, was enough to take any family through a night. It would be dry come bedtime. Jessie stood singly in the kitchen. Adrian, newly awake from his afternoon drink, entered from the front room. He squinted to see who could be calling at this hour. Yet expected anything.

"Leo! What in God's name? Why you here? And who's that behind? Let me get on my glasses." The liquor while mostly a dead force within Adrian had residual strength to preserve irritability and keep vision struggling. Adrian's glasses were in his shirt pocket. He stood before his cool interlopers, then, in his kitchen on the weakened legs he could no longer trust. He gathered poise, by going partially bandy-legged.

"Answer me. Ah, no! God, tell me things aren't amiss here – Daniel? You couldn't have gone up and back that quick? There's no way in the world?"

"I didn't go up. I didn't make it over Smokey."

Leo cleared his throat.

"Tell me where he was supposed to be going?" said Leo.

"Tell you where was he supposed to be going! To bring some help to our son is where."

"I'm bringing him in for illegal trade, Adrian. He tells me one of your boys was hurt."

"I'll say one was hurt. If getting a good goddamn well part of your arm blown off is hurt!'

"Adrian!" said Jessie with pleading nod for the backroom.

Daniel spoke, but what he said was perhaps to Jessie. At least in her general direction. "Was on my way," he said, offering the slow revealing headshake of one uncovering rampant injustice.

"For Christ's sake – Leo!" said Adrian. "This man was going for a doctor!"

"Calm down, I didn't know he was."

"He didn't tell you? What did you turn him around for?"

"I told you why. You don't know these fellows, Adrian. Not the way I do. You can't trust them far as you can throw them."

"Let him go now, then."

"Don't know if I can. He's got stuff on him. I'll have to report it."

"To what! My young fellow, out there, shot, lying in a steel bunk, in such a way that we don't know if he's going to make it through the night and you have to report it? He was going for a cursed-eyed doctor! You understand? But, do you?"

"I do. I do now."

"You always were a maligning prick you, now look! Jesus, I say, in heaven. Look!"

Frank heard, plain as day. He heard voices grow tumultuous. He heard his mother utter a phrase indiscernible at grappling followed by bangs and smacks of a wall. A general falling of two men then, a scuffling at the knees on slippery linoleum of melted snow. There was swearing, threatening, long-pent accusations. A poker was grabbed. Jessie's scream had that put down. Grace intervened, her young voice adding miserably to the scene, crying in paroxysm which seemed the core element to quell it. Female sobbing then, followed by increasingly lowering voices then the dying, the death of passion.

A throat was cleared. An outside door opened. Someone spat beyond the porch. No more came. Not from the kitchen. A horse whinnied, up at the road. Its driver swore for its silence then hawed as crisp hoof-fall on crust began. More than one horse. Sleigh runners, too, rushing sweetly over snow.

One brother in the kitchen spoke in consolatory tones, in sum and mortification. Then definitely there was nothing more – in the way adult kin can offer nothing more, in a kitchen, near a fire, in winter, poor, with alarming things freshly said and freshly done.

ᴰaniel Dunphy had escaped, his illicit cargo gone. Adrian and Leo had fistfought. Adrian had swung to make contact during Daniel's getaway. The brothers sat strangely abreast now on hard kitchen chairs. Each knew defeat. Fleeting promise had come once more to right all, in a wholly questionable just world. Frank glimpsed this sitting abreast when the door to the kitchen opened and his sister Grace entered with Claire Dunphy. Grace spoke to the darkened room.

"You hang in there and never mind those pack of fools in the kitchen. They got no more sense than a bedbug."

Frank looked up to see his sister tilt toward the lantern. She increased the wick and he saw how taller she had grown. It became the most private of scenes when his sister and her friend came forward, stood abreast preserving the comfortable distance teenage girls keep from each other, those holding trust for one another. The kerosene burned. It lit inquisitive rigid faces that would stay forever thus, long as lantern wick burned and kerosene climbed. Any adult world was miles hence, beyond a closed door where clumsily it licked self-inflicted wounds, all lightness of step and being long removed.

Grace saw for herself the beautiful look in Frank's eyes. The look she would come to recognise as one of permanent hurt. But her brother's gaze rested elsewhere, upon the newly sloping front of her best friend. It was a gaze of admiration, in part. I can understand, thought Grace. Claire Dunphy is the beauty of Ingonish. Prettiest girl North of Smokey. She is darker than most anyone here knew a person in winter to be. Those definitive black eyes smooth as liquid glass. The eyes to covet, wish for.

The young Claire smiled at Frank, as pain and fear dribbled from him like water through a cracked cup. He looked up at this remarkable face, at the strange bridge passing now into improved land and leaving this behind. Instantly the profoundest of thoughts arrived: that there was this in life. To have a girl, to love a girl, to go through all, with her, for her. To touch her when you want and have her touch you. To call her to you and have her gladly come. How alone, this was enough to cast off any early chains that come to bind.

Sister Grace removed herself half a step. She saw what was going on. She had come into the backroom to reassure her brother after the kitchen scuffle. To explain that it was all right again among father, mother and uncle. To explain the boys were still bringing medical attention and Daniel Dunphy was gone for help still. She said none of this. Instead, silence held the moment. Leave her brother to his contemplation of her friend. Give him this. The girls, having stepped into the sacred backroom where girls never went – that alone won the silence.

Claire smiled. "You'll be all right, Frank. I know you will."

Frank watched only her while Grace turned, looked to see where they kept their clothes.

twelve

The moon was two-thirds through the night sky. Smooth-bark beech allowed starlight passage of its canopy. It was beyond midnight and Daniel Dunphy had crossed the top of Smokey. The earlier ruckus and late hour made him apprehensive about having his horses go down over the mountain. He carried hay in his sleigh, some of which the pair had eaten during the unexpected trip back around the harbour. But they were tired. He stopped the sleigh to decide. If he kept it slow he could get down. There was rustling. The stepping of an animal? The cautionary retreat of the moose, at last, one grazing a nearby fir? By moonlight Daniel saw two forms refuse further step, pause, like lost folk.

"You two only here? I thought yas would be well up the North Shore by now. Which is William? I can't remember the other's."

The boys left a thicket to take on the easy appearance of the starved and the frozen. Daniel had his stallions draw the sleigh forward.

"I'm here to give you pair a lift into town by the urging of your father. First we got to get down from here, though. Think the two of you could go ahead of me? Watch where snow hides any holes? Horses don't travel down hills all that well, nothing does. And these fellows, they're played out. I've got glass aboard I don't want jarred, there's some sandwiches too. But we got to make bottom, all right? Yas cold?"

"Chilled to the bone. Fire didn't help."

"I didn't see a fire coming up."

"It was too little."

"I'll tell you what. Get us down the other side of this and I'll make us a fire that'll roar. We'll eat and get warmed right up."

They descended the backside of Smokey, tinkling and crunching marking progress. When at the bottom and having travelled a frozen river a piece, they set up camp before the sea. As his fire built heat, Daniel passed over wool blankets. He handed a boy each a seal-meat sandwich his wife had prepared and he saw how sleep stole over the young mugs. They shared a tarp in the firelight and chewed, but sleep came at intervals to wreck them. Daniel told them to get up finally, to get on the sleigh and find a place to lie properly.

"Rest all you can, through of what's left of the night, because before first light we travel hard."

Daniel turned to the ice floe and saw it bite the shore. Hefty pan pieces decorated the beach till all went out of sight. It had to be minus twenty, and without a breath of wind. He saw trace horizon cloud to the east, never to the west or north, not with the mountain. With light broke, they would make town in a good five hours from here. The boys had been useful on that mountain and would prove moreso the rest of the journey, up and back. Those horses had not been without danger passing down that ravine. First thing in the morning I'll tell these two the good job they made, but this big man is himself weary. With the tarp under him now Daniel stretched out and slept in the snow. Stars shone and a full moon hung innocently in the allotted west, to remove all doubt – which can linger these winter nights.

Sleep was short-lived. The fire sank out of sight to die under an oblique falling snow, rushing for inches. They had built on wet ground, according to the depth of the hole. Daniel stared till no flames came then got up and broke limbs with his hatchet, off a dry windfall this time to get a solid blaze. William woke to snapping. "What a walk we had. Dad let us go in a storm. He was half foolish to."

"He was making a move, young fellow."

"We got lost then had a proper fistfight. I think I got a baby finger broke. We had to go back down the mountain at one point just to climb back up. At the top we stood under a tree that broke the gusts and we lit a fire, but then one of us backed into a big bough that slid snow all down our necks and put the thing out. We travelled opposite the North Star, and were some old glad to see you come when you did."

"This is the woods, bai. Not home, where we know every nook and cranny. But wake the other, will you? Brother, she's frosty yet. See the glimmer over the ice? That's daybreak, believe it or not. Not purple yet, but she'll break before we know it. I'm pushing these animals. I got to get this ride over with."

"They don't belly down, when they sleep? Ours does."

"No, these stand. They're the wilder version and have more sense of the predator that might be lurking nearby I suppose, especially out here in the hinterland. I saw them bed once, but most rest comes just by stopping. Tell me the name again of the one who was shot?"

"Frank. Mom cleared us out of the backroom when they brought him in. They got him on a bunk."

"He the youngest?"

"Yalp. He was trying to make it up onto the first field of Middle Head where the summer fish shacks are. He wanted to get home by the trail when the rifle let go. Struck him fair in the muscle of the left, then he swam."

"He what! I didn't hear that part?"

"He swam. The drift ice moved off while he was out. He had to make a break for it by getting in the water at the beach. He couldn't take the cattle road back along Middle Head. Too weak to climb the banks. He made his decision out there on the ice. He used his good arm I guess. The big mystery is how he got the twelve-gauge back in. Clifford was going into kill him for having that out."

"Why? It his?"

"Pretty much. He's the one who travels with it all over hell's creation."

"You fellows are hard nuts. I'll say. But ah my, never have I heard the likes of going in the water in these temperatures. What kind of stuff is that youngest fellow made of, anyway? The heart! Getting in the icy ocean this time of year, living to tell about it? But that situation of the ice pushing off, what he faced, is exactly what I'm afraid we'll face. It can happen here just as easily, and more, and I don't want to be out there with the horses and sleigh should she decide to. So rattle him. I haven't a clue where the winds are coming from in this hollow. I will when we get out of it. The tides, I know. High, is about right now and should stay so in our favour for a good four hours."

When the boys were on their feet Daniel told them to flap their arms. He showed them how to beat hugs around themselves to get the blood circulating. The boys did what he said then got back on the sleigh to cool under blankets as the horses stepped gingerly for the declination to the beach. The rocking sleigh entered a granular salt surface, righted itself then moved easily. Its master kept the shore close where he could. In many parts they simply travelled sea which had ice formed so thick it sat on bottom. The welcome sun lifted powerfully, then broke out everywhere. Its made sparkle and shadow of all the misshape further out, before advancing, in spots. Glimmer on white landscape effected a trimming of the eyelids. Each fellow looked through narrow slits to maintain general study of a lovely world so far from home. Black dots were soon adult seals barking at a whisking sleigh. Fleshy mothers and mewling pups maintained distances according to pup size and its ability to defend itself. Crows cawed. Without shadow, wings spun in the dawn sky above a coyote's seal kill. But the eyes of curious pups glistened in a sun departing the floe, a sun ending much camouflaging allotted white coats. Eagles hid nothing of their restlessness in tree perches, but rather adjusted balance on large boughs whereas coyotes, slunk shore. Each predator was encouraged at the prospect of feasting on the day-lit floe. And, naturally, always ready.

Sun shone hard on a frigid landscape inland, of snowy trees and nearer frozen-sand banks. Wind flew brashly over faces to make the sleigh ride all excitement. Daniel turned elegiac at the glee, he shook his head: he knew talk of this would be property of these boys for years to come. It was a fine moment and enjoy it they should. He sped up, driving the hell out of the horses on a neatly frozen sea between beach and floe. He wanted to warm the equine hearts, to test the good ice shoes into which each was shod. Snow flipped from runner and soon the going became that of the best of the straight roads travelled by fast wagon in high-summer Ingonish.

The sleigh flew over a frozen ice road laid between floe and shore, one guided now by green bough, the work of the Scotchmen who lived very privately on their large granted parcels along this North Shore. The Scotch had their rounds to make as well as any in a community and so took advance of what nature provided even if for shortly. In patches of untested grip, across this wind-swept ice road, signals were such that days had passed since anyone had been out. The boys hooted. They were impressed by the excellent beasts that drew them, their returning eyes always coming to light on the workmanship of the sleigh before squinting again like men at a solid white sea. Daniel laughed. He felt goodness at witnessing boys take departure.

The party drove till midday, slowing only at the appearance of the town of North Sydney. They came ashore over the breast of a boat slip. With silent darkened boyish wonder then, particularly at tenement housing, industrial buildings and smokestacks, the three northerners entered town proper. They exchanged one hard-packed road for another then selected the widest and most active street, coming at last to Alice Hale's Hotel. They drew up alongside its windowed facade, stepping off the sleigh with legs uncertain.

"Alice has red hair, bai's. Hereabouts, they call this place the Rusty Nail. That other wonder is the Balmoral, too posh for our humble footsteps."

Daniel took the boys up broad steps. Their boots crunched salt-grain and gravel. He had the two remove their headwear inside then got them situated at a table in the dining room.

"These two are froze to death," he called to a waiter, repairing nothing of his speech. "Bring them a plate of codfish cakes, each, can you? And a piping hot pot of steeped tea?" Daniel went outside to see to his horses, promptly chilled at stopping. They blew streams of vapour and awaited guidance. To a curmudgeon stable attendant full of compliment for the breed, Daniel commanded fresh water and hay cut from the previous fall. Dry blankets, too. The man bowed and winked as above rose steam from expansive backs and slick thighs. "Leave the sleigh out back I say." The horses were led away to hotel stables. Daniel returned to the dining room.

"Those're quite the creatures," he said, his feet turning for the window. "Conquistador and Piaget. They bring us here with speed, or what? I love those animals with all the heart in me. Say my name in farewell too, when they go. You fellows will be all right here. It won't hurt any of us to eat from a clothed table. I got to disappear for an hour to run two quick errands. One is to get a hold of that doctor for your brother; that's primary. I'll try to do both jobs at the same time, but if he gets here before I do talk to him. Tell him all what occurred and that I'll be right back. Keep an eye on the street for me. Don't talk to anyone."

The big man left. Dignified moustache and gold-rimmed glasses newly donned, yet his entry into the deeper street scene evidenced a theft of his significance. He trod and tucked a collar in among strange women of double bonnets and strange men of bowlers with earflaps, a few just as big as he.

After an hour, by indication of the hotel clock, each boy having eaten and done a magnificent job of implying that sitting here was the most natural thing in the world and that perhaps both belonged, they at last started to writhe. Wood seats without armrests. Legs needed stretching. They watched blankly as single customers came and went. They watched the door blankly, the clock, the street. The odd dolled-up woman came and went. No great numbers seemed to use this place. At last Daniel returned.

"What! He ain't here yet? The doctor?"

Daniel whistled curtly to a new lone man working the bar. A pocked head rose from sundry accounting. "Fishcakes! Hot tea, my man!" Daniel asked if the boys wanted another plate before lowering the finger completing his request. The boys looked at each other: "Full," said Clifford. William nodded a russet head in assent. Daniel nodded that he believed them, but in his chest knew otherwise; his experience taught him that neither boy could know what full meant. He held up two fingers to the barman, wove the hand clockwise to indicate inclusion of the boys. He sighed then sat with thick fingers and thumbs knitted on his belly.

"That doctor. Connelly? Hate him already. He's got flat-tipped ears. Trust anyone with flat-tipped ears like you would a rabid dog. Turns out he's not the guy I knew, but some sterling bird. The proper doctor is on the other side of the island. Cheticamp. Look bai's, I ordered for yous too because I didn't come all the way into town to eat alone. No man with a half notion of grace does that. I ordered two plates but will eat only the one, see. If I'm still hungry I'll put in the request then work on another. A person has got to have all he can when he's away from home. You know that? So, enjoy yourself, hear? A person doesn't know when he'll pass the same way twice. Not in this day and age he don't. Knowledge of that alone will bring you farther ahead in life. I'm footing the bill. You two helped me last night and a lot today. Coming ashore was no easy task."

The food arrived and Daniel divided the grub of the second plate with his fork. He set the plate between the boys who were slow to start, but mindful of the other once begun.

"Bai's," said Daniel, with drama. "Look around. Tell me what you see. No, let me tell you. This here's the spot where I screwed me first woman. The Alice Hale. Rusty Nail. You get it? Right above here I banged her. That was back some while ago. Back when the wild blue streak of hell hit me. A person doesn't know which way to turn when that hits. But hits she does."

William's freckles waited. Clifford's tongue touched his lip. The moustache of the interlocutor appealed greatly. Daniel sat with ear fur-flaps up, half-cocked. He was eating and soon realised it, so he removed the headgear. This was a different breed of man altogether from men the boys knew. He sat better, for one. Deportment was his, he looked you in the eye at points beneficial to both, to illustrate better what he said. Without warning the boys then knew disappointment – they would never know whiskers like these. Full facial hair was not on their father's side. Nor their mother's. Moreover, their forebears included no lives lived in which the first screw came at a hotel. Each boy deduced privately the correlation between a good moustache, the fuller life.

"Screw? Me son, that's all a fellow ever did! Then, it was. Anything that walked I took a crack at. Never more than one at a time, though. A fellow has to keep his dignity. A man losing dignity in bed with a woman is a man lost altogether, far as I'm concerned. Thing is, every fellow goes through that patch when the wild blue streak of hell hits him. It lasts two maybe three years and begins right around the turning of twenty. Which is just up the tracks for yous two. It's the most natural thing in the world. Don't fight it. Don't let it Lord over you, either.

"Ah, the smell of this place alone. Can you smell? Spilt hops. Rot that collects in the corners and never goes away. No mopping of any kind gets it. Smell alone brings them times back."

He cut fishcakes with his fork and chewed a piece. Jawbones worked. He blew on hot tea and gestured with tines.

"You boys will go through what I did. Mark my word. And if yas don't – look out, because there'll be hell to pay! Denying nature is asking for troubled growth. Or, what's worse, no growth at all. Here's what to do. Get in one fight. With fists, a haul-down where you get properly smashed in the mouth, but once. Second, a night of trouble with the cops. The reason doesn't matter, let it be the fight. Finally, one night of screwing a woman whose name you don't know and won't learn. Those three things. After that yas'll be prime. Do what you want with your lives, then.

"Some fellows, I know, get stuck in one of these periods. A lot do in fact, I've seen them. They end up living in a shack somewhere along a shore or in a wooded valley. We got them around home. Ha, that's the queer part of it – the socialising they did earlier, not knowing when to end it, finishes with them being alone, dirty and drunk. Anytime, be it night or day, they can lay their hands on liquor, they will. Black out what they threw away, see. What they were supposed to only move on from. Yes. That I do know. They lose appeal for women, of course, and so end as hermits. Every community got them. Never learnt what it is to trust anyone. Don't go that way, bai's. For the love of God, steer well clear of that manifestation."

The bootlegger paused with infectious calm. He sipped tea then looked around the empty dining room, but did not seem to see it.

"The others of course are, and I hate to say it, your father's breed. The ones to stay with the first woman they bed. Nothing wrong with that. It's just not the proper way to go. They're in as much trouble as the hermits. More! Do they learn what it is to taste their own blood on their lip? To have authority wrestle you to the ground? Bang Betty Ann, or Bertha Blue? They miss the humility. And then afterward, watch how they shy away from all scenes where one might have to stand up for himself. They never sample from the buffet of strange women, but tramp through lives wondering how things would have been if they had. Trapped like the ice we travelled over, they get, except that ice frees itself. In a way they do become hermits, of their own. In their minds, they do. Lives of dependence. Can they turn around, to say boo? Without first getting consent from the wife? The ultimate victor? No and nope. Their kids give them grief. Wife, family, Church – but there's the highlight. All dominate. They never break free. I don't feel sorry for them, everyone gets their shot. Which is my point here. You got yours coming so act on it and take it. But let it pass too.

"Don't hesitate. Keep shoulders back and your mouth shut till you're prime ready to haul off and smack someone who deserves it. But, where I say! Where in the cursed-old-dying-frig is that fellow to bring us more hot tea! And the doctor! One or the other don't walk up to the table soon, you'll see a smack all right! I'll get up and fire a chair through that window to begin. That wet-eared doctor. Oh, Lord dying. If I have to go and find him a second time, he'll be getting his teeth to drink. The day is good for travel yet. Which is what's plaguing the soul out of me. We could be over Smokey before midnight, we get away in the next hour."

He jabbed his fork into his final bite of mashed cod and potato.

A long-coated man entered the hotel lobby. A sharp-eyed man with clean face and trim sideburns. He took off slender gloves and, placing one over the other, set the pair on a leather medical bag at his feet. He stayed with his bag, choosing to peer from the foyer into the dining room, past cleaned spectacles. He saw. There were no patrons beyond the three. It was early, inclement and not a pay day.

"See that," said Daniel wiping his mouth with a napkin opened large. "That's repugnance there. He spots us. Just wants to make a show of it."

The doctor gave attention when Daniel established a bland eye, when he wrenched his head backward. The doctor passed tables with drawn chairs while the boys saw first-hand how one man, without a word uttered, could be bound to another. The doctor brought bag and good posture. A paper-thin scar was on his lip, his trim nails with babyfied cuticles.

"I guess you're the party, how do you do? Doctor Connelly. Henry."

The boys duly took the hand of the doctor. The first handshake of their lives.

"Listen," he said. "You need to know I haven't made a call like this before. The regular doctor servicing communities north is absent. I am interned at the hospital only. How far is this exactly? There's a stipend for travel, you see. They need to know. At the hospital."

Daniel tapped a finger to end the waiter's pouring of more hot tea. A second plate of fish cakes that he'd intended to divide with the boys had arrived. He wiped a mouth already clean, pushed his empty plate aside. He skillfully removed a potato crumb from his moustache.

"All right. Now you listen to me. Think you can do that?"

"...I can do that."

"Well. This here is Clifford Curtis. This here is his brother William Curtis. You got my name. We're up from Ingonish and outside is a sleigh set to take you there, and us. You're about to take a little ride. These gentlemen have a brother in dire need, otherwise none of us would have made the none-too-easy journey. You're a doctor. That's how that part goes. Now. Mention once more this subject of stipends between here and the completion of your journey and I'll personally take pride in beating the face off you. If you only knew how tempted I am to beat it off right now. Rise from my meal. Dance you in the street. Come on – pout in defiance. Stipend...."

"All right. I shouldn't have mentioned it."

"No you shouldn't. In all decency. Now, these boys here and I will finish our food. You stand over there or you sit and join us. You might want to eat. It's no skip down the lane. And if you're worried don't worry – I'll supply the meal, stipend."

"Enough, mister."

"The thing about money is – you listening? Thing is, leave it out till it becomes the topic, on its own. That's the art. Learn that if you learn anything, as doctor, as a person."

Doctor Connelly, red-faced, turned and walked away. He stood at the coal fire near the entrance where he set his bag at his feet. He looked through a window at the street after taking off his glasses to wipe them. He replaced his glasses and did his best not to think about the treatment he'd received. He had heard about the communities, had heard about the gruff. He did think, however, of how he was trapped. Medicine. Perhaps it was not the thing to have gone in for? Wind flew down the flue.

"*I* say, fine way to get started, eh boys?" said Daniel, chewing, stopping to pick teeth with thumb and finger. He removed a wisp of bone. The boys smirked and Daniel smirked. "Eat, we get the hell out of here."

Daniel paid the bill at the table and they met the doctor at the door. The four stepped out into a frigid afternoon entirely sunless.

The boys undid fresh hitching at the post while Daniel yanked to tighten belly harnesses. The horses snorted and raised hoofs while a much lighter sleigh now sat under a snow's dusting. "One of you young fellows sit up here, with me. There'll be too much wind I fear. We'll need to break it, for the man who needs his accounts balanced."

"Enough mister. I said, enough. So lay off!"

Daniel laughed heartily into a town whose streets had quietened and cooled. William, the more social, faced the sulking medical man. He had wanted the front but Clifford's narrow shoulders had that. Daniel dropped earflaps, snapped reins and sang, "haw!"

thirteen

In the dark, after a day of good travel conditions, the sleigh stopped above the home of Adrian Curtis. A lantern deep within the home lit its window: poor light exiting exposed how the home was built, especially where the common room of night was. Roped to the hitching tree, the horses lowered heads that strained tethers. The boys had wiped them down before tying on blankets. Nearby, spruce was limbed high enough for animals to get under so it easily allowed for people to pass. "Can you boys get some hay and water together too? That'll be your last job of the night, I promise," said Daniel. He moved ahead with the doctor. "We'll take care of them," said Clifford touching the unspent dollar in his pocket while William worked. Clifford wondered what to do about the money now that they were home and turmoil continued. William wouldn't forget it. The family was never not in need. He would return it, first chance he got, in the morning.

The boys caught up to the slow men under eight-foot snow banks; passing them at the doorstep and continuing to the cabin where they would borrow hay from Sally. The men had poor luck with the latch. It was jammed in its casing and there was danger astride ice formed on the threshold: latch work was made tricky.

"Those fellows gone? Maybe they know the secret?"

A flushed, shaven Adrian appeared at the door. "Wait, I kick it open." Daniel and the doctor stood back then entered, stomping feet on a springy porch floor. They removed headgear, scarves and mittens.

"How do you do, Mr Curtis? I'm Henry Connelly."

"Doctor?"

"That's right."

Adrian took his hand as Daniel waited for the two to go in ahead. He looked behind – a set of wall-mounted antlers had jabbed him in the skull.

In the corner of the kitchen on a wood chair sat a smaller Leo Curtis. Bent, forearms on knees, he made no eye contact with Daniel, who stood proud at the closed inside door, a hand high on its jamb below slackened coiled door spring.

"Jessie? You here? Get together a cup of tea with the hot water for these gentlemen. There's stew too, fellows. You got to be half-froze."

"Bit later for me. If it's all the same," said the doctor who puzzled at the odd ring of his voice in this thickened light and heavily scented kitchen. Coal burned. None took off footgear. A sink with no faucet had alongside it large jugs. A blanket covered a doorway. A puddle stood at floor centre. Not so much as a radio played. Oven bread had been recently withdrawn. The doctor breathed wood gases.

"All right. I will have tea, but first things first. Where is he?"

"Out here," said a subtle Jessie, mortified at the state of the house during the visitor's calling. She hadn't thought of how she would feel. She shifted weight, holding the fingers of a hand, her wedding band like iron. The doctor turned and smiled at the matron; noting the Irish mouth and persistent black eyes of a cornered animal. He would remember these eyes when encountering other mothers whose houses he would come to visit. He wore his long coat, but felt its frosted ends could be chilling the place.

"Grace?" said Adrian. "You get the tea together for the doctor while your mother and I take him out to the backroom. And for Daniel here too. Did you happen along the boys, Daniel?"

"They're outside tending the horses. Brave lads, them. You should be appreciative."

"I am."

Doctor Henry Connelly watched where he stepped. Somewhere, a dog lay growling; clearing nostrils tenderly, he tensed in uncertainty. This really was the end of the world. Kitchen heat warmed his bare head and made his ears itch whereas his midsection felt no heat at all. His coat was unbuttoned and he thought he might pass the outerwear – Daniel kept his on.

All down that North Shore, following red clay cliffs and those slate ocean banks, the doctor felt as if he were approaching a place from which he would not return. Then, coming on land where they had – at a frozen river gorge from which they climbed the tallest mountain he'd seen, sleigh runners riding dangerously upward for the longest time till summit was reached – only then silence broke. He had spoken to William in the twilight. The boy heard, but also added in parallel context: "This is not impressive, or nothing." The boy's smile softened him. In it was charming innocence and great patience. How this boy had survived, let alone the other, and so graciously?

William widened his eyes at the doctor's speech and a ready rugged tongue was present, characteristic lively gesture to add, ability to listen. Yet nothing further was said. Milburn MacAskill, the regular North Highlands doctor must have made a career undertaking such adventures and coming to know these folk. He never spoke of it. As for young Doctor Connelly a deep prejudice was much apparent. He supposed Highland people to be ignorant, and desperate. He expected no dignity. Hamilton Hospital in North Sydney was as far as he had got in his treatment of patients, having finished medical school in Halifax only the spring before. His summer was spent in Outpatients where he worked under tutelage and general supervision.

But the harsh beauty on that shore ride. The barrier of barriers, Smokey Mountain, climbing from the sea. It got more and more isolated, and thus lonely, wondrously shut off from the world. Uncivil land locked in entirely by winter desolation. From the sleigh, leafless forests stood stick still, forests certain never to know a degree above zero. Simple tight dwellings passed view. Pitch roofs of green, red and black asphalt shingles. Smoke rose from what looked like railcars abandoned in fields, denoting the densest of spruce. Pitch-roof protected these railcars, never to be linked. Never to arrive at any station. Smoke chugged nonetheless, indicating that Determination lived here. And, no medical facility? To wait for the circuit doctor to arrive? All hopes invested in the seeing from the road the red flag of need.

This house was one of those, and Doctor Henry Connelly was inside it. He stood among wood, coal and a people who toiled away their hidden days just to keep from freezing. Twelve-by-twelve pitch, seven-foot wall: shelter from the storm. They stored, shot, salted dried staples at the periphery of existence. The dangers in such a life, and tonight, evidential.

The doctor stood in the backroom, where another wood fire burned, where air afoul of rancid flesh met them. Jessie brought a lantern forward and waited for the doctor.

"Oh, I see," he said toward a better-lit lower bunk. "Keeping you out here are they? With your own private fire." Henry Connelly felt the forehead of the boy who lay on his back with covers drawn to his throat. "Yes, nice warm spot all right. Frank? I'm Henry. They tell me you had a mishap." Frank looked up with glassy eyes, unable to speak. Mililica, curled under the bunk, jaws on a forepaw, growled at the soft-faced stranger's advances. Adrian hissed when the creature started, then openly called it out from under the bunk. By a handful of its fur he got it to the door where, letting it pass to the other side first, he booted what he could of it into the kitchen, catching only a tail. Regardless, it yelped in retreat.

The doctor felt for fever as Jessie stood alongside. She could have told him there was fever without his having to check. She knew her son fought the battle of his life, that he was using the heat of his body to drive out what chill he had contracted. She suspected the ocean brought the fever, but the accident made the battling all the tougher.

Connelly faced her, lips pursed in sympathy. He winked both eyes.

"I'm going to lower these blankets. It will be better to have those girls wait outside, with any tea."

"They won't enter here," said Adrian.

"When did it happen again?"

"Evening before last, forty-eight hours now."

The doctor lowered the wool cover and breathed in gases of putrid infection.

"What's this? Who put this on?"

"I did," said Adrian stepping forward. "It's what they were doing overseas. How?"

"Were they?"

"Was it bad to do so?"

"You were treating it." Then, "if you could, a little room please."

The doctor grimly slackened the tourniquet and looked under the dressing. The flour had not caked because of generous yellow pus. Applying two fingers to the inside of the wrist he checked pulse by a pocket watch. His weighty stethoscope came forward.

"Little more light possible? Mrs Curtis?"

He pinched the skin of the forearm, pulling it forward and letting it settle. Dehydration. He studied fingernails and marked blue black colouration. Destruction of circulatory pathways. Cupping a hand over the boy's open eye he waited for reaction to candlelight.

"Please. No!" said the doctor. "Hold the lantern away. As I do this."

Jessie gasped.

"Sorry, really. But the candle does it, I have.a light, but the candle does it, I caught the wax."

Jessie bowed and was careful to do as bid. Shadows climbed the wall. She felt light of chest in this company, but also ready with detail of how the boy had come in. She recalled all symptoms from onset till now, yet ventured nothing. Too much had been ventured. The arrival of someone with real know-how meant intervention could die.

"Good," said Connelly. "Frank? You're tougher than any I know. Hear me? Frank? You just lie still while I go out and have a word with your mother and father. That's the boy."

The adults left and, when in the kitchen with the backroom door closed, the doctor used two fingers to indicate he'd like them to pass as a group to the front room. He avoided eye contact, crossing the floor as clergy do altars. Jessie and Adrian followed closely.

With the three stationed in the front room, in a darker space away from the fire Doctor Connelly touched Adrian's shoulder, "Sir, you're played out." Adrian became erect, opened his eyes better. The doctor looked around this drafty section of the dwelling. He felt taller and heavier a man under its low ceiling. Quick intimacy formed in the near dark, it persisted enough for whispered speech to develop. Jessie came abreast her husband as the doctor put his lips together for her, here, too. Their pairs of unknowing eyes watched the visitor.

"I wish it were anything other than what it is. The plain and simple of it is, we are late getting here. There's been no circulation to the lower part of the arm, and for some time now. How long is of no value. It cannot be restored is the hard point. No blood in an area causes capillaries and veins to collapse. A tourniquet is customarily temporary. Used with serious blood loss."

Adrian straightened.

"Effective, just *too* sometimes. Seepage from a wound is not so bad a circumstance. Seepage goes on for years in some cases. A hospital would have been the place, but we'll not dwell on that. Listen, damage does not end there. Collapsing of the capillaries is moving upward. Tissue is something to be constantly fed with oxygen carried in the blood; it is something that will destroy itself if it doesn't get it. And all the while, pulse drops. A left arm comes nearest the heart. From what the sleigh-driver Dunphy told me, before coming, I did anticipate severity. I can say I came prepared. Listen. It's a hard, hard course we must take. But we have to restore a good pulse or we'll lose him. He's in danger of not snapping back, do you hear me? And as I said, no hospital's near. He can't travel, I'm sorry, the two of you. But, as a physician... it has to come off... tonight."

The doctor had soft sandy hair and full lips, his forehead was tender as shortening. For Jessie it was a forehead never to know worry. She was turned, to the blackest wall, unable to express herself properly in this damn house with these damn people filling it. Adrian put his hand on her shoulder in a way he had never, and yearning was such that she wished only to be taken properly, overwhelmingly, to be held. The hateful constraints placed on a person with others present – this damn, damn business of having to act just so!

"Come now," said Adrian. "We pulled together so far on this, Jessie. Jessie? It's up to you and me now. You heard him. He knows what he's doing, he wouldn't have come all this way if he didn't know what he was doing."

"Just like that, Adrian? A look, a decision? Adrian? No more discussion on it?"

"I wish there were time for discussion, Mrs Curtis. How I wish. There's not. All I can tell you is that this is what I know and that I can say no more on it. But take your moment."

Neither party spoke. The moment lengthened, to become of no value.

"The pulse is low, we got to move."

But Henry Connelly need not say another word, medically: he felt all too well their trust. His training would guide him from this point during the events of the night to follow. New to the business of house calls, realising suddenly where he stood – like these northern parents he too felt forced to invest all faith in what he knew.

"There's one more thing, I'm afraid. It was a rush job getting here. I have the surgical tools. I do have those, all right. Just. And how I hate to say it, no anaesthetic. Doctor MacAskill was in Cheticamp. I went to his home, to his personal cabinet but his wife had no key. The sleigh was waiting, nightfall approaching. We had ice to journey over. I just didn't have time to go to the hospital. I hoped all the way down it wasn't as bad as what it is."

The parents listened, with nothing to add.

"Get the young people out then," said the doctor to Adrian. "But out entirely. Keep the men."

Adrian's face was ill with the tiny authority bestowed it; yet he would get the kids out. The face had enlarged. The eyes especially. They searched the world tonight through cleaned spectacles where sketches came fuller and weightier but in matter-of-fact suffering, induced by these mysterious casts of Fortune working against him to make him finally feeble.

He entered the kitchen and spoke to his sons at the window, including in his speech the two girls who had come to settle near the stove. "Claire. Time for you to go home, dear. And you other three are to go to your Uncle Leo's for the night. He'll take you partway across the ice then leave you to come back here."

"No," said Leo rising from the table. "I won't take them partway, I'll take them the whole. I got to let Gloria know what became of me today, last night – tonight. I can't be sure if word reached her. You know how she gets, you above all."

"He operating then? The doctor?" said William, perking, effecting a general silence.

"You'll be operating you interrupt me again," said Adrian. "Get moving, mister! Dress along with the others and snap to it."

"Without a bite?" said the son. "What's a fellow supposed to live off of, air? We never had a mouse crumb since lunch."

"I told you – eat that fried baloney sandwich your sister made you. But eat it on the way. Come on now, I'm not saying it again, you young people get dressed and clear out."

Leo took opportunity at the door to speak directly to the self-possessed Daniel. "Nothing is over between you and me, Dunphy, hear? You slimed off the hook this time, but mark my word, from here on in it's my sole ambition in life to nail you to the cross."

"I don't doubt that. Someone like you likes to keep sole ambitions in life. If you had let ambitions lie, though, our situation might be contrary to what it is. Carry that with you. And, oh, listen. Take a good look in the sleigh when you're outside. You catch sight of anything untoward, beyond tarps and ropes, you let me know, will you?"

Leo put on his cap and buttoned his jacket. He stepped into the porch – further along this theatrical stage of his own ridiculous making. More steps. Through the first door window he could see plainly the profile of his adversary, then nothing, and no one, as he turned to check the weather. Snow. The single accomplishment of this night might be merely this job entrusted him, of getting the kids across the ice and into his house. No, the return, there was that.

Inside, in the heat, Daniel faced the doctor but took in the young as well.

"Adrian. Get your brother out there to take my rig across the harbour. These young people don't need to walk, especially the boys. But Claire. Once you get home, run over my place and tell Eloise where I'm at. That I'll be here the night yet."

The young people buttoned up. In the porch they filed past Leo who with cocked head saw through the glass the busted nose and good skin of the bootlegger. But Adrian suddenly stood before Leo. He had come to mention the offer of the sleigh. Nope. Leo would take no rig. He didn't know the horses. He didn't want the responsibility. He wove an arm. They would take the shortcut down over the hill to the shore then straight across the harbour. It would be just as fast. When Leo left the house he glimpsed Daniel through the glass and pointed a finger. Daniel nodded, fist up against an inside wall, steady on his feet.

The outside door closed. No bang. Snow fell.

At the kitchen table the doctor had an arm through his jacket.

"Tell me. How old is he?"

Jessie waited for the removed coat, communicating a surplus before answering.

"Fourteen. Tonight."

With dropped eyes the doctor passed the folded coat. He sat in his white shirt and suspenders. He drew his chair in and tenderly cleared his throat. He ate stew. He picked up sliced bread to butter it when Daniel reached across. Daniel touched his shoulder. The doctor looked up to see who it was.

fourteen

*L*eo got up on his horse. His heels touched its sides. Clifford stayed near Claire as the group moved into the downward frosted forest. The night had picked up a wind that circuited spruce crowns. Trunks groaned and ice in birch shook jingles of frozen limbs; the sky wore wedding veils of star fabric and a full moon had a pretty ring around it. Claire said goodnight at the Woody Shore then stepped into the wind bent thickets. Clifford made no extra effort in farewell and there was no speech from any crossing the ice.

*C*limbing the path, the group waited at Leo's door as he led his horse across to his barn and into her stall where he covered her. A frosty view of the village proper was back across the way they came, a dog barked. Leo opened the house door and inside stood his wife. Gloria Curtis. In apron and housecoat, a straw-haired woman. She was visibly ill with distress and equally horrified at the prospect of being hospitable presently. With hands binding apron, she looked as if she were drying weapons for use. The unblinking grey eye suggested loss of reality; she looked above heads to the forty-five degrees of winter slope – upon which the door was closed. She blindly addressed her husband: "And you? I should haul off and smack you, mister."

Turned to him, she said, "I don't know what's stopping me. Since yesterday morning – gone! What would you have a person do? Beyond break with worry."

"I sent word."

"I got word. What's word? I told you never to leave me over here alone on this hill, at night. I made you promise *before* we married. It was the one thing I asked you and you broke your word. I was worried sick to death, you hear? I dressed, went down with the kids to see to your load of wood crossways on the road last night. No sign of you – not a print. What was I to think? I didn't know what to think. Whether you were among the living or the dead. Whether the banshees took you. Well, answer. Tell me where were you. You can't disappear like that, Leo, do it to another, not to me. You were home always before dark. And this brood here? What're you doing with your brother's kids?"

"They're here for the night."

"Oh yes now."

"Oh yes now, is right. Adrian's youngest boy had a mishap with a rifle. A doctor from North Sydney had to be brought in. He's over there now tending to him."

"Doctor MacAskill?"

"Connelly."

"Who's that?"

"Gloria? I don't know, Gloria."

"Who's hurt?"

"Their youngest."

"Bad?"

"We don't have to go through it, do we? I said shot. That bad enough?"

"You didn't say shot. Shot? Still, where in the name of God are we going to put this contingent to sleep, that's what I want to know? We have only the room for our own in the household, you know that better than any."

"Sort it out. You'll just have to sort it out. I'm going back."

"You're going *what?*'

"Back. They need me."

"Yes now, you're not going anywheres again."

"No? No? Watch and see how I'm not going anywheres again – just take care of things here till my return. Can you do that much? Show some hospitality?"

"For the love of God, Leo. I'm to deal with this on my own? I asked you where you were and didn't yet get a proper answer."

"I told you where. Take care of them, then you go have a proper lie-down."

"Where am I'm going to put them? Six already in their bunks, you can't expect me to wake them and double them up with their cousins."

"No one's asking you to wake anyone or to double up anyone. Fix up the wood room. I'll be back when I get back."

"Listen, mister. That saucy mouth we can dispense with. If you're going – go, but don't be the type to use backtalk."

"Gloria?"

"Gloria what?"

"Grow up. A little."

Leo went out the first door, pausing in the porch to get on his toque and to firm up his laces for the foot journey. He eased the outside door shut.

The kitchen preserved a lingering cold at his departure. A higher ceiling was inside, with brown cupboards, plenty, built up to it. The visitors stared at these. Their own cupboards had always at least one door swung wide open.

"That man," said the aunt. "Come on. I'll set yas up in the wood room. No, back out here, off the porch. Back up. No, let me ahead. He works out here. Has a stove that's operational. Can one of any of yas put on a fire? Nice question to ask. You bunch must have been putting on fires since yas took your first step. The door to the outside is draughty. Oh, what a man. How does he expect a woman to cope? He likes to bring in the bitter, all right. Here – what's your name – William, Clifford, Frank? Here, ah, grab that tarp off the wood and get up on the counter, yes, hang it over the door casing. You're Gracie,

I know. Stand here, you. No, like that is good, ah, what's-your-name. There should be nail heads. Are there? Push the material through. Don't be afraid, it's only tarp. Here. All right then. Like that is good. There now, that'll break the wind. Listen, any of you have anything to eat? We're all finished up here, a while back. The kitchen fire's out for the night. We don't keep one on, not through the night we don't what with the chance of fire. I'll whip something together if yas want it, how about if I do that? Say the word."

The faces of the three did not stop following their aunt as she spoke and flipped open a hand. They managed to avoid direct eye contact till she'd turn to confront one with a question. The woman had poorly etched shoulders, a crooked back climbing to an all-white, bumpy nape. She was a bigwig in the church.

"Well?"

"We ate."

"What did you eat?"

"Moose steaks," said Grace.

"That what you had?" said Gloria.

"We ate moose steaks," said Grace.

"I suppose."

She studied these children of her in-laws.

"I hardly know you three from a hole in the wall. I'll leave yas to it. It's the one night, better be. It won't kill any of you. The outhouse is out that door. Go down over the bank to the edge of the trees. The door to it gets drifted in, so does it here. Don't any of yas break it either, either door, by forcing your weight or hauling, hear? Kick the snow away first. There's a pitcher of water in the kitchen. Use the bread knife alongside to jab it if it's frozen. Don't wake anyone. I'm a light sleeper as it is. It was young Frankie, who was hurt? Where'd he catch it? His foot? He pull the trigger or did one of yous?"

"He did it to himself."

"Jesus, Mary and Joseph! What next? Nice time of year for something like that to happen. Poor little fellow. What a sin. Dear God in heaven what next. I'll say a prayer for him tonight with my beads, but it's beddy-bye for me. I'm half-snow, half-ice just standing here talking to yas. Now also, I say, don't get up in the morning by yourselves. Wait till your hear me roaming, hear? That all right?"

"All right."

"Go to sleep then, pull over you whatever you can find. There's his sweaters and oil skins hung on that spike over there. No, forget that – heaven help me – let me get proper blankets. I don't know where my head is. Ah, how he asks a person to perform. How he expects it."

The aunt came back with good wool blankets, folded. She instructed them to get in the corner and sleep along the partition where it was warmer. Use their jackets for pillows. She apologised for no mattresses, but repeated that it wouldn't kill them.

"In all my born days I never once had to sleep on a floor. I couldn't do it. Supposing the world was coming to an end. I'd stand, wait for first light. But I ain't young, am I? You young people can handle it."

Her back was to them again. Sloping shoulders and white neck disappeared for the night. A hurricane lamp flickered on the counter, alongside the blankets.

The siblings had never slept in a house outside their own. They waited against the partition, half-blankets under them as cushion. When no more sound inside came, they drew the blankets tight to their necks, tucked them under their behinds better. They turned talkative, humoured and yet kept voices at an all-time minimum. Life from here on in, it seemed, would be only segment after segment of adventure like this. William spoke of the big trip to North Sydney where snow buried motorcars, and one puffed on a street. He spoke of the flush toilet that ran everything away. He spoke of views from atop Smokey and of their racing slinking coyotes along the frozen North Shore. Clifford looked around. This part of the house was no warmer than theirs; it was colder. The walls were painted. Pine trimmed door and window. The smell of varnish got in his nose. Stacked firewood against the opposite wall appeared to be dry. Maple, it looked.

The boys got up and lit a fire with no kindling. There was newsprint. The wood chunks had the tiny cracks in their ends to prove seasoning. They selected the smallest. The two did not work the fire but instead sorted the blankets better and got under them: having spent some minutes inside a house, chill had entered their bones. With the newsprint consumed, the draught not set properly, the fire died and with backs to the partition they watched a black stove. The three stretched out then to lie in a sausage string. William had turned the lantern low. It was up on the counter, too high and too far for anyone to stand and put out. It was so cold an arm couldn't be drawn outside the blanket. There was lantern kerosene to last the night.

"It's coming off," said William.

"What?" asked Grace, and Clifford.

"You know what."

"Just shut up about it, bai" said Clifford.

"It was in their faces. You saw? I know you saw. I know I saw."

"Go home, fool. They'll cut in and dig out the pellets like a partridge cleaning. They need men around to hold, while the doctor works. He'll pick out the lead then dab the whole thing with alcohol swabs. Be done of it before heading out at first light."

"How about stop talking about it?" said Grace. "How about that?"

"I'm saying I saw their faces. Each one was right... petrified."

"You two didn't see it," said Grace. "Not since yas got back. I did. It was puffed and grey, looked right dead. That what you want to hear? Now, can we shut up about it?"

She got the silence.

"Where you going?" said Clifford, to William who had dropped his warm blanket and stood on his feet. He adjusted his toque and pulled tight the cuffs of his mittens.

"The fuck out of here, is where. Something just bit me! I don't know what else would be living in this frost! And that crazy old bitch of an aunt. Gloria Hystoria. That's a witch if ever there was one. I ain't sleeping under no roof of hers. You hear her? Or the likes of her, before?

"Soon as we're out for the night, yalp, me son, she'll be back in here with a bread-knife pulled. Slit our throats one by one. She'll use what she's got to break the ice in her pitcher. See the eyes? Like something straight out of the belly of hell."

"Lay back down, bai. You ain't going nowheres. You're staying here, with us."

"Am I? With you? I had enough of you the whole trip. I'm going to find out what the hell's going on back at the house, too tired to sleep now anyway. You don't honestly think they sent us on a trip to North Sydney where we could have got chawed to pieces by wolves just to have a doctor swab alcohol on a cut? Poor old Dad – he could have done that much, me son! Also, it's warmer outside than it is in this barn she has us lodging in for the night. She hates Mom. I don't know why, but I know it. They all hate each other, here. And those cousins in there, sleeping in their beds. Each one slimier than I don't know what. I ain't waking up to have them piss-mires lord it over me. Eat breakfast, with them? Their cold-sores staring at me? Yalp, not in this lifetime. Call me what you want. Prejudice? Then prejudice it is."

The other two got to their feet and stepped from their blankets.

At the door, under the tarp, Clifford shoved the younger William who reached for the latch. "I'll do it, fool. Beep out of the way."

Clifford used the weight of his leg, stepped a foot into the bottom of the door. No sound came as he expertly guided outside snow. But its buildup on the other side allowed a mere ten inches for flight. Each squeezed through as delicately as thieves. Then, out in the dark, joyous in deep descent, they peered back up at the squat house. Three or four times they peered, till down over the bank at the road, they saw it no more.

The trio travelled the black road then dropped over the treacherous bank of crust forever touched boldly by the northwest wind, to arrive flatly on the ice, at last. William spotted their tracks of coming ashore the day before. Sweeping winds and blistering cold had removed surrounding snow to create raised pads of their prints. The travelling of them partway was speedy, reassuring. The moon was gone. Grace encircled her throat with her scarf then got it up on her face as the shore got behind. She felt terribly exposed out in the middle, but beamed at the expanse. She had never travelled with her brothers. One was forward, the other aft. Her left ear, facing west, froze. It brought nasty night through its hole. She saw only to the right, to the black ocean. She tried to turn left when William cracked a joke. Out in the very middle, wind drove through them like swords and lances. It whipped eyes to seal them. It died only inside Bradley's Point. Each blinked to break ice bits formed in lashes during the crossing.

They waited in knee-deep snow. They were under the spruce, well back up on their own land. These spruce were the ones to catch the brunt of the brutish Northwest. They faced the kitchen window. Snowdrift starting at the road and long as a sea wave, swept the breadth of the field. It gave a balanced five-foot ridge under the spruce. The three chose spots. They settled on jacket backs, snuggling bottoms deep in order for the whipping wind to pass higher overhead. Their bodies, protected like Arctic dogs then, were safe from all gusts tormenting the lonely field. As children they had come here to spy on the house. They knew the internal views afforded. Tonight a trapezoid of kitchen light ran out to greet them in the snow. A second box tenderly reached out past the backroom's window summer fabric. The backroom was not the scene. It was where exits were taken – from the scene. An item fetched. A moment taken. To recover.

Adult figures anchored the kitchen. They dipped and swelled and swayed at intervals about the table presently pulled from the wall. Heavy dull heads bent powerful necks, they also rounded shoulders. Postures wove in and out of the light.

How the wind howled. How it drowned out the heart-wrenching screams and the eroded endurance. There were wails and then nothings to compete with it. The trio could not see plainly where the group worked. Shadows betrayed them. Or rising curtains of snow. They bent, twisted to see. They saw where the surgeon kept himself, the city stranger apt to saw bone. He worked over – was it, packed snow? A cloth-covered board? His back was to the glass. A bottle dabbed a cloth. A bottle raised. But they saw the doctor bend, because the group had bent. They saw his presentation, both hands passing. The severed arm of their youngest brother.

part II

fifteen

The blistering sun's rays made it week five of a hot spell to beat all records. Roadside grasses wilted. Laggard horses and cows drew what fresher grass grew from perimeter sod of buildings. The windows and doors were flung wide at the Fairway Market. Flies entered freely to buzz down aisles or hover at counters. Flypaper hung as if photographic film; elongated and faded, catching no legs, no wings. The place was deserted – for all were out behind the store at a rare gathering: a competition. The question among staff was about to be put to rest: whether the new employee could perform a certain feat of strength. Money had been collected five dollars each put up as the employee did a wide-arm circle. Crumpled bills were placed atop a wood barrel; a rock added for good measure, though not a breath of wind stirred. Storeowner Reuben Burke, with brown-spotted neck that filled out a white dress shirt, commanded attention.

"All right. If we're going to have at it, then let's have at it. Here's another crisp five. I'm in, too."

Rueben wanted the contest over because today was the day of the big order. Since morning, the delivery wagon had been running trips back and forth to Dunphy's Wharf, where the trade and passenger vessel, the *Aspy*, was docked. Servicing this northeastern section of Cape Breton Island the cargo and passenger ship was crucial to normal workings of life in the region. Undergoing recent repairs made her weeks late with the summer order.

The bet was to determine whether it was possible to hold horizontally, for sixty seconds, a sack of flour weighing one hundred pounds.

With one arm.

Patrick Robinson produced a yardstick to ensure a straight line was kept. As senior staff, Patrick had been the one to arrange the bet, he had put up the initial money to counter the staff's dismal prediction. He was unable to match Rueben's new stake.

"Take it out of my hide, Rube," said Patrick. "Which you do anyway. I'll honour it. You know yourself I will. Other takers? The boss's words, then, let's have at her."

A certain young mother and wife knew nothing of the event. She had entered the empty Fairway Market with her little girl and stood, confused. "Anyone home?"

Claire had come in for a bag of doughnuts and a carton of cigarettes. Her husband would be in from fishing before long and she wanted something for his tea. She paused at the fabric of a newly arrived bolt leant temporarily against shelving. Heavier curtains would suit the kitchen window, the shining sun and harbour reflections have all but destroyed the lighter. Claire looked around. This store was usually a centre of action no matter what the season or weather. She didn't know what to think about its abandonment. And she could have anything she wanted! Except that eyes always watched somewhere in Ingonish, especially in a public building. Dallying at the counter she tapped a finger and looked at unopened candy in plastic containers.

"Good thing you don't see these, my little Dawn Marie."

She looked at Dawn, the little girl had been putting up an awful fuss lately when she saw a thing she couldn't have: the terrible twos, did they never end? The big order must be in, thought Claire. People will be stocking up for fall, which is never far, though the heat wave would have a person believe the contrary. Claire heard the clamour of voices out back. She reached for her daughter's hand.

"Come you."

The backs of heads greeted Claire, the napes of necks and shoulders, tense in observation. "What's all the fuss?" she asked the hermit, Cod-Liver Al, who needed his tobacco and canned milk too. He smiled his oaken teeth at her, his stocking of coins drooping from his hand. She stepped away and raised Dawn, who had tried to touch the rolled-up cuffs of a boy standing near. Claire's eyes met the source of the gathering: the eyes of the source met hers. Standing bolt upright, arm out and straining, was her brother-in-law, recently returned from time working in a lumber camp in the Highlands, Frank Curtis.

Frank gripped a corner of a sack of flour, the commodity caught like a piglet snatched promptly for ill doing and held at arm's length. The audience wore a rigid rapturous face that felt his strain, while a marshalling Patrick Robinson held up a yardstick to verify position was maintained. Timekeeper Victor Shea peered into the face of a pocket-watch. Frank moved his eyes from Claire, his purple smile again intent on his sack. The gleam in his eye alone seemed to garner sufficient power to carry him through his ordeal. But he shook at the hips, the strain manifest here, the odd body position he worked to keep, wanting this. He made a hot sun hotter. Claire lifted Dawn from hip to ribs.

"Hold her, Frankie boy! Hold her, goddamm it all!"

"Ah, who's here with the mouth? There's kids!"

Emotion swelled. Gatherers clenched fists as time elapsed; it was the kind of spectacle all little places would recount time and again during cold months and long seasons. A shush defeated a murmur begun. "Cursed be to hell. Will all of yas just shut up and let him do it! The shusher, too." People had tried the quiet approach, but sixty seconds was a long, long time.

Someone ahead of Claire spoke: "He's carried the weight of the world on him for so long now. This should be a walk in the park." Old Peters woman, Matthew Peters's wife, Pearl, said that. Up in her

nineties now, what went around in her head could only be slow coming, slow circulating, but truthful; she may have only now realised the
event was underway. Cod-liver Al winked, twisting his head know-
ingly. This gave them much.

The timekeeper tucked his timepiece under his chin. With closed
eyes to hear, and hands raised, he counted down the last ten seconds,
digits descending into fists. Removing his watch, he studied it and
made drama of a thumb pressing its top: "And... Stop!"

The crowd let out a genial sigh when individual cheers rose like
popped corks. A child wove the yardstick, sword fashion, while a single hand shot from the corpulence of the crowd, clutching the money
from atop the barrel. The hand of Patrick Robinson.

"Did I tell you we'd do her, Frankie bai! Heavens all mighty – I
knew you had it in you!"

Storeowner Rueben Burke approached. He held a pinched hand
out for the bills.

"Pass them, you! And you better be sharing this with Frank!"

"I am."

"I'm the one to make it official. As all events of note need officiat-
ing – stand aside, stand aside!" Rueben creased the bills and passed
singles to Patrick. The rest he held up with two fingers, for Frank.

"Listen up!" said Rueben. "Here – you two! Put that down!" Two
kids had raised the flour sack, which leaked, their mouths circles of
floodlight guilt.

"I'm seventy, seventy-seven now," said Rueben, clearing largely his
throat, at the crowd.

"Hush now. I'm trying to have a word. I said – all, right! There,
that's better. As I said I've been in this racket all my life. Been around
all sorts lifting and carrying the heaviest kind of merchandise you
can think of. In all my born days though I never saw the likes of this
Frank Curtis. Come here, Frank. No? Stay there then before you collapse altogether. Nope. I never knew anyone to hold a hundred-pound
sack of flour out straight with two hands, let alone one!"

A squawking cheer, the pounding of fists into hands, superlative
whispered swearing. Frank smiled bashfully at the admirers with an-

cestral features and charms coming to the fore. He mumbled thanks to the boss and shook his head at no one in particular, to himself perhaps. The effort had left him somewhat sociable, a feeling to which in large measure he was not akin. He winked at some waiting singly to catch a good glimpse of him. Against orange crates he leant, his chest heaving, the winded spell slow to pass. Someone touched his shoulder, as if for luck. Another smiled, wanted the eye contact.

"No one disperse yet!" said Rueben. "We ain't done of it yet. It is a hundred and one degrees out, I know, but I want a word more. As I said, no light thing, a hundred-pound sack of flour. You saw him. This Curtis digs in and waits. Bulldog-fashion. Sinks the teeth in and holds on. But here's what I'm coming round to say.

"Sunday next, North Sydney Forum, there will be a big event. Now I don't want to put any pressure on anyone. And I never mentioned it before, ah, Frank. But you see, it's their yearly arm-wrestling tournament. You've done some of that. Surely to God you have, it being all the rage now amongst you young fellows now. Your strength? You'd be hard won not to press a prize-winning steer onto its back. I was going to suggest it, is all, Frank. That you go there and represent us. You showed us here today what you're made of, so I want to sponsor you. Send you to North Sydney. To compete!"

The crowd stood poised. Claire put down her daughter.

"What do you say to it? The biggest show in the Maritimes. None from here can say he ever went. Never had the money. The ambition. You got the strength. We can show them what we're made of down here, North of it all. I'll put up passage aboard the *Aspy*. She's running errands down-north the next couple of days but she'll return. I'll put up the entry fee. We'll even see what we can do about springing for a room for the night."

"Where you getting the money?" came saucily from the crowd.

"I'll tell you where," came just as saucily and remotely. "See what he wants for a can of tinned milk!"

"Hear!" said Rueben. "Pipe down you and – you! I'm trying to do a turn here. What I charge for a tin of milk ain't no one's business but my own. We're lucky to have this store down these parts. I'd like you to see how life would be without it!"

People sighed and swore, in half-breaths.

"Don't listen to them, Frank. They're what's not uncommonly known as the rabble. Come now. I won't be offended, but what do you say to it?"

"Person could give it a try, Rube."

"Hear that! That's the stuff! Give the chap a good old-fashioned clap, come on now. He's got the courage where few have it. Frank Curtis – the bulldog!"

The crowd cheered then left the boiling platform.

Frank walked up to Claire.

"What did I get myself into? Say, there's someone getting big."

"Better not be talking about me, mister. I'm putting on few. I know I am."

"The girl, Claire, for Christ sake. I was talking about the girl."

"She has a name, Frank. And it wouldn't kill you to use it."

"Yes, but what is it?"

"Frank Curtis! Some uncle you are!"

"Been away, Claire. You know that."

"Dawn Marie, after my grandmother, Marie part anyway."

Frank and Claire watched the child. But how so powerfully built Frank was now. Broad of shoulder, handsome, thick chest. Eyes like the night. Each kept faces on the girl. Claire cleared her throat.

"Haven't been over the house since you got back, Frank? Clifford's been asking after you."

"He has! I don't believe it. Haven't seen a soul, Claire, tell you the truth. Too busy fixing up the old place of Dad's. Took no time for him to let it run all down to hell, Mom gone. He never was one for taking care of things. With her gone he's worse than ever."

"Ah, Frank, it was some terrible to see her go. Young yet. And she didn't go easy."

"I was home. I saw. She didn't."

"We all saw. It was for the best."

"Oh, it was."

142

"And now you're working here at the Fairway?"

"If you could call it work. I just started. I like it. I don't make enough to start my mansion on the hill, but she's a place to come to every morning. That's plenty for a fellow, for now."

"Ah, Frank. You were always easy to get along with. Everyone says that. Don't drink, smoke, don't curse."

"Curse? Not at all, by the old dying."

"See. That's the thing right there – a person's nature. Being good-natured makes all the difference in the world. You get along properly with people, out in society. It's a knack not everyone has."

"I'll take your word on that, Claire. Clifford fishing these days?"

"Some days he's out. Today, he's out."

There was no more to say, then. Fortunately, Pearl Peters was bent nearby. Her diaphanous head-cover stored her blue hair, a dye job gone awry. A fuddled gaze watched, as one lost to the world. She eyed packets of worksocks. She touched stapled orange rubber-gloves.

"Won't be needing that stuff, Pearl. Socks, at least. Not in this swelter." Frank smiled kindly upon her. She didn't know him from a hole in the wall. She looked at his front then into his eyes. Had he said something? Had she herself said it? This was the Curtis, everyone knew. His appearance disconcerted her.

"What did you say to me?"

"Nothing, Pearl – I said it's awful hot to be thinking about heavy socks."

"It won't always be, awful hot. It will always be, awful cold. That much I can guarantee you, sonny. There's a good price on this stuff. I'm just trying to remember who it was I didn't get Christmas presents for, that's all."

Frank looked at Claire, enlarging his eyes to look like his father, Adrian. Claire tried not to laugh and Frank tried hard to look serious. The two were forced to play out the moment in their eyes, the thought of this old woman preparing for something so far away, when molasses ran thin and stretched flypaper caught no flies. But just then one landed on paper. A leg joint worked, wings buzzed.

"I'll drop over," said Frank, moving from Claire. "Tell Clifford."

"I'll tell him. You tell him! You should see your sister Grace too. Pregnant again, big as a house this time."

"I saw her. She came over the old place to see me and Dad. Brought her little fellow... ah, Rodney."

"You got *his* name. She didn't mention that. She minds the heat, she told me. I can't blame her, I do remember how that part was."

Frank nodded and wondered what smooth gesture or word could cut correspondence here; he *had* been getting away. Arm akimbo, wristwatch tightening, he saw his sister-in-law bend to fix the girl's bonnet, drawing her face close for reassurance.

"Claire?"

"Yes, dear?"

"Tell me her name. I got no luck with anyone's since I got back."

"Jesus, Frank! This is your niece! Dawn Marie Curtis."

"I won't forget."

"Better not. Well. Lots of luck in that competition. Clifford will be interested to hear about it. And come over soon as you return. Let us know how it went."

Frank grinned, and simply turned his back on his sister-in-law, telling himself not to look over his shoulder, not to watch her shop further, see her movements at the counter.

He entered the storeroom where the high temperature and new stock made the place feel more cluttered than ever. But things were to be done here, in the organising of old and new stock. It was Frank's territory. People left him alone here. He made some uncomfortable out front, he knew, those who didn't know him directly – which meant the younger of the village now. Sundry others. He had gone in on the flour challenge for that reason, to get to know folks. He was twenty-two, strapping, easy-going, six-foot-one in bare feet – it was high time to show folks he had humour. Which so far turned out to be his greatest of strategies.

Frank used the stepladder to get down old stock, dusty buckets of riblets. These had to be sold. Riblets were pork ribs in preservative, a Sunday favourite among Ingonish families. Buckets were kept at the foot of the counter, near the entrance. Halfway down the ladder, using a thigh for balance, three buckets in hand, Frank tilted his head in a half-cock. He ducked to see into the aisle. She was gone. He straightened, the top of the door casing then facing him. The storeroom was hot as the dickens. He turned toward shelves, shaking his head at the words shared with his sister-in-law. No. He just didn't like to go over to Claire's. He didn't like to see his brother – they were never close, cool since the accident. Mainly though, it was Claire. Frank could not take being in the same room with her. They were mute amongst others, but all too talkative when alone. People knew this. They had to see it. Rurals folks were supremely intuitive.

Also, Clifford drank his evenings away. He had trouble rising to fish in the morning, to participate in the sole activity that brought the family food to its table. He had drunk heavily before leaving home, before Jessie died.

Claire's beauty had faded none. Her hair had gone from flaming to auburn, but those eyes; still made the world vanish. And always – the analysis to follow. What passed between the two? What was said, and how?

Frank had been sure his time away to work in the lumber camp would have blotted the impression she made on him. Hoisting with pulp hook countless timbers onto winter sleighs, the dragging of branches year round atop rough ground, handling of his end of the cross cut saw – he had hoped that these would erase feelings aroused and lingering after even a moment shared with her. The comfortable silence in the bush, each man letting the next perform his job. A place where you were left be. Where reassurance came. Confirmation that life could be a light-hearted affair. It erased nothing.

While Frank's body had turned to iron, he hoped his mind might do the same. Not the case. Today showed that. She showed that. Perhaps nothing could purge you of another's hold and it was only a thing to accept, to bear as all was borne. She did grow stout. Did that help? He had removed his eyes from her while they spoke, but looked accidentally when she bent for the child. He had tried to sense her new size, to take her in a little at a time, peripherally.

145

And yet, she too changed in his presence. It was not imagination – she clammed up with him near. A little uneasy perhaps. Many were. Especially as he was so full, strong and alive now. People spoke of the satisfying proportions of the boy, now a man. Proportions. Form. What people saw as correct, true, sound. The Claire Dunphy he knew, she was not one to be uneasy. No. They shared a talent all right. But when had it begun? The night Grace brought her out to the backroom, is when. The accident. She was just beginning to take up with Clifford. Something had passed between Claire and Frank that night. Damn it – she kissed me at the shore. And, well... William liked her too. She liked us all. Still, it was the backroom. That little girl, Dawn, how much she looks like Mom. A little Jessie. What a piece of work, be that the case. They say I was the one to look like Mom.

"Frank! Big-shot status means you can go slacking off? I don't think so! Bring those dreamy eyes down here and move those pork barrels and flour casks off the back step!"

Derek Campbell, Assistant Manager, the figure who seemed to be in all places at once. "Come on I say, we need the space. Another wagon'll be here in a minute, so let's hop to it. Everything is to be inside by nightfall."

"Coming."

Frank carried the three buckets of riblets by wire handles to the counter. He said hello to a family up from down-north. They grimaced and winked somewhat, but kept eyes averted: peripheral were creatures here, so peripheral behaviours were practised, expected. Frank didn't mind.

He went to the loading platform where the sun shone mercilessly onto the back property corner. Crickets whinged and bottle glass glinted. Not the slightest replacement of air came. Clay the colour of weathered shingle denoted the wagon's turning space, wheel track and hoofprint remained. Trembling aspen stood opposite, their leaves silent – the logging fellows called these trees the "Waggling Tongues of Woman," an Indian expression, apparently. One fellow claimed they spun in no wind.

The driver must have gone to the fore with his load, thought Frank, with goods that needed to be sold quickly. He walked around to see the horse that pulled the wagon, its tail striking half-heartedly at flies. No driver in sight. Frank's father would be excited about the North Sydney trip – he had been there; as for Frank, any notion of the city came in bits and pieces of conversation gleaned, of glanced-at photos in the *Sydney Post Record*. The radio did broadcast one program about Canadian cities, only the fall before. It began in St. John's and went clear across to Vancouver. Radio came in clear as a bell up in the Highlands.

North Sydney was no city. North Sydney was a town. He would be all right in a town. Multi-storied buildings, thirty or forty feet at most, jammed together. Noise, commerce, motor cars. Purses to breasts, children alongside – the way Claire went with Dawn Marie. Heat. Nothing worse in the world than heat, thought Frank Curtis, as he climbed the steps to the Fairway. Nothing worse. But it would be difficult he knew. There. It would in fact be impossible to be anonymous.

sixteen

When Frank got home he saw his father splitting wood, in a jacket. Frank had just swum the Fresh Water Lake. Twice a day, before work and after, he swam from Jack Doucette's Cove to the beach and back. Just looking at his father in the extra layer made him ill.

"What're you doing with an axe? Dad, me son, she's high summer!"

"We got to keep ahead of things, Frank."

Winded and sweating, Adrian tried to rock the tool. It was buried in a green chunk of knotty spruce. Seeing this diminutive version of his old man, Frank could not imagine that he himself would ever become this. His father had never regained the weight lost when Jessie died. During her final days, he had in no ostensible way given way to grief, but rather stood firm as an oak. The wilful man had always been against the church, yet he put up no fight when the priest came to guide the family through the wake, and through the funeral. Dressed in his own father's suit Adrian stood in the kitchen each of those last mornings, listening, obedient. All that was asked of him, he did. Never returning to his old self showed a structure undermined, a bridge condemned.

Frank put what he carried on the step. He went to the splitting block and Adrian stood back as his youngest worked the axe to extricate it. Frank caught the handle low and lifted the whole thing over his shoulder and head. He drove chunk and axe down at an angle to the block. Jammed still, Frank's anger rose and his father stepped further back, placing knuckles on hips and blinked.

"How did you manage to get it buried so deep is what I want to know!"

"By starting in the first place I suppose. I wanted to get it out, but only lodged it deeper. The maul is somewhere here. Just leave it, Frank, it'll dry and split by itself. You get in more trouble as you go along, with this green stuff."

"Don't I know it! Because that's all we ever burnt! Stuff held together like this. Ah, you miserable bastard!" Frank freed the axe and stuck it in the chopping block. "There now. You leave the wood. Save this foolishness for cold weather."

"I will, Frank. I will smarten up. But look here, bucket of riblets! Sunday's a ways away," Frank.

"Sunday? Forget Sunday, I say we cook it up tonight."

"We can do that. People got too many expectations for that day anyhow. It's no better than the rest. Sunday is no more than a day."

"I don't know what you're talking about. Whatever it is, it has got to be some slight against the Church. We'll feast just the pair of us. Come inside, I got some news."

"Bai – tell me here! I don't like it when someone says they got some news then invites you inside to tell it. So, what?"

"Rueben Burke's is putting up money to send me up to North Sydney. There's this arm-wrastling competition he wants me to attend."

"Attend?"

"Partake."

"Arm-wrastling? Suppose. You have to split the purse with him?"

"Never asked that."

"Well any arm put before you the way that axe was just now will be torn asunder. Must be all that swimming you're doing. Those push-ups I hear in the morning. And what's the Fresh Water Lake and back, got to be two miles? They tell me you cut through it like a swordfish. Arm-wrastling? You never arm-wrastled, did you Frank?"

"In fact I did, at the work camp up in the Highlands I did. The boys hauled up this wooden barrel outside the cabins, and they'd take turns on it. First going off I only watched, but then this one night, after a plate of beans, I said, 'Come then boys, I'll take on the champ.' This farmer's son from Margaree, Bucket-headed Ben Dauphinee was champ. He put them all down like he was snapping spaghetti for boiled water. But he turned up his nose when they said he had a challenger. 'Him? What's in the old hell he going to do?' he said, staring up at me on the top step where I was thinking – give me the chance and you'll see what! I was strong, what with working in the woods. Though I'd only been there a short while, at this point. He was ten years older than I was and had this mono-eyebrow running the gamut of his forehead. It was hard not to look at when his eyes were on you – and you daren't laugh. All of us were misfits of some kind, up there in the bush: hair lips, premature balds, giants, dwarfs. Still, good fellows. He agreed in the end, we squared off.

"So his hand goes around mine. I knew right away by the feel of his thumb he was made of iron. And honest to God, like trying to bend a crowbar set in cement. I glanced up at the bucket head. I never thought farmers were tough – they're as tough a breed as God ever set on the face of this earth. The savage nearly kilt me. Me son! Right away, he robs all my strength, my arm dipping like a barometer needle going from fair weather to bad. I held him – I gained on him at one point. But no sooner had I then he got his arm to climb back to scratch. The other fellows hooted and this drove him on to no end. He swore, spit, put on the steam like you wouldn't believe. Then all expression died away when he jammed my arm onto the barrel ledge. What a jarring! Thought my body was broke in half! In the dirt, toppled like a pair of pants lost from the line. I couldn't use my arm the whole of two days."

"No? No, those farmers aren't easy."

"That was meeting one. Later, after I got to working in the woods and built up real strength it became a different story. Thirteen, four-

teen hours a day, hauling pulp and tangled branches, turns anyone
into a clear brute. Especially the one clearing limbs, which is where
they stuck me, piling all the brush they cut. I did fifty chin-ups a day,
when no one was around, from beech branches near where I worked.
The only thing that would hold me. Getting ready for him is what
I was doing. Defeat drives you, when you're young; I know. But the
knack of arm-wrestling is technique. My French bunkmate Hyacinth
Boudreau from Isle Madame told me when we were in the grub room
one night, 'There's a way to not getting your arm tore off. You want to
hear it? It's by... waiting. Only that. Release what you got, but after.
After you tire the other fellow out. It's no different from when you're
with a woman – you got all the time in the world provided you don't
get excited first going off – tell yourself to save it for her. And when
she ain't expecting it, nail her."

"Nice language in front of your old man."

"Sorry, me son – it's the woods yet. The shoulder, Hyacinth said.
That's the storehouse for power in any kind of arm-wrestling. Not
the arm at all. Still, wait first. He demonstrated what he was saying
with a soup ladle. I watched and because his eyes were criss-crossed
it was awfully hard not to keep from laughing, especially the poses
he struck. I tried what he said – but on him. Then and there. Neither could put the other down. We ended up on our toes, gripping,
grappling, tearing, ripping, dipping. A bench breaking, pots clanging,
glass, silverware. Us straining like fools. A cook with a beard on his
neck rushed in and tore a strip out of us, gave an awful tongue-lashing
before firing the pair of us out. 'And you're going to pay for damages!
Look at the salt! Look at the salt! Spilt salt, on the floor!'

"Oh, but it was worth it! Jesus, the laugh we got. And I beat him,
Dad. Hyacinth Boudreau was the first, though he would deny it. And
those French, Dad, they're are as strong as hell too."

"I heard as much."

"The end of it all was this final night when Bucket-head was packing up to leave. Off to help out his family in Margaree with spring
planting. I waited by the barrel and when he came round the corner
I said, 'Little rematch, in parting?' The eyebrow thought about it a

full minute before Dauphinee dropped his duffle bag in the dirt. 'You didn't learn your lesson first time? Come on, let's get it over with. Weasels like you must like being showed the foot over the hole.' The others gathered in a second. The two of us locked arms.

"Well, sir. Again, from the start he nearly tore it from the roots. I could feel each ligament in my shoulder rip. Be patient, I told myself, looking over at Hyacinth who was nodding as if to say, 'That's right. Like I said.'

"We went at it a full twenty-five minutes with neither slacking. And I held him fine – till from nowhere the audience raised this crotch-grabbing screeching and hollering the like of which would drive any animal within a mile scurrying for its life. Bucket-head had put on the juice. I couldn't believe but I was holding him, because that's all I wanted to do. I struck, after I felt him back off. Oh, Dad, the feeling, to take him down. To have that arm smack that half-inch barrel ridge. Bucket-head Dauphinee from Margaree. Beat, at last! I put my hand down to raise *him* this time but also felt, for the first time – the awful feeling it is to beat a man. Stays with you. And this poor guy had been leaving. Leaving, now in disgrace. He grabbed his duffle bag: "There'll be a rematch, piss-ant." But all knew there never would be. I got him to shake my hand in the end. I left the Highlands shortly after."

Adrian put an arm back to raise himself. He straightened from the step.

"That was some story, Frank. But let's go inside, a big drop of rain just struck me on the forehead. It was too hot. I knew the lightening was coming. So you beat him, eh?"

"Fair and square."

"I know what you mean about the bad feeling for the one defeated. Overseas, I beat the head off this fellow going on about Cape Breton-ers. It was nothing so civilised as an arm-wrestling match. I just took him outside, cracked him in the mouth and gashed my knuckles. No wait – that didn't feel bad! That felt right good!"

They sat at the kitchen table and listened for rain on the roof. Tea cups were empty. Each watched the mist cover the windowpanes when Frank got up and took vegetables from the bin. He used all of his hand when setting the knife over an onion, when pushing the back of the blade while fingertips held. He cut four pieces, tearing peelings free with his teeth. He spit scraps onto the counter then cut potatoes and turnip in this fashion – which he didn't peel, but left for each fellow to cope with at his plate during the meal. As Frank cut the carrots he thought of how his father never spoke of peelings in his food. And carrots had a gummy peel.

The hotplate was on the counter. Ingonish had its own electrical power plant now that the national park had moved in. Electricity had been hooked up the year Jessie died. She would not use it and never did get to like it in the house. Getting it put in perhaps had been done just to keep up appearances. But she was in much pain then. Adrian liked a light bulb at night, but only at intervals of a minute or so, long enough to find the lantern or the oil. He loved radio and would listen to that. William brought him the electric radio for his birthday and Adrian plugged in for half programmes. Unknown costs of appliance operation harassed him. "I like to see how much a thing costs before buying it." Adrian had only ever worked seasonally, baiting fish traps, carpenter's helper. He never had a dime. Mostly, he could not get beyond the thinking of his parents – go without, scrimp, save whatever was left for later once the basics were taken care of. This was the way to live.

The cord bound, Frank saw his father observe the struggle. Frank got the plug in the socket and from below the cupboard took out a pot too large for the heating element. He ran water from one of the mismatched faucets into the pot then set it to the hotplate, centring it as best he could. On the shelf, where the radio sat, was the box of salt.

"I thought riblets had plenty of salt," said Adrian. "That's what they preserve them in. Rock salt."

"You'll get rock salt. Keep commenting while I'm working, not lending a hand."

"I'll shut up."

"Ah, salt, what's a little more. Salt won't hurt a man, especially in summer."

"Frank, enough! She won't be fit!"

"I'll change the water! Rinse the meat! But after the Jesus boiling starts – how's that!"

"You got a dirty mouth, Frank. That there's what you should be rinsing. You're out amongst people now. You got to smarten up. Some, at least."

"I wonder where I get it from?"

"What? I don't curse no more."

"No, eh? Tell us another one – how would you express yourself, if you didn't. You are right, though. Working in the woods ruint me. I'm not the same."

Since Frank had come home in the spring he had done the cooking and the cleaning. The winter before had been his father's first winter on his own. The old man wore a prickly beard when Frank had showed, one shooting out like stripped wire ends. Frank lent him his razor. His own had gone missing. He'd been living off tinned corn beef and boiled potatoes. He ate eggs that spent the winter in the cellar. And he didn't wash the dishes. Knives, forks, spoons and pans were let soak in a plastic bucket by the sink. He wiped them, he said, and Frank saw the bath towel. "Whatever you cook is boiled or fried. That sterilises what you eat the food with." Her gone, his son back, Adrian had slipped right back into the state in which he had lived his life: dependence. Someone to care for him. How immediately he passed over the run of the house. Frank could only think that a person's cooking and cleaning habits demonstrated a person's frame of mind, his will to live.

"Some help here, Dad, could you? In the very least? You can't just sit in your chair. I'm out working all day." The dog stirred under the table. It tried to stand then just dropped to the floor.

"I just don't want to get in your way, Frank. You know you're better at that stuff. I lost my glasses in the last pot of stew, remember? There was corn jammed in the wings for a week."

"Sit there then, sit. No – get the broom and dustpan. Clear these scraps I dropped, from off the floor. No one can work with things at their feet."

"That much I can do."

Adrian was slow to find the broom. He looked everywhere, twice, and when he did find it he looked for the dustpan.

"Top of the woodstove!" said Frank. "Under your catalogues and burning papers. I don't know what you were doing with it there."

"Me neither."

He aggravated Frank by jabbing the broom at his feet. Frank stepped back with the knife and a hunk of cabbage as his father swept. Peels stuck to the floor and wouldn't go in the dustpan on their own. Adrian bent. He had to get down on one knee.

"That's what you hate worst, in life, bending."

"Guess who came in the Fairway after the sack challenge?"

"Who?"

"Freda MacDougall. Her mother was an old flame of yours."

"Yes now, I'd have anything to do with her – she's too young, Frank."

"I said, the mother!"

"Oh."

"Freda has these new glasses and those big googly eyes of hers are bigger then ever. She comes up asking what's going on, why the commotion, who's going away. I try to go back to work but she chases me all over the store, springing on me whatever question comes to mind. And this patient way about her, listening till you finish. Drives a person batty."

"What's wrong with patience? You want that in a person."

"A little is fine. But she doesn't leave you alone when she's got you in her sights."

"She must have the hots for you then. Sounds like it. Take her, me son. Her mother, when she was young. Oh the juggernaut that was. One look at her and both legs turned stiff as a plank. To look at her now, she's not all that bad a piece of gear. There was a time though when I would have been happy to roll off her and into my grave."

Frank nodded. Graveyard talk. They all use that, they all throw in the towel at the end. Does that alone come to preoccupy the mind? Any word you can get on the topic? I hope to hell to have a little more wherewithal.

"She's a terrible gossip," said Adrian.

"Who? The mother?"

"Yes the mother. It's what happens to the good-looking ones. Looks fade and they realise they got nothing. They strike out against the world with what's left: the tongue. The only reason anyone ever paid them any attention was their looks. This is what they realise. It's an adjustment. All they have to fall back on is what they can say about others, never learnt common decency like the rest. And they suffer, for it. Your mother was a bit that."

"She wasn't good-looking."

"Hear! You want your teeth to drink? Who says she wasn't good-looking? She was no Myrna Loy, but she was all right. What idea do you got of her? You were the youngest. You don't remember her, really young. But what am I doing – putting her in league with this other? Your mother had virtue. She didn't participate in community gab – beyond the quota, I mean. That's the good thing about you and me. We can have an evening of talk and not hurt a soul. Enjoy ourselves just fine."

"You run a lot with the women when you were young?"

"There's a fine question to be putting of your father. More of the stuff you learnt in the woods, I don't doubt. No, your Uncle Leo was the tomcat, not me. When he was young there wasn't the pocket of a fur coat he didn't get all riled up over."

"Dad! I'm putting a meal together."

"What! What's wrong with that? It's true. Him and Daniel Dunphy were after the same girl for the longest time. That's what started the rift between those two, I figure. I'm sure of it. The heart has got a lot to answer for, in the end. Lives wrecked by it."

"That so?"

"One way a person can look at it."

"Saturday evening is when I leave. I sleep aboard the *Aspy*. She docks in North Sydney early morning. But I guess there's nothing open at that hour. They told me just to hang around the docks; that there's always something interesting happening there. The competition is at the forum on Sunday afternoon. Runs toward evening. I get to sleep in a hotel. Spot called Alice Hale's."

"I know the Alice Hale. Rusty Nail. Alongside the Balmoral."

"If I can get passage back early though, I'll skip the hotel."

"Why, for heavens sake?"

"I can't stay in a hotel. You get your throat cut in a hotel."

"You do not."

"No, never been in one, tell you the truth."

"I know you haven't, which is all the reason to go in one. Why on earth? Enjoy yourself! Man, dear! Once in a lifetime trip, this is. Paid for, and you've never done anything like this."

"How will you fare out? Me not here? You'll burn the house down."

"I'll fare out just fine, Frank. I don't need a hand here. It's the one night. Stay on. I want you to. Mililica is here and what better company is there than an old dog? Go learn a little about the world. William's home this weekend. Plenty of talk there, about his military training. They're shipping him off to Europe next month. Word is that general conscription is coming. They pass that and your brother Clifford qualifies. Be interesting to see them make him go. Those politicians use that conscription business as a bargaining chip, I figure. To lay their hands on whatever power they can. It's what they did in the last war, how I got to go. I didn't like it one bit at first, forced enlistment. Once it's set in motion, though, you get caught up. Then, in the end, you find it the thing to mark a man. Going off like that, going off anywheres. You've got to answer the call when she comes."

"*The* call?"

"Ha, no. Every couple of days something comes along to spoil whatever you got going. New decision to make. No, I mean heading off gets you prepared to handle the future. Your trip to North Sydney is that. It's as much as any overseas jaunt – more! You're tackling it alone, you."

Neither spoke on. Frank's condition had surfaced. Simple speech, circumstance, certain looks raised it like the dead whales the other nosed to the wave crests off Smokey. Grandfather Augustus told the story. It was the one thing Frank remembered of him. The whale floated for weeks in the sun while sea birds hacked its skin. When it began to sink its family edged it up in attempt to get it to breathe. Augustus had seen it over a two-week span, rowing out to the fish trap off Middle Head. He knew below was its relatives, because of sizes and markings. "Dying on land is to fall to the ground. Whales don't know when another dies. Or else, won't admit it."

The Canadian government would have no fighting men with one arm. The recruiting officer who had come to speak to the young fellows of Ingonish had taken Frank aside. "I guess I have to lay it out for you. The Allies would experience distress to see fresh troops arriving, not whole. Morale would lessen. Morale wins wars." The officer told Frank to stay on at home, to help out his family all he could, for a tough time was also in store at home. Good fellows were needed right here! Frank got the job in the woods then. He sent money home. The fellows in the woods had similar stories. One had scoliosis, another flat feet. Near sighted, far sighted. Misfits. The army took William. William had come with Frank to see the officer. William knew the decision deeply hurt his brother. He never spoke of it. That showed he cared.

Frank watched Adrian set the broom and dustpan against the wall. It was Adrian who had remarked how great William looked in his uniform, standing in this very kitchen, one month past. Frank had been trying with little luck to bake bread that day.

Mililica raised her snout. The cooking food gave off aroma, with the present slopping addition of riblets. Adrian sat at the table and put his face in his hands. He straightened then and leaned far back. He stared ahead.

"What now?" said Frank.

"Frank?"

"Right here?"

"Something I want to say, Frank."

"Say it."

"I buried it with her."

Frank looked.

"With *her*."

"What are you going on about now?"

"You know what."

"No, this time I don't know what."

"I kept it in a heavy bag down in the cellar for years, I wanted to have a service for it. Something. Then I decided to leave it where it was. Then, Jessie was after me to get rid of it. Get it out of the house. I don't know how she found out. When she passed on, I set it in the rough box with her, just outside the casket. No one knew what I was doing. They thought I was putting in an heirloom of sorts. You've got to have respect, Frank. It's the gauge I've tried to keep my eye on in this later part of life. You'll find that out."

"Let's just eat."

"I'm sorry, Frank, I shouldn't have opened my big mouth."

While lowering the plates of food Frank was overcome.

"Where are you going, ah... Frank?" asked Adrian. Frank coughed in his fist and stepped outside.

Day was over. A damp filled the yard air. At the corner of the house, with arm raised, Frank saw the chipped paint. He saw the shingles below it where the boys had pissed and the paint never taken. The wood here was harder than any ground around. Any wood. He looked toward the harbour then traced back along to the cliffs of Smokey. An early evening moon in its stillness skirted the ridge while behind, north, heat lightning broke and streaked. Frank urinated, wiped his fingers in the grass then went inside to eat his supper, he only had a light shirt on. Not having a fire on in the house these days chilled time taken over an evening meal.

seventeen

$\mathcal{P}$assengers aboard the *Aspy* looked toward Frank, and smiled. He turned to lean on a railing: imagining it was first passage for many aboard the ship.

The *Aspy* steamed out of South Bay while Ingonish inhabitants ashore enjoyed a summer evening. Smokey's lofty red bank ledges climbed down to the sloshing brine, with each the dusty residue of unsold chocolate blocks. High above, a capping field delineated an end of mountain forests. Visible from houses along Ingonish sandbar, this field was locally known as the Green Spot yet it deepened to a more memorable gold in autumn with its grass getting as tall as it would. A standing passenger spotted three adult deer stepped out to graze; one deer kept its head high on alert for predators while the pair lowered necks. Frank had seen these animals the past few evenings when walking the Fresh Water Lake barachois. He had told none, not even his father, and so faced disappointment at others now learning of their existence. He wanted to come out here and shoot one, to surprise the old man. To pay no attention to government hunting regulations, but simply shoot it and haul it home through the brush or – lower it over the ledge to a boat and into the hands of someone arranged to be there. He and his father could hang the carcass in the cellar. Together, they could salt the meat like in the old days. But the flies were terrible in the woods. The cape had its bears. Frank could presently see the work, to haul an animal off the mountain, especially alone. He squinted: chill wind rushed over deck.

"If there's a prettier place in the world I'd like to see it!"

A heavy-set woman had addressed Frank. Bracing the rail, she wore a black dress draped like a curtain, one oddly staying where it came, down her front, lifting only at her shoe tips. Strips of grey hair caught in her bun needles got freed by the wind and carried over her face. She grimaced then made her mouth into an impressive O to show how she was troubled by the sea and its wind. She wore a silver crucifix, prayer beads, almond-shaped eyeglasses. She raised a hand to grab her habit.

"I'm from Sydney, by way of Port Hood. Sister Sarah Samson. I was in Ingonish with the other Sisters over there, from Glendale. We think it's just grand down north here. Another country altogether. I told them at the Ingonish Glebe that I wouldn't mind coming here for the winter. Do you know what they said? That I had to go on a list. No one wants to give up their place!"

"Never imagined there'd be a list to come here, Sister."

Frank trimmed his eyes seaward. Like his father he didn't go in for the Church and therefore felt uneasy in the company of any who made it their lives. The instant friendliness unnerved him, always had. Porpoises raced the ship and much, much further out a Finback broke portside to blow a spout. People rushed over.

"Ah! I missed him!" said the Sister. "They told us about the whales, that they blow spitballs to stun the cod. They spin around schools to confuse them and when they breach they smack their tails to get more cod with shock waves."

"They're interesting, all right."

"I'm sorry. I didn't get your name."

"Pardon me. Frank Curtis, Sister."

"I knew a Curtis – oh, feel that! Land sakes it's rocky out here, rounding Smokey. Better go back in to where the others are settled.

We're trying not to hog the benches, but our legs are far from sea-worthy. We wanted the air, because who knows when a person will get a shot at that again, fresh like it is? I didn't see you at the parish hall bake sale yesterday? We hardly sold what we had prepared for it. We've got the remains with us. Each is trying to cut down; carrying sweets I'm sure helps. Come get some squares when you're inside the cabin. You want some now?"

"I'll be along, Sister. I'm fine out here for the time being."

"You're shy to approach, that it? I'll bring you some."

"Don't do that. I'll be along."

She did not leave. Frank turned to let the air rush over his face and to twist his cowlick. Seeing two children at the bow preparing to spit over the side, he pointed, to warn the Sister. She had seen. The children waited at the slim bow, fascinated at how the wind broke spit into glistening streaks, often with four corners, how it collected and rushed astern.

"Need help getting back?" said Frank. The Sister shook her head no, then paled in the shadow of a passing cloud blackening heavy star-board equipment. She took Frank's arm when the ship cut through a series of waves and a sickened look appeared on her face. Frank re-alised she had been afraid all along, that she had come out solely be-cause he had been here and she felt incumbent. She tapped his arm, "I'll go on my own from here, Frank." Her fellow Sisters who had been keeping an eye on her watched the retreat, over the deck and back to them.

Frank breathed in the cool marine air, recognising this distinct qual-ity that signalled fall. A cormorant twisted above whitecaps, as his mind sped back, to a full autumn a few years before, October. The leaves were at their peak as he stood with Claire Dunphy at the corner of his house. She had arrived after dinner to ask after Grace. "She get back from the nuns in Cheticamp? I can't believe that!" Clifford fall fished in the village of Neil's Harbour, fifteen miles north. He stayed there nights.

A beautiful Saturday afternoon, no one home. Grace was actually in North Bay learning to make a quilt from an old Protestant woman; Jessie was at church with her walking-friend, doing the Stations of the Cross. Adrian had left early that morning to work at the A-frame a rich fellow from Sydney was building over by the Clyburn River. William picked rocks off the road at twenty-five cents an hour.

Exceptional, warm, expansive. Lightning had cracked over Ingonish at mid-morning, startling inhabitants and prompting mothers to have their children draw curtains so they wouldn't go blind. After the storm cleared and curtains drawn aside, the sun in a seasonally lowered altitude made her appearance. Light struck mountain indentures to create visceral shadow. It turned damp foliage to a dazzle that let mist rise and break. Near the Curtis house were the brasses, coppers and ores of ground foliage. Undergrowth was just as much the spectacle, though none gave undergrowth its deserved attention.

"I'm heading to the shore," said Frank.

"Mind if I come along?"

At the end of the clothesline, the two moved into grass that wet their thighs. Jessie had put out a late morning wash and white bed sheets lifted high and slow on the rope line. They flapped sprinkles of rain left from the lightning storm and, for long moments, appeared as if sails broken free of stays. Amid washing and a summered woods preparing for dormancy, Frank spoke: "This path to the shore used to be good. As children, our bare feet pounded down across it to make it hard as a rock. All prickly now, so go slow."

"You're so lucky, Frank."

"How?"

"No worries."

"None at all."

"What I mean is, not yet. You're still in a good time."

They stood at the outcropping of granite which Frank's family called, simply, the Rock. It was an over-the-bank dump: where hills of frail tinned cans, rusted bedsprings, iron bed frames, half-buried bottles and a wringer washer lay strewn. Frank and Claire stared down into the heap as – for his part – Frank sifted with eyes a full minute, searching for items of value for some ongoing project. There was no ongoing project. Claire looked away, taking both faces to high points across the harbour where Smokey's ridge traced inland to Robertson Mountain. Two eagles spun, leaving behind a perfectly blue sky, eager for mountain shadow. Rushing wings became planes as tips showed best the skill of downward passage, that the slightest pull resulted in the full exploration of some new caprice of direction.

"That's what I mean. There. See how one follows the other when there's the entire sky to fly in? You have that, an entire sky."

"All have an entire sky."

"Which is where you're wrong. We bind ourselves, Frank."

*O*bliquely descending the Rock west, they passed a greyed delicate handrail free of bark and listing in its rotted supports. Frank had made the railing, as a kid, the day his mother and father had travelled to the Mabou wedding. Frank had worked the whole day, it was his first big project and no one had expected it of him. The anomaly forced presentiment from the start. He used an axe, maul, hammer and galvanized spiral nails. That day was the only time his parents had ever left Ingonish, together. They stood at the road to wait for their ride. They returned, quietly, and never left again. Adrian had got drunk over there and on the night of the return was hung over in such a queer way that he couldn't speak. His lips wouldn't work. With long face at bedtime he only stared in pout when anyone told him goodnight. They said he was poisoned. He stayed up that night and made noise as he moved about, going down the cellar. Something had happened. The galvanized nails had rusted on the hand rail; desiccated, it still denoted the path.

They crossed flatter ground, approaching a fieldstone foundation, a place called the Old House. Two bushy crabapple trees stood west here and, laden with overproduction this year, the feeling was that the trees had gone amiss entirely of roaming nature, of deer and bird. Yet, anticipating the greatest of attacks, these bushy trees merely waited in paralysis. Apples wore red blotches: since the sun never hit with the power it had for other property points; its attenuation could not significantly ripen fruit which hung fast to stems, resisting fall.

At the Old House, Claire stood perfectly alongside. Out of the corner of his eye Frank caught her rising chest. Orange hair and brown freckles gave the vernacular of colour more meaning than anything of the field. But each looked away, to experience with brand new eyes this world never viewed. Frank stepped forward, got up on the concrete. But she came along. She rose to walk the foundation as well. More rubbish was inside this hole, tins wholly brown from rust, firmly fixed where tossed. A finger could puncture a side. Oil carburettors lay in the open, stovepipe lengths, steel hoop liners for wood barrels. A pair of oil-barrel stoves were buried at diagonal corners. Bedsprings were strewn. Rancid grease mixed with seeding grass.

"You know what? Frank?"

"No, what?"

"I always thought you were the cute one."

She was on the far wall of the foundation, when she spoke. She laughed and held branches of wild cherry from her face to preserve her view, but also to keep from falling. "You never say anything. It puts the grip on a girl – which you might want to bear in mind, for later. No girl knows how to approach a guy who keeps it all inside. Bewitches the life out of her. Guys blabber – they do, all the time. Clifford's quiet. Not William! That's where the family tongue went. He ended up with both your shares. But he gets too personal, that one. Grace is no vault, though she comes off as being one. When it's just the two of us she talks a blue streak, I can't get her to shut up! Is she ever funny. Girls are just not interesting, Frank. They aren't! It's why they go for guys. Must be."

She came around the foundation and jumped into spiky grass.

"Can we go to the shore – I mean, right down? Clifford never took me right down, Frank."

They went through lush grass, into the shadows. They took a path now grown with wine-bark alder and thorny raspberry. Vegetation clutched. Frank's sleeve caught and stripped fully away then. He had to stop. Claire forgot her own plight and reached to free the sleeve, help tuck it in. "One time there were paths of all kinds going to the shore," said Frank. "As kids we cut up the woods down here too, like a warren. The paths hardly remembered now." The two kept to one that ran straight below, stepping off only at the Black Mud Brook where each dug stones out of the mud with the toe of a shoe. The stepping-stone bridge was washed away. "Once, that raised the water level enough to make a skating area. I fell here one day on skates and split the back of my head open." A filtered sun came: a blown-over tree had opened things. "I remember," said Claire. The dapple became glimmer on fleshy white birch. She kept her eyes away.

Nearing the shore, an iodine breeze struck, damp harbour air rushed over wrist and neck. A fresher rush caught both, then stepping out on the sod bank, its ten-thousand copper needles afoot. Shale fell into the water, but around the side, past where each used balance to hold horizontally; a falling tide allowed them to get down on shore proper. Crunching seaweed marked progress. At the Cove, Frank stooped to pick up a bubble portion. He broke one in a crackle when he saw that Claire was right beside. Breathing. The two stood in a sun chamber, a stiff harbour breeze backing off. But Claire pulled away. She had experienced a misgiving and so hid her face from him.

"What's wrong with you?" said Frank.

She shook her head – but his black hair, dark features, just so remarkable. His proportions. She wanted to say this, aloud. That his coming features now pushed through her like blades. She lost her balance, hands went out.

"Watch it. You all right?" said Frank.

She felt she must look older, in the cheeks. So many moments of her days now are filled with the rawest of emotion, coming at the most unforgiving of times. It was hard to cope. She hoped it was not a condition, that there would be stability of emotion one day. She had openly told herself not to worry: it was best to give no attention to unstable conditions affecting the here, the now. Womanhood in youth rattled the soul.

Looking across the unstill surface of the water she experienced all its depth, all its expansiveness in her chest. It was as if suddenly she were assigned to hold all this water in her arms. To hold him in her arms. She felt weight in her breasts that *seemed* to bolster confidence. Frank, to go through life, how? She blinked out harbour brilliance, the clam-flats west. Claire was the one with the handicap. Hers, hidden from the world. A capricious nature. It tempted, then got her in trouble. What she would not do for permanence of disposition. Yet she had it, with Frank. She got away from herself with him. And a word need never pass between the two. Just this resilient calm. Was there a more trusting soul to walk the face of earth? Was there? While she followed, featureless, a dummy?

"You read the paper, Frank?"

"What's that?"

"Another war in Europe. Our British dollar, government, law and all that, are tied to it. They're getting the hell bombed out of them, losing the homes they live in. In the last war men here were rounded up. Your father, mine. Mine died there. There's talk of it happening again. I don't care. How can a person care when it's beyond their control. Accept is all you can do. Me? I just want to settle, Frank. Marry is what I want. Get the thing over with."

A cloud spot of pitch raced over a high mountain point. The two watched. But Claire approached now. She stumbled less on the rocks under her hard, flat-soled shoes. She took Frank's hand, releasing his grip on a stone, raising him from where he squatted; the stone fell with a click. She put both her hands around his, making him come along past the Big Boulder. Frank did not speak. Looking sidelong at her elegant shoulders he wanted to tell her he would marry her, right now, on the shore, given the chance. He would say he had not known till this minute. But the grand scheme seemed possible here at the tides. He felt it in his groin, and it spread. He wanted to say, that someone like him would be a good option. Someone like him could dedicate a whole life to another. Not all can, could.

"I could marry you."

Claire stopped, painfully relaxing her hands: the two had not quite made it behind the Big Boulder.

"Frank, ah… that's not what I was after. Frank!" She looked into his face, her eyes containing the compassion of a young mother. "It's just not what I meant, at all."

She shook her head merrily at the thought that would be back to haunt her so often, in time to come. She clicked her tongue and decided it would hurt none to smile for him once more, to look into his eyes and smile. She kissed his cheek. But he turned, athletically, kissing her mouth. Heat moved up her legs, too. Oh, the heat. The heat was all.

Grace called.

They turned.

Grace was down off the sod bank, wholly visible on the shore.

Claire, yanking hands free, turned beet red. Frank quickly got his hand out. In approach, Grace dropped her head slightly under pretense that she hadn't seen. She came in her swaying manner, brushing with her fingers more of her sweeping black thatch of hair. She could ask what the hell the two were doing all the way down the shore together. Easily, she could. She was soon before them, matronly. She wore a chain straightened by a crucifix. She stood in front of Frank to look at him squarely, searching his eyes to get at once many answers to many questions. "Whew, she's nice down here," she turned. "Everything so close. Look at the colour across the water. I'd love to go over there when the leaves fall, roll down that mountain, through them."

The three walked rocks, ending somewhat cleanly the first of Frank's accompanying trips to the shore, and behind the Big Boulder.

The *Aspy* entered the heavy chop of ocean. The sea wind was deeply cool, though high summer remained ashore. And yet, summer was perhaps a dream of shore – the general truth more likely that this cold persisted out here, just off their homes, just off their lives. Summer might have only ever been mere suggestion.

Frank saw seabirds shoot from cliff ledges. The *Aspy* steamed along the backside of Smokey now, where young in nests waited, adults hovered, high over sloshing hunting grounds. On this side of the mountain an entire ocean south lay before the ship. Frank had never seen it. The village fishing boats: had they come out this far? There were no tales of it? But he had not frequented wharves.

Deck benches sat vacant. The nuns were in the passenger lounge, vigorously praying, or vigorously consuming fudge. Frank let go the rail and took a few steps. The wind rose harshly to play with the lounge door as he handled it. Inside all play died: all saw him. He bowed, sat alone in sun entering thick glass. He scanned lesser heights. Mountains flattened inland; light remained. Light here was in fact that of the North Shore. A place where so much more could be gotten out of a summer evening, he saw – free of deep shadow, free of sheltering mountains.

eighteen ·

Of all shape and size, folks milled about the North Sydney Forum. Such an expansive structure; Frank wondered what held it together. One chicken-wire window alone was as large as a wall of his house. He stood before a table adorned with a thumb-tacked festoon of red. A hand-written sign read, COMPEDATORS.

A whiskered muscleman behind wanted to reach the table. He wore a light cotton shirt, which from the back looked to have been pulled on over a rock pile. This man alone could yank the building down, thought Frank, waiting, watching to see what the muscleman did. Seated at the table, two officiates took note of Frank and one, elbowing the other, pointed his pencil and whispered forward to the muscleman: "See him, Tom. He's the first we're putting you in against. It will have to be a right-handed match. You can use your right, eh, Tommy? What?" From nearby came snickers and Frank lifted an eyebrow good-naturedly to show he understood the humour of a joke. Muscleman Tommy left.

"This where I sign in?" said Frank. "Here's my registration form, paid."

"Paid registration form," said the man with the pencil, who eyed the document. "Whose signature is this?"

"Rueben Burke's, owner of the Fairway Market in Ingonish."

"Oh, you're all the way up from down there. North Sydney must be quite a sight for you then. Lights, electricity. You people got a road down there yet, or are you still swimming it?" The fellow alongside refused to look, but shook his head in delight and laughed in a bucking motion. Frank gave no sign of condoning this remark. People behind were mute.

"Stand over there," said the registrar. "We start in ten minutes. Now don't lose your heart and go running away with your tail between your legs. There's a lot that'll want to see you here today."

Frank went where bid, to the competitors' section. Arm-wrestlers seemed to know each other here, or at least took ease in becoming acquainted. Frank stood off to the side near a loading door.

The first match began on a table erected to the sternum height of most men. Sawdust was underfoot; elbows rested on lacquered leather pads. For grip, granular chalk was provided. Two wooden pins were atop the table, dowels for left hands.

Competing were staunch fellows and when the first arm was put down the faces of the waiting men returned to those of little boys, pale and impressionable. The audience knew the men who fought. They called out first names in support and guidance. They liked Tommy, who winked, who raised a chin. Referee Sammy Halborn, a narrow-shouldered officiate in a bushy red moustache to contrast the orderly black and white of his short-sleeved shirt, liked to walk backward, to make the table a constant study. Using two fingers he brought new pairs forward to take position at the arm-wrestling table. The curt blow of a white whistle initiated the grapple.

Frank could only look on vaguely. He had not recovered from the registrar's comments, searing words branding his memory. The ogling in the forum was discomforting. His stomach churned as perimeter children pointed, and sundry women shook heads to show disapproval of his being involved in the sport. Audience men smiled most eagerly while pondering tongues pushed high under lips and out at jaws; blinking was profuse. Frank realised for the first time that there was no protection here, everyone could gawk without license.

None knew his background, none what had happened. To be anonymous, he learned, was to allow a singling out for conjecture. "It's not Ingonish," an *Aspy* passenger had said on hushed arrival at harbour entrance. And Frank had paid heed, but his lighthearted ways and good nature fell entirely away. A town was a cold-spirited place. A town was a place shunning.

An uncommon feeling of spite washed over him; he despised these bunched-up queer mugs, the shabby dress and bent posture. No eyes were pretty, no eyes welcoming. Moreover, the building stank. It was too high to take any enjoyment in. This was a money-grabbing scheme, he realised, swallowing bitterness, keeping perfect malice for the men who had signed him in, who exemplified best what breed of people lived here. Frank moved a foot toward the loading door, eyed its bar. Go there, he told himself. Go through and disappear down a side street. Let the world do what it will; none will see you go. Not true. Eyes were on him; all would know of his flight. And? What did he care? Ah, damn them, he told himself. Not me to go cowardly like that. Because that's what they mean me to do and I travelled all this way. I'm paid for and to hell with them. Let's see what the world will do to the fellow who stays this side of the door.

"Curtis" was called and Frank, telling himself to lose, but to lose well, stepped forward. People laughed and shouted, "At last! Here we go! Lord have mercy – watch this!"

At tableside, Frank refused to look into his opponent's face and therefore would never know the eyes behind his first professional win. Frank focused on the chalk when the referee took his hand and roughly to place it into the other's.

The forum swelled with enthusiasm. A pressing of bodies began toward the action as if the crowd itself were commissioned to compete. Shoulders swayed. Groins tightened. Men hired for control stirred from lazy carriage. Frank knew he encouraged the swell, but incredulous faces got too damn-well close. Leering began at this young clean-cut handicap none knew.

One arm. Ha! Whose idea of a practical joke was this? The irony! But also, delight at the prospect. All good shows had to have some element of the freakish; this was fantastic! And so flanking Frank, circumnavigating the clustering front for the other side, partisans aggressively became intent on seeing with unobstructed view this particular match and what would happen here.

The white whistle blew, Frank snapped the man's arm down. "Yah!"

Roar charged the forum, a pent wind loosened. Defeated was Billy Taylor who with round eye and gaping mouth stood wondering what had happened. And despite looking the type born never to smile, referee Sammy Halborn could not help one broad one forming across his face; he bit for it while red facial hair spread like copper wire ends. The crowd jammed the table, then looked on incredulously as Frank went off to the side to stand with men who had not lost. Mute men who laterally studied him.

Frank snapped down three more arms and the initial technique of using his shoulder and speed proved successful. He discovered that by hooking his left heel in the table leg while positioning his right foot behind allowed for improved balance and better overall rushing-strength. His entire body competed, like the good singer who sings not from the mouth or throat but from the core: the stomach and the anus. His reaction time, after the white whistle blew, was like lightning. Frank had stepped away from learning he had taken in the woods. What need was there to recall it? These men were not wilful and his wanting to beat as many as he could, while he could, kept him from needlessly holding back.

At least two competitors contested decisions, brothers MacDonald from Whitney Pier, the first inspiring the second to voice complaint. Fingers got raised. They did not like this foothold of his, at the leg of the table. Referee Sammy Halborn was patient then addressed both: "Perhaps Mr Frank Curtis here doesn't like the fact you get to use your left hand on the table pin! I'm allowing it – do what you want with the table, long as it's arm against arm!" This silenced the pair and wholly encouraged the lusty crowd. "A match can't end that quick!" protested the brothers. "There has to be struggle! He's using some slick manoeuvre to unfair advantage!" Referee Sammy Halborn raised his hand as if to smack the face that said this and this charged the crowd to no end. The MacDonald delegation of two walked out of the forum, each with a small leathery bag grimly clutched by hands in handstraps. "They're making it... a mockery."

Mass over mass hooted approval. Faces wore bemused reddened cheeks and perfectly enlarged eyes. But behind those eyes mental notes were busily being copied out, busily detailing every moment here; the turning of the name went over in their heads as precious content built for conversations to come, soon, and in years to come. Controversy, just the element to bring precedence to an event. Shoulders rode kids. "You're in the way, you! Set that youngster below, or so help me – this is no place for them!" A finished bingo game across the street brought a mob bunching at the entrance. Crowd control men worked left then right flanks in attempts to keep people reasonable. More control men were required. A bitter argument arose over a dropped soda. The audience swore, shook fists. The town had waited since its inception for such an event, in which the underdog won, in which life made sense, for once! Bullhorn blast: "Can we have calm please, order! We *will* continue!"

Frank went on to win two more matches. He was given longer breaks as competition narrowed. His arm ached miserably. He let it hang, made fists. He looked up at the towering chicken-wire windows and saw that they were blackened, that full night had arrived. "Curtis" was called. He leaned forward, face-to-face this time with someone he knew: the bearded muscleman, Treacherous Tommy Shanks. The final match had come. Champ, against the one-armed fellow.

Muscleman Shanks spoke before allowing his hand. "Beat me and you got my solemn oath that I'll be taking you out behind this forum to beat the face off you." Frank took a breath; saw the beard was wispy. But Treacherous Tommy winked and Frank wholly knew kinship like no other. Hands grasped. The mustachioed mouth clamped the white whistle. A singular voice rang: "Enough of this, Shanks – break off that arm remaining and send him home with none!" There came quick booing and hissing at this. The head that said it fell beneath blows and boots. Buttons snapped and blood showed on a scrawny, disorderly face, freeing itself in manic struggle, fleeing to get some distance from the fray; he was lost in the crowd. "Rat! Don't mind that!" Yes. None of that was the general impression. Respect reigned, for both men here; each had publicly proven his worth. The whistle went shrill.

But shrill stayed long in Frank's ear as he discovered that the physical laws of earlier matches were not applicable; this man's arm would not budge. Frank drove at a stone wall. Muscleman Tommy Shanks smiled with small teeth to see Frank learn how predator cornered run-down prey, how run-down prey looked up with ultimate knowledge of their relationship: here was defeat. Acceptance.

Cheers, wails, choking cigar smoke, acrid mass sweat was stifling. Frank saw the table, the chalk, the hair on his arm when hoots and hollers moved far-off, muffled as if in carpet, escorted behind closing doors. Yet two spectators sounding unreasonably close broke through:

"Tell me once more, his name."

"Frank Curtis. Ingonish."

"Ingonish you say? But he just doesn't give up, does he? That alone makes him a mention. This'll make front page of the Sports. Watch and see, it doesn't."

Frank pushed for all he was worth yet the larger man's arm held as if secured by foundation bolts. Frank was forced to draw it out, to remember the lumber camp strategy whereas the tendons of his arm, inflamed from accumulated pushes in earlier, quicker matches, needed a stamina he did not possess. He was unsure how to answer the call ... poor old pitiful Dad, you – here? The convalescence, after the accident, a winter spent in bed, building strength, mostly of mind. Time then was like time now, an item to break and know by its conceived components: moments. Yet even that wasn't working. The arm dipped horribly. Think of nothing: regain the bit lost. And so Frank held, tasting sweat in his mouth, with lungs burning as drops stung his blinking eyes. Hold, hold till the basic calculation comes at least: that the body weight of his own was three-fifth's this man's. That energy there was burning up far more than energy here. This machine was leaner. Frank could go further, on less, if only he held.

Treacherous Tommy Shanks no longer grinned. His face was amber, petrified in distaste, fear. A smaller man's muscles held him, solid. A smaller man with inner strength few men knew. That wolfish kind, where hungry soul dwelled. Where the sated never prowled. Tommy could lose and this crowd was behind the newcomer. Tommy knew the value of patience, of drawing a match out – it was just not coming. He could end it, if he wanted. A shift in balance to the other side where he could drive like a bull. A transfer of weight, to redirect the body, the ultimate counter.

Tommy shifted. Frank felt it, instinctively. Here, right here in pushing for the end, where a man is most vulnerable in his bid to end all struggle – Frank had missed it. The shift was all too brief, a slackening. Knowledge was gained. Would opportunity return?

Singular shouts. Thirty minutes had forged. And, as it did the fighters, fatigue set in among the audience. All fought this fight. It was key to appreciation of what it meant for adversaries to meet in the fore. No imagination needed.

Tommy grunted. Blew voluminously and snorted his unclean air at Frank's airway. Frank cleared his nostrils of it. And how he held, he didn't know. He lived for the shift in weight.

When it came, visibly pronounced this time, Frank struck. He moved the brute Tommy upward, dancing the whole right side of the tremendous body to make it appear as if total mass were ripped from its antipodes. Tommy let out a horrendous cry as he listed beyond the point of no return.... What is it, he thought, clutching the tableside, eyes abulge. His left hand, holding on, embarrassingly? What? Not that I am down, surely? But what in the world, now, where legs buckle and a cheek is on the table? He puffed chalk, experienced only shock at how utterly stripped he was. No. Can't, can't be. The sport of arm-wrestling, gone, no longer his. Never. The greatest challenge he would meet was his defeat. Here he met it, with awareness and, alarmingly, no suffering. Treacherous Tommy Shanks. Done! A single. Bravo. No more.

Frank fell backward and dropped a destroyed, extended arm.

Someone caught him. He looked up dolefully as all around territories erupted in cacophonies of disbelief. Explosive bellows came, expletives flew recklessly upward. It gained strength, cohered. Strangers hugged strangers, arms partnered, shoulders wrapped as if like drunken men gambolled down country lanes. Fists punched palms; spread fingers piggishly pulled for ceilings. Old and young blasphemed in elation and every mouth twisted in joy. The country had been sailing too long with poor helmsmen into the fog of a European war; there had been worldwide economic depression; high unemployment to dog the working man. People had been weakened by loss of purpose. Capitalism burst hearts. And liquor, that great charmer, had embezzled its way too easily into striving lives, lives too ravaged to fight off its enchantment.

This, a society of underdogs! And here! Look here! Champion of their own kind! Ha! Arm-wrestling, sport of sports! The best there was to pit man against man, philosophy against philosophy. Here, hope! The latter part of the decade had allowed this. Hope, victory! Arm-wrestling the rollicking rage: hard times had produced it. One night at the forum and there comes along a poverty win that none can take away. Poverty! Government, powerless. Labour unions blind. Long struggle of the meek and the true has not been in vain! Summer ends with truth – that all any in this world need, be it young be it old, was the triumph of the human spirit. And tonight all in attendance, bear witness. No Second World War would come. No further Depression could lay a finger on us, not the way it has. There would be work. A fellow could feed his family. A drink could be enjoyed. Couples could love. Families could get along. Here was victory! This fellow with the one arm wins the sport of arms!

"Cur-tis! Cur-tis! Cur-tis!"

Darrel O'Leary, sports columnist with the Halifax *Chronicle* got to Frank. O'Leary stood smiling, holding on, waiting for his chance to speak. "The Maritimes of Canada – its new winner," whispered O'Leary and a swooning Frank heard it, but as if it were just the two in a small room, or an inner voice forecasting, diagnosing. The newspaperman tried to take his hand.

"No," said Frank. "Please. Not the hand."

"Of course. You're damaged. O'Leary, Frank. I work for the Halifax paper. I heard this arm-wrestling stuff was catching on, but, heaven on earth – and you sir just turned it into wildfire! Can I get some information? Not now, but in a bit? Look over there, to that fellow. He's going to snap your picture. Important not to blink, Frank."

Honourable Jerry Hines, arriving late, stood on one of two crates, taking the microphone from the master of ceremonies. The corpulent politician twiddled his fingers, caught and raised Frank's hand, while producing a silver trophy and a cheque for five hundred dollars. Hines was unsuccessful at gaining sway over the crowd. The member of parliament was pshaw-ed. He fumbled poorly at a second microphone handed, then simply passed Frank his rewards. Frank had trouble taking them. "Here! Silence! Here now!" said the Honourable Jerry Hines eagerly into the better microphone. "I am forced to say ... shut up a minute, will you! Give the man his glory, I say, listen now. What's that? Feedback. Ow, that's hard on the ears. Give those back here, Frank?" The audience, warming to the scene, laughed as Frank handed back the trophy, but with effort stashed the cheque in his shirt.

"Couldn't blame you, fellow!" said the Honourable Hines. "Don't blame you one bit – that's money, that. You have our hearts, Frank, so give us this moment. The whole event tonight was carried on your shoulders. Yours alone. Get him a crate! And you saw it through to completion. How does it feel to be the new – ladies and gentlemen – the *new*, undisputed, Champ of the Maritimes!"

Frank tried to say a word or two, but feedback made daggers of his attempt.

"That cheque in your pocket for five-hundred smokers is well deserved," said Hines. "But I say, be quiet! Folks. Folks. Folks ... Frank Curtis here is from Ingonish. The strongest man in the Maritimes is from Ingonish!"

The crowd opened fists and spanked hard perimeter chairs. They hooted into hats. A bench was thrown against a wall and one area dramatically hushed because sleeves rolled and bare knuckles squared off. Police had arrived and with bats quelled the scene. Frank was taken off to the side for photos with better background. "How was the arm lost?" said O'Leary, the question coming loud, the answer being noted even before Frank spoke. Frank painfully wove off further questions and O'Leary was sympathetic, as was the whole world tonight. Frank looked past him, toward the ceiling rafters where two fellows working lights raised caps.

Frank was ushered outside and down the main street to where the Alice Hale Hotel stood proudly, though dwarfed by the Balmoral. A local Sydney newspaperman wanted to talk, but more casually, as if the two were long acquainted.

"My father was to Ingonish once, Frank. Travelled over Smokey, he did."

People following ahead walked backwards, others stepped along coyly on the other side. A bagpiper played out a raised window. It was a chill night, none minded. Boys threw rocks at cats and leapt into alleys to check on their success. Bottles smashed. Cranky motorcars hooted a-oo-gah horns. They had come to race in the street but presently crept at parade speed. Honourable Jerry Hines pressed the small of Frank's back, his good-looking daughter accompanied him.

"I'm the MP, Frank. You need anything, anything at all, hear."

Two pock-marked, wiry young men going by the name of Wallace followed, "We love arm-wrestling. Never miss a match. We live for it, eh, Jimmy? We wrestle each other every day of the week, morning, noon and night. Stop only to recover. He wins, I nail him in the mouth with a left. He'll do the same. Custom. What do you say we carry you, Frank?" When Frank said no, the hungry pair stopped dead in the street to howl properly at his refusal. They knew they were frightening him. One smacked the other hard on the back of the head, they grappled then came along. Both listened with strained faces when someone spoke, then broke apart in more laughter. They ran across the street to chase two kids who sauced them, but promptly returned.

"Treacherous Tommy Shanks had it too good for too long. He'd given up on his training. We need a champ who knows what it was to pay his dues. Stay hungry. That's the only man a person can trust."

Inside the Alice Hale, the bartender glared at the Wallace cousins. And they at him. With an eye to the window, at a table near, they resumed explanation of why they were so passionate about the sport. Each fought back tears when they said, how on a Friday evening when drinking, they used to challenge neighbours into the street because the blood was so hot in them. Arm-wrestling cooled it. Made them men.

"There was no arm-wrestling. If a neighbour did show, though. Just good old-fashioned face smacking, then." The elder of the pair showed recent cuts on his wrists from cop bracelets.

Halifax newspaperman O'Leary, fascinated, scribbled in a notepad open on the checkered tablecloth. When tables had glasses of beer on them, Honourable Jerry Hines turned and patted Frank's knee.

"You feel fine, Frank Curtis? Because I know I do. I don't come out to these things. But you got to keep a face on this and that, I find. And speaking of *find*, you're quite the find, my boy. The sports world won't know what hit it. You'll see. This will mean an awful lot to an awful lot of people. Before you board the ship for home, though. I wanted to tell you. Hear? They have girls here for one purpose or another. Hush now. But yes, they do. Don't imagine you have that sort of service in Ingonish. Now don't you go looking at her. That one's my daughter, see."

The daughter grimaced and Frank laughed along with the father. But later that fading night, when the *Aspy* had her ropes thrown back and the ship was easing herself out into open sea, Frank looked up from mid-ship deck. He studied the windows of the Alice Hale, the Rusty Nail, the third floor in particular, where he easily located the room he had been in. The one with its lights now extinguished. Oh, he felt fine. Fine all right, sniffing his nails, loving their strong scent. He dropped the hand, turned for the inky sea. He did feel fine, but not from liquor. Frank Curtis did not drink.

nineteen

From his bed, Daniel Dunphy could see out the window, set dead centre in the pitched ceiling. This window faced the front yard and when installing it the concern had been leakage. Daniel had been mindful with the tar and flashing and though water had never come in, he checked frequently with a tracing finger.

His fists pressed the mattress as he turned to Eloise lying on her side and with her back to him. She had worn her housecoat to bed. He wanted to tell her he had just been watching their son Edward, but she was too still. Edward was not as tall a man as Daniel, though he did fill out the lining of his new fall jacket. He was broader of shoulder. Eloise had consulted the Eaton's catalogue to buy him that wool jacket, after Edward had said he felt too old for catalogue shopping, for his mother's involvement.

On his feet now, Daniel could see the yard below, but not the near ground beneath the window. He leaned, held the window framing. An eddy of crisp leaves rose under the carriage wheel, swept as if by a phantom broom to settle at the spokes. Edward appeared, carrying his duffle bag. The team was hooked and ready to go. It was 1942: Edward was off to a European war; Prime Minister William Lyon Mackenzie King at the helm of a Liberal government.

Having slept his first night this fall in his longjohns, Daniel felt
the tight fit at the wrist and ankle. He reached inside his crotch and
dug out his penis. Still staring onto the yard he urinated into a wire-
handled bucket alongside the dresser. He was careful to strike the
bucket sides, to keep himself quiet while his wife lay in her bed. He
shook himself, but well; he was an older man now and it was a harder
thing to keep clean. He turned, bent and lifted flannel pants from the
foot of the bed then, sitting gently on the mattress, drew out the laces
of his boots before tapping Eloise on the buttocks.

"Up now. He's ready out there."

"Little too tired this morning. Blood's low. Put coal on the fire,
can you? And, don't forget your pail there."

"He'll be wanting to see you."

"I know he'll be."

Daniel came down the stairs and entered the kitchen. He stoked
the fire, then added coal from the full scuttle Edward had brought
in from the shed. Daniel filled the brass kettle and carried it to the
stove. His kept his hands on its cool sides while it heated and while
water beaded on the grates. Eloise had said this for years – that she
would be getting up later; would not be coming down for breakfast.
Daniel had hardly expected it on this morning. Her blood had never
been what it should, diagnosed young as having low-pressure. "Up on
a mountain is where I belong," she'd say. "And here, sea level, far as I
got."

Those hand-rolled cigarettes she carried from room to room did
not help. In the end, she always got up. She always came to clear the
table. Daniel thought it was the good French sleep that held her so,
that made her say what she did. It could have been the way she was
raised. Daniel noticed long ago that the French slept a longer morning
than the English. The French didn't need the afternoon lay-down.

He took his pail out the back door.

When he returned, Eloise was standing at the stove in her housecoat and his slippers. She had added a half scoop of coal and now
greased a cast-iron pan with white lard. She crept down the hatch for

eggs and sausage, as Daniel lay out good clothes for the trip. Two of the Curtis boys would be travelling with them today to the train station in North Sydney. Those fellows had also received official word by mail. Both families had been over the letters, checking departure times against what the schedule in Halifax would be for catching the Queen Mary and her subsequent churn from the continent.

Edward entered by the front door and stood not so near his father. He had with the black features of his mother's line this morning. "I think we're going to have more of that rain." He bent to the mat to take off his stall-boots and, opening the porch door, set them outside. His mother's people had the coal-black eyes and the thick skin without blemish. Their looks arrested people, if entering a room too fast, or coming too quick upon one on the road. Edward shaved now. He kept his hair short, combed and parted to the side. He showed Daniel the toilette he had bought himself: mirror, tweezers, razor, file and nail clippers. Daniel wanted to tell his son that Napoleon carried one of these. In gold. Daniel spotted the blue beard in the young face this morning. He smelled lotion.

"I saw you hook up the horses. Good to have that done beforehand. The bits at their jaws and leather at their backs gets them excited, raises their heartbeat."

"Then it won't only be mine that's raised."

"We're all anxious. The whole community is, but a lot is pride. Think of it as an outing – no more. Heading up the mountain with your friends for a couple of nights. They'll have that thing put to rest by Christmas. I've been following along in the paper what's going on. The Germans want France. Old score. But with England and now Canada on board, the Yanks to follow, they'll be licked in no time. England's the major player. And what's stronger than a country owning half the world?"

"Owned, Dad."

"That's what I said."

"You didn't go, last time?"

"To no fault of my own, I was influenced. Or, no – I'm tired of saying that. I had my own mind about it then as I do now. I will tell you something. I always felt bad about not going. No one along the whole of Kelp Cove did, except my half-brother, Charles. I guess we felt we were above the duty you owe a country. Isolation keeps you at arm's length. And there come too many opinions concerning how you should act when a thing major goes awry anyway. Who owes who what. I got caught up. I had a big mouth. They sent the military down to round us up and all we could do was nod our heads and wink sarcastically at the sight. One guy poured alcohol in his eyes, another burned his feet. Recourse like that left us with not a drop of integrity. Thing is, government, we felt, couldn't give a damn about us. There wasn't even a proper road built here. Still isn't! No proper medical care. A pesky school the Church had far too much involvement in. Some weren't paying taxes – some aren't now. Long winters here saw little outside help so when they came looking, when their policies got hooked into overseas affairs, we turned our backs on them. Not everyone, I should say. This war doesn't seem to be going that way. Firstly, they're doing a better job of managing people."

"How do you mean?"

"Managing to get you from us, for one. And without any debate on the matter. You're a smart fellow to have. Your mother and I will carry our heads high knowing you're over there fighting for the country. Repairing a hole in the wall I made." ·

The water was slow to boil as the brass kettle was too full. Daniel stepped up, rubbed his palms along its sides, as if to encourage heating.

*H*e carried the hot kettle to the sink where his wife stood near the window. She smoked and watched the grey harbour. In her hand was the heavy glass bottle with a wooden crucifix built inside. This was her ashtray. She wanted the ash built up to bury the icon and she often shook the bottle lightly, checking contents, as any drunkard might his drink.

"But this is not the first trip I made with those Curtis boys. Ho, no." Daniel poured water onto the tea leaves in the porcelain pot, leant backward to allow steam to pass over his face. "I rode the same two that one time on the sleigh, remember. To get the doctor for their brother. I found them atop Smokey half-froze in deep snow. You should have seen their frost-bitten mugs, how forlorn they looked to see me coming along and then – to get the chance to climb aboard! I'll tell you they liked that sleigh. We rode full bore over the ice, Piaget and Conquistador, the Thoroughbreds hauling to beat hell. You were a boy then. But so were they! Yes, bad shape all right. I wouldn't have asked them to do what their father had. But that family has always been a little more hard up than the rest. Good people but – like the rest – struggling more than what's called for."

Daniel stood by the steeping tea, inhaling largely the scent of its bitter leaves. His wife was at the stove, slowly dishing up eggs and sausage from the pan when, for the first time he could remember, Daniel had nothing to add. The same man who began conversation at the breakfast table and orchestrated it through till night was as mute as the leg of a chair. He sat at the table, blew on his tea and looked at the plate of sausages, the eggs set before him. Having lived a life of proving that a man must impose his will, to get anywhere, to benefit his family, he no longer saw it as such. There was no will to impose, for one thing.

His son was going off to fight on the other side of the ocean today, a rifle strapped to his back, a metal helmet set on his head – nothing more than the material of army issue to protect him from catching a bullet, a shot from a stranger whose tongue was foreign and so couldn't explain what was going on to save his own skin. Daniel had not tried to talk the boy out of it and the result was this: this day of his leaving them. Son, like wife, was never the kind to do injury. Each lived lives of order – to the letter. And yet here, Edward going off to point a rifle and get tired of *not shooting back*, as Daniel once had had it explained.

The family ate their last meal and though plenty of time remained, Daniel got up and stood dressed for the outdoors, complete with leather driving gloves. In the porch, he nodded to Eloise and took her shoulders. It was Edward's turn.

"You get to Mass. Promise your mother. Also, you'll respect your-self over there."

"A letter. Every week, after the first."

Eloise searched her son's face only to find her own lost days. Through the open porch door she experienced the cool fall in her nightgown, it entered to touch all at once a thigh. She would go back to bed. Pull up the sheet.

"Goodbye, then."

"Yes, bye."

Edward felt her eyes on his back as he walked and the weight of what those eyes saw bore through to his chest. Unnatural fatigue came in his shoulders, centred below his neck. Daniel walked along-side while the certain spying of his mother continued to plague the son. She was at her window, Edward knew, now that the outside door was closed. She was at her favourite spot, her chair by the stove. Any-thing that caught those eyes from there was long the subject of medi-tation. In the carriage, Edward turned to his seated father. "Could you go, Dad, for the love of God, quick? Could you get us turned and out because that was the hardest thing I had to do yet and so long as we're in the yard it's not over."

Daniel snapped the reins and hawed. He drew the bit firmly left. The aligned horses responded with a skip to a trot as the carriage emptied stillness from the morning. The rig traced the property's rock wall. "Whatever happens to you from here on in might not measure up to this," said Daniel. "And you'll have an easier time for it."

"Keep going, Dad."

A vacant road waited along the Woody Shore. Carriage wheels fell and rose in mucky potholes past dwellings of puttied panes facing the harbour at high tide. All around, trees sported seasonal coats, of one hundred thousand turned leaves at a glance. The eyes could have what they wished of replete mountains and valleys basking in this gorgeous attire. The sun struck hard at one point to produce sil-ver flashes, then centralise what looked to be washed woodland. The shimmering harbour marked the considerable distance to the clam-flats and rain in the night had left a resilient forest to fall sharply to shore. All would make for exceptional deer hunting as luscious apples hung now dampened in the wild. And yet such beauty mixed with the morbid tinge of departure. A holding back was the first truth: that the heart never gave over fully to beauty. How? When a fall storm was always brewing with slanting rains to strip cloaks and leave brute trees living, but bare.

They approached the Curtis property and they felt less awful, as their departure had now its first event to provide some distance. Passengers inside these walls would likewise say their goodbyes to homes and people, and thus the second truth: that the pain of others was by far a better healer than time ever was.

Claire and daughter Dawn sat in the Curtis kitchen, alongside Clifford. The little girl half-attempted to crawl onto Clifford's knee, but refused to vacate her mother. She wanted both. Clifford drew his chair in close and set her between.

Lucy Hawley, from the head of the harbour, sat on William's lap. He had his arm around her and an open hand lay on her lap. Lucy had balled toilet tissue to her eyes. William's freckles had all but faded, so too his free-spirited ways, the rough talk entirely gone. But this affair would see little talk of any kind.

Grace and her family sat on the hard-armed sofa hauled in from the living room for this family gathering. Grace's husband Charlie was an older but capable man. Poor vision kept him out of the war. The couple had two children, the youngest Patsy, who stayed between her parents, orderly, dressed prettily in white gloves and Mass clothes. Grace still went for the Church. The eldest of the new generation was Rodney. The auburn-featured Rodney liked Uncle Frank, his quiet ways. He looked to his mother, Grace, when Frank winked at him.

Frank stood at the stove, his back to the scene. He wore the suspenders his father had wanted him to try. Removing slightly the grate with the lifter he saw the dry stick of beech burn and he heard the inferno roar. He crinkled his brow, spit slowly into the fire when Edward and Daniel walked in the door. The seated looked up, as Daniel remembered to duck his head though he had only ever been in this house twice.

Clifford and William rose as one. They got their government-issue soldier bags off the woodbox, but then dropped the bags at the foot of a coat-rack Frank had built. The two went through the pockets of their military jackets until they located their identification and travel papers. Looking these over, they exchanged nods with Edward Dunphy.

Daniel lifted his chin elaborately in Adrian's direction across the kitchen.

"I read where your boy Frank here is going to compete in the Nationals. We got quite the celebrity now in this here town."

But Adrian only looked to his departing boys. Daniel saw how hard it was on them to be leaving their young women behind, especially Clifford, married to Claire, his niece, his own flesh and blood. Their tiny daughter would find time terribly long. She loved everything about Clifford, it seemed – she was forever looking up after him. She knew something was changing.

"No, you're right. All fellows in this kitchen are celebrities," said Daniel. "Of their own accord. You don't got nothing to drink, Adrian? Toast the gentlemen off proper?"

"Drink! You? Asking me? I wish to God I had something to drink. There's not a drop in the house since Jessie moved on to greener pastures. Do you? Nothing in your rig, is there?"

"What do you take me for? In my rig.... Ah well, we need nothing like that. You got water. What finer drink is there than water?"

"I can name one – I can name more than one."

"I'm sure you can. No, let's make it water, have a dash of that, forget the old tea for once. A proper gesture of some sort is called for. Are there cups to go around?"

"Grace. Get down everyone a cup."

"Asking decently, still, I see."

"Grace. Don't be like that. We're under pressure here."

Grace measured out thirteen cups and glasses of different shape and size. Adrian kept the pitcher ladle ready to drink from in case

Grace had counted wrongly; or they were short. Each person in the house rose, the children especially reverently.

"Here then," said Adrian. "To the boys. To Clifford, William and Edward. Back soon fellows. Your home and people wait with a Highland welcome."

The drink was drunk with dignity and purpose before porcelain, glass and tin were set again on the table. Everyone moved out the door and in the open air breathed deeply before surrounding the carriage. It was forty Fahrenheit, a brisk East.

The horses stomped hooves, but held ground. It was often at this point, during the local farewell that the most wholesome conversation began, when laughter came freely and the best stories recalled. The girls said private goodbyes to their fellows. The older men focused on fixed points in the copper-coloured fields, or the spruce crowns, the roofline. All daughters wore sombre faces that suited their clean, formal clothing till one women broke and the children came on loudly. The lips of the men reduced, paled. But the carriage then drew away with creaking, before hooves picked up and steel pins of hubs left the autumn day their intolerable whirr. No one aboard looked directly back at the null gang, waiting till its majority broke in varied retreats for the home. Frank and Adrian stood fully at the road to watch the carriage round the bad turn.

"I feel low, Dad. Only that."

Adrian turned eyeglasses toward the remaining son; Frank noticed his father had shaved for the occasion, missing grey nostril hairs, missing them for some time now.

"I know, Frank. No one can blame you. To feel low is all there is at times."

"I went to see that fellow when he came, they wouldn't hear of taking me. I wrote the MLA."

"I heard all about that, Frank. You told me yourself. You've had it hard up till now. Best just to forget about a lot of things. Come inside, where we'll have a bite. That slaps it in the face."

The two walked the path then came over the flat section of the field before heading down into the door. The families had missed

Mass in order to see the boys off, but a Sunday dinner was lined up just the same and there were the girls to cook and minister to it. Adrian had planned a little speech, mostly about the war being over in no time and that they put out the professionals first. He was tired of such talk – and ceremony.

In the kitchen, Frank saw his father quietly waiting for the food. The women, not without some consolation, were at the stove and sink, although in shells of spirits. Frank would lord over this group. He glanced at Grace's husband Charlie, who craned his neck at the brother-in-law's eyes upon him. Frank gestured a goodwill welcome to the man. Rodney had been spying; he took his eyes off Frank.

Claire's head was lowered, she stared into her daughter's just washed cheeks. Frank could not see into Claire's eyes. He did remember Clifford looking at him right after speaking to her, before mounting the rig. Claire merely attended her sad little Dawn. But Frank too was leaving. He had forgotten. Competitions would steer him clear of this.

The wait for dinner was long. It was a relief to bow heads and be led by Grace in prayer. Everyone believed in God over turkey with cranberry sauce, over mashed potatoes, carrots and boiled turnips. Lots of salt and pepper were available. They prayed openly for the success of the boys, then privately that winter would not strike dastardly without them. Frank eyed Grace through the prayer and he knew now – that Claire watched.

twenty

Clifford Curtis put his head out over the chain-link border of Café Hilvessum in Holland. He searched the street for his brother. The two were on military leave and had not seen each other for one year. Dehydrated, Clifford suffered a splitting head and mild insanity from heavy drinking. His spirit was waylaid. William was nowhere in sight.

With a touch of anxiety, Clifford's mind travelled to the year before, when the bootlegger had taken them to the train station in North Sydney. It rained sheets. Deep puddles had formed in the wagon tracks along the North Shore. Clifford, William and Edward Dunphy wore military berets, the bootlegger his fedora. The felt berets only redirected soaking, as drops cruelly pelted foreheads and passed over eyelashes. Whereas the stubborn leaves of Ingonish trees had remained, North Shore's foliage had finished for the year. It was the day before Halloween.

"This muck puts me in mind of my cousin Milburn," said the bootlegger. "It was pissing that day, when he came to the house toting his violin. 'I want yas all to know drunk today I'm getting! No, I'll take no more of it'."

"'No more of what, Milburn?'

"'Why the beauty of trees,' he said. Oh, how we laughed.

"'What!' he pipes up. 'How can any with a proper heart take it? Today's wet. Yesterday wasn't, no, not a tear got shed, and when I was at the shore carrying rocks to build a wharf below the boathouse didn't this warm harbour wind come to take the life out of me!' A hand on my shoulder, a voice whispered, 'Take the moment. Look around here and know just this.' It was that wind that puts a person in mind of all the lives he lived beforehand, ones that had you doing God-knows-what for God knows who. Straight down the harbour it came to set whitecaps at my feet. But then it dropped off and the sun hit. It struck the crimson maple to warm everything just so, an oven open, heat moving off baked bread. I would have raised a hat to the Maker, but didn't dare disturb the scene. Not a soul, and across the harbour, the sight of those mountains. Oh, I'd be happy if I never ever saw their other side. How misty-eyed. The soul of an ant was stirred. And to smell those apples on the clay bank. I shut my eyes to it.'

"Oh, the laughter, to hear him. He looked at us and smirked realising what he said but, as usual, only after saying it. You got to understand Milburn. He was our village poet. One that even went as far as to write things down. On occasion he brought us what he wrote, to read aloud. No one in a community pays a fellow like this a hen's tooth worth of attention and yet – there's always one. Thing is, you do put in a favourable word, then look out! You'll not be able to hear yourself think. They'll fill your head with phrases you think are coming from another tongue. They'll mangle definitions of any word you thought you knew. That was our Milburn, anyway. Good to have around, when you were drinking.

"We knew it was more than wharf-building and the beauty of the leaves that troubled him. The start of Ingonish Centre – where a young Stockley girl lived – that there was the source. Her family was down over the Nook, in a big grass hole just past the graveyard. A sprawling lop-sided blue house anchored there. Milburn had been to the house the week beforehand to play his violin. Beverley, her name.

"Her people were crazy about Scotch music and welcomed any-one with half-a-notion to play, which was what Milburn had. Half. About a lot of things. Oh how he talked about that night, how he had played for this Beverley Stockley. His concentration going all to pieces, when she entered the room. The one time he was called to give his best performance and he mangled tunes so fast people didn't know what they were hearing. If he took his eyes off the fingerboard, apparently, he couldn't play a note. Even his feet, necessary to provide brotherhood, they betrayed him.

"So this fall day – harassed by the leaves – he arrives at our place with three beer bulging his belt. We're in the kitchen, in the left half of the old family home, what came dragged across the ice. He offers us a sip. And, nodding our heads, we let him go to it alone. He gets the taste next and proceeds to down his stash like it was going out of style. 'No one minds if I go out for a proper nip?' he says, disappearing outside to come straight back in. He had his pint hidden under the step. A weekday, quietest time of the year – hard liquor, the last thing you wanted tampering with your spirits. And he's at it, full bore.

"Milburn Dunphy had to be the worst there was for liquor. Leg-endary. Man, dear. Smell the cap and he was loaded. So, straight into the maelstrom he's headed. He starts putting his hands all over us. Some are like that. Need to use both to help them speak, think. His face distorts listening to any reply to his babble. Still, we couldn't re-sist the company, what with not so much as a peep going on, near and far. A feed of lobster was set on the table and he ate his fill. Back then lobster was eaten when there was nothing else; it was food for the poverised – whoever that was supposed to be – we were all hard up those days. Shells crunched. Keeping his drink handy, he dug in.

"'No, I've had it with the single life. I'm determined to ask for her hand. Give me a slew of kids in a pioneer house up that valley, with her, I'd be all set. I'll build it.' He stood. 'But that's it for me – I'm heading out. Obliged, for the grub.' We got after him to sit back down, to get to the next room to sleep it off. You can't reason with a drunk. No. Swaying like an electric cord, half tears, half bliss, awash in the love of his fellow man he said, 'You might be right. I ain't going nowheres. I will, though, step out to the outhouse for a wee minute.' We thought no more of his going, which he did, because in the middle of the floor was his violin case. Nope, no ears would be graced by those strings this night. His beer bottles stood on the table. Not his pint.

"Well, sir. Straight for her house, drinking what he had left along the way. And when he came to the Glebe, what did he think he might do but stick his long face in the window facing the road to see what the nuns were having for supper. Nuns. Habits off. Sitting at a big table of chicken and potatoes when that white face appears. 'Ahhhh!' he says, fingers dancing above. Up they come, door round back bursting open. As a coven, they charged the corner in their long dresses. He lit out of there like a man possessed, tearing past the statue of the Virgin and down over the gravestones. I guess he got cut to pieces falling into a bunch of wild rose bushes, alders and crabapple trees. And him, an altar server! Them grooming him, for the priesthood at one point!

"He made the Stockley home. The family was sitting down to their evening meal and, as chance would have it, Father Patrick Mac-Donald was in for his weekly visit. Milburn bowed in the kitchen then turned for the porch to go there and sit. No one followed, to attend to him. The heightened effects of the booze came all at once, memories, intentions, regrets and dreams: what any poisoned mind conjures. The family asked young Beverley to go out to him. Did no good. She couldn't get him to look up. He spoke into the throat of his coat saying, 'I'm all right.' Then he rose. 'I got to get to the woods.' She saw him stumble down over the bank. And he ran, fell, got himself up and in behind a spruce tree on the slope, he relieved himself. But didn't he not exactly get his trousers right down. Ah, me son. Wet leaves underfoot, staggering, uneven land, didn't he go and lose his balance altogether. He tumbled down into that big hole the land is on, rolling, spinning, splintering, the world gone out from underneath him while he clutches his suspenders as if they might stop the descent. He come to and got himself upright. He didn't know it, but he was in worse shape than ever a fellow could be.

"Did it end there? Ha! No. If only the world *did* work that way. He goes straight back up to the house – though I'm sure he wished ten-thousand times over he had turned around and beat it for home. Or, a river.

"Head to toe, fouled. And it has its way of working itself around, apparently. In his own mind he was fine as roses. Leaves, is all, he imagined. And leaves is what he was peeling off outside under the porch lantern. He figured he would enter now, but through the back door where the dining room table was set and an intimate meal was in progress, Father Patrick at the head.

"A formal dining room was in that house. I remember. Lace tablecloth and brass candelabra. Milburn jars the back door and, arms outstretched like the Egyptian mummy, he walks in, mouth squared and one eye peeping. I guess the family knew a mortification such as they never did. They couldn't comprehend it! In his mind this was the greatest lark the world knew, and their reaction ... well, it encouraged him! He got to the arm of a chair that someone had scrambled out of and began talking. The family bunched up across the way, bowls of soup below. He begins to wonder what people were in the world for, anyway? How life can be lived, but well? He grabs a drumstick, dips it in cranberry sauce, bends his head way back and swallows a scraggle of chicken or turkey skin. He then took a big satisfying bite of meat and next cleans it to the bone. Which he inserts through his fingers and makes out he's smoking a cigar. The candelabrum he uses to char the end of the bone, dousing himself with wax in the process. 'Ahh!' He blows imaginary smoke, smiles for everyone like an aristocrat."

"That was it! Patron of the house old Bertrand Stockley got to his feet. He swore to high heaven then surged forward, like a wave, into struggling arms. Wife Margaret flew out to the front room for her poker. Which she swang. Someone had to take it from her. 'Get him down! Down to the Clyburn!' they shouted. There were no volunteers. Good thing, shock of that water alone would have brought his end – if that wasn't their first intent, mind you. He went from chair to chair, as chair by chair, was vacated. He finally settles in beside the priest, who has held his ground so far; not so much as bat an eye. 'What it must be, Father? To be a Father, Father. Minister to a community so far north of it all. To guide us meek and sinning through all the tough times? Put people in the ground without lifting a finger? It must be only the most important thing there is.' That struck some odd chord with Father Patrick, who pushed his chair back and with beaked nose and biting tongue commenced to throttle the youngster's throat. He wrung that neck I guess as if it were carrying air to the Devil Himself. Milburn turned blue, allowed the choking at first. They struggled to work the priest's fingers free, whereby a dissembled Father Patrick straightened and stretched a long arm with denouncing finger. 'Straight to the belly of hell is where you're going, mister! And your kind!'

"'I don't doubt it,' said Milburn.

"Oh, our poet! Condemned! But Father Patrick, now – he lets out a string of curses such as to make the most hardened of criminals cover his ears. I tell you, it was a night to end all. The priest grabbed his hat and stormed off. Someone coaxed Milburn outside. And one of their young fellows was assigned the task of marshalling him home – to follow, at least. A fresh switch in hand. The girl he came to see? Beverley? She stayed in the kitchen this whole second part. One good thing.

"Ah my, when he got home and his mother saw the state, straightaway she upset him into the woodbox. He looked up at her and experimented with an obscenity that I won't soon repeat. She struck him with a full haymaker where he lay. 'Get out!' she said. 'I'm putting the run on you! You're not to set foot in this house ever again, hear! Take those books!' He spent the night in someone's hauled-up boat down the Woody Shore. Next morning, he clears out from Ingonish, not to return. He was gone I don't know how many years before I saw him again. It was in Ontario when I was out on a business trip. He was living with a woman who already had seven kids by another man. He stepped right in as father I guess. But he was hardly the fellow I knew. His face was shaved, puffy, hips wide. Shame, there. Because I don't know of any poets who are anything but thin. No high talk, whatsoever, even with prodding. Walking around in baggy pants, a belt of early holes dug out with a knife. He was on the last hole. Not a word about home. Poetry, ha! Dead! I didn't know the man.

"Listen. I'm telling this with purpose. Keep in mind the power of liquor. Milburn, poor Milburn. And, of getting smitten, above all. Stick to what won't hurt you. Build your rock wharf. Stay on the shore. Trouble comes when you step away and go back up in the woods. To the house, and beyond."

This story came to Clifford lately. He woke to it. And with the hangover particularly bad this morning his ears rang with it. Clifford looked around the café. He saw breakfast patrons and waiters.

William passed a hand over the rail, "Good day, me son." Clifford stood for the firm handshake then waited in good posture as his brother passed through the foyer.

"Jesus! When's the last time you slept?" said William looking his brother square in the eye.

"A while – I had to stay awake waiting for you, didn't I?"

"Got a little lost."

"Sit, take a seat."

They faced each other and William leaned back in his chair. "Boys, oh boy. Some place, eh? Clean. But, here together, overseas. I haven't seen you since the Queen Mary docked in England. You remember the last time we were in a restaurant together?"

"I remember. You're heavier than you were, Will. Than I ever saw you."

"It's from eating. The food here is just grand, I find. A fellow can have whatever he wants, often when he wants. Here. Look what I got the old man in a little shop, coming around the corner."

"A book? What he's going to do with a book? I'm doubtful he reads."

"He does. I think he does. It can't be all that well, mind you. He's always valued them. That I know."

"Their pages, maybe. To start a fire with. Pass it here."

"Hands clean?"

"You'll find out I smack you with one."

"Here, then."

"Poetry! What the old dyin' is he going to do with poetry?"

"What anyone else does. Look at it. What you and I are doing right now. I glanced at a page in the shop. You can get something out of it. Slow, you can."

"Adventure books, all I ever went in for. Something with bite. I'd do better with French or even German than tackling this."

"Still. Keepsake, in the very least, and two-hundred-and-fifty poems. Hard to get more value than that if you're buying a person reading material."

Clifford slid the volume back toward William. It stayed between them. Clifford had done well to hide the effort it was to converse.

"Yes, it was something to get this furlough together," said William. "All the Cape Breton Highlanders are here. Lord, the parties. They never stop! You'd swear the war was over and done with to see them go on savage like they do."

"It's a time, all right. Listen, Will. I ran into a little trouble and got a small favour to ask."

"What?"

"What do you mean, what?"

"I mean, what?"

"Hear me first. Jesus. One of the company fellows, he got killed last week. He went too near a foxhole and fell. Bayonet up through the groin from a gun positioned upright. They carried him back after they heard his crying out, but he bled to death on the table. It was a foxhole me and two others had dug, partially, a place where we were keeping a few things. Handguns, watches, couple of souvenirs. Someone must have leaned a rifle up like that without removing its bayonet and the poor bastard, come along, probably to use the bathroom, kicked it out. We were going to sell the property. Someone was just about to pick it up. We were to be done of the business, for good. We figured we could do a little well by the stuff, manage a couple travel bucks is all. The military doesn't leave the goods rot in a field of action. You know that? They get men to round it up. Us, for example. We didn't figure a little skimming was stealing. If it is, then the military is the biggest thief there is. What happened to that guy was an accident, pure and simple. A case of wrong place, wrong time.

"On account of the trouble, though, they're investigating, see. The other two lit out leaving me alone in the unit. But, I want to make out like I lit out with them. They only have the name of the fellow signing for the shovels. They got my name, Curtis. What the talk is, anyway. They probably won't check and will just drop it. Still, let me have your tags and documents just till this blows over. I'll get them back. There're other Curtises in the outfit. Everybody's known by their last name or a nickname, anyway. I checked. No big deal. I got to make it look like I left is all. But right away."

"Jesus, Clifford, that's not allowed. Always, always, always something with you."

"Allowed? What's allowed got to do with one brother asking another for help?"

"It's the military. They've got lists. Proper lists. They'll see right through it."

"They won't! And if they do, I'll take quick action when it comes. There's guys crawling out of the walls here, it's a huge outfit. And you and me look so much alike, especially with hair shorn like this. Our eyes and eyebrows are identical. And that's all they ever look for. They'll never know. I'll flash them the tags. I wouldn't care but I got a kid at home. So come on now, I'm in a scrape. Hand over what you got and don't be a prick about it. Take mine, here, for safe-keeping."

"What if they ask me about my name?"

"You lie. That so hard? Why would they ask you? You'll have all my identification. For Christ's sake! That so hard to give a fellow a hand? Come on, quick, I'm hung right the hell over."

"Always schemes with you. And I'm the one to get tangled in them."

"Oh, I forgot ... you never do anything wrong. You and that little brother of yours, pictures of the old lady. Do-gooders. Listen, the world ain't set up to always do right by it. Learn that and you'll get a whole lot further in life. Now, my head's split wide open. I'm in no mood. Give us here what you got so we can get on to having a talk between brothers who haven't seen each other in a year."

They exchanged tags.

"Papers."

"You said you'd flash them the tags."

"Look. William...."

William passed what he had and straightaway Clifford had the waiter bring a bottle of red. The brothers lit cigarettes from one match then waited for the light talk. They drank glass for glass, but William sat out a glass at the arrival of the second bottle.

"Mind if I fill you up?" said Clifford. "Come on. It's all right, me son. We'll take her easy."

William tapped two fingers on the table and looked over his shoulder. He listened for the wine to enter his glass.

"Got a letter from Claire," said Clifford. "She wrote all the Ingonish news. Weather's turning. It's all shadows now. They got some good swordfish this fall and the harbour has a flotilla of military ships in it."

"That's a good deep harbour, that."

"It is, deep."

"I did read a newspaper from Canada," said William, "an article on the arm wrestling. Chicago, he's in now. The fellows he's lined up to fight are all Americans. They gave a whole extra two sentences about him." The brothers watched patrons eat their poached eggs and crumbly brioche when Clifford suddenly turned. "I told him not to take the gun that day. You remember I did."

"What I remember is on the mountain, climbing the trees so we could see him better out on the ice with the dog. When we get down, you tell me to strap in the load so we could take off and catch him. Then, suddenly, you said there was no hurry. We both heard the shot. I didn't know why you suddenly had the change of mind till I myself checked the safety catch later. I shut up on that account, too."

"He was bugging me. He had his warning. Should have listened."

"Listened! To what? Who listened to anyone back where we grew up, half-savage? He was young, out to prove himself. What happened to him could have happened to any of us. With him, there was help."

Clifford stared at his brother and William looked away.

"Call him 'The Bulldog'," said William, his face trying to find the other's. "After his technique. Wins by holding out till the other guy shifts balance, they say."

"Maybe his own will get shifted one day."

"I don't know what you ever had against him."

"I got nothing against him."

"No? But that is true – I never thought of that – his own balance going one day. Maybe he doesn't have to worry, what with the way he is. He gets in there and holds. Rearranges nothing, till the other shows weakening. Takes stamina, they say. I'll tell you one thing, he's the toughest thing on two legs, that I know. And it's not just one brother saying it about another, either. I always had a private fear of him, ever since I grabbed him once to teach him a lesson for something. He had only the one arm then, but he locked me in such a way that I was useless. He set me down like I was nothing more than a load he was offing. Grabbing a hold of him was like grabbing a hold of a tractor and trying to upset it. I didn't touch him after that. Because you know yourself...."

"Finish. What do I know myself?"

"He didn't lose consciousness that night. That's no detail to be forgotten. Must be worried of him around Claire, that it?"

"What are you talking about?"

"Nothing."

Clifford didn't pursue. He turned to the street and blinked a black eye. He never liked to talk about Frank. It spoiled things too readily, ended distance too well. But then any closing distance slipped away again, of its own accord, in a bottle of wine. Brother nor wife touched him here. He filled glasses. Frank wasn't even in Ingonish. He was travelling in another country for his sport. Frank was as far away as they were, in one sense.

Clifford and William saw the breakfast crowd leave. They sat through a waiter change then through the lull before midday diners. The brothers sifted faces and fashion when customers did come. They listened for snatches of a foreign tongue, brushed unnecessarily at their uniforms, drew a thumb across name tags. William had slim cigars. The wine had a sedative effect in strong daylight, which can be a good time for drinking, with control. The sun warmed linen. Their table was freshly supplied with a burgundy tablecloth and white napkins, both sitting back deeply, for the linen change.

"We can get whores," said William.

"What for? This hour?"

"To screw. Every hour's ripe for that. They're not expensive. But then, there's plenty of free stuff around, too."

"Work and politics, in the free stuff."

"Like your handguns and watches, you mean."

"You want to hear more about the letter from Claire? Got it in my pocket."

"Tell it."

But Clifford said nothing, did nothing, as a new avenue of happiness opened for him upon seeing his brother reach a capricious hand for the third bottle, set between them. Always good to know another stumbles. Sun hit their forearms and in the heat of it, both spoke of tattoos they wished to get while overseas. Two fellows from William's unit entered. William stood sloppily for them and whistled shrilly at their drawing near.

Soldiers, how they love to see each other in likely surroundings, knowing what good company each makes for each. Clifford didn't go for their talk as much as William. These soldiers were unmarried, which, though good company, made them poor soldiers.

twenty-one

$\mathcal{F}$rank woke to clean sheets in a Chicago hotel room. His right shoulder pinched. His middle two fingers did not straighten on their own. Sitting up in bed made him wince. He looked at the left, at the stub, which gave its own share of trouble, the largest share. After all this time, more than a decade, the deepest ache came from below, from that which was memory.

He would do what his mother had helped to discover, stand at a mirror, hold out his arm to let his brain see two, two hands. He carried a compact for the purpose now. The reflection could miraculously ease the pain. Since becoming wholly involved in arm-wrestling, in the past year especially, the condition had worsened. He wondered why intense pain came at waking. Being away from home didn't help. He rubbed his shoulder and neck where arthritis centred. Uncapping the liniment he kept at bedside, he spread it over both shoulders and waited while surveying his hand in the compact. Drawing on a white shirt over his undershirt, he stood, walked to the window.

Chicago: lifeblood of the United States. Cargo from the Great Lakes, hub of Midwestern agriculture – each contributing to the nation's standing. Soft man, Wade Miller, the Pudding from the competition the night before spoke of this. New York was catching up; it had its Brooklyn Bridge and Empire State. Never, however, could or would it contain the life force that was Chicago.

Frank took the mirror from the bathroom and brought it to the window. He looked down at the grey streets. Telephone and telegraph wires obscured his vision, a dead pigeon dangled in the lines. Automobiles raised street dirt, as exhaust coughed from tailpipes and transmissions jerked laden frames. Pedestrian men wore brim hats and tight-fitting gloves. Women walked in long coats flattered by dress hems. But there was a knock at the door, and Frank set the larger mirror face down.

Into the room came a robust Chinese with bushy eyebrows. He eased forward a linen-draped cart with rising breakfast smells. "Chew," he said pointing to his nametag. "Chew, like food. This fresh fruit, but also have coffee. Eggs and bacon with fresh bun inclusive. Congratulations on your victory, Mister Frank. Here is newspaper I have brought. It say you are come from Canada. That so? But so far out on Atlantic Ocean! My cousins over there at Vancouver died on Canadian railroad construction. Tragedy. Would you sign this, please?"

Frank was handed an early calendar for 1944. He set it over his right thigh, squeezing it with his forearm as he wrote: *All the best, Frank Curtis.*

"No, no. Bulldog! I like Bulldog, much more better."

Frank stared. He had signed soup labels, bankbooks and dollar notes. Amendments. Everyone wanted amendments. He avoided, when possible, to write a name; rarely could his attention be kept long enough when someone spoke one. People had unique spellings, always some attached distinction.

"You defeated American Champ, Bulldozer Lawrence Reid last night. Nasty end," he shook his head. "Seventy-one-and-one-half minute, but finish like a lightning bolt! Audience cannot remove eyes when someone fight with Bulldog. Is that right? And watch for his final victory push. Sensational! I read, for Allied war someone like you comes along to increase spirit. This morning in my walking to work I have seen two boys set up orange crate. Two more wrestle arms over wood barrel. Others ... please pardon Mister Curtis ... but others leave this sleeve out, for memorial purpose, tribute. To honour you, whatever. You will be in Chicago long? Many people want to meet you. And womans? I can get for you, already."

"Chew – I'm leaving for New York, Chew. I have to get ready for my train. Here's a quarter."

"Of course you have got get. New York has world final. I don't know why Chicago not get finals. New York is near to Europe, where is the hot war. Japan involved now. Cities close to war do best business. Then, of course, worst. I will not see the exclusive New York match, so take my luck with you. If there is anything, push service button please."

𝒲ith the attendant gone Frank looked through the food. He had hoped to spend the morning feeling good about his win but this man had spoiled that, mostly with his exuberance, his frankness. Frank was reminded of all he was involved in – this circus – and the next match, only two nights off. This one has to end it: loss is imminent. But children mimicking. What next? The craze that is in arm-wrestling, spreading from central Canada to just now catch on in the United States. It had been huge in England, before the bombing. Perhaps there is a correlation with a country's war involvement? Frank had stirred up the craze. People waited in line-ups three days to get a ticket promising an event with The Bulldog on the card. Radios featured documentaries about Frank Curtis. Exposés and commentary were featured on a controversial programme called *The Curtis Participation in Sport*. He was scheduled to appear at Radio City Hall before the New York match. They asked him to choose three of his favourite composers. The request worried him. A Hollywood film was being shot, not about his life directly, but everyone knew its basis. And, it was true – what they said: that it was the best escape from the horrors of the European theatre. Pitiful stories ran daily about accounts across the water, from a continent darkened by war, ravaged by a dictator whose rejection from art school set off a blitzkrieg of injury.

Frank could hardly control how people reacted to his wins, especially children. Pressure mounted. Suspicion rose as to whether promoters were rigging the matches, putting in lesser-than's to secure Frank's continual victories. The sport could easily fall apart were he to lose now. People wouldn't know what to do with themselves. Perhaps, none was like him. Or, that all men did allot themselves importance, that they only hoped became them. These were the radio programme views. He thought about the match of the previous night. He hoped to hell no criminal charges would rise out of the "nasty end" this Chinese mentioned. A group of concerned citizens wearing placards and waving signs showed up at each match now. Last night their cameras flashed. They had frightening faces. Rakish.

His father would have listened to the match, on a Canadian broadcast. All Ingonish would have tuned in. Never had anyone gone so far. Done anything close to this. Save, those boys in Europe. Those dying boys who never got these hotel sheets. But the fuss: musical entertainers, jazz artists – the best of the country played at the matches. Lead actors, Clark Gable, Rita Hayworth, famous politicians – all dressed to the nines waved from box seats. They stepped forward and stood publicly with Frank, shook his hand, smiled for cameras before speaking favourably to journalists with scratching pens. Frank was also making a buck from something that took no time, only strength.

At the window he stood to eat a bun, but it fell. He kicked the bun across the room and winced, "Ah, Christ!" Internal damage from the previous night. Had to be. He blew. He could have won that match early, but had held on, for show. Bad idea. Something could have happened to his neck, his spine – something *would* happen if he kept this up. The awkward way he positioned himself, and for so long. How can the body go on? He soon might never again walk straight.

Muscles never gave trouble; ligaments gave it, the joints the muscles fought from. Muscles go on forever. Like a knot in firewood. Last night at the hour mark, he looked across at his opponent, Boston's Blond Soldier, Bulldozer Lawrence Reid. Taken out of the war, where the boy had lied about his age to get in, Reid was brought in for this single Chicago match. He did not look the brute. He stood at Frank's height and build except that his shoulders were planted like wharf posts. From the get-go, Reid was mercilessly aggressive, wieldy and, unlike Frank, hardly road-weary. The young blood moved Frank, who was forced to make an uncharacteristic drive for defeat at the hour mark. This cost him, dearly. It had been too early to try him. But he shouldn't have tried him at all, because he could not budge him. His arm was shamefully forced to retreat to centre – where Reid's wrenching counter did not rest, but went beyond. Frank lost two inches of declination in Reid's favour. No one saw, but Frank had to give it his all just to bring them back to scratch. The soldier saw. But with eyes too eager he gave it his shot to end Frank's bid and it was then that Frank felt the shift. He knew opportunity had come, but only while the fight of his life was on.

They went at each other a full ten minutes more; a brand new match it seemed in which anything was possible. They fought with twists and grapples neither man knew to exist in sport. Frank shook off the passions and returned to his proven method of letting the opponent tire, of letting the other man finish himself. Yet, the soldier, coached too well on Frank's fight likewise slackened. Frank's style, was too well known.

Bulldog-wise, none had seen the type of fight Frank Curtis next switched to. He rose in a sea-surge to win. New material for the papers: unprecedented courage. A mustering to get out of a bind. Formulaic fighter no longer: a chess player, thinker. Frank learned on the spot that these later wins only meant a change of tactics. Successful leaders in a military campaign must know how logic enters, then forbearance. Competing for the great had always meant the slimmest of margins to win, luck being the deciding factor. But for the very great, luck was no factor, only presence of mind.

Frank struggled afresh, teeth grit, as pundits witnessed this emergence of a new champ: multi-disciplined, mature. Gamblers, predicting a downfall and staking more and more on it, sweat once more over Frank Curtis. The labourer in the cheap seats, the housewife by radios at home, the child wrestling in city lanes – each knew the underdog, the quiet champ. But this fresh fight? Where did it come from?

In the end, Frank never did put down the soldier's arm.

He snapped it.

Final competition. The World Championship: New York City. Frank's name led the bill at Madison Square Garden; tomorrow night was the weigh-in, the press conference to follow and the night after, Scandinavian Yon Per, the first off-continent contender. In a photo posted in Chicago this challenger was written up as The Black Swede. With pursed lips and rumpled forehead the man evinced a pair of jaws like crossing railroad ties. The Black Swede, Yon Per, a full nine years older than Frank, ate one dozen eggs and two loaves of bread for breakfast; he consumed fourteen potatoes for supper and a pound of butter a day. He never trained, but since the age of ten had worked a life in the woods. Frank posed in thought. From his experience, the man stronger than he who ploughed the field was he who fought the war. And stronger than both was the man to take his living from the woods. Frank lit a filtered cigarette, poured coffee in a queer cup shaped like a soup bowl. His throat was dry. Turning off the valve to the hot water radiator he listened for its dying gasp. For his dying gasp. He did what he did in every hotel room then, when disconcerted: raised the window fully and knotted the curtains. He had never got used to the heat of buildings. He washed at a basin when his cigarette was smoked then ate a frosting-coated croissant while packing his bag. He did his one hundred push-ups and five hundred sit-ups then left the hotel and caught the train for New York City.

The train rode through the night and part of the morning, bumpily east, before easing into New York's Grand Central. When the train doors opened Frank felt every bit of the country he had travelled. But then, outside, he saw New York stand impressively before him. Manhattan! War was here – in starched uniforms men wore crossing streets, in war effort posters flapping on lampposts or stapled firm to power poles. Frank started down Fifth Avenue and boarded a streetcar for the Chelsea Hotel. At the front desk a note waited for him:

Wade Miller. The Pudding, thought Frank, the same man from the Chicago event who compared the cities so well. He's here? He did say something about managing him, but this? This is harassment.

"I see you got my note."

Frank turned and saw Wade Miller stand in a fashionable navy-blue double-breast with high collar and slim necktie not exactly hiding the top button. The shaven face was rosy – the high colour of the carnation in his buttonhole; the nails clipped, filed. "That is one lonely trip," said Miller. "That Chicago-New York. Come to the bar, one deserves only to relax after that leg. The body needs a break, Frank. Not to mention the mind. Don't worry about your room, I checked on it."

A porter came for Frank's bag.

"No, Frank. Let him have it, Frank. He'll only put it behind the desk till you're ready to go up."

"My wallet, photos are inside."

"It's a hotel, Frank."

With his back to them, Frank removed his wallet. Wade Miller looked at the attendant and raised a chin, communicating inequality here, of the city versus the country sense. "I'd still prefer to keep the bag," said Frank and the porter bowed.

"Well then. The bar?" said Wade, and Frank nodded.

They entered the Eden Lounge, the hotel bar where a huge green apple hung from a plastic tree whose trunk was vine-wrapped, and a sword, buried to the hilt. They sat at a table with a half-empty cocktail glass and a dish of shelled peanuts.

"...Fifteen percent! That's simply not enough! Frank? Ludicrous. They ought to be paying you – that's hardly paying you! We'll talk about it. We will. It's paltry compared to what the door takes. The truth of the matter is – and I would be concerned – that you're the main attraction, plain and simple. Double it, without batting an eye, I could. Give me the word and it's done. I could get handsome takes, at least decent, Frank. And proper billings clear across this country. Back across your own. Marquees all the way. I know the Barnum and Bailey people – well, very well, in fact. The lift of

209

a telephone mouthpiece puts you on their card. Circus act, true, but the Greatest Show on Earth, let's not forget. Pardon the in-discretion, Frank. Frank? But did I say compensated? Handsome as the devil – dealing at the front end, that is. With a proper sign-ing, that is. Which is where I come in. Pull your chair in. Further."

"This place is jammed. And what is it, eleven?"

"New Yorkers for you. They're a people who are convinced the end of the world is tomorrow, sunrise. Opera crowd too, I expect, by their dress. Now, Frankie, if we do work out a deal I have to give it to you straight. You'll be embarking on a life of the road. And nothing sedate, I'm afraid. The rest of the world can have it to their liking. But the man, I feel, on the move, is the man on the move. The profit-taker. Travelling affords the greatest of pleasures available a fellow, provided he go in style. And, ho, sir, I can arrange style! No – simply not to be tied down is the answer. Not enough can be said about it. Is it in the species, for heaven's sake, to be bolted with lug nuts? Jammed, like the legs of a park bench? Darwin and all that? Look how we're built. We've kneecaps to protect forward motion. Elbows to nudge past. Too many a good man gets coroneted into his wearing of the millstone: house, kids, gal. All that. They lodge there and rot like sugared molars. That same fellow does get sprung ... when asked to fight in a mucky war, on the other side of the bloody Atlantic! Cre-ation! No, what I'm proposing is civilisation, intellectual development and a side-stepping around 'settling down' or 'being a patriot.' I mean, fill your pockets with fruit overhanging the road. Then beat it quick. Don't get stuck in a bend or a bind. Tell me whether living is a thing other than that and you will see someone refuse to believe he who says it. It's how I go. Merrily. How I *try* to go."

He coughed into his hat.

"Hear me now: I wouldn't give up what I have for the world. No! Man's a roamer. And freest when he does roam. Sense of worth comes by putting one foot in front of the other. Chinese and all that. He is able to learn, to help, to have a viewpoint. It takes courage. You have it. I've seen it. What's your drink? Frank? I'm getting wound up – and you're not paying a solitary dime either! What am I saying? Why, Frank Curtis doesn't drink. I read, I read. Powerful thing, this day and age, not to. I'll give you that, and that well-deserved, I will. I rarely hear of it. They say P.T. was big on temperance. As for me, a splash or two enhances life. I would be a smaller man without a tinkling glass near, but that is me, the Miller, and not you, anyone else. I don't expect it to be anyone else. I gauge. The key is to gauge. It changes your thinking, I find. And tell me a day when there is not a need for that, eh, fellow? A change of thinking?"

"Jesus. Do you ever shut up?"

"I talk, Frank. I do."

Frank had been feeling low but the remarkable company ended that. So harmless. The banter, immediate. Wade Miller did not come across as the sharpest knife in the drawer. He certainly didn't look it; though he tried. He was eager to make a friend, to find one with whom to share his thoughts. He was the type to latch on to the first stranger he meets – who needs to. Yes, you see them on trains, park benches. Look cool, till you say "good day." Then, look out! Frank had met them on the road, the radiant heat type that draw you in but any real warmth is practically in their flames. Step away, you chilled. Wade Miller wore hair oil and his nose was broad like a prizefighter's. His thin eyebrows left a couple of hairs to fill in the gap, and more prickly wisps stayed at his earlobes. An unlined forehead marked him. Frank looked around; others wore hair oil. Wade paid no mind to others; his eyes were solely Frank's property. The big green apple above. The sword. The place set Wade Miller down in his element.

"All right," said Frank. "Call that fellow over, I will have a sip. My first."

Wade touched Frank's arm. "Frank? Don't do it, Frank. You don't want to. But do, and I'll eat this glass! Ho! Frank Curtis. No – really, don't Frank. You hardly know what waits. A guy like you is fine the way he is. A fine fellow is. Stay that way. Believe me."

"I want a drink. No one wants to wake one day and find they never lived."

"Now, that – that is splendid! Never heard it put that way. Be it the case, then, I'll get more in my glass. I'll finish this and top it up properly. Because it's the greatest honour there is to share a man's first drink. Back home in Iowa we drink our first out of a shoe. Better not try that here. We don't want to get chucked out onto any frosty New York cobblestone, my friend. No colder sidewalk exists than Wall Street down around the corner."

Two fluted glasses of gin were set between the men. Each got lifted with ceremony. Wade, putting the stem neatly to his forehead ridge, shut his eyes. He winked at Frank then laughed smartly when Frank leaned back after his first taste of alcohol.

"You don't like it! You don't! I didn't figure you would. The tongue is not what's it about, though. The feeling, Frank, be present for that. The allure. And it's instantaneous."

Wade inserted a cigarette into his holder, raised a brow at Frank and pressed his cigarette tin forward. Wade lit his companion's with the blue flame of a silver lighter.

"Now, Frank. This is gin. Its flavour comes from the irrepressible juniper berry. The potation itself has been all the rage since the turn of the century. Wrong! Since long before that! New Yorkers swim laps in it. If it doesn't grab you then there's wine. I was going to suggest wine because with wine you're never let down. It has class … in a glass. Not unlike the man I'm sitting with. I can drink a gallon of wine without moving a toe. The worst wine will ever do to a fellow is make him converse better and prompt him to squeeze the shoulder of his adversary. Gin is my companion. And as companions go you're never left high and dry, provided you don't petition too much of that companion. To respect gin is to have a friend always near, one to trust and turn to for solid commitment, passed and beyond this craggy world. Hell, fellow, when we had Prohibition on a few years back, gin was my, and most everyone's, soulmate! We never drank so much, as when we quit! No. I consider it divine wash, that which settles the soul. Drink up. It's made specifically for that."

Warmth settled into Frank's heart, enough so that everything seemed possessed of deep meaning.

"Then you like it? Tell me."

"Well enough."

twenty-two

"But Canada must be quite the place! What? Fresh, clean. All those lakes. You fellows have a king too, don't you. And no doubts about the war? But Frank Curtis – you're the talk of the town. Boy, oh boy, what compunction! There's more talk about you than the construction of the Brooklyn Bridge, the marching of the elephants after the tragedy. Look around. I don't know what my mug is doing alongside yours. You're cause for the gawk. You and your hearty Canadian appeal. No … I mean it. I bet you got a gal in every port! At the trading post, the pick of the pelts!"

Frank laughed, at last, and Wade Miller smiled with even teeth and eyes that glimmered: he was being laughed at, and, yes, had been getting ahead of himself for some time now.

"All right, Frank. You know the truth … I'm only partly sensible. I get a little wound up. But I mean what I say. And you can't take me to task on that. But there are gals eager, what with their fellows off to Europe. You the Bulldog. Me the Miller – left to minister to a whole country of filled drawers. Women loosen grip in a drought. Biology left them that way. My oh my, Frank, I have to say it. You're an ace of a fellow – I don't care! I don't meet anyone, anymore. Not to converse with on the level of an intimate. Stiff, is what is out there.

"I feel I can say anything to you and get it right. That you will take it right! And that's rare, to find an intimate. When you do, treat them with postmaster respect. The city does, in the end, promise the intelligent conversation. I die if that's not there. All may *be* country folk on the inside, but what draws and keeps us in the polis is the conversation. And my belief is that there are only few meant to come along for you. Oh, happiness now! I'm having another. Will you have another with a man who begs the company?"

"Can't hurt."

"See? There, you said something again. I'll wait till the barman spins around, comes down this end. What do you say to our arrangement then? We can give it the smallest of go's. Merely to test the water between us. A water test can't hurt. How can a water test hurt?"

"Shouldn't."

"Right there, like that! Man providing accommodation for opportunity rising, allowing to come what is to come. None of this lay-ing-down-pipe-programmes, of fear and fuss."

Frank put the last of his first gin to his lips because another had arrived.

Ah, this stuff, he thought. How light becomes the weight. The gentlest of reassurance, this spin on matters. It might very well be the big answer to the complications a fellow faces. I might have at last learned why they go for it. I *have* learned! Nor, does it need be the mess, it is for some, a man need only keep perspective – *this* perspective. Setting aside his first glass Frank took a big swallow of his second and received a slap on the back for it.

"My, oh my, company, and how it excels," said Wade pushing back his chair, standing. "Listen up! I know how curiosity has its bite on you all. So let's put it to rest. Ladies, gents, it is true. This here is *the* Bulldog, right here with us, sharing a glass. Would anyone care to join me, in raising an elbow, spending half a wink on our Canadian darling, Frank Curtis?"

Lipstick parted and gloved hands took dainty champagne vessels. Gentlemen tapped cane tops and smiled pearl-barley teeth through expansive moustaches. One showman wore a monocle that crept upward. Large winks and ho's came freely from various quarters. Opera. Frank raised his glass and sailed it in a half-arc, in so fine and easy a manner as to reciprocate the approval. And how comfortable it can be to show gratitude? Frank tilted his head and returned winks, deeply comfortable under his canopy of gin. But during applause, goodwill, its gentle recess, a flat-chested blond walked into the bar. Glasses tilted, but mouths froze – and no longer in regard to Frank – but for the porcelain dish dolled-up for the world to see. Forgoing two stools she stepped to the bar and, turning sidelong, leant against its wood. She was not far from Wade, from Frank, who each swallowed in turn.

"See that?"

"I am seeing it."

Her face implied a thing or two was on her mind, a furrowed brow attempted only further, to the beauty she was. She wore a green-chassis skirt, slim-shouldered blouse, tight string of baby pearls. Classic charm was hers, that of the screen actress, where silk neck and high cheek carry the burden of grace. Frank watched Wade as each moved Adam's apples in the offing.

"Help me, Frank. For the wind's been ripped from my sails and I'm bound to strike port. You ever see them put together quite like that, way up in Canada?"

"Can't say I have."

"The face is… I will say, demure."

Frank took his arm off the table in order to elbow his companion: she had tossed her hair back to look over her shoulder, the play of it ridiculous, but winning the success it had hoped. Wade winked both eyes at nothing then sat up straight. He coughed, touched his hat to his knee then took matches from the ashtray. He stood and walked to the bar with his cigarette tin. Frank could hear.

"The plain and simple? You are something else," said Wade. "Care to join my friend and I over there? That there, is none other than Frank Curtis, and I'm speaking Bulldog. You have to know of him. Smoke?"

"Thanks mister, I have my own, when called for. Now, would you be so kind as to go back to your table? Leave a woman to her thoughts?"

"Erred. Do beg your pardon, miss. In any case, we're right over there."

Wade returned the distance, traced the brim of his hat and coughed. He sat on half of his seat and rotated his glass. He fell into a funk which made Frank twist with joy, wishing wholly to pound the table.

"You hear it?" said Wade. "You did, I know it! 'Leave a woman to her thoughts.' Oh my. My day is gone now, wreck and ruination. Leave her to her thoughts. Ah, Frank, does one need suffer such declivity?"

The woman paid the two no attention. Thus driving the two mad. They could see by the way she eased out of her leaning that her breasts were not small. They were full; but had been strapped back merely in some fashionable brassiere. She wore the device in such a way to snug the pair, but with shoulders, drawn back....

"Bizarre," said Wade. "But the flat-chested flapper never really did leave. In fact, it's a fashion back in full force. Which makes it about right – all fashion repeats itself every twenty years. That only makes this one doubly dangerous. Dessert, before the main course. How she pulls that off!"

She approached the table and each man dove, mute.

"Fellows. I am sorry. I will have that drink if it's still on."

"I thought you were thinking," said Wade, waiting, open-mouthed. "Thinking about coming over to smack us one."

"Waiting is what I was doing, in the lobby, for someone who didn't show."

"And what a Philistine he must be!" said Wade, timely standing, pushing in the back of her chair while she grimaced at the two. "Don't you worry, honey. Everyone's a no-show these days," he said. "Common decency has taken a back seat."

Frank had come to his feet as well, feeling the weight of his coat, waiting a little too long for her to push into the table better.

"Much obliged, fellows. Mine's a gin, with crushed."

She looked at Frank's front a moment, this gentle occupation he had with his sleeve, this pained swarthy face.

"Well. So," said Wade slapping his palms together. "What station in life does your charm occupy?"

"Come again?"

"Job? Actress? Off Broadway would be my bet."

Her eyes were softly on Frank.

"You got it," she said.

"I knew it!" said Wade. "There's intuition. I should be at the games! Soon as I laid eyes on you I said to Frank that, here is no common beauty. I said something like that, Frank? Didn't I? When she walked in?"

"You did all right."

"And I'm guessing you're his manager?" she said.

"Now what gives you that idea? That I have anything to do with Frank beyond the relationship of pals?"

"That tie. And you use his name like it was going out of style."

Her voice was raspy, an accessory to heartening good looks that plainly and for all time weakened men.

"Ah, detective as well,' said Wade. "That tie? What do you mean, that tie? I'm highly insulted. You're clearly on the attack, it wasn't me who stood you up."

"No one stood me up, mister."

"Stop! Let's stop. We're off on the wrong foot. Wade Miller, and pleased to meet you. And yes, I am working out a business arrangement to *become* this fellow's manager. This is Frank Curtis. Undefeated Canadian arm-wrestling champion. In New York to fight tomorrow night in the World's."

"Hello, Frank. Good to meet you both, boys. I'm Della Rae."

"Della Rae? That it? I mean, no last of it?"

"Washington is my last name."

"Presidential. Don't you think that sounds presidential, Frank?"

"It sounds a good name all around."

"The stage likes it," she said. "No doors closed yet."

The lull came. Frank put his hand out for her glove. She looked at the hand and said, "Oh, all right then." She shook it and Wade

Miller followed suit: "Yes, how did we forget." Frank ordered drinks. "Watch him go," said Wade, but when the drinks came and Frank reached for his third, Wade took his arm, "Easy, chum, I say. This ain't no fountain water."

"Of course it ain't no fountain water," said Frank. "Who said it was fountain water?"

"All of a sudden so knowing?"

"I am going easy, pal. Relax."

But Frank spun in his chair and began to orchestrate conversation, starting up dashingly then increasing in pitch and volume.

"That's some accent you got there," said Della Rae Washington. "Are you sure you're not from Ireland? Lots in this city are."

"He's from way, way up in Canada. Up where icebergs press down from the Arctic Circle with seals catching a ride. But, by gosh, how he can strike down a man's arm."

"Pfft," said Frank waving off the topic.

"Tonight is his weigh-in. Preliminary stuff. But we need him there in decent form. Frank? You hearing me? Because you're going to feel this already, my boy. Those last were doubles."

But Frank was further along than Wade could know. He hadn't slept, hadn't eaten, the train provided poor water. And this gin, unbeknownst to many, was unlicenced. Frank got to his feet and went to the bar where he pressed against his elbow and called harshly to the bartender wiping a glass at the opposite end.

"Eyelashes! Yes, you! I'm waiting. I saw you look when I came in. Want to make something of it?"

"Frank?" called Wade. "Come sit here, fellow. They'll be by, with a tray."

Della Rae turned and lowered her head. Frank continued.

"Come on, me son – fill … my … glass! That's your job! And get more for my friends while you're at it. Hoo! Hoo!" Frank pounded the bar then lifted his empty glass to toast the house. Patrons stirred, some, to reciprocate but then saw this for what it was: hardly genuine, spontaneous – not one of the sprightly acts to preface a session. It was common drunkenness, where nothing original nor charming had ever lived. And yet, tabloid. Frank put his glass down and setting his elbow on the bar, raised fingers to invite a match.

"Eyelashes! Take your crack! I'm the one with something to lose. City fellow – talking to *you!*"

The porter entered with a bellhop. The bartender nodded. They began the removal of Frank.

"Wait, wait! I'll go. I need to go. Let me get my bag. Can I say goodbye to the people at my table, can I? Well, can I?"

The porter went for Frank's bag. "I told you before – and you didn't listen too well – I'll take the fucking thing!"

Frank tore the bag from the employee and swung it at him when a large hand clamped his shoulder. Frank got himself freed enough to turn and saw that it was a fully regaled police officer, standing with hat, club and badge. "How in the hell you get behind? Where's the magician?" said Frank. "I'm going." He was roughly ushered into the lobby where he was asked pointedly to leave the building. Wade intervened, spoke eloquently, even brashly, explaining of some condition of Frank's that provoked the rash behaviour.

"I heard of it," said the hotel manager, arriving, emerging from his glass office. "And no, it's not so uncommon this condition, is it? The condition of getting sloshed at noon. Out, the pair! The Chelsea is hardly your venue. So get in haste along the street. You'll find your place."

"Sir. I say, sir?" said Wade. "This here lad is only all goodness. It was his first attempt at liquor and a failing one. My fault, entirely. He just lost his head. I lost mine. He's from Canada. The borough is just too much for him. Can you give him the one break? Let him go sleep it off? I guarantee you a full apology when he wakes."

The Chelsea manager stood with buttoned jacket, with sleeves fitting perfectly at the wrists. He wore well-cuffed trousers moreover and a deep-top necktie. A speculative man and slow to react unless provoked, he raised a finger at the police officer who maintained grip of his bat and Frank. "As he's already in. But get him up to his room. And afterward, you sir, make haste." With hot palms the manager returned to his office. He had taken the booking himself. He had known of this seedy underworld of arm-wrestling and was deserved of self-reproach. It would be this one time, he promised himself. After that, clear policy implemented at the Chelsea. Tight ship, no matter the racket.

*F*rank woke to a light knock at the door. Four hours had gone by and his head swam, the air, chill. He lowered his arm from his eyes. A hotel room. He wore no shirt, had merely warmed the bedding. He turned his head toward the window then back for the door. His sense of self was broken and nothing could deal with the arriving, heaping remorse. A driving headache got him upright where he took his undershirt from a post then grabbed his long sleeve. He put his feet on the floor, sighed. His bag was precariously set on the table ledge. A proper knock came as he turned over a shoe – then a rap.

"For Christ sake! Yes, yes, yes – come in!"

The door was bolted.

Frank stood with the doorknob in his hand to see Della Rae Washington in the hall. She wore a new outfit, blue calico dress with black cat sweater; silver earrings hung, a loose bracelet near fingers pinching a lobe. "Thought I'd come by." Frank saw that she came to his chin while he stood in sock feet. He left her the door. Closing it gently, she followed.

Frank sat unsteadily on the bed, all the splendid untruths of alcohol killed in him. He looked up and saw she was more beautiful in sober daylight. Younger, delicate as a pussy willow. Wholly attractive. So much so, he feared her and yet was thankful to have been chanced a sensible word, to apologise, show her *some* civil manner was possible.

"Ah, me head, me head. Don't stand. Sit. There."

"Thought you might need these," she said, her raspy voice resounding in the nearer space. She opened her hand above his and dropped three aspirins. She unbuckled her purse and took out a tiny bottle of milk of magnesia.

"My mother gave us that," said Frank. "What else you got, cod liver oil? No, I can't take any of it. I feel like hell on earth."

"Which is how you should feel. You've got company. Half the population in this town is waking up from a one-thirty."

"A one-what?"

"Drinks after lunch. You started before that."

"My watch got screwed up on the train. It's hard to adjust. Well, I won't be waking up from no one-thirty, two-thirty, three or four, ever again. Mark my word. Dirty dying old frig, the state."

"Dear me, the way you *do* talk."

"Dear me, the way *you* do talk."

Frank sat up straighter and decided to play it silent. He kept in mind how his father was fearful around women. The shoulder hurt. The cop's grip. If he were alone he would straightaway apply his menthol creams. On the bureau sat his compact mirror. But the woman played it quiet too and she made no effort to leave. She waited on a word, perhaps, one upon which to build a departure. Frank drank from the bottle.

"Keep that," she said.

"The taste hasn't improved. Della Rae your name? I do remember that much. Where did you say you come from again?"

"I'm a Midwest girl."

"Was there a cop there? He learn my name?"

"Uh huh." She lit a cigarette and blew smoke agitatedly before studying the room. "North Dakota, to be precise. I've been in New York for exactly one year."

"The time my brothers have been overseas. They're in France fighting the Germans."

"Paris?"

"Did they get that far? I couldn't tell you where. One's an RCAF pilot. The other, regular army, ambulance."

"You didn't go? Well, no. I guess you didn't. Sorry."

"Why sorry? I don't care, they couldn't take everyone. Don't be sorry. Tell me more about this acting business. I never met anyone who was an actress. I'm shy even to speak the word. Are you in the pictures? Ah, this head. I've never even been to the pictures. I see the movie houses, passing in the street. The entrances where you go in,

I see. When it comes down to it, I'm too bashful to find out how it works."

"Try walking up, buying a ticket. There's a start."

"I know. When you've never done it, and don't know what to expect – I hesitate, then don't bother. I got to get over that, in me."

"We all do. I was new here. It wasn't so long ago. No, I'm not in the pictures. I've met an array who have said they'll get me in. Watch for that, while you're in the town. There are all kinds who say they will get you into things. No – acting is about patience I'm finding out. Much. Still, there's far more here for someone starting out than there ever was in Chicago."

"Chicago? I was in Chicago."

"Finished with the bottle? Put it there. I'll pick it up."

She crossed the room and drew a curtain, her nails tapped the pane. She came to stand room centre when, spotting the ashtray, she soon carried it to the sill where she set it down. She showed herself fully in the light of day. Frank did not think she was any older than he was, just unattainable. But the light of day was failing, Frank saw. And she knew this – the dying light gave her the confidence to stand there. A silvery aspect came to her cheek; it traced her jaw to give it the weightiness of a good machine part. She put up a bold index finger on the pane and drew a face in its condensation, in a lower corner where mist and bead collected.

"You want to get something to eat?" said Frank.

She lifted her chin, for him to continue.

"Another area I have trouble coping with. City eating. But I got to get something in this stomach. And I wouldn't mind the company. Ah, this drunk business. What a lonely prospect."

"You want me to come along, to order for you, I suppose? I can manage that. There's a decently priced diner around the corner. But, that friend of yours, Wade Miller. Quite a card. He says he can get me in the next major New York production. One out on Broadway proper. As a fill-in, he said. I didn't take him seriously till he mentioned the director's name and what the director looked like. It surprised me that he knew."

"That guy's no friend of mine. I only just met him. He followed me from Chicago, thinks he can make a buck off of me. A little too over-the-top for my liking."

"You think so?"

"In honesty, I do. He keeps popping up like a weasel wherever I go. Wants to *help*. I don't trust them. Not when they come that smooth."

"Perhaps I shouldn't have given him my name and number."

"You did? Ah well. I'm sure, he's harmless. Talker. And there's plenty of those. As you said."

"You think he's harmless? You're right. Everyone talks. Little comes of it."

The two sat in the diner, with menus open. Frank looked out the window at the motorcars and pedestrians, all cast in a drizzling neon backdrop. Night falling. He suddenly understood the lure of the big city: how complete anonymity is fixed amid its crowds. It freed you, ultimately. He turned to Della Rae to learn better of what they might have in common. Della Rae knew horses. She'd grown up with her own Lusitano mare she named Lucky Charm. She had cared for Lucky since she was a little girl. She saw the mare born, its dropping to the ground then getting up to walk after its first half hour of life. The wild, the reason to run from predators. Lucky Charm hated the winter cold; bobbed her head like a rubber boat whenever Della Rae called her name into the stall. Della's father was taking care of Lucky Charm. In the opening of every letter from home the question rose as to when Della was coming back. Lucky missed her.

They laughed at the unique flavour each had for elaborating on subjects of interest. Frank learned of the involved process in making goat cheese, that some crops hurt soil, that limestone was added to restore a field. He said he would love to give the farming life a whirl. While travelling by train, through Montana, he had come across a flatness to the earth the like of which he'd never seen. He was over-whelmed by just how far the eyeball could travel land without hitting anything substantial. He spoke of his arm. He felt compelled. Della waited here for him to finish. She asked about the sea, whether waves topple houses. "We don't live in fear of waves. Waves are the beautiful part of a coast, if you're close, at night, in bed." They compared winters, each excelling at describing frost. In light spirits, they parted for the night at the Chelsea entrance. Frank stood to finish his cigarette. He had nodded when she said she had to be getting along. He told himself not to watch, as she crossed the intersection, but he did allow a look at her using the sidewalk opposite. She had a lovely, private way of navigating her person through the mean city: in no want of protection from any man. Frank sensed then she well knew his eyes were on her. When she was gone, he tossed his cigarette into the gutter and reached inside his pocket. He touched the piece of paper upon which contained his best prize yet. Her particulars, her handwriting.

twenty-three

"There's got to be a thousand! Ringside alone!"

Wade looked through a break in the curtains. "I'm about to lead the Bulldog down through the hordes. What do you think, Frank?"

It was the night's final card: the Main Event. Frank felt better for having Wade along, it tightened officiality. The largest numbers yet were in attendance, seventeen thousand tickets sold. Frank had not looked, but knew the human accumulations by the tension in the air. Wearing a red satin robe with initials in gilt, he refused to put up the hood. Wade set him straight.

"Suffer the hood, Frankie. Combatant enters arena with intrigue. People respect only the mystery. Part of the show. You can't let folks down, not you. All night they've been witnessing South American matches and listening to showpiece tunes."

Frank pinched the hood. "I just never liked one. Listen, bad nerves tonight. You don't have a nip, to tide a guy over?" Something erupted well below the curtains destroying a lull neither knew had been present, like a gunshot or fireworks. A crowd's roar ensued.

"The Black Swede, entering?"

"Positively."

225

"You have that drink?"

"Ah, Frank, what do you need it for? Because I don't advise it. Very well, cheap one. But wait! They're supposed to give us the signal to go – there it is, right now. Here, sniff this up your nose."

"What is it?"

"Don't worry."

"There's trickling. I like that."

"What they use in soft drinks. Halfway down is a post. I'll get the cap off on our way and you duck in behind. And, a sip, Frank. Finished with the ointment? The spermaceti? Come then, we got to go now. Hear that, sonny boy! That's your name – at Madison Square Garden!"

They descended spacious concrete steps, his hood up, Frank's heart raced, his mind sharp. He looked to his feet for balance when another roar struck – for Frank. Deep below, a canister at each corner, the ring spat fireworks. Sulfur travelled. Frank was stopped at the post where he swallowed a mouthful of gin and had started a second, when Wade yanked the flask. "Not on the night of your life!" Frank pinched his hood forward as he walked through jamming masses of bad breath and yellowed faces straining with mad all-too-familiar eyes; arms reached, fingers spiked, whistles went shrill. The two pushed in descent through claps on the back and a continuous thunderous beating of ten thousand immediate palms. But they got stopped at another post, where Frank huffed and asked for the flask. Wade shook his head and waited. Two men near spoke in exceptionally clear, whispered voices: mad psychics bringing their communion:

"I do have to laugh. They call it a thinker's sport, at the level it's grown."

"Chess game, I enjoy when they liken it to that. But why not? Established moves. Certain strategies. How to proceed, is entirely your own."

"And there's no cheating."

"Can there be?"

"No, there cannot when the calibre is up where it is. It's why I come. One result. The imposition of one will onto another."

"...Frank! I told you, I poured it out! Give that here... Frank?"

"What about the other!"

"There's no other! The racket – I swear, they're going to destroy the place!"

"He's big! Don't worry! Did I ever have trouble with the big ones?"

"You test that, sport!"

Exiting the stand melee and approaching the ringside floor, they passed jostling wealthy patrons with glinting eyes. Tuxedos, gowns. Frank wondered how far removed this experience was from that he was born into. No crouching under thickets here, no leaping onto harbour ice. No wood, no fire. No blustery stepping out to feed the horse. Yet all seemed placed, known.

The crowd went berserk to see the two robed men turn from their oblique entrance ramps, to make for the ring. The men climbed ladders to a raised floor, a transformed national boxing ring in which ropes were removed for proper viewing. A massive poker player's lamp, a man's height in diameter, hung above to light the competitor's table.

Names were called, hoods thrown back. Erect attendants were passed hollow robes. In wide wool woods-pants and suspenders, the Black Swede took the opportunity to raise his arms in planes and flutter fingers. This brought the adulation sought. He closed his eyes in joy, swayed hips and proved himself to be the showman. He and Frank stood in the obligatory white t-shirts: World Federation Issue. But the Swede had made holes in his and the sleeves of which he presently tore free and flung in Frank's direction.

Acrid air climbed the skin and, with chemicals charging vessels, Frank felt grand. He saw cigar smoke rush the ventilation system, clouds through steel girders as sweet tobacco leaves flamed. He wanted to inhale it all. How would Adrian's face look to see all this? Would he know where to look?

In the ring, smoky light dropping, thunderous applause abated. Humidity came to the neck. Frank knew the moment. He remembered stance.

But the Black Swede lifted cow eyes. There was hissing. He drew out paper matches tucked in his belt buckle. He lit the cigarette stashed behind his ear and drawing deeply let smoke drift from a cavernous mouth, a rising of freezing ocean vapours. Bending slowly, he unlaced a leather boot and with it threatened an audience quarter, before stubbing his cigarette on the sole. "Yon Per!" he shouted to no effect. He put the unfinished cigarette behind his ear and with boot on, unlaced – straightening a massive back – he opened eyes wide and rushed his opponent, stopping only feet away to glare into his eyes. With less than startled face then, he turned, scratched his buttocks through burn holes of the loose wool pants, closing eyes to its grand feeling. Fingers aflutter, an oceanic cacophony of sarcastic laughter, female voices cutting through with irreverence – a general debacle of debauched adulation, he smiled wryly. To Frank, specifically, he showed a busted black tooth probed by a tongue. The Swede then set his elbow on table. He bent and thrust buttocks outward to establish spinal comfort for the match.

"Yon... " he whispered, "...Per." He lowered his head.

Famed Yankee referee Alexander Clayton climbed the ladder, to walk the ring backwards. He shot to the competition table to establish two brash hands on the Black Swede's forearm; Clayton waved a large "No, no": the large foreigner must know the Ref is not ready. The Black Swede backed him off two rapid steps with a heavy, crab's forearm. The audience adored it. There were screams, shouts, selective swearing. Frank was struck from behind by a paper cup, with something in it; this prompted him forward. He stumbled, clasped the Swede's hand. Referee Alexander Clayton, embracing pathos by becoming a part of it, blew shrill his Federation-issue whistle, chopped the air, commenced officially what had already begun.

Yon Per: a man to waste no time. With his rear out and wriggling he drove lumbering strength, letting depart from his girth the greatest "heaves" and "hos." The blather irritated Frank to no end whose ear was necessarily forced in close. Yet Frank had known mean behaviour. He worked, consequently, to remove sound and sight. He looked at his arm to create fibres of strength, by studying its physics, its follicles, veins. Vision could do that.

In mid-grunt the Black Swede thought, but just what is this now? Am I not international champion? A tooth. A baby tooth, to be hauled out – from a little one-armed man. The Swede threw joyful weight, from this side and that, maintaining balance like the most skilled of technicians, the tree climber. No, trapped bull! He was in a wood pen, whose sides he must burst, and would, in a moment. Tooth, you! Fused, not ready to go! The Swede's wife Klor had the tooth job, the baby teeth of their nine sons. Yon Per was asked on occasion to lend support, after a day in the balsam forests, to yank a tooth she could not budge. Klor wanted children with straight teeth because her own hadn't been weeded. The children squirmed and screamed in agony to feel their father's brutish digit enter an undeveloped mouth, to make rack and ruin of the entire set, while he pulled.

The big man of Europe pushed, twisted, hauled, got toes involved. He bent low at the knees. Nowhere? Ah, little bar of iron! Attached to floor, foundation, core of the earth! Yon Per knew not to slacken. He also knew to keep the crowd involved. Wriggling, forcing upper body – as if up through a tight hole, he kept up the show. Twisting pressure, just under maximum, maintaining off-rhythms. His second wind would come to uproot anything put before it; his second wind wreaked twice the havoc of the first. Waiting for it reduced drama. So The Black Swede snorted and burst in frightful paroxysms satisfying first himself then the excitable multitudes.

The men grappled, held, jaws worked. But the senior of the Northerners – was he whispering instructions into the ear of the junior? Moans suddenly stopped, the crippling wait that both professional competitor and educated audience knew so well, had begun.

Viewing the match from the fourth row were Wade and Della. They stood abreast, unmoved by the spectacle, as if custodial wards to all, as if word had long been used up and any further relationship consisted of this dull, godly survey of the world.

The caged timepiece clocked the men at forty-three minutes. The crowd seemed to note the lapse all at once, as there came that unique universal surge of emotion known only to arm-wrestling. It made livid the round arena, the Garden, tonight with its quality of surrendering torment. Patience swelled to burst impatience when the Black Swede let out the most egregious of cries any were likely ever to hear: his euphonious "Muaaua!" The cry of the aggravated soul, the lonely bobcat slinking across its barren slope, windswept in the awful, utter dark. People hushed. The Scandinavian tussled with an all-out attack of strength, managing to move hands swiftly from their zero, to three inches of favourable declination. The brute drove on with all remembered strength, with everything used to cut those one-hundred thousand trees, hack their one-hundred million limbs in the forests he slew, in woods entered beastly with double-bit and crosscut. He gained one whole other inch, lengthening the shadow on the table.

The crowd knew instantly, the attack was on and their man about to lose. And so, in collective gasp, they watched panic-stricken as Frank Curtis lost ground, as the precious arm they loved so much slinked away from its sleek, altered body. And the Black Swede knew, the only road was this – and he could never go back. As if, a churchload of paid mourners then, he wailed his anguish and rocked it, but suddenly, to gain no more ground. He shouted, over wasted hell! Hollered to denounce Satan from his seat in Pandemonium! Wished to terrorise the very roof off this round garden, square garden, and eat all inside! But could not. Here was seizure. The unnatural strain on his amassed spinal column, its awkward positioning in frozen advantage – the brain shouted out merely one thing! Shift, balance. But to shift, was to die. No! Not here! Not at this point, no death; the little man and his miniscule forearm will be returned his inch, then suffer twelve in defeat! And so, the game was played perfectly: with no rules. Only instinct. All known had to be thrown out because to risk was to live! Obey. Rule. Never be King! They said this minor waited for this, just for this. No! Fight cannot be left! In no arm, ninety, plus thirty, degrees in disfavour.

The Swede lifted one buttock, kicked his right foot back, mechan-
ically lowered the second buttock. He then watched horror-stricken
as his great gains melted away. He watched in petrified disgrace as his
arm approached the ugly ninety degrees of equanimity – too soon,
and below his nose! Too soon, where he averred never to see it again
– in the spot where it had slept away the brutish part of the night.
But then he saw to utter visceral displeasure that it did not wait here,
no. Unceremoniously, no! Not without ill humour, it continued past.
In disbelieving, wondering, malefaction the Swede saw how the baby
tooth bit him. How it dragged him down dastardly over another plane
on a journey the proud years of his life hoped never to take. And Yon
Per's heart ruptured to see all will leave him. To see mortal arm and
mortal hand in this living other, its instruction downward into the
real-life drawing of the simplest storybook. The hairy backside of a
heart-broken wrist awaited plunge to the cool leather mat connected
to the bell. Held, held, held – no! There it was....

*A*n uproarious cry that choked lungs, made larynxes raw, rose to
beat steel roof girders, to shake miserably the colossal edifice with
the reckless joy of society gone mad. The single greatest witnessing of
human triumph! Kingdom come, indeed! At last, how life was lived!
Meaning all at once! Countless years of the fruitless searches. The
writhing on beds, the waking to another dull hour in which clothes
must be yanked on, shoes tied, faces washed. To clean, to eat, to say
nice things. Work. Love in bits. All burst at once and in it, the answer
all fought so desperately to know!

Della Rae beat hands and blasphemed openly. Teeth bared with
white glisten, cheeks breathlessly high in rouge. "How great a thing
– how great! Jesus damn, halleluiah, in heaven! Did you see it? Did
you see the thing? An end to beat all bastardly ends! Ding!"

*T*he broken Black Swede, tall tears in beautiful eyes, laughed, kissed
Frank's foot because this simple man had come to release him from
the spell that had kept Yon the great lonely figurine. Yon Per goes
home to Scandinavia. Yon Per goes to sit and consume twelve eggs in

peaceful swallows; nobody would knock. Nevermore come the worries about the sorcerer to arrive one day and remove what we must primordially, preciously guard. He kissed Frank's ear. "You are strong man now." The Swede then smiled for the hordes to show his busted black tooth before gaze returned to his victor, just once more, from this wonderful, downward sweep, this plateau of defeat. He extended both arms, hands.

The crowd raged like a hurricane sea.

Few would remember how Frank bent poorly at the competitor's table then, as if puzzled, searching vacantly for money dropped. Few would note how he looked drunk moreover, trying desperately to assemble some sense, some courage to move on. Frank was hurt awfully this time and in loopy crowds he alone would carry that knowledge.

The old trick: taking over from master of ceremonies, New York City Mayor, Fiorello H. LaGuardia, clamped onto, then raised, the wasted arm. Frank tried only with futile deliberation to coax "The Little Flower" off, to pull free his mangled paw. But the five-foot mayor was all-powerful. In top hat and brash coat, virile, holding high his microphone – the instrument on command for this travelling circus – LaGuardia about delivered, into the device, the booming words to go elsewhere. He pushed the little switch.

"Ladies and gentlemen! On American soil! Frank Curtis, digging in tonight! One and all. Come, find your programme. The Bulldog *does* win his bone!"

Frank was shoved the solid-gold belt: the giant buckle's engraved taut arm in the V, its fist squared like a hammer head. They held the glimmer to him, pressed it to his chest before coarsely removing it. A distant chorus began to sing that ditty composed solely for the champ, that one printed on the evening programme. Growing in popularity the piece was now note-worthy, and most recently recorded by a black jazz group from Detroit, The Happy Haymakers. Seventeen thousand plus joined in from the start:

"...The man of the land who lives by the hand. Who does what he can, our dear friend – Frankis Curtis, Canine! Whose jaws get entwined, to take adversity sublime, and never ceases to tear that thing, to pieces – Frankis Curtis, Canine! Frankis Curtis Canine! Honour thy mother, but love thy father, obey, pledge and stand free. Protect our home while – we're away. Then show again, and again and again, our pet, that every dog has its day!"

Sung by New Yorkers, a race impassioned and staunch, the piece sounded far off, deliberately haunting. Perfectly gladiatorial. But, the song through, the Garden did not empty. People needed that glimpse of their hero of heroes. Brass-buttoned police stationed in full regalia braced at Garden exits, sporting polished riot gear. Units were over from New Jersey tonight, and from Boston town. In packets of sixteen they stood, force-poised, expectant of the worst of scenarios. There had been progressive trouble at previous events. And yet, these law-upholders broke smiles not heads as they alone got the best sight of Curtis: now entering the wildest morass of the night – the main exit north. Groomed officers with shoulders taut, with hands on long black bats and shields; these kind uniforms winked at the Canadian windfall. The reach, even to shift hats then, get better light into the eyes so as to see the handsome lad. Camera bulbs flashed, bursting noises were left, to ride over caterwaul and jeer. Frank met Wade.

"Hide me." Frank bent, drank all he could from Wade's flask then straightened. Della Rae's hand had found his, "Easy." Space formed for the couple. An interview on live radio began, Radio America with national host Willy Walkerton:

"Do we have him? We do! So here he is, radio listeners, the gentleman himself, Canadian Sweetheart, Frank Curtis. Bulldog, listen Sweetheart, will you be going to Europe to head off this war for us? Take care of this Mr. Hitler?"

"I got my two brothers doing that."

"You do! Ha! Holy Cow. Well, if they are anything like you, Sweetheart, those SS Nazis can begin running tonight with their tails between their legs!"

"I'd like to say hello to them, William..."

"Frank? Frank! Ladies and gentlemen... Ladies and gentlemen, we had him, we lost him. Oh, but there, the north entrance of the Garden, by the wall. He's at the War Memorial Anchor and they're coaxing him, the champ, to lift it, believe it or not. Mayhem, folks, sheer mayhem, you'll just have to take my word! I don't believe it myself that, Frank Curtis, new world arm-wrestling champ is lifting the memorial anchor. The coaxing is too much. And he has it, too. Well, they have it. Oh my, getting it on his back, somehow? They're helping. Every move is a photo for this kid. Frank Curtis, hoisting the Memorial Anchor, onto his shoulder. After what he has been through tonight – but there he is, and he's doing it! With help. Frank Curtis, giving us a post-show here at Madison Square Garden in New York City, Manhatten, folks, defeating the Black Swede Yon Per in the greatest single-hour struggle the modern world has witnessed, and this is Willy Walkerton.

"And now – celebrating by lifting an iron anchor of, who can say how many hundred pounds over his head. One-handing it. No, little help. But oh, the spectacle! People are gone mad, mad for this Canadian, I say. Mayhem galore. And he's holding it, for the flash bulbs. It has got to be three hundred, more!

"Oops... Uh-oh.... Oh my, oh, oh, oh, my. He's lost it. Lost the anchor, folks, it got away from him. Ugly scene. It has slammed the floor, the Memorial Anchor has fallen. A chunk out of the floor. No one hurt, they had been giving him room. The champ, is he ... no? No, not hurt! Thankfully. Is he...? It is indeed hard to tell, listeners. Apologies all around. It took out a chunk of the concrete, tagging his shoulder on the way down I'm afraid, narrowly, so narrowly missing the foot. No man would walk again. Dangerous play, and he is favouring the shoulder, the left, ladies and gentlemen. But there, incredibly, raising the arm to wave. Now this is sports-card material. What a night for the Garden! What a night, oh, oh! Willy Walkerton for... for Radio America.

"Ah, but here it is, their cheering, that roaring reminiscent of the Roman theatre. Their Bulldog song, once again singing his glory. Yet the champ is no longer in view. Goodwill is, in plain sight. A scene to be possessed only of the modern city. And New York, our home, has it tonight! You can hear their choral feast with full bursting lungs. But the man has gone, and that is it. The long black car has taken him from us. Good night, Frank Curtis, Sweetheart, wherever you are. Our new world champ, bringing the belt to North America, listeners out there.

"To repeat ... Canadian Frank Curtis beating undefeated world champion Yon Per of Stockholm, The Black Swede, in fifty-nine minutes flat. We watch. We stand. As the modern world basks in this overwhelming glory ushered in by one single man of the frozen North. Frank Curtis."

twenty-four

The Rolls Royce waited under vying skyscrapers made less tall but more looming by night. An expansive reception was taking place at the Waldorf Astoria, where chandeliers burned and Broadway sensation Montgomery Clift had arrived with entourage. A photographer for *Vogue* was busily snapping photos but *Time's* man, Mike Villermet, sat at the bar waiting for the shot of the year from the star of the night. In a backroom with plush carpet lounged Frank, drinking champagne in peace. Wade had remained quiet, but for too long now.

"It's the time, Frank. We got deals lined up."

"Can't, Wade. Physically can't, everything hurts. You saw the gouge that anchor took out of my shoulder. Whose stunt was that? I'm beat to pieces."

"It's not hindering you from raising a glass."

"No one said he was dead."

"You're tender, I know, but it's recuperation soon enough. Let's get this tidbit out of the way. Your drink, good? I'll fill mine up when you're set."

"That trick."

"No trick. Listen, there's too much going on out there to know what this is all about, Frank. Timing. Much of life is timing. We got to get deals out of the water, out of the air, and into stone. People talk, talk and talk but only ever act with signatures on paper. I'm staking, too. We can wrestle right across this country and back across your own. I said that. Right up to your front door. There's never been this opportunity, in history! What was your take of our purse at the Garden? Six thousand, mere. We can double that right off, now we can. Two weeks hence can make tonight look like a handful from the cookie jar. San Francisco, Los Angeles. They're mad for you. Next month, there's a lineup in Europe. I know we can get it. For the troops, with Bing. Dietrich mentioned you. Noël Coward. Think of the troops. They deserve to see you – your brothers. It could resolve the conflict sooner. Well, it could! Morale brings about ends. Morale, alone. No one else need get involved."

"I can get us out? You are *not* trying to tell me that."

"Of people and their stories, I'm telling you that. It is what moves us, Frank. That is what I'm saying."

"Where is it you think I grew up, Wade? In an abandoned well? Keep countries out of a war! Ending it! Home, Wade, home. This foolishness has to end. I'll be crippled for good, I keep it up. You saw the x-rays, shorn ligaments, unstable joints, doctor shooting me up."

"No match for will, Frank. What someone like you got. Give it a month. Let's ride this together one month then pack it all in, once a nest egg is established. I don't have the experience other guys might. But there is a good feel between us. Let's get you primed for life. Everyone has to want that. Your father, brothers. Grace, your sister."

Della Rae squeezed through the door. A bulb flashed. The man set there, security, turned for signal, allowed her entry. Frank looked up while Wade stared ahead.

"Please, Della – now?" said Wade raising an open hand, a pen in its fingers. "I brought Frank in here for a purpose." Wade waited, ministered to a smile, seeing she was so pretty; Frank adored her. Frank put his arm around her, but gingerly. He allowed her in at his ribs but it was too much, so he tapped her, had her sit aside. "You *can* take care of this," he said smiling, rocking an empty glass. She filled it then got in close: she too felt good about things, and her slim frame did indeed cradle Frank's though, yes, now was not the time. Frank smiled, his thinking changing in her scent, to become frivolous.

"Set for life!" he shouted to no one. "But that *would* be something, eh!" He laughed and laughed while Della Rae looked on, believing her presence produced in him this jocularity, so, she laughed back. Wade nodded and smirked. Della Rae looked into Frank's eyes, in a bid to make the world disappear. Wade removed himself a step, swallowed disgust, weighty contract drooping in hand, a bent head glowering.

"Pass the fucking thing here," said Frank.

"You mean it?" said Wade, turned, walking to the fore, carefully pressing back empty glasses and full toward centre table. He reached into his sports coat for his fountain pen, where he had just returned it.

"Another autograph? Wade? That what you said?"

"Nothing more, Frankie."

"Sore, honey?"

"Not with something of your softness ringside."

Frank copied out his name in the three blanks indicated by an X. Della Rae took the pen and witnessed the contract, at the same three points. Wade reached out his hand for his pen then held Frank's hand.

"No jarring."

"This? This is a business grip."

"Don't know if I like the sounds of that."

"Drink up, high times."

"They do get high, all get a piece?"

"Oh, Frank! Leave me out of it, no!"

"All get a piece," said Wade, watching the two kiss for the first time.

"Dell?" said Wade. "I'll leave you here with Frank, to explain an item or two."

Wade crossed the carpet.

"Dell? Who's Dell!" called Frank. "What's he mean calling you, Dell. Familiar, all of a sudden."

Wade was past the doorman.

"His way," said Della Rae. "Forget Wade Miller, Frank. The crowds got to him. He received a sharp elbow out there. I wouldn't worry. They wouldn't let us in the first three rows, he's sore about having to sit with rabble. You were amazing. I don't rightly know how a girl is supposed to act sitting alongside a Champion of the World. I will tell you one thing. The feeling I do have is not horrible."

They kissed again, but Della Rae pulled away when Frank pinched a breast roughly, reached for her crotch, tearing a hem.

"You *are* fine enough for that," she said, standing out of his further advances, raising all the sweet feeling with her.

"I'm no whore, Frank. If that's what you're thinking."

"Just your mouth. No one's thinking anything. Give me a drink."

"I'll be in the powder room. I'll be out front."

"Why? Come back, I was kidding."

"People want to see you at the bar. I'll meet you there. I want you to try a highball. They're new to me, but seem the best of all drinks."

"Highball? But that's what I want – to do."

"Frank."

"So, cat, is it? Play the cat? Play it."

She was gone awhile, but outside, at the party, after talking and receiving clustered congratulations, Frank spotted her across the floor where she wove the drink she had for him. She was standing near an actor. Two-bit. The drunk standing near Frank made better company. He and Frank clinked glasses. "That one is taken, my victor friend. But look at her. The plum of the slickest cocktail in town. Wade Miller."

"Come again? How's that?"

"Wade Miller. Cue Ball. He loves to brush up against the highs, and the lows. Be the last on the table. A better choice might be wife, than date. They're hustlers from out Chicago way, by reports. You'll see her with a second guy every so often. She's named the Eight, I think it is, Ball. He's never far. They like sporting events. He hires her out so goes the talk. But that accent of yours? You have to be from

Massachusetts? You're an Irish from Boston, I know it, I can tell you are! I know New England. I know their mean-spirited winters."

$\mathcal{F}$rank reviewed the drunk's words the next morning, when boarding the first train out of New York City. He was travelling to Boston, where he would make a connection north. He stared out his train window, awed at the activity for the early hour; dark winter skies threatened snow. But passing railcar, streets, buildings below – nothing looked to know snow; all was shabby, grey, dessicated. Cold, but not snow-cold. The station temperature read 22 Fahrenheit. How a man can run off discreetly in these big centres, thought Frank, till he saw a boy in a Boston suburb, one arm only through the sleeve of his jacket. Two of his friends dressed likewise came up. The three extended twisting sleeves, took loose right hands.

The lightest of flurries struck the Boston train shed. Frank had a four-hour wait before the next train. He walked the grim streets and heard in use a scouring accent of unsuppressed vowels. New York had threatened bad weather: Boston had it. Frank felt the snow travel his nape. Iodine was in the air, the ocean a presence here. He saw chilled gulls soar, their caws ricocheted from cornerstones. Frank had slept the night with Della Rae Washington. She hadn't liked his hand on her throat, at first. It was the way he reached it, he said. Every inch, every way he'd been the ram for her. Got belly full at the buffet. His groin was sore. Her smell was on him. He lifted his nails. He let her know nothing of what he knew about the scheme. And she had volunteered nothing. She seemed ill at ease. Why? To be following through on her part of the bargain, with a man like this. But then, she didn't have to follow through, so why did she when the deal was sealed, the signatures drying? She was grateful. She was in love. Grateful sluts in love, what next? She was wet, eager to begin. That said something. It said: that all travel the straight, all travel the crooked. She removed a short hair from a lip, to speak of love. Frank had the whole night through promised her the world. Did she mind hearing it? Her husband didn't; it was his expression, the world. Frank took his merry good old time, filled her up. She worked, not him.

He spat phlegm. He lit a cigarette at a shop window when inside, on a ledge, a porcelain ballerina confronted him. His mother. She would have loved that. There was the taking it to her grave, though she lay under three-feet of snow, and with other things, already pressed in against her.

Snow swirled at the shop door, someone wanted to pass. Frank tucked in his collar, moved out of the way. He swayed past a newspaper stand where the morning edition of the Boston Globe still sold. The last copy. An entire front page, a ridiculous man struggling with an anchor. Frank coughed out his cigarette, kicked, scuffed it. He'd sign his name a thousand times over – to whatever X they told him. What did a signature matter? It mattered nothing. Not to him. Do they have any idea, from where some of us leave? Frank turned leeward, cowered in gust and ache.

twenty-five

*V*isiting with her new baby, Grace said her hello to Adrian then explained all that was going on in the community. Adrian moved off the step to let her above and from the ground he listened to his daughter, his arms akimbo, saying, "I see. Yes. Go on. You don't mean to say?" Grace thought of the timidity of men around a baby. She saw how her father was trying gently to sneak off toward the back of the house. She clicked her tongue, and went inside where she stripped away a shitty diaper on the kitchen table. Her eldest child Rodney entered and sat at the window near the stove. Jessie's spot.

"Why didn't you come when I called? Reaching the age you don't listen, is it? Get through that, mister, and quick! Also, stay out of that ditch when I tell you!" With shifting black eyes and perfect sharp nose Rodney was the dead, spitting image of his grandmother. He left his chair for the porch then reappeared with a piece of firewood. He began smacking the door casing.

"Out there with your grandfather. Get! You're beginning to plague the soul out of me. I'm heading down to Claire's for a visit, where your sister is, so you be good here while I'm gone."

Grace put the baby over her shoulder and went outside. "I'm leaving for an hour!" Adrian was down at his woodpile; he poked up his head. "You see he doesn't get his clothes dirty!"

"Where *you* going now?"

"Pay Claire a visit, down the Woody Shore."

Adrian looked up from his sawhorse to see his daughter make her way, waddling up to the road, hips rising like cow scapula, new baby in her arms. Rodney stood at the corner of the house, on higher ground to show his full height for his grandfather.

"What can I do for you, sir, with that rake in your hand? You got a stance like I'm supposed to back off. A challenge, you want? Come on, I'm ready." Adrian pulled the crosscut out of his log and raised it. But the boy stepped out of the cool gable shadow, in swift motion advancing forthwith his rake. Adrian backed off.

"You little bastard, calm it down. See? Look... unarmed. What side of the family you belong to is what I want to know? Not mine.... So she left you here, did she, for my amusement. Come on then, we'll go inside. You can read to me from that book your uncle William sent."

"I can read."

"I said you could."

Rodney fell back and waited for the senior like a regular gentle-man. His grandfather did not reach for the boyish hair when rising and passing, telling himself, don't be joking with this kid, with any kid any longer; they go through stages when they're as invincible as Samson. And besides, could I relate to my own when they grew, let alone others? The old folks are loving, yes – out of fear. In the porch he sniffed the baby change; talcum was on the tablecloth he saw, on his way to the sink. "Poo, Jesus! You smell that? She do that in here? Why, I want to know, when it's where people have to sit, to eat – when there's a whole house in here to operate from?"

Rodney waited deadpan and Adrian experienced misgiving, again.

"Your bread is flat," said the boy, eyeing two experimental loaves.

"Flat! Is it now? Well, that's what you might be too, you don't stop looking me straight in the eye. Look away, you're not supposed to look anyone right in the eye. They don't like it, I don't. Here, eat these pantry cookies I got down the Fairway. There's no cow's milk, only the canned. You'll drink the canned, mixed with a little water. I'm having tea."

"I'm having tea."

"Have it. Go ahead – if you only want to ever stand five foot tall."

"That light overhead isn't screwed in, it never is."

Rodney pointed at the bare bulb in the ceiling, directly over the long table.

"For a reason," said Adrian, who pulled up a chair, a swivel that twisted miserably. He had his grandson hold the chair – told him to let it go – to go hit the wall switch.

"You'll fall. You'll kill yourself if I let it go."

"Flick that switch till I finish here, or you'll be the one dying all right. And I will fall, I keep up on this thing."

Adrian screwed in the bulb past the click of emerging electricity.

"There. Hold the chair again, 'for I twist. That's the boy. I don't put it on all the time because it's a hundred watt. Too bright, hard on the eyes. Now where you going? For the book? All right. Good. No, don't look in there, there's private stuff. It's up above, here in against the radio. But you get it."

Rodney waited for the chair then took the book from the radio shelf. With good posture he sat, studying the inside cover, the inscription his uncle had written overseas.

"Where's Holland?"

"Overseas. Alongside France somewhere. Europe. I was there."

Adrian brought the teapot then profaned because the holes in the canned milk were plugged solid with yellowish caking.

"Ah my, how quick how quick these seal up, with sleep in the eye. Enough to make you hang your head, and cry. Pour – pour! Let me get the bread knife. I'll make a hole a ladle can pass through."

The boy read in clear soprano.

"Ah … no … Rodney. Not that. That one's foolish. Makes as much sense as a bedbug. And you read that, day before yesterday. Give us the one about the nuns sinking in the ship. Them all going down with it. That one has a story a person can relate to."

Just then there was a rare knocking on the outside pane of the porch door.

"Who the hell? Here? This hour?"

Adrian put down the bread knife and tinned milk whose pouring holes he had greatly enlarged. Outside on the porch was the postmistress, blue lipped, waiting on the first step, a brown envelope in hand. She was frozen in the gable shadow. November had given some snow, stuff that didn't stay; but the air in the sun was passable, most days. The postmistress's lips dropped like rained-on violets. But where was her best friend, her hand-rolled smoke?

"Day, Mildred."

"I'm done out, Adrian. Give me a minute, will you? Here. This came officially, but the fellow bringing it couldn't understand the simplest of instructions on how to get here on his own. He was petrified to death you had a dog. Last evening he was bit on the calf, to the bone, coming down the North Shore. And this morning he had to pass through that gauntlet that's down along the Woody Shore. He took the wrong road, but wouldn't be returning the way he came, he informed us. The dogs – the mountain! By the *Aspy* was his only way out, supposing he had to wait on the wharf till spring."

Mildred handed the business-sized envelope marked:

CONFIDENTIAL

"Looks important."

"All I can say is people are getting them, Adrian. All I can say."

"They are? Well then. Sorry you had to make the trip. I don't get down the mail often as I should. Jessie always made the run. Will you come in, Mildred? That's the boy you hear in there. He's reading."

"I hear him."

"My grandson, ah... Rodney. There's tea on. You'll have a cup."

"No I won't, Adrian. I got to get back."

The postmistress climbed to the road. When further along she took out her tin, on the flat, in the sun. Smoke trailed her. She moved on leisurely, enjoying late-year warmth, the breeze at her face; but went straight back down the road. When lost to sight, when the trembling aspens covered her, Adrian studied the correspondence.

He went inside, stood over Rodney, who used a finger to read.

"Shut up a minute. That woman came a long way to deliver this. We have to have a look at it."

"You want me to read this poem or to not?"

"I want you to shut up. And, look. I'm getting tired of these disrespectful ways of yours. I'm the adult here so smarten it up once and for all. Here. My eyes aren't what they were. Read this for me while I get my glasses."

"Do you have a letter opener?"

"Guess what? Don't have a letter opener. And you wouldn't get one if I had. Rip it apart with the hands God gave you. Here, pass that here."

Adrian poked his finger through the sealing flap and drew harshly down the envelope. He removed a well-creased paper, flapped it twice and studied it. Seals. Acronyms.

"Here." He at last handed it to Rodney who received it respectfully. The boy put his finger on the addresses.

"Get on with it. Leave that part alone. Tell me what it says? Tax bill, is it? Because if it is, my day is ruint altogether. They'll have it soon where people won't be able to live down here anymore."

In good posture, Rodney looked up, his skin taut in the browning expected of a child after a summer out-of-doors.

"It's got Uncle Clifford's name, Grandfather. He was diseased in the war."

"Give me that, you. Where? Where's his name?"

The boy left the chair, stood and pointed.

"There. And here. Look, 'diseased.' Here."

"Diseased? What in the hell?"

Adrian sat and studied the letter, peered up at his standing grandson. He hadn't had time to find his glasses.

"Jesus, bai. You out to destroy my nerves? Are you?"

"What? I'm not making it up! It says it!"

"Read it to me, aloud, all of it. No! Come on. I'll get my glasses after, we need verification. Maybe we can catch your mother before she gets too far. Merciful Christ, what a day, what a day."

"I'm telling you the truth," said the boy who, then overcome, began to pout, then sniff, understanding along with his grandfather the import of the letter.

"Now, stop that, now. I don't want it. I only want to check what it says. To be sure, hear? Rodney? Stop it."

"It says what I said it says!"

"I know but I think it says more. I just want a grown-up to look at it, is all. Okay, fellow? Chin up."

Rodney took the back of his wrist from his eyes and the two left the house.

They passed down over the field to take the shortcut through the falling woods, but the path was so overgrown with goldenrod, raspberry and alder that they became ensnarled every which way they turned. Both had arms protecting faces when Adrian called for a halt. "Let's get the hell out of here before we're sliced to ribbons. Back up, I say. We'll take the cursed main road."

They climbed the field and started down the road, taking the shoulder, walking in silence a long way till they came to the Woody Shore houses deep below the look-off bank. The wind and sun had free reign, as trees cut by the first Portuguese for boats or for fire, had never grown back. The houses, set on descending ledges, glinted in the sun. Red, yellow and blue were favourites among these fisherman, tints to become means of identifying houses during workdays on the sea; fishermen got a sense-relation, to where their homes stood, their backs to the land. Smoke climbed half chimneys and in the near harbour, plumes dissipated, leaving the pleasant scent of the year's first fires. November, 1944. Frost crystals in mud.

"I don't like it down there," said Adrian. "Too steep for me. Have my neck broke in no time. You go, ah... Rodney. Go inside the blue house where your mother is and bring her up here, like a good fellow. Tell her I'm up here."

"There's a dog down there."

"There's more than one, me son. They won't hurt you. And if they do I'll come and put the boots to whatever's chasing you. Go! Your mother and the baby got down. Go."

Rodney descended the hard clay path denoted by sporadic grass tufts. High above, Adrian saw distant ocean breakers wash in the tight harbour entrance to penetrate a calm water that quashed its force. Foam bits floated, sliver flashes struck. The path Rodney took wound its way to water's edge, its small stones long kicked free by climbing generations, by tired soles tramping a return. Adrian could not see his grandson, then heard a dog go berserk. He listened for the charge; for the moment to go mute. The dog was told to shut up – from deep within the house clusters. And, remarkably it did, though the communication subsequently commenced a canine chorus all along the Woody Shore. Adrian blew, to clear his nostrils. He shifted his weight.

Grace began the hill. With all dogs barking, stirring themselves into a fury, Grace huffed and puffed to reach the summit.

"Better be important. You couldn't come down?"

"I don't have my glasses."

"Yes. Right. Because you might be seen, is why. Ah, you and your queer ways. And, are you getting better with age? Not one bit. I have a baby down there, Dad."

"Read this, Grace."

Rodney rose, to stand alongside the pair. Grace held the white paper, in a fist when breezes arrived to blow it. She flicked the page, started at the part she had read. She grimaced, then looked at her father in the whitened way of the grandson. "True then? Grace? Tell me now, because I want to know!" Grace's face wore all the work a lifetime had given. She put a finger and a thumb to the bridge of her eyes. She looked again at the latter part of the letter, tried not to tear up in front of Rodney, yet the silent spillage that comes with the direst of moments easily betrayed her.

"Oh, Dad. She was just talking about him down there. He's in her thoughts, there, now. As we stand up here, Dad."

"Ah my, he was my eldest. Here, Grace, come now." But Adrian did not follow through, with the taking of her in his arms, despite much will prompting him. He turned rather, to take the moment for himself. "Young fellow," he said to Rodney. "Stand over there. No, back here then. We got to tell her, Grace. But you go, will you? I can't attempt the bank. Ah, to hell with it. We have to tell her right away. I do know that much. But I will take Rodney back if that's what you want, Grace. Should I come, or not?"

"Of course you should damn-well come, he was your son!"

"Calm down, I know he was. We'll all go then."

The three descended the path to the blue house with white trim when a yellow cur slinked from a hidden yard to head them off. Adrian lifted a leg and let a boot fly for its cowering backside, attempting a striking that in normal circumstances should effect all the hilarity in the world. The dog retreated without murmur, through a passageway behind Claire's.

The porch ceiling of the ancient home had the adults bent upon entrance. Then, over the threshold, in a dim passage, each grew taller. This was the back-end, the old section built away from the sea.

They stepped up for the kitchen, into which none removed footwear, but stood rather in what they wore, feeling awkward yet justified. A window, horizontally set in the deeper down-set living room, permitted sparkling sunlight, harbour deflected, to penetrate. It threw diamonds on pink asbestos wallboard. Dazzle travelled to where the three waited, wrists and necks wearing its bounty. The kitchen was warmed by the light. But the broken wind, blowing on the hollow bank high above, blowing the entire season, was missing. It made footing unsteady. Baking powder worked, yeast worked. Baby pabulum was in the close air. Adrian saw Grace's baby, laid out on table, cloth-diapered, squirming on a towel. It was a swollen-cheeked year-old infant child with black eyes oblivious, top hair curled, infantile ears, itsy-bitsy nostrils.

But in the draught of the open door, the sense of people having come in, made the infant child kick its legs. Its feet swung as motor parts, miniature fists pounded air like pistons. The little thing continued this way till it frightened itself with its enthusiasm and began to wail. Grace raised the child to restore calm, precisely when Claire appeared in the hall from her back bedroom.

She had gone to change her shirt – the baby had spit up on her – and to get Grace the promised letters. She had explained how the letters were funny in parts, and wanted to read bits aloud – if it were not too forward. The pages had been alongside her bed, to where she could turn and read, during her afternoon lay-down. Clifford was not much of a writer, but he was improving. His most recent was three foolscap in length and included the drawing of a bridge, and rushing water.

The beautiful Claire, Claire of the fiery hair, the prettiest girl North of Smokey. She stood in her own kitchen, wore her own mail-order tan slacks and short-sleeved V-neck. A sweater to match. Never a tall woman, she had lost weight. Had devilish eyes. Adrian looked at the glamorous daughter-in-law, she at him. Presentiment of change was all through him he knew, and he felt bad for it, wishing now he had washed. He noted her concern mostly, this immediate prescient ogle at his simply having set foot in her home. Yet, she refused direct question, for the moment, as to what was going on – and so the process had begun. Her whole person suffered intuition, with shoulders drawn, clavicle ridges exposed. Adrian saw more: he saw how these nicely cut, trim features would presently be chipped to learn the Truth arrived – how those features and to whatever they had aspired were about to shatter like a mirror. He wanted to turn away, be away.

This is what Grace could not understand. Why it was, that he could not witness these moments. He had lived longer than they! They didn't know, can't know. There was no strength left for it. Did they try to understand? And now, look here, wedged in to watch the breakage of features that, till now, till this mini-conspiracy orchestrating itself in the kitchen, had had the world before them. He prepared for the chipping-by-occurrence. Use of that same cold chisel carried for everyone alike.

Grace hushed the baby, put it in Adrian's arms.

She turned to Claire and took both shoulders. Claire listened, as they all listened to how Grace told it. There then came the mournful common plea that completely silences latent clicks and drumming hums found in every household. A plea to silence far-off choral dogs, wind brushing a house corner, to make the kitchen the most horrible of all places to be in: a single step forward, now, would bring a falling that had no end, and Adrian, here – holding a baby. He saw Rodney look away, as he himself had, the grandson then meeting the grandfather's glance. Atavistic features clear in both. Claire writhed in Grace's arms; Grace could not take her completely: the letter was in her hand, she did not want it crushed. But Claire held her own correspondences. With rolling shutting eyes, Claire flew disoriented, became wholly unmanageable. She soon dropped what she had. Yet her mind was clear, she knew the attraction her twisted shoulders had – even here.

Adrian wanted to step forward, to help both out of it. But his legs stood rooted like wild cherry wood in their loose pants. He pointed, pinched his fingers in cue for Rodney to take what had dropped from Claire, and from Grace, which the boy did, gathering all up well. Grace was here for her childhood friend. Poor Claire. Claire, who clammed up and just would not get up off the floor, a posture broken, posture supporting new knowledge, and for good.

Grace was not without strength in reserve. From the floor she raised and set her friend on a kitchen chair and held on, till Claire regained some sense. But sense came as madness, creeping over the face like the reaching legs of a huge spider, returning any look upon it a sight most unnerving. She bid hello to Adrian. To Rodney. She spoke at them, to explain how plainly none of this was true: Ha! And thank the Lord in Heaven, too. She would read her letters now, as proposed: if the others didn't think her too forward. Rodney? Thank you. These letters have travelled all the way from, Overseas. Did you know? There's this one to begin, it arrived at the post office on Tuesday. Claire would work her way back through the others, by way of date. That fine?

She read an opening, then fell off in mid-sentence to weep, to shake uncontrollably. She ordered everyone – out! Blasted them, first with eyes a thousand miles away that rolled to search ceiling plaster, eyes avoided presently: as if the most mortal of hazards. Her spine twisted in the chair, raking back spindles. Grace raised her voice at last, demanded control be taken! When, just at that moment, who but daughter Dawn Marie walked into the kitchen. She had been down at the water's edge, her first time alone, playing, getting her blouse dirty with red clay. The child removed her single-strap black shoes, set the pair neatly, on the mat. A narrow-shouldered youngster, she stood abreast her mother.

"Oh, honey."

"Why they here, Mom? You crying, Mom?"

"Oh, honey," she said unable to give more. "Oh, honey."

Dawn Marie came around to stand before her, a hand to a shoulder, comfort afforded the woman, but the hand especially, too much to bear. Claire looked steady at the child's eyes, "Daddy was hurt."

"He's not coming back?"

Grace reached for the tiny closing hand pulling free. She clutched it tightly.

"He is coming, Mom? He is coming."

That was as far as Claire got with the girl. Grace in plain whisper finished the job and the child threw a tantrum, returning that it was lies, stupid lies. That she wanted everyone, out! She pointed.

"Come, hear! Smarten up I said! Listen you, you be strong. Don't then."

Through fat tears of post-acceptance, the girl said: "I will be."

"Go home, Dad," said Grace. "Take the baby. I'll be there when I can."

Adrian felt the plush of the baby blanket at his neck. He smelled burp. He kept quiet. He made sure he did not squeeze too much, to begin. He lifted his chin for Rodney to follow. But when outside, the shock came: that Grace asked *him* to take the bundle – up the hill.

twenty-six

Adrian would have protested this allocation of responsibility. He had held babies, his own. He understood how they were cared for, but to carry one up the Woody Shore hill? It worried him. The child was quiet now, could it be counted on to continue? It was a long way home. With Rodney in lead, Adrian stepped from the corner of the white-trimmed house and into a salt breeze over green grass. The yellow cur watched from its neighbouring yard, silent and comprehensive in its fear. But no bark, no chain reaction.

"Go up easy, Rodney, I say. Case I drop her. She's without a murmur, let's keep it that way."

They ascended, stopping for Adrian to catch his breath. Rodney showed how to use the long grass tufts. At the summit they looked back out over the smoking chimneys of pitched rooftops. They listened for the sea while Adrian took his moment. "No dogs went haywire, one good point. She's taking it awful hard. Ah, how much more, for a person? It doesn't surprise me how much."

They kept to the road, when it turned midday all of a sudden. The sun no longer hit wagon tracks as it had in summer, to light ruts and potholes. "These winter shadows. The speed they creep in! It seemed like only yesterday we were dying of heat. Stay close to me, bai." The grandson followed, but eyed the footing to come and was set to speak of anything wayward. Ground foliage held autumn brass and fall copper despite the leaves down everywhere: a feature of November. But someone approached on the road. A husky man. Adrian trimmed his eyelids, then shook off a prescience that hit. He would have to speak to this person to account for himself. But it went beyond that. He stood paralysed, the event of the Shore coming in storm force with the horror of the child tumbling from his arms, that of his falling with her, to crush her. Oh. This hour of day? This *day*? But one of his grown sons, approached! A loud raven crowed, adjusted on a branch; a harsh sparrow flitted in crispy leaves, deafening sounds both. The features. Clifford? I witness his ghost? It has to come only thus: real as life itself is real. Eyes are playing tricks, coincidence and consciousness: coinciding. A stranger – had to be. But the stranger had the air, the walk of one who belonged too well in the region, one away, tramping now preciously through geography entirely known. Shadows fell, the cracked crackled. A rushed breeze stirred fallen foliage. High cloud sailed.

"Grandfather? Why you stopping?"

Who said that! Who spoke – Rodney? The boy doesn't see it coming? I'm in his way, am I? Adrian needed to shake his head properly. He looked down, blinked. Baby. Apparitions. No one was coming. Bear in mind, this child he's carrying. That the peculiar activity of holding an infant, alone, meant no dream could be present. It was the fall air, outdoors, consistency all around. Dreams come in bits. Why had he not eaten? Because lately there was no cause, just no cause. He looked up. He saw the winter coat. The empty sleeve.

"Grandfather! From the radio! Uncle Frank."

"Don't shake me, kid! I'll drop her – yet! But you're right, all right. That's just who it is, thank the Father in Heaven."

Frank called out hello and increased pace to meet his father, to help him over the marsh section of the road. He touched with a heavy boot for dryness and tossed down his heavy pack.

"Dad? What in the hell? And, with an infant in your arms?"

"Take her, me son, take her. Don't drop her. Here. Jesus, bai, I say, Jesus. Your looks have changed. You'll never believe who I thought it was, coming. You got your hair all short?"

"To look a little presentable. Who, who did you think it was? Good day, Rodney."

"We heard you on the radio, Uncle Frank. You have your belt?"

"Not on me, no. What's going on, Dad? Something's up."

"Give me a second, I'll tell you. Oh, I've been on edge, worried about dropping that bundle all the way up from the Woody Shore. She was right good. I'm amazed."

"Quite the way to greet a fellow, I know that, passing him a newborn."

"That's Mary Anne, your niece."

"She ain't the lightest thing in the world. My shoulder's shot, from my pack."

"It is? Bad news, Frank. And I'm sorry to have to dish it out here. Your brother Clifford, overseas. We just got word. And I wish to God the word were otherwise, but he's gone, Frank. The government letter came this morning."

"What? When? Clifford?"

"I don't know when, I don't know a thing. Let's just get to the house for now. I'm sick of this business and want to get home where I can sit five minutes. Think, for five."

Rodney watched Frank, as Adrian went behind and fitted the boy with his uncle's pack. "Sure you can you carry it now?"

"I can carry it."

The company followed the shaky black spruce with rising iodine harbour breeze penetrating to reach them.

"How did you know where to find us, Frank? You just happen by? Or suppose you went to the house first – someone at the Fairway told you, I bet. Near the Post Office, that place. They probably all know down there. Down-the-road knows your business before you do, especially when those large letters appear. Ah, Clifford. I need a moment, Clifford."

"Frank, Dad."

"I know it is."

"I should go back. See Claire. What do you think?"

"You mind following us home first? I haven't had a bite since yesterday evening, not that I'm hungry. But I got a fairly good scare back there on the road. It played me right out for some reason. The young fellow needs to be fed. Let the girls cry it out. There's no women tougher, but they need their cry. Your sister Grace is with her."

They came upon the sloping gold grass of Shea's Field where each was presented the supreme view of the bouyant Atlantic and Smokey Mountain floating on it. Precipitous cloud in floral hue, laced with chipped pitch, hung over the mountain visage. Spindrift broke at the Gut.

"I don't know how close you two were, Frank. You and him. I suspected there was bad blood. He was never an awful fellow. Not for all his silent ways, he wasn't."

Frank favoured his shoulder, adjusted the baby.

"That where the anchor caught you?"

"They broadcast that?"

"They broadcast that, and more than that. It was in the *Post Record* and the Halifax paper, two days running."

"I read the article for Grandfather," said Rodney. "We listened to the radio that night, but the static broke everything up."

"You ever look like your Uncle William ... ah, ... Rodney. Dead spit. No. That anchor stunt was me showing off, someone else too eager for a photo. They lifted it onto me, then let go of it. A spiteful move, but spite never seems far off. Foolishness. I'm home for good, got a little money from my time away. A racket, all that, and nothing more. All it ever was. Shifty people in a shifty world. You hear from William?"

"Not a word from William, for a long time from William."

"You all right, Dad?"

"I'm not, Frank. I'm not."

They moved over level ground, past the wild rose of dry ditching. Not a petal hung: burgundy, berry-shaped hips merely, set for birds that winter. Trembling aspen twirled scant leaves. Their light rustle dropped whisper and sigh. A general hush came among the iron undergrowth. Houses appeared, curtains drew.

At home Frank began a big meal with cans he had brought. Mary Anne whimpered in her fatigue, but soon drifted off between a couple of thin pillows with the stuffing gone, found on the front room couch. They had put her in the dog's basket, using a clean towel, then decided to keep her visible. Frank raised the basket to the table. He caught a section of the baby blanket on a nail under the radio shelf, building a tent to provide shade from the 100-watt bulb. He was mindful of the likelihood of suffocation from material. Spoke of it, touching the nail head.

"There a bottle? Formula?"

"She didn't give me one. She'll be by before long. I think there's Pablum here, but Frank, get on that chair and unscrew that bulb. The doorway bulb is more than plenty."

"Leave it on, Dad. I've been too long out-of-doors and today's no day to keep in the dark. You got dry wood?"

"I do, I'm doing well with the wood."

"Have bacon any in?"

As Frank prepared the meal of corned beef and Irish stew, he stopped to look below. Mililica was at his feet.

"Don't tell me! That thing alive yet? It has to be ninety-five."

He gave the dog a section of bacon fat and she carried the treat under the table, where she growled, convinced someone approached.

"She must get that behaviour from you, Dad," said Frank. Mililica munched the fat.

A sombre, more efficient feel was in the house, thought Frank. Possibly, from the new location of the furniture in the kitchen. The coveted wood chair, previously positioned between stove and window, had been taken out and shoved behind the table, where it pressed the wall, its arms out of sight. At the stove and window was a cushioned chair: slim, floral, ornate. Frank would take this away, as it posed a fire hazard. The sock-box was near the table, pulled out from the wringer washer alcove: within reach. News of Clifford made this a stranger's home. A day or two would settle the news, when time came to nudge it aside, some. Frank watched his father. He had planned right away to tell the old man of the event befallen him on his trip. It mattered none. None of it mattered.

There were potatoes, pickled chow from a jar. Adrian kept the HP sauce to himself, at his elbow. The bottle's white cap was not screwed, but set crooked on top. This was custom, in advance of Frank's return. The long table wore the pattern of a huge sunflower in its cloth cover. Frank finished his portion and got up to rinse his plate.

"They didn't say, how, in the letter? Who's got the letter?"

"We left it. She does, your sister, Grace. They addressed it home here. No, nothing about how. That would be a lot for them, Frank. To speak of every case."

Frank had been drinking liquor. Adrian smelled it: saw the zealous hand gesture. Frank had the half-flask tucked in his pants pocket but it jutted through material. He knew he would go out into the backroom, stash it in his hung jacket. But not before he sat longer with the others. He called down to the dog, when pulling in his chair. She started a steady growl after Frank let up on patting. "Now you shut up, you," said Frank. Adrian looked up. Rodney did not. The dog's dim recollection and curiosity translated to uncertain behaviour. The animal squirmed from under the table and looked up at the three. What were they up to? Rocking its way to the stove space, it got under the cushioned chair, with a sigh.

"Dad?"

"What?"

"Pass Rodney the HP. I see he wants it but won't ask."

"He'll ask if he wants it, that fellow."

But Adrian did as asked and the boy put brown sauce on his potatoes.

"It's a sad business," said Frank.

"Sad is right."

"We'll pull through. Don't you well worry about that."

"Pull through, Frank. That's all we ever do. Pull through... we're experts. I'm not thinking about it. You shouldn't."

Rodney finished his plate then stood over the sink. He reached the long way to open the faucet, which poured cold water over the dish. The pump in the cellar cut in and, running to regain lost pressure – finding it again, it clicked off. Rodney ran the water longer than necessary before finishing with the plate, knife and fork. He washed his hands with soap then dried them on a dishcloth. The men paid attention: the boy was hardly afraid of the home. He had the freckles, the brazen looks of all his uncles. The baby on the table squirmed. They looked. Dark features there made their study of the world. The flue caught the wind east, as dry wood spat, as the pump, from its second running, clicked off.

twenty-seven

Frank came to see Claire only on the day of the Mass for Clifford. Circumstance made him uncomfortable: history. But this was also his first time in their home. Claire opened the door.

"I thought I would see you before this, you were one of the ones I wanted to see before. Come in. Dawn Marie can't be alone, I myself am dead on my feet in the evenings. Otherwise, I can say we're holding it together."

When Frank sat, Claire asked him to stand, to come see Dawn Marie speak to her dolls; a make-believe tea party was in progress in the living room. The little girl kept her back to the kitchen. "It's the first time she's out there on her own. Must be your presence. I told her you were coming. My God but children can be a source. Stick them in a twelve-by-eighteen tarpaper shack, raise them and they'll find some way to while away the darkest hour."

Claire spoke with good eye contact except for pupils going larger than Frank remembered. His father had been right about how sorrow, strictly, affects the face. Hers was sallow – less distinctive in the way strokes of signature become over time. Shoulders were drawn ahead as if roped, neck taut. She was thinner, shorter; coif lacked lustre, beauty marks at temple and chin all but faded.

Frank stayed only as long as it took for a cup of tea, but returned before week's end. There were jobs to do around the place, tasks she had set aside for her husband's return. She asked Frank if he would not mind somehow shovelling the truckload of the winter coal in through the cellar window. She hadn't got last winter's inside and the snow covered it, giving her an awful time; she had to break through with a pick. Frank borrowed the short-handled shovel of his father's to get the load in, one pail at a time. It was slow work. He found a five-gallon Planter's Peanuts bucket and, by lowering this to the inside frost wall sill, walking around to enter the house, he was able to crawl the bucket down the ladder, backwards. Coming in the house frequently furthered an ease forming between him and Claire. She laid newsprint down in the hall for him to walk over. He had the coal in by December.

Claire's people took care of her. Frank silently watched how the Woody Shore folk were good to each other. Her uncle, Daniel Dunphy sent over dried cod for the winter and four cords of seasoned spruce logs. He knew Frank was around the place and so came personally to ask that Frank might buck up the firewood and get it into the cellar alongside the coal; extra sticks could go in around the woodstove, the porch. To ensure stove-lengths, Frank measured spruce chunks with the handle of the axe. A bush bucksaw he kept filed did the work. He was conscious of Claire and Dawn Marie in the window, watching him work. To chunk the heavy wood, he used a splitting maul his father had found and had fitted with a hickory axe handle. The splitting maul slammed through the widest of chunks, turning the otherwise heavy ordeal into the mere making of kindling. Frank worked tools at half handles. The very biggest chunks required the iron wedge. He was unable to hold the wedge till he learned to strike the surface with the axe to start a split.

The cordwood took weeks. By the first day of winter he had finished all splitting and in three days got most everything in out of the weather. Christmas snow arrived in timely but lasting fashion, turning bluster to bitter cold, recalling promptly-forgotten frozen waltzes that wound at windowsills and brushed door boxes. Claire motioned to Frank from the kitchen window. She had tinsel in one hand, a tea pot in the other. He entered and smelled the fir tree, felt its humidity. He saw the threaded popcorn.

"I can't take the house," Claire said, in the kitchen.

"What's wrong with the house?"

"Nothing is. I need to get out. I'm not the type who finds it easy not to see people, not to be out amongst society. In my twenties yet, Frank. Couple years older than you, look all you done. Surely that's not all life has to offer a person."

"You've done a lot."

"There's a Christmas tournament, at Mary Helen's. Pairs cribbage."

"Pairs cribbage? Now – look out!"

"Why? The winners are to be crowned king and queen. I wouldn't mind going, I mean you taking me."

"Now look out, Claire," said Frank leaning in his spindle-back chair past its squeak. He drew on his cigarette and squinted an eye in corpulent smoke: he had rolled a tight one.

"Claire! Have a little sense! How nice would that look, now."

"How nice would what look! How? What? Afraid of being the subject of attention? They're already talking. Those with no life of their own. Not to worry, none of that crew will be there. And to hell with them if they are there. A person will never do a thing again, if they have to consider first what others think. I'm just glad to be considering about going out at all. Shows I'm coming along."

"You are. But let's keep to tea, for present." Frank set his cigarette in the beanbag ashtray, then raised it again. "And her? What about, Dawn?"

"I can leave her next door. They got kids."

Claire measured out the pot. Frank lifted the tinned milk to blow caked holes.

"You were planning on going whether I went or not. Weren't you?"

"It's better to arrive with a partner, for cards. I knew you would. You got spine."

Frank shook his head, blew on his tea and sipped.

262

The night was a Saturday. Outside, frosts of high altitude winter trickled down the atmosphere as if soot shaken from a flue. Tall, over mountain ridges, impressed stars waited like poked holes viewed inside a kettle. Crackling footfall reached chill ears and gloved hands pushed as balls, into pockets, forearms going tight against ribs. Frank spoke of the minus twenty-one degrees. He was glad for it, for its ability to clear the head. He was aware too: it kept them close.

"Frank?"

"Right here."

"Nervous?"

"I am. Always was. To be around people, no matter the occasion."

"Ah, don't be. Silly card game. By the way, no liquor."

"Why you telling me that?"

"Why? Your clothes, I smell it all hours of the day off them. Your cheeks are beginning to develop those little veins. I'm the one picking up your coat when you leave it on the chair. Your tiny flask, you carry … right … here. Feel, here near your tin of smokes." Claire held the back of her glove at Frank's left side, brushing till she raised the flask an inch.

"Your equipment, mister. Never was. Keep it from the rest, not from me. I know what's going on. I just don't speak of things."

"The way you're not speaking of things now. And, care? All of a sudden?"

"What do you mean, care? It's high time someone said something."

"I got my reasons, Claire. Never healed, from the start. I planned to have it checked, few times. Arm-wrestling ruined it altogether. No time given to get over the tenderness."

"That helps?"

"Better that than anything else, I found. I've looked … waited."

"Suit yourself. I won't speak of it again. You know I won't. You're entirely your own person. I'd see a doctor if my body was giving me trouble. Take the proper route."

Frank halted. They had reached the Fairway Market where no electric light burned in winter and the blackness and cold made the community fixture all-but-lost to close alders and dead snow. Frank undid the top button of his jacket.

"You'll catch your death, you. What?"

"I want to show you something. A thing you might not have seen."

Frank reached inside his jacket and took out his silver flask. He held it in his armpit while he bit off his glove and, with his teeth, he unscrewed the cap. He upset its contents, a thin dribbling beginning into snow. Shaking it empty, screwing its cap back on, he chucked the vessel up behind the Fairway.

"Not done. These too, because one doesn't seem to ever want to miss the company of the other."

He produced his cigarettes, not his tinned hand-rolled but a package of store-bought. End for end he held the package, when from top down he curled his hand to snap and crush bodies. Not one to litter, he returned the destroyed cigarettes to his pocket. The flask would be found in spring, used again; he had bought that in Boston. As he did up the buttons of his coat, Claire stepped forward.

"Let me help. No, never saw the likes of *you* before."

"Nothing has me, Claire. I have been fortunate about that."

"You showed it. But, Jesus…"

"But Jesus what?"

"Liquor, I can see. But a full pack of smokes? Store-bought? Never crush store-bought, Frank."

She rapped his chest and smiled easily into the dark before bumping him hard with a right shoulder, knocking him flat on his back. He got up, snapped his glove at her as she pushed away with a squeal that echoed over the baby mountains of Park Headquarters. She returned to him, shrugged her shoulders and took his hand, after he had bitten the glove back on. "Frozen?" she said, holding the gloved hand in both hers, rubbing it, then keeping it a considerable part of the way down to Mary Helen's. Nearing the two-storey, she felt the need to adjust her scarf. And clearing her throat, she touched her collar twice before returning her hands, to her own pockets.

*P*artnered at the slim card table, sitting opposite, the two glanced at one another. During play, they made faces and kicked legs under the table. When waiting out a game, they sat in silence on red spindled chairs set up at the entrance. The feeling was that other players encouraged their closeness. Winks and nods came as what could be taken as approval. For what? Players stood generously aside for the two to pass, as a pair, when there was a change in seating, another game to commence.

Hostess Mary Helen kept laying down her cards then forgetting where they were. She rose to tend to the two big pots of tea she had going, or to remove wax paper from another tray of egg and tuna sandwiches. The folks at her table hollered at her, she hollered at them. "Land sakes! Factory wheels need grease! Operation, production! I said I'm coming!" But she'd hurry off again. "Enough!" they shouted, "How do you expect a serious game to be played out with your rising?" She laughed and laughed and thought – the wonder in having guests over! If people knew! If they knew! My rising?

Father Archie MacDonald arrived with three nuns, and sporting concessions were made to get the clergy readily and fully in on the matches. Father Archie had brought his own deck, a brand spanking new one. Great to-do was made of this, hoots and jeers came.

"What's wrong! A man taking pride in the playing of a hand?"

"Long as it's not money he's taking, in the playing of a hand!"

"You'll get money!"

The black-attired nuns in horn rimmed glasses frosted yet, felt good at being inside, out of the cold. They had marshalled through deep snow from the Glebe. Never overly warm in garments parish life afforded them, they nevertheless had taken the extreme trek in happy stride. They were elderly, the trio. "We doubled up our nylons! How can cold bother us, the aim being cakes and tea!" They laughed with closing eyes, with reserved smiles, unpainted lips, and wetted teeth. Each wore identical plush-lined buckled boots.

The nuns knew Claire. Knew of her. Claire had come from the most extraordinary card players North of Smokey. Her grandfather, namely Malcolm Ranald, was the best card player in Ingonish. Claire explained, and none doubted, how the family gathered around the kitchen table, four feet from the wood stove every frosty night wintering up at MacGean's Interval. She was a child, but remembered how the old man was given a deck every Christmas. By Easter, he had the ears worn off.

"Yes. He went around with ink on his fingers, black on his tongue. He loved Solitary. We thought for the longest time something was wrong with his head. He liked to play cards. All are notable for one thing and the best stick to the one thing. Group games could hardly be played, sensibly, what with the ears worn off. Didn't stop us. Playing with decks like that teaches earnestness, remembering what was played beforehand."

"Anyone ever beat him? Malcolm?"

"No one ever did."

They looked at Frank, they didn't mean to. He waved.

Frank switched his game, to one of memory. In conjunction with the consistent play of Claire, the two began a winning streak. The tally showed they led at break, then a few more games made it impossible for any to catch them. They took the tournament, becoming king and queen. Mary Helen, in possession of a hand-wound eight-millimetre movie camera, brought the device out for the final game; her aim to capture every face. When the crowning was over and the parade began in which pairs strode in linked arms around the living room, she was ready. All were morbidly shy; some horrified to see the lens point their way. Maynard Doherty assisted Mary Helen. Maynard Doherty had come to the card game, singly. Mary Helen instructed him on the proper way to hold the rack of lights, to ensure suitable illumination was got for filming indoors. "Lights are what make the star, Maynard. So get up on that chair or I'll brain you." Maynard had to leave the floor, get on a spindle chair, with the blinding bulbs, the brightest and hottest any had ever seen. Squinting subjects added a comedic effect to whatever was being preserved.

Frank managed to avoid much of the filming by making a trip to the outhouse. In the spirit of friendliness, he walked toward Maynard who had climbed down. He asked if the lights were hot.

"Hot? Only as the hinges of hell," he said. "That's all, for frig sakes."

Frank held his crown against his hip. He and Maynard were peers. Both had stayed back from the war. Maynard may have thought Frank's question came oddly in relation to the issue. His people were touchy, it was common knowledge. Frank's brothers had gone. One brother gave his life. There was talk concerning Maynard, of feet, fallen arches – a twisted spine, even. His condition could not have been too poorly; he shovelled Mary Helen's walk, got up on her roof to clear the snow.

"See that knuckle. Melted."

"Quite a gadget, that movie camera. Sorry, I've never seen one before."

"People have them. Your Claire looks the happy one tonight."

"She's not my Claire. She needed to get out is all. I've been helping around the house, getting her and the little one set up for winter."

"Might be winter a long time."

"Might be. Claire's on her own. It's tough even for people who have someone with them all the time."

"She won't want for long, perhaps."

Frank had been looking away when this final unkindness came. The burnt finger, no education; these left a hole in social skills. Frank left it at that. Fortunately Cletus Williams was nearby and, having just put on Claire's crown, began to act the fool. He fluttered both eyes and leapt, waltzed his heavy paunch toward centre floor and bent low before taking off in a pirouette. When space was available, Mary Helen wove roughly to Maynard. "Cletus! Do it again! No, Maynard, up on the chair again. Hold them straight this time. Down. Direct them down, I said."

A winded Cletus leapt a third time, to move for a lady who was no longer capturing, but directing.

𝒜 sullen Frank exhaled vaporously. He tramped over snow crust. Desire came plenty for the spilt rum. He'd fight it, in the spirit his father, ironically, had mentioned – of knowing only to pull through.

It was the walk home, and he and Claire were distanced. There was no wind, dim stars twinkled. It had to be thirty below. Yes. To get through all the years, to pull through. Was a mind free enough to pull through? Ever? Frank had been trapped this past while. Half-drunk. One pays vague attention to a world around them, half-drunk. There were deaths in the community he learned of only much later. There'd been the showing up to help out Claire, nothing beyond. Except this, talk, what he sensed in the later night. It had been going on awhile.

Claire coughed. She suspected Frank suffered the liquor; his sudden taciturn manner told her. Desire had to run its course, like all things. Claire had not expected the two to be paraded around Mary Helen's living room; and a second time before leaving; and in front of the clapping fold, in front of a chittering camera.

"You know I've always liked our chats. You got your daughter to think about."

"What do you mean? Why you speaking of her?"

"People can make it tough if they want. No matter what you think. I know it. Talk hurts. It cuts people down. That priest didn't even look me in the eye."

"How can he – when the old clown has one that wanders? Oh, him. Forget him. What's bringing this on? Someone say something? Did they?"

"How long has it been? Hardly a season, Claire. Stop and think a moment."

She shook her head, clicked her tongue.

"There's marriage. Maybe in the spring. If it'll lighten the burden, make card games right."

"For Christ's sake."

"I'm only offering to help out."

"Nothing happened!"

"Not in their minds."

"Whose minds are the concern?"

"Our own, Claire."

"I never had time, Frank. You got things confused, again."

"I shouldn't have said anything. It was just some decency I thought I was offering. I couldn't care less what others think."

"Sure, you couldn't care less. Decency. Listen, don't think about me. What we got – had even – was friendship, Frank. Something never found between a man and a woman, outside the larger ordeal. That might be the most precious of all there is, to have. I believe it is. You ruining that?"

"How's anything ruining anything? It would be helping."

"Not helping...."

"I come down the road every evening, Claire. Your house is close to those others."

"Well, I ain't moving it. I ain't making that walk up the hill. Stay home with your father. No one needs you to come. No one asked you to. He needs you more than I ever will."

"Him? He doesn't need a soul, him. Tough as nails."

"Exactly how you were supposed to be. Too bad you weren't, Frank. We can't just concentrate on getting through the winter? That's all I want. What I want above all. I'm lonely, yes, but I want nothing more. Better you don't come around no more, then. And I don't like being put on the spot, hear me?"

"Spot? All right, I hear you."

Frank lost this one, yet felt the ease at having cleared the air. For the rest of the journey neither spoke and Frank thought of how he had not planned to say what he had, that the thing came like all utterances of will: without petitioning, and in preface, to change in life. She was right about one thing. He was hardly tough as nails.

The two moved for the last of the Woody Shore. Distance and time cooled nothing in their hearts. They followed the road, its tracing black ridge of harbour ice pressing hidden into the snowdrifts on land. Low tide: reshaping, ice accommodating ice, receiving more of the freezing influx that never ceases in the early black broken night.

At her door, Claire lowered her eyes in goodbye. Frank refused them. He got his face under hers and his mouth on her mouth. She pulled away with a muted cry then slid through the door soundlessly.

Both hearts sped. Both waited, with wood between, till a slow latch passed over and clicked downward.

Frank walked in the soft steps of the thief after fresh crime. No one had seen, windows were black, latent fires minimal, or latent fires cold: an air with only brief traces of wood gases. The hour, witching.

In amongst the trees, below the road, the shape of his own home then, in the emptiness of frigid night. Frank went toward it, thinking of commitment – of taking care of oneself too. A sound person is necessary, to create accord with another. Still, why was it men looked so hard to find women? And why after finding them did they stay with them so long as they did? It had to make sense, he knew. Down the banked path to childhood shingles, walls, a roofline allowing a draught of smoke. Here, a fire burned. There needs to be allowance, to help the other. Acknowledgement. Society steps in and it did, seemed to, tonight. Comfort, alleviate suffering; it can only be condoned. She needs a strong back. She's right. It is the best thing.

The inside latch of the door was not over. It was the outside clasp that had frozen; the difference in temperature between this side and that caused the freezing. Frank turned away and pushed through the thigh-deep road-facing drift to come to just above his father's window, his pillow. He beat the pane.

"That you?" came instantly from within, below.

"It's me."

The old man was not alarmed. He came eagerly and in self-possession. He wholly liked to see his son, and hardly minded a disturbance like this, at night, in winter. Being disturbed here is often the best thing there is in the world. Ah, how lonely a proposition, to bed singly in a house once full, the darkest hour of year having returned for you and all you have. "You'll never believe who I thought it was, at the door."

twenty-eight

The village pushed through the frozen season. And the month of May kept its promise: to ease snow back up the mountain, to bring down in rills, chill waters falling. Warmed yards began around houses and green shoots shot past burned or flattened or yellowed grasses. It was the third Sunday in May and the parish priest had brought his Roman Catholic flock onto the strong beams of Dunphy's Wharf. The occasion was the yearly blessing of the village fishing fleet, the spiritual appeal for good catches and reasonable safety among families possessed of fishing territory and gear. The day gave high sunny ceilings although a fresh wind stripped nearby airs of pleasantry. Old men rowed skiffs through the bottleneck inlet or had young sons of improving strength draw oars. Families perched on sloop bows or settled in behind rowing spaces and sterns. Young children, who clawed the breast, lowered drooling mouth, and with increasingly less innocent fingers poked the directions boats did not take.

Frank and Adrian had come, with Claire and young Dawn. The little girl wore the frill dress and white gloves her mother had purchased from the mail-order catalogue in anticipation of the girl's First Communion. Both Frank and Claire thought they would have to work on Adrian, to coax him to attend the ceremony. Surprisingly and with little fuss the elder agreed, despite twenty-odd years of avoiding the blessing of anything.

The four joined Grace and her family on the wharf. And, along with other broods, they gave their all to Father Archie MacDonald, who presently, with widening purple robes of gesturing arms, gathered petitioners forward. A robin's-egg sky fixed heights then, a stiff breeze in it giving promise of steady passage for fractured cloud. Maintained at a seaside altitude, a less oblique flag flapped at the storage building's peak before stretching eastward. Reverend MacDonald took up his stainless steel aspergillum from its stainless steel aspersorium, which a senior altar boy, his first mustache noticeable, had positioned in tilt. The priest flicked his club and internal reservoirs wetted with holy sprinkle the marine wood, while his murmured cleric oaths went again without question among patrons of sidelong vessels tied wharf-front and wharf-side.

"Hold up, Father. Straggler."

The congregation craned its neck, stood on tiptoe to see a final dory row the inlet. It came bow-first with rinsed raising oars spilling brine. The rower gave the suggestion of pride, of skill, through the wind-touched water; he drew a dignified, trained shoulder. A low cap worked his peak, but did not hide the barber's recent clipping; shearing done to document the high white nape of a sinewy neck. The tardy rower offered back only. The tarnished barque was wholly unfamiliar, save to one family whose members knew the craft well, and better yet, its association.

The profile slid before the arrested flock and eyes shifted focus from this boater to this family presently most stirred, most forlorn. Eyes compared ancestral traits, here, to gain fairer assessment in what they saw, there.

Adrian looked and, for the second time, felt this whole-body clutching, the breaking fear of reality gone haywire, of distortion imposing on him its belligerent spheres and cranky squares. Too often, important meaning comes, but why at the public moments? And, why, profound meaning manifesting itself through shoulder shudder and spine spasm, to unravel at his feet the maze string denoting no longer where he had entered?

Instances of old age, he knew. Or the phenomena, at least. But this was most disconcerting: to disturbingly dream reality out here on this wharf. Approaching was his son. Clifford – in the fishing dory the son built, a vessel laid up since the war. It had been an error on the road that day – with Frank. Surely to God it is erroneous now. Yes. William, of course. I always got those boys mixed up. People did. William. Second son, back from a war officially over some time, though the community had sighted stragglers. William, bringing his dead brother's boat, in dignified gesture of commemoration, signifying his own heartfelt return. New strength, this gesture: that which he picked up while away. Yes, William would take on such a project, yes, after hard travelling overseas especially. Adrian had the poems dog-eared. He had them tucked in beside the radio. At night he studied their inscription. He loved his son.

Father Archie MacDonald, open palms raised amid brash whispers, lowered vocals to a sepulchre strain, half-waiting himself for the drama to play itself out. The youngest altar boy, a trailer, had opened at the green ribbon the pulpit bible – the King James. Perhaps a little audacious, a little too weighty for such an occasion. The tome. The boy strained under its spine. Father MacDonald fully paused then. He would wait: a moment at least. A priest, of course, faces like instances from time to time, when calm, decent ceremony best shelters vested authority under threat. "Close it," he said, intimately. "Close it, lower it," he nodded to the altar boy.

The latecomer slid into view, to dock. Congregational men bobbed heads in the general direction, while women of the same held fast their troubled faces. Children were discomfited: first, this attention paid the priest – now, patience, in secrets undermining.

But all got underway again with an, "Ahem," and the ceremony did undeniably bestir with a priestly: "Well... then...," although, try what he may, the cleric MacDonald could not regain utter control. Gravity had resulted at the boatman's arrival, gravity putting to voice a much harped-on suspicion of late, one Father MacDonald with an intensive ear picked up: "*The two were – are – living together. Blood.*"

The whisper of a single name then. First names volleyed. Yet the man in the dory waited respectfully at docking beams, at bumping treadless tires. A hand was near, but he had not yet committed himself to the iron ladder. "*This was Clifford! This was not the middle, this was the eldest!*" Those who never left the community swore such; their eyes were not to be deceived. Whichever brother, the facial bones cut some – awful gaunt representation of what was – or, misrepresentation, be it the case. The whole aspect in a man, altered; swayed greatly from any Curtis line, from any endemic Ingonish character. This was a ravaged soul, that which a ravaged body merely supports, as a mouldy stick might laden plants.

The majority took its impression while Father MacDonald, housed six years, therefore still relatively new to the parish had the sense to be patient, in the unravelling mystery, the removal of shroud from the newcomer. A priest simply submits to historical involvement, at times. Military digs, shoulder boards, under a long rain jacket: the erect rower poised in perfect, powerful connection. He had to be one of the region's own. The priest embraced, perhaps for the first time, the disquieting truth that one must: that he and the Church could not ever wholly gain possession here. They stood outside, knocking in plea at heavy doors, soliciting from the threshold among the nodding company of other outsiders never born to this soil.

And yet he went on, in unwavering voice. He wished the most hearty, most bountiful season of catches ever, as was due this humble village fleet during the coming good spring weather. The altar boy's arms failed. A buckling elbow brought the book down. The priest raised a chin, had the senior boy take it. No, keep it. With rough dashes of holy water, he nodded, tapped on the closed book, terminated the ceremony.

Children broke rank. In cheer, in play, they chased over the renewed hallowing of a wharf. They had made it! All the way through the second rite! The first, a regular Sunday Mass, till midmorning – hadn't that been enough? Then, this! Matrons slapped young heads, maintaining a keen, furtive eye on the latecomer. Light began the speech in their tongue and soon unwavering revolutionary opinion came of child rearing, brisk temperature yet, of washing sheets with success now that winter was done, of bingo wins and losses. And yes, of course, fine days to come.

The thin fellow climbed the wharf. The thin fellow bent, turned to better secure his boat, working bony hands to rope an iron stay, keeping sharp shoulders to the crowd. Say nothing. Look to none in particular.

Brave patrons of the wharf, in pairs and threes, feigned no talk on secondary topics. Their stares closed parameters. Chief Brendan Neil, a blunt man – this side of ceremony; a reformed alcoholic by conviction, a community notary, rocked forward. The matter bothered him heartily and, as acting Fire Chief of the Ingonish Beach Volunteer Fire Department, well … he had to say something. He knit knuckles.

"Jesus, how I hate to ask. Is it Clifford? Or the brother, William?"

"It's me."

"I know that but me which?"

"Clifford." It was a hollow, wispy voice.

A light handshake. Its initiator, Brendan, then took the man's forearm as well. Others lined up behind the Chief to greet their community member back from the war: revelation, broke wide.

Clifford agreed five times to his being the man each had "from the start" suspected he was. "Yes, they got us mixed up," he was at last cornered into saying, but to them as a group, most approximate, most intimate – a concerted knitted brow followed this knowledge. Confusion cleared, to make visible this deeper sense of what it was to live – a sense that none articulated, except that it might be approximate to… well, the pool in a rain barrel. Yes. Joy and sadness, above all, life's ironies, mixed deep below. Oh, it nourishes us. It also keeps its mysterious colours. You can't take it to bed. A rain barrel.

Clifford Curtis was no longer what he was. Clifford Curtis had left a broad-shouldered, sharp-eyed hunter, a man of the water. He returned a potato jacket, emptied of fruit, spoilt, ready to discard – broken and roughened by what a person must inevitably face, over there: out there, up over Smokey. Men paraded, but Clifford left them a consolatory brow, an upward chin. Lines furrowed his forehead.

He walked to his wife where he put on, then took off, his cap and looked, lips tight. Dawn was alongside, below. Putting a knee on the hard wharf, Clifford got down to aim attention with less provocation here. He looked too intently into the eye of the daughter. However, she broke.

"Don't cry, Dawn Marie? This is your father. I'm home, now."

Dawn could only press against her mother's skirt and, try as she might, she could not hide with hands and cloth her misty pupils. Clifford stood and squared once more to Claire. But she dipped forward, eased to his shoulder in feminine falling, her whole person overcome. She cried lavishly. A little *too* perhaps for those peering from less discreet angles. Were these even real tears?

"Take it easy," said Clifford, to her. "A lot in one day, I know it is. Come now. Claire?"

She responded to the name. He pulled her back, took her shoulders side-on; then saw his brother.

"There he is. The champ. How are you, Frank?"

"Hello, Clifford."

"I followed your competitions when I was able. You're not on the road?"

"All that was all a while back, Clifford. I'm going back out soon, though."

Clifford nodded and reached for his father's hand. "Come here, you. Jesus, Dad? You're paler than a slice of white bread. Come on, old man, give us both hands." Clifford held his father's palms although his eyes travelled back to his brother whose own eyes had not left their mark. Clifford winked at the stay-home brother, raised a chin. Frank likewise. The men then looked away.

Everyone waited and waited in roof-baffled wind, below a flapping flag now; the shock of Clifford's arrival had stirred up such queer community sentiment. No one knew what to do! It was a miracle …

wasn't it? Ah, but now it was William never coming back. And who in their right mind didn't like William? The freckles. They turned to the priest for some edifying look, wink or nod. The priest only turned to a close church member, the young-shouldered schoolteacher Sister Elizabeth Crowley. Sister Crowley let Father MacDonald in on who exactly this was.

Play of the children failed: their own gossip displacing it. They looked to this man who was supposed to be shot clear dead in the war, killed by shrapnel, gassed to the lung walls. Did he have metal in him? On him? But the baffling wind got stiff, it struck from the north: a wharf end most highly susceptible to exposure.

Rising red clay, unwanted from a steep dirt road wended and stung eyes. Hats had to be held in now-varied road ascents. Heads dipped. Cursed wind, plague of the heart.

Clifford got introduced to the loitering priest, but just as soon turned in answer to a question concerning his boat. Clifford used improved volume here, said he would leave his dory just where it sat: tied up. "Let the saltwater in, soak her bottom. She's been hauled up these years. Wood swells in water. Seals the cracks."

Final boats shoved off. Hangers-on cleared. But the priest spoke to sparse others, casually, while beginning his own assault of the clay hill. He moved among others, taking also advantage of exposed sidelong roots, of getting a foot on known bared rocks, tufts. With robe ends in his hands he climbed, and burdened trailing altar boys took up their own robes where they could. They unsnapped top garment snaps, to free their throats at least.

Clifford wanted Claire for a private moment, to ask what he might do: whether he should go home with her or back with his own gang. It was poor strategy. Claire Curtis was his wife and although emotion was high, and yes, there had been a lot for one day – the course of events to come could hardly be uncertain. Facts were facts. So he petitioned none, put forth nothing; instead, he found himself sauntering along in her empty company toward the Woody Shore. In his hand, Dawn Marie knew only reluctance so he let the hand go. A half-committed Adrian came along, in rubber boots with dress pants over their tops. Frank watched them go. He sung out, saying he had to stay behind, would go rather in the other direction because it was Sunday and he had a telephone call to make at Mary Helen's. His old man returned a mule's look, gave a slow head shake. His sister Grace, who held his shoulder, was surprisingly near. She whispered Frank his name, then nodded: said she had to go with her own family up the wooded path that met only later the clay road.

All out of breath, Frank slowed to a walk. He was bound for Mary Helen's all right, home of the village telephone station. He was all out of breath because he had run through the spruce woods, doubling back to Claire's where he had removed his belongings. He stashed maul, wedge and axe in the near woods. He stashed items of clothing in the woods higher, in long grass near the family tree whose poplar bark still wore scarring initials of childhood. Clifford would see his yard – he would see wood cut, grass trim, tools forgotten. He might know. He might not. Except we are brutally intelligent. None might ever breathe a word to him. Such was handled such. Such was kept buried, through the worst of times. Or, sealed behind knowing walls.

Mary Helen. Mistress phone operator. The retired village schoolteacher whose parlour wore a wall switchboard of protruding wires greeted Frank who bid his hello. He saw above her the formidable instrumentation, the bold brass earpiece, the black porcelain mouthpiece. Stationed for operation. But Mary Helen kept hold of Frank with her liniment hands, with her ringless fingers that did the dialling. He saw her bracelets. Neither spoke of his last time here: Christmas, the card tournament. The King, Queen. Mute communion could be deafening.

Mary Helen soon sent the call through to its main operator in Baddeck. Abruptly she explained to Frank a second time about his taking the earpiece in his own hand, here – getting up good and close to the mouthpiece, there. No. Yes. Bend down. Also, not, not to be afraid when someone on the other end picks up. Speak loudly. Holler if you must, if the connection is not all that great.

Mary Helen closed the kitchen door behind her. A voice picked up, distorted, delayed. Wade Miller? Yes. Frank Curtis. Indeed. I remember. Frank Curtis, how could anyone forget Frank Curtis? The same who walked out on a deal, on a signed contract. Yes. Still there is something possible. Della Rae? Pow! Long, long gone that one and good riddance, too.

"Frank. You will have to take the initiative of securing passage. I'm not set up so well as I was. That will change. You just get yourself down here, Sport. That will change."

A sharp pencil, stationed on a notepad, on an oak desk, under a green banker's light. Frank wrote out the address. What? Pardon? Yes. Frank did have something of his winnings yet. For passage, some. He spoke nothing more of it now, and if so not loudly. "Yes, I'll call soon as I get to New York. I'll hang up now. I'll sign off now. So good-bye to you."

Thanking Mary Helen face-to-face and passing her her mouthpiece, Frank asked how much for the call. She produced a hard-cornered ledger with listed prices but first she entered the new call, its duration, from whom, to whom, when. "Twenty-two cents a minute to New York City, U.S.A., landsakes that's dear. Hope the Yanks don't get all of that." She held by its brass casing a wind-up alarm clock. "Still, a call's a call. Must have been business that one. So far, long distance-wise. That's usually worth the investment."

Settling the account, studying its receipt written in school teacher's hand, Frank nodded deeply.

"Come in here. You'll stay for a quick game of crib?" She was already inside. "Hot cup of tea? Did you get to the Blessing of the Boats? My, my. I didn't bother with it this year on account of my knees, my rheumatoid arthritis. Look, copper bracelet, each wrist now."

The telephone rang and Mary Helen came forward to answer it. "You wait right here now. Promise me."

"No, no tea. Ah, Mary Helen, you just go on now, answer that. I've got to be on my way as it is, Mary Helen."

She refused him, she stood instead staunch in the hallway as she spoke up into her mouthpiece. She wove a hand for Frank to go in, sit down in a chair. She saw determination, put full eyes on him, leaving him a woven finger as her face formed careful study of the switchboard, making herself then smaller in the entrance. It was a dignified face on the phone, aged, replete with compassion. But she was learning something from the call. Frank straightened on the spindle chair, smelled shortbread cookies, removed his eyes from the ebony prayer beads on the table to look at the low counter pantry. Solace in old age, plenty to defeat right off the rough moments that come. And he could wait here a moment, in her warm home. He could wait all the moments. He had to wait this. Mary Helen had singled out Frank as a boy. She'd always kept in reserve that private double wink, or kind word when they met out amongst people. She took out that extra moment with him. She saw through to his heart. Mary Helen had a piano in her parlour, lid closed. He'd seen it coming in. Frank had played the violin for her once: long, long ago in a school performance at the parish hall. She taught him notes, here. He remembered the chipped middle C, real ivory, its tiny linear cracks making it real, the middle C, a cracked tooth. He heard the note at will.

Poised and listening, the woman said in a haunted voice now only a word or two toward the mouthpiece. She pressed for her caller to call back – later. Frank was up, he had got around her; had eased the outside screen-door open and waited on the veranda, hat ready. It was not right to leave a person, however meagre the visit, without the standing goodbye. Mary Helen had learned what had befallen the community. Shock was on her lip, travesty. She knew William. She had punished William in school on many an occasion for being the fool, for his blasphemous mouth. News had travelled fast, yet she must be the last to know. Who would call her? From where?

"You won't be staying?" she said, a face wearing its study.

"The cards? Ingonish?"

"The tea."

"No, no tea, I'm afraid. That was a fellow I talked to, in New York. There's work down there if I want it. Dad could use better help, and more than what I bring in. I could use better help."

"I always thought you were the bright one, Frank, of the family. I want to say bright goes beyond being smart. You listening? There's a light in you."

"I don't know about that. I do seem to be the one things happen to."

"Peace with your maker, keep that. Always stand your ground for what you believe in. The rest doesn't matter a straw, hear?"

"I hear. I hope it doesn't."

The old woman closed both doors. Frank felt her eyes on him especially at the crossing of the kitchen window, where view faced the long distance up the road.

"The day is done and the darkness Falls from the wings of night
As a feather is wafted downward From an eagle in his flight.
I see the lights of the village gleam Through the rain and the mist
And the feeling of sadness comes o'er me That my soul cannot
resist...."

The poem by Longfellow. She had him remember it as a student. She was his teacher at the time of the accident. She had taught him the musical scale on the school piano, that she never let go out of tune. She had brought him here. He secretly had tuned the violin, touching the piano; five notes beyond the chipped C was the A. Second string from the bottom, the A. He had hummed the A all the way home. Her disposition never faltered, even upon first seeing him the way he was, when first he came back for the school year. He had touched her prayer beads today, at the table, had pinched them. Can I carry their pitch? They were of hard ebony, like black notes, sharps, flats. She must invest in the beads. Many do. Many must. Nothing is really the whole white notes, beyond sound.

That night, Frank needlessly explained the rising circumstance to his father as rain struck and the rain barrel filled. Adrian understood. He understood well and, while listening, his face wore more of Mary Helen's expression: the one of no protest, the one possessed of the knowledge held expertly by the elderly. Some young could also know it – or recognise it – young who had a hard go of things from the start. Trial was in the expression, the patience for bad times, the patience for the doling out of good and bad with as much equanimity as possible: meal helpings, in large families, where one mysteriously always got just that little bit less than the others.

Frank patted Mililica, a kitchen dog a long, long time now. She no longer smelled wet. Curled under the chair by the stove, she waited, mostly. But she half-raised her head in attention presently, between the table surface and Frank's face. Adrian leaned at the stove, warmed himself, put an arm over the stove back, the fingers going empty. He stared at the mutt.

Frank said: "Fellow does get to keep his integrity."

"That he does, Frank. Foremost. It's how I would look at it. How I *do* look at it, and intend to."

They stood on Middleheader's Wharf next morning. Across the inlet was Dunphy's, the scene of the Blessing of the Boats: no boat, with wood to be swelled any longer. All boats were gone. Frank waited till the *Aspy* blew her final blow before boarding the gangplank.

"Might be gone a while this time, Dad. I'll send word, couple of bucks when I can. So don't fall into the habit of not going down to the mail. They'll send it back and it'll get lost, hear? Buy a few groceries whenever you go for the mail. Stock up, me son. That's how a person best gets by."

"I'll go down, Frank. You needn't send me a thing. Frank? I'm sick for what happened. Sick like I never was before. This will make it a whole lot better, you'll see, on them. You have always been good that way, doing what was in your power first to make life easier on all involved."

"Best not to get in the way."

"You're right there. If a person can. If they can they're a whole lot further ahead."

"Grace promised she'd keep an eye on you. Don't go hiding when she comes up the road. And promise you'll go and live with her when winter strikes."

"No, Frank, I'll promise nothing of that sort. You're asking too much there. Ask something else and I'll do my best on it. Living with others... I don't like to stay with others, Frank, you know that yourself. Can't take a ride, even. A man belongs with his own roof over his head, else-wise he's done for. I won't refuse their lending the odd hand, here and there. That's as far as that goes."

"Go ahead."

"You were always good to me, Dad."

"All right, all right. I don't like to stay with people myself. Well, it's time. Take care of yourself old fellow. Dad?"

"Go ahead."

"You were always good to me, Dad."

Frank watched from aft-deck as the old man in gift-given suspenders climbed that muck hill out behind the wharf. He was going up for better view of the ship's break of the bay. You're tough, Adrian Augustus Curtis, bare-headed in the sun. In spring rays beating worn shoulders, in a brightness that forces the eyes shut. Trims them. It is something to have sons. It must be. Is it Adrian? Dad? Frank stood watching as long as he could, till a nodding bow rounded Smokey Mountain and, once there, bashed deliberately and for entirety the full belly of an open sea.

part III

twenty-nine

In the gently-white schoolhouse on the hill, children were expectant. A whole second period was off due to some special visitor, a retired boxer or some kind of fighter travelling schools to talk about his career. No one knew the name. He was supposed to be famous.

In file came the legs, streaming down into the largest classroom, the basement, the new physical education room. Scrunched faces saw the stalwart stranger in dim light under the steel stairs over which they had just come. Seated inside, on bingo chairs carried over from the parish hall, the children then sat uncharacteristically with hands in laps. He looked scary. He came forward, to make first the doorway small then nearby desks, the blackboard and finally the teacher Mrs. Warren – who had pushed herself into a left-handed desk. Principal Westaver waited in introduction, saying in their rustic midst was a world champion, an all-around solid fellow, "So you kids be good." Principal Westaver left the room and stood in the hall alongside the suited school official travelling with the champ.

A thin cap, like a welder's, twisted in the brute's hand. Clean bulk overalls, straps tightening at the chest, legs short. Red face, lopsided nose, gold tooth. One arm.

"Good day, young people. I'm Frank Curtis. Golden international arm-wrestling champion. I don't know if they told you, but I grew up here in Ingonish. Don't let my appearance fool you, I'm nervous. Seeing all your faces, knowing family traits in them brings me some confidence.

"I turned fifty-eight this February past. And that's not kilograms on the new scale. Everything seems small here, but that's the work of your memories. Yes, weary road all right. The last part of my life was with the Barnum and Bailey outfit in the States, but long after retiring from the professional arm-wrestling circuit. Now I travel on a circuit around the country to give little talks. I did get to see a good part of the world. The world got to see me. I've been to the bottom of Chile, the land of fire. South Africa, where I stayed in a hotel built in a tree. It was never easy for me to speak. We'll see how I do here.

"Faith to begin – faith to end. My life of travel, if there was glory, must seem a good one, but I've had knocks. I was in scrapes I never thought I'd get out of. I pulled through. When I hit the road for competitions after the war, older than what you are now, I got involved in alcohol and drugs. Women, too. I'm supposed to talk about the drinking. So, sorry to the principal, what's his name out there? Sorry.

"A man trips, falls and looks around to grab what grows near, to break the fall. We got appetites. For food, yes, but for other things too. Appetites know only to grow. They are our selfish parts. When they grow, enjoyment fades. After a while you look for the initial pleasure.

"I tried to get away as far as I could once I left. I wanted no one around me I knew. I succeeded. Little did I know, that when you lose family and community, you lose identity. A person's worth is identity. Keeps your nose to the grindstone, identity. When I got signed on with the circus I got carried away like a blade of grass caught in a wheel. Oh, sure, there were good times. I won't deny it. Adventure sprang at every turn. Adventure and liquor. When you start waking up in strange surroundings, craving anything that will get you through the next few hours, you start to hate the sight of day. Last thing I did before bed was make sure I had a bottle for morning.

"You're young. You must have heard of rock bottom. You might know what that is. I don't – and I've been there. They want it to mean that when you have nothing left, you can climb upwards, get better. The problem is, there *is* no rock bottom because there is no bottom. The fall through hell has no floor. You just keep going. "You're at the perfect age to steer clear of what I got mixed up in."

"Faith, I said. Family, community. Some of you will leave, others will not. Whatever you do, bear in mind family. You were put in this group you're in so work through the trials. Everyone has trials. Your choice, to make the coming years ones of promise, or waste. Easiest thing to heap moments with torment, if that's your aim. I was not able to say I was happy for the life given. I learned what it was to raise my head in public, go out among folks. My purpose here is to change one mind. We have a moment to educate the world, a lifetime to educate ourselves. Stick to school, kids. Or else Frank Curtis might come and beat you up!"

Frank looked around at the beautiful washed skin, cheeks and foreheads hardly harassed, hardly spoiled heads of hair. Did he sound convincing? They wrote that for him. He remembered the privilege to be allowed to come around to these buildings at first, to enter the tidy warm spaces and see small faces give all their wonder. The pleasure to be a teacher. To every day set foot across tiled floors and make your life one of spotting early promise and whipping it into shape. But the heat of the buildings!

Frank had gained more from the kids than they from him, this past year and a half. He felt guilty: here was unfinished education he was getting. Young people gave him strength to stay on the right road. The taste of liquor called and called. So, they reminded him. He touched the flattened beer cap he wore on a chain around his neck. That was coming off soon. Meeting Sylvia-Ann Parker at that church social in Buffalo. Her poking him for his story, encouraging him from the get-go to do something with his life yet. He had "Sway." It was from her he got the hand up out of the ditch, or so the story goes. Sylvia-Ann Parker set up his first talk at Alcoholics Anonymous. It was there Frank met T. G. Betts, administrator with the New York Board of Education, a gent who had witnessed first hand Frank's wins back in the forties. He knew who Frank was just by looking at him.

The circuit began with schools in the Bronx. There was no sleep the night before his first talk. He rolled badly in his bed at the shelter, ravelling and unravelling sheets. So badly he croaked for a drink that night. He wept to drink the tears. It was late, nothing was open. The taste would always be with him, they promised him. All tastes were with him. The pressure to perform had returned; that was the real source. He muscled through the night, muscled through the nights to follow. He talked a squeaky fool, but they clapped.

A girl shifted. She looked the shyest of the lot but held her hand high. A white face the oval of an egg spoke.

"How did you stop?"

"You a Cameron?" Frank asked.

"Yes."

"Thought so. See – I am home. I get that question. By focusing. By making all else secondary. Don't have the first and you needn't worry about the second. Two sips for me, beer, wine, spirits. Watch Mr. Jekyll come to life. Personality goes. Mean, selfish actions come. You want to erase all hours set before you. You want from people what they could give you. You become a manipulator."

"When did you quit?"

"Twenty-two months back. I remember the moment. I was leaving jail in the States – hauled in disorderly in Saint Paul, Minnesota, during the starkest winter imaginable, a cold snap that killed two homeless, on their feet. I would have frozen in a snow bank myself. The cops gave me my boots, belt and jacket back. I started out the station, but hesitated at the entrance, where heat lifted the radiators. To go back into the cold was the last thing I wanted. I studied the wall, a bulletin board. One poster, a campaign to chain up your dog, had a woman's face on it. My God, eyebrows. Jawbone. My mother. Dead in my tracks it stopped me. The thought of her, here, this juncture in life. Nope. The past is never done with you. "Get that hair cut, Frank. This the way we brought you up? To look like the last rose of summer?" Her voice. I misted up, but turned up collar and tramped boot, out into the frost. It was a sign. I believe in signs. A person needs only keep an open eye to catch them."

This story began a flurry of questions, to which Frank gave short answers. Interest centred on his arm-wrestling career. No question came as to what happened to his arm. He never had that question. By the end of the allotted time, hands still raised, he called it off.

"Back to your regular day, now. It's good to have a regular day." He nodded to Superintendent Tate, of the school district, who broke from the principal.

Tate, clean-cut, articulate in a necktie, lean as a bean, asked the children for a really good round of applause. "Thanks for your enthusiasm, children. I've been travelling here with Frank Curtis this past week and can only say he is a gentleman among gentlemen. He intimated to me that he was delighted to get a chance to speak here at home. I hope his delight matches ours at having him."

Frank presented a fist to the discerning children still caught up in wonder. Faces here broke apart in broad uncertain smiles of forming teeth. They read his knuckle tattoos. What they spelt. He winked on his way out and the children would never forget the fierce gaze, the busted nose. His face was remote from any they knew. His form of speaking, the quality of whisper yet with good volume. Mannerisms: how he held himself half-turned; how he moved eyes from small to large. His person evidenced a wide world – vast, adventurous. They had been fortunate to have him come. But these hints, really, such prophecy? Were more pugnacious strangers to come, damaged but personable? More messages mumbled?

A bell rang. Lunch can lids snapped. Dark and light half-moon pastry plastic got sheared. Distribution began of the wiggly milk bags, from the school milk programme, their puncturing straws sent to work. Hands shot through sleeves of jackets left unzipped. Boots got retrieved from the great pile deep under the stairs, slipped over newly-wetted socks. Games of recess waited outside. It was a Friday, the herald of leisure and excitement even from this early age. Promise of weekend lived in the air. That man had been frightening, threatening. It had been odd having him here in the schoolhouse on the hill.

In no way did he fit. In no way did he seem to be from here. But he wasn't; he went away. German Ball. Hopscotch lines etched in clay with stones kicked free. Marbles, spunkies, friends and bullies.

In the plush front seat of the expansive Lincoln Continental, Tatess-poke. His hand was on the wheel, Frank's door unclosed. "A positive no, Frank? You sure you can't, because I can drive down here in three day's time and get you. There's the whole of Newfoundland and Labrador to cross. Twice, St. John's and Labrador City, both called for you. There's the high north, the native communities. Awful trouble there, Frank. With their young people. Inhalants."

"No, ah, Greg. Thanks all the same. None of this is me. You heard me in there. I knew I'd realise it best coming back. No, last stop is here. I got family living yet I want to look up. My roaming days have reached their end."

"Just like that?"

"No other way, than just like that. At some point."

"I'll press you no further. Let me at least give you a drive to, what is it, the Woody Shore?"

"Done with riding in these too. I was never all that fond of motorcars. Hard on the groin. I want to go by the old paths, on foot. See how things have grown. I'm not going to the Shore, anyway. I will get my bags out of your trunk."

They went around to the back, and Tate put his key in the lock. He passed a duffle bag and lifted a small suitcase by its handle.

"Not much to what you're carrying. Two bags?"

"Yes, and it took a lifetime to get it down to two."

The Superintendeant took Frank's hand. He winked and twisted his head, then got inside to start his engine. His properly-inflated tires soon crunched loose schoolyard gravel before dipping into potholes endemic to parish hall parking. Superintendent Tate worried about broken bottles here. They held dances down here. He'd heard how wild a folk lived in these parts. There were fires, riots. He studied his rear-view, saw the bulkhead champ go. The survivor. A buoyant form passing through the children, beginning the steep falling bank beyond the school grounds. What kind of life must that have been? And no mention of the real time. The hard time? Does he admit to it himself? He sounds to have got religion. I don't believe it. He has to eat. We all do. Ah, my.

The Superintendent was just about to lose sight of Frank Curtis when he saw the unsteady leg buckle. He braked, shoved up his gear-shift and searched all mirrors, his hand was on his door handle. He eyed his side mirror. Did the children see it? He stood outside. Dust rose to his eyes. God knows how drinking, drugs, women and the rest ruined those legs! The Super held the door handle. He called: "Hey! All right?" Time in a cell. I suspected he was guilty, like the rest, like the whole island did, and both countries. Those malformed are guilty to begin with. Turned out he wasn't. The children kicked their ball high. There he is – up.

"I say, you all right?" Tate called. The legendary anchor-bearer waved. Second-degree murder, guns, hot tempers. Yes, brush off, make your way. Suitcase lost down over the hill? Letting him speak, true like that! The mention of women! Dope! I believe it: he wasn't even to the upper fathoms of the man who spoke. He just skimmed the surface; Frank Curtis was a frozen ocean. That heart, hardly breathed open. Yet there was that calm in him, calm like in no other. Priest, free-spirit, mucky-muck – none has his take. Straightforward on the slightest things: mealtime, sleep, speaking, listening – each definitive beginning and each definitive end. Never more than one helping at a meal; his washing with hot cloth before bed; the need to shave before anything else in the morning. Institutionalised, I guess. He had slept at the Tate's house the full week and the television had not come on; here was a real old-timer. I had to press him on it. The radiation bothered him, he said, from TVs. Seven days: no memory of having spent so much time with any man. It had been a week of half-dread.

Did he get a taste of Frank Curtis? A flavour? Not a drop. Home to Karen, an hour to Baddeck on the new road. Thankful I have her. Home to the house where it will be just the two of us.

Loose gravel ended; quality radials took firm grip.

thirty

The ache of poor circulation to his arm pulled him awake. Frank tapped the back of his wrist on the wall then raised his hand to the faded curtain. For the first time in years he heard the tick of his watch in this dead silence. Where was he again?

The backroom, where he slept as a boy, but without the iron bunks. He lay instead on a single cot stationed below the window that faced the line of spruce, now with spreading branches. They never grew all his childhood. From here he saw their crowns.

The floors sagged in the old house, he knew that. The evening before, he had put a foot through and had fallen to the knee. He had to grab a doorknob not to go deeper, to extricate himself. Sections of panelling were nailed over storm windows outside. These he yanked off with the help of a rusted hammer, then hauled inside, staggering pieces over the sagging kitchen floor and hoping joists had strength yet. Peering through the hole he'd made, he saw, then felt, that the near joists were dry. It was but two-by-four framing? And, holding all these years? He started a track through the living room with the paneling, through to the toilet his father had put in. He climbed down the cellar hatch and found the water pump. With his candle set on the dirt ledge behind the hatch ladder, he felt along with spread fingers to where the cast-iron pump casing had been split, where water long unemptied had frozen to split the housing. He laid a track out to the backroom last, to where his luggage sat near the bed.

Moisture had remained trapped over the years. It had damaged the house sill. The worst thing in the world was to board up a house from the elements, to lock in the wet. Respiration was a challenge, in a musty house. Frank had lain on his back, opened his mouth to catch air falling from the three air holes of the storm window. He had left the porch doors open through the night. Fetid must remained.

March, April, May – May. Soon the good weather of spring, but it would be a long time or never before this place freshened. The old house might not have been his best choice. Too big, for one. By cordoning, he could fix up a section, in the spirit of the old fellows who stayed on in a family home vacated. The house sat below the paved road. Near the bad turn, vulnerable to travelling motorcars at these increased speeds. In the night he had noted how the cars liked to barrel up the clam-flats, accelerate out of the bad turn then fly down the road. Speed to places like this.

Frank reached the medicated cream set on a chair at bedside. His copper bracelet cool on the wrist, he rubbed cream along his armpit and over knotted scar tissue. It burned where skin met the pit hair; that place had been raw a long time now, and the absent arm ached evenings and most mornings. It had ached this night through, while unseen and now disturbed creatures made changes to their rafter homes. But this morning, where are they? Outside, daylight foraging. It had to have been squirrels rummaging. Did they never sleep? Rearranging, re-packing, adjusting till a man goes batty? Frank's presence had upset them. They were a wilful creature. Had babies. But, the sound of a brook? The little one down behind that broke in spring? He and William had some great time skating on that till that one day his feet came out from under him and he bashed the back of his skull. Or was that down the Shore? It was me? His mother Jessie ran out he knew, lifted him off the ice. What's that? White-throated sparrow? Its shrill five notes just over brook trickle. Yes. Wind too, brushing leaves of trembling aspen: trees tall now. He brought his head forward to see what height he could: but the storm window had too much ribbing. These poplar trees brought the sound of heavy rain. His old man had told him the Natives called these "The Waggling Tongues of Women." Twisting, hushing. Shushing with no breeze up. Was it the old man? Great name. Someone had chickens, too; a big rooster crew down at the Woody Shore.

Frank listened for the squirrels. Summer would drive them from the rafters. That, or a gun.

Drawing aside some of the same bedding he had slept under as a boy, he fixed a section of the cot before pulling on pants and fitting on shoes. Shoes with a buckle. He had slept in his sleeveless T-shirt and so was chilled. He got his leather toilette bag out and stashed it partway down his front pocket. He wrapped a towel around his neck. With hand taking his belt head, holding it habitually after it was through its loop, he proceeded over the darkened panels. He let go of the belt, reaching the first doorframe. There was creaking, but not breaking-creaking.

The first steps of morning also recalled the tenderness of the syphilis. For the past two years he had been swallowing spoonfuls of quinine to reduce its symptoms. He had left off on that recently: the medication in pure form rendering his speech and thought overly deliberate, then, altogether washing it out. He learned quinine was in carbonated drinks so drank them; soda water with ice when he could. The syphilis flared up from time to time and some nights when it was bad he could not sleep a simple twenty minutes. The burning sensation brought its incessant desire to urinate. Nothing was more painful, and then – no spillage, not a drop, as the bladder was never full. Doubled over, he would curse aloud. The bladder so easily tricked him into thinking it was full. Inflammation effected the trick, by producing muscle tension. But the brain was tricked into many things. He himself consciously fooled it, by looking at his hand in the mirror to show a pair. Also, the temporary wearing of the sling at times: same effect, a lessening of pain. He had always hid both from people. Memory pain. But, of that – memory pain – he was growing less sure now. Travel never helped conditions and he would go nowhere after this. The school visits were done. The ride hitched. He was now here.

*O*utside, he deeply breathed the yard vapours of May. They filled his lungs with sweetness – a detail he'd forgotten. He set down his toilette kit and towel to remove the backroom storm window under which he had slept. He jammed up a shovel blade to do this. The structure came away easily with the wall rot plus the window's weight.

"There now, air – get inside all you want."

The point against the side of the house, down past a prior year's bountious goldenrod, where he and his brothers had once urinated, had blackened shingles. He got soaked going in, his cuffs and thighs taking on heavy dew. He got mixed in a patch of burrs – huckle-buckles, as he recalled them. They clung to his pants to make his thighs itch. "Cursed hell." He stepped into a tangle of the field where he could piss, in peace. But nothing came. And then, ah … there it was. But a buzzing was near, though far-off it sounded. He saw below that he stood adjacent to working hornets, their papery nest built in tall grass. Sunshine hit. Shaking himself with care he eased away but turning – someone approached the property at the road. A hornet at knee height understood his start as aggressive. It raised itself the foot and a half needed to sting the nearest exposed skin. "Ah! Merciful Christ!" Frank jumped back, then turned away toward the road and having begun for the house, the visitor didn't know what to think: this old fellow yanking on his fly, hopping over grass like a man possessed.

Frank was stopped at the step. He looked down, turned, dipping his penis back inside his underwear this time, zipping the trousers. The red-faced guest waited ten yards off, elbows out.

"Not coming down?" said Frank, seeing the man stand in the posture of his own people.

But Frank had to use much of his body again – to swat impressively at a passing housefly he was certain was another hornet: "Come on you! I'll squash the life out of you! Oh... just a fly."

"Get stung?"

"Yes, and by the biggest kind of hornet, right smack you-know-where!"

"Ah, me son. Suppose."

The young fellow offered his hand. Frank looked at his own then gave it.

"You're not Grace's? Not Rodney?"

"Yes sir. Your nephew, Uncle Frank."

Rodney wore a pirate moustache, with reddish tints. A digital wristwatch was in a leather strap the size of a slave bracelet. His looks were good. Frank noted the eyebrows, cheeks. He had some size to him, not overly, but a good sharp eye. One aware.

"They're out, the wasps are."

"Wasp? I wish. But how are you doing, Rodney, bai? You're damn-well a man now if I ever saw one."

"Thanks, I guess. The old lady sent me over. Here's some toilet paper. She said you got home, yesterday, was it? She asked me to come here, get you for a bite of breakfast."

"How the hell she know I was home? That quick? No, don't an-swer, me son. Things haven't changed. People know what you're up to before you're even up to it. The talk at the school, must have been."

"You all right? Want to sit down? Here, sit on the step. It'll hold."

"Yalp," came the endemic drawn breath of sarcasm. "I'll just sit: that's the stuff. Oo, we!"

Frank couldn't get over the young man, Rodney, here beside him.

"Time went. Listen though, I'm dying for a cold, cold drink of water. I want to get my neck and face washed too, before I head out anywhere. Come on down to the old well with me. Just down over the hill. I don't want to meet with some other foe lurking in the thatch, so you come. That old shovel, that no one stole, there. Grab that. I hope to God the spot isn't grown over that much we can't find it."

"What?"

"The well."

They passed rampant weed and tangled raspberry. They moved under curling alder leaf and brushed back fiddlehead fuzz or dead ferns with copper fronds. Wintered cattails climbed to their temples. Squelching turf told what was below, bog, muck and, soon enough, their proximity to the old well. The new well, situated under the well house, contained water for the house, but it was far below the floor-boards and there was nothing to retrieve it with – as Frank had discovered in the near dark the evening before.

He bent low, pulling back ornamental grasses to view the pool. The barrel sat solidly, buried, convex sides still preventing any sign of cave-in.

"Will you look at that. The real old-timers got all their supply here. My old man, your grandfather, lined it with this wooden rum-barrel when I was a boy. He was good at projects like that. He kept this as a back-up, in case we ran out up at the house."

Rodney remained taciturn – as both had – on the trip through the undergrowth. The silent decades between the two stood as powerful obstacles. Frank felt he had let too much silence creep in, before reaching the water.

"You're not married, Rodney? Kids?"

"I'm not, no. Suffer shyness, I'm told."

"Ah, that's no crime. Too much coaxing, of a fellow to go out and meet the world, far as I'm concerned. Look, same speckled black blue water. That of a smelt's back. We called this the Fountain of Youth as kids and believed it to be so."

"Must feel odd, being back. Never heard tell of anyone gone away long as you had – and then return."

"Familiar, at the same time. Like the next day even. I'm hardly back. I got to relearn everything, not just place. Tell me what you think of the well."

"I knew this was here. I fell in it one day running down here with my sister Betty and her friends. There was a crust of snow just heavy enough to carry us, but I stopped pretty quick when I came up onto the rim, she's deep."

"That must have been a nice smack, sides sharp, strong as they are. Jesus, how everything is matted! See, where the snow was. Things will grow. We wouldn't have found this a couple of weeks from now, after the plants found their roots."

A knee in the muck, Frank skimmed green and brown scum. He bent almost ceremonially to scoop water with a cupped his hand. "Ah, now that's water." The wooden perimeter rose not four inches above the ground at its highest – buried chards had battled rot.

"How barrel wood lasts. You couldn't break it. Look. Must be the alcohol they store it in, what? But I knew that. See here, how the spring breaks, the slightest bubble, swelling. Your great grandfather Augustus witched this with a rod. The old man and I dug down. He put the new barrel in, two, maybe. Some job that was, the rocks we took up, the crowbar work, muck. He was set on maintaining it. Wanted one of us to build down here I figure. Many times I thought of it, this very spot. Building. It came quick to mind, as early memories do. Woods, especially. The woods stay clear as anything no matter what your state of mind. Where you find yourself on the planet. Geography. Your very own nooks, crannies, stream and stump. All gets clearer the further you go."

"Bearings, is it?" said Rodney, and Frank looked up to see his nephew's face not yet tampered with, though it could have been – he was no child. He knew his own to be dastardly in the morning gleam.

"I came by the old place," said Rodney. "Few times. I came to clean brush. Not this spring, I didn't."

"She's grown up, all right."

"The snow's hardly gone. It's in the woods yet."

"That so?"

"In the mountains, all kinds. Mom hated the sight of the old place, she'd say, whenever we went past. My plans were to come with a scythe. Trees around the perimeter of the place were getting high enough to cover the windows facing the road. The soil must be extra good there. Why, I don't know. No one thought you'd be back."

"Least faith in those closest. I was always coming back – a person is mistaken to think he can leave. The trees took off around the house like that because of the material thrown in against the walls. A soft, clean dry dirt, a form of insulation to keep places warmer in winter. Little banks run the base of many an old house around here. They wanted the walls buried, against that first six inches of real moisture. Ah, that is cold!"

"What are you doing?" asked Rodney.

"Going deep."

Frank had his entire arm sunk in the well, he spat grass and leaf.

"There, ahhh … there! Sweet Jesus, the frost!" He drew out a slimy rope that soon brought up a linked chain.

"What the hell?"

"Rodney, catch hold."

The two drew on the chain, getting soaked and sloppy, Rodney straining and feeling just how rigid the chain got when his uncle alone pulled. They rocked and racked the chain, hauled till a sack of slime broke with blue black mud upon it. Rodney didn't say a word.

"You're not going to ask?" said Frank breathing hard.

"I want to. It weighed a tonne. Not an animal? Felt like she was caught down under a boulder."

"One I put there. Open it. I got a knife in my shaving kit. Wash your hands first, wash them as you go along. Try not to get it too wet inside."

"What is it? Not the bones of something. Look, lettering, an old mail sack! What the hell?"

"That was for its metal loops. That material is the best there is."

Heavy construction plastic was deep inside the sack, under layers tied, taped and sealed. Rodney had to work to cut through. He reached inside and brought out a wad of money.

"Jesus! This you hid in a well?"

"Winnings," said Frank.

"Winnings?"

"From long ago, Rodney. I kept it all. We aren't fools around here."

"How'd you manage it? There's American here too. A lot is American."

"You carried some. You don't remember? The day we learned the news of William, or of Clifford I should say."

"I remember."

"When Dad was carrying the baby. It was in the sack we fitted you with."

"I remember the strain on my shoulders, coming back."

"You were a regular soldier."

"What if you never got back, Frank? There's a pile here. A pile!"

"It's smaller bills. I had, not coming back covered. Let it drain. Let's go have a look down over the Rock."

"Is it safe, on its own here?"

"Has it been all these years? Let it dry. Jesus, you look like your mother. Come on, see the best view in Ingonish. I just hope that's still legal tender."

thirty-one

*L*oons sobbed. Rodney and Frank lifted their eyes from the Rock to the shrouding mists of Hawley's Point. The few heavy clouds were in a dead sky, but a stiff harbour wind blew low and contrary to the sea keeping the day chill.

"Must be ice on the Freshwater Lake," Frank remarked. "When the loons arrive and they can't get in there, they wait it out on the harbour – fishing there, till inside clears. They don't begin young until they can get into fresh water."

"The lake? The lake's open. The last of the ice down there went, I would say, a week ago now. We had two straight days of rain, spilling buckets. You couldn't set foot out the door."

"Any boats in the water?"

"Some have theirs in. No one has started fishing yet. It's the repairing of nets, the getting primed for the season. You see lobster traps stacked where they're dropping in ballasts. Men are either in their yards or down on the wharves every day now."

"Early like this is good to catch the mackerel off Middle Head. They have a scale over their eyes right after winter and so can't see dropped nets. They sail right into danger."

"Never heard of that."

"It's what I heard. I paid no attention to fishing, growing up. The little I do know I gleaned later. Nature will always interest you – rough way to earn a living, wet rain down your neck, cold gnawing your bones. Want to head up? The loons are gone." The two brushed alder aside and returned to the well. "Going to have some of the water? It'll keep you young."

"I see now how it might."

Rodney got down for a sip. When he was up and out of the way, Frank took off his outer shirt and set it on a limb. In a sleeveless undershirt he got down to wash his neck. Rodney saw trickle cover the arm's tattoos. There were three, the first starting at the deltoids, and moving down. Each was encircled, with an oblique strike through it, left to right. One scene was a cocktail glass; another a pill bottle; the last a lusty mermaid. Plainly written across his knuckles: b.r.e.a.d. In ink faded blue, these ideas, all. Two copper bracelets jangled at the wrist. Frank removed his watch by biting the leather strap, this simple action jiggling muscle mass at the triceps. And his shoulder, set like ripe pumpkin ridges, worked hard. The uncle was rumoured to have killed a man. And another in jail.

"Quick shave before I go anywhere. Do you mind? I like to be clean."

"No rush."

Rodney studied the mountain tops but also stole glimpses of this peculiar act of shaving. After a brushed soaping, with pursed lips, Frank scrapped a bare razor blade at his neck; a piece of mirror set in a tree. But where the blade went, he would station three fingers in cream, feel for new areas as he went along, the intent hand crawling like a spider. It was slow work in frigid water but he cleaned himself directly, trimmed the sideburns well and under the nostrils. "Returns a fellow his mind. I could have done it over at your mother's. Been too long. She's timid, her. Did I say, timid – what's wrong with me – she's a wildcat! And with a raised family, I expect she's worse than ever. Sentimental. She is sentimental, I know."

"Not many that aren't, Frank."

Frank looked at Rodney at this, used his shirt end as a towel: "People are, all right. I don't hear noise from the gypsum mine. Can't be too early in the day yet, can it?"

"The gypsum mine? The gypsum mine closed down I don't know how many years ago now, Frank. A fellow was killed down there."

"Was there? I never heard."

"I can't say if it was the reason for the closure, but one was. Could be why the loons are in the harbour: being quiet, with the plant gone."

"Could be. You're aware of your surroundings, Rodney. That's good. I was like that – they told me I was. Look, knees soaked through like a hobo down off the tracks. Come on then. Can you take the sack?"

"Like old times?"

"Like old times."

The two got lost to fight bushes to win scratches. They pressed through to destroy wintered reeds and ferns, going entirely off the old path to where alders swallowed them.

In the field, they turned to face what and where they had broken through, hardly noticeable in the ten-foot vegetation.

"Staying a while Frank, or... ?"

"If for good is a while. I'm building a house and you're helping me."

"You are? I am?"

"Yes sir. Been too long without blood around. No more."

Scant sun hit the roof. They studied the gable end where a metal wind vane churned to offer some direction. "Set that down, if it's wet. Your Uncle Clifford built the vane before whoever put that one there. Him and William set it on the peak one windy fall day. It lasted through the worst kind of storms, though only made of wood and a nail in the propeller end. Everyone heard its whirr every night. They fell asleep to it, woke to it."

The sun broke, faded white walls received it to make it a house warmed. Houseflies buzzed. The backroom curtain sucked in, popped out, like a stray sail in a port breeze. Frank would tie that in a knot, first chance he got.

"Where you building? Or fixing this up, that what you're doing?"

"This place is shot. In want of a bulldozer. Down the Crick, just before the Sandbar; not all that far from where you fellows are. Dad left me a strip just big enough to put a place on. I require nothing of size. He wanted to live there himself, first going off, raise us there. Yalp! The old lady would hear of that, all right. No, she wanted to be well away from any cutting ocean breezes. "The Sandbar? It's cold and barren as the day is long," she'd say. Well, I don't know where she thought she was relocating to! Where isn't there cold and barrenness around here? Up in the mountain valleys, maybe. Dad said she needed the road. It was true. Her favourite place was at the window, there. I can't imagine what she'd think of the clean strip of asphalt, the cars. When the house is done at the Sandbar, right here is where I plan to start a gasoline stand. I do. Be the first to catch tourists coming into Ingonish."

"I suppose; it is an idea all right."

"People still get their gasoline off the wharf?"

"They do. But there's a garage in North Bay open now."

"We won't worry about that. That's miles, in the other direction. We're south, despite the grim look of those mountains."

"How do you know I'm not working some other place, already?"

"Your handshake. Skin's not beat up, and unless things have changed, a job around here is a manual one."

"I was lined up to work at the wharf."

"The wharf! Go away with ya. You don't come from fishing people. Your Uncle Clifford might be an exception, his notion, at least. And I don't know why. He can't swim a stroke. No, many think any real life you make for yourself here has to come from the water. That's not true. Make what life you want, where you want. But leave the sea to the others, bai – those better suited. I'll pay you a wage."

"Let me ask the old lady?"

"Your mother? You're a grown man?"

"Her roof, only polite to pass things by her."

"You'll have no trouble with her. I'm her favourite. She ever mention that?"

"I didn't hear her."

"Well you could lie about it."

"All right. I heard her all the time."

The loons called in mourn and haunt, falling, fading, far off. A flap, trickle, long lifting.

"There!" said Rodney pointing out the head of the harbour, past the corner of the house, where the pair sailed into view, evenly distanced, making slick return to the agate surface of Hawley's Point. Their wakes eased. Rodney alone watched. Frank was taking a leak.

*F*rank set a foot on asphalt. With hand in pocket, he walked between the double lines and whistled, tapped the ball of a foot. "Clear rig, ain't she? Never expected all this modernity, what! Hard, flat. There was a time this here was nothing more than a meat trail."

They stuck to the gravelled shoulder.

"I play the harmonica," said Rodney.

"Nothing wrong with that instrument. Music is in your people. I remember an old fellow once telling me playing music was like shaking hands with the devil. Never understood the meaning. Comment on its power, could've been. I knew scales. I knew them. There's nothing like music to shut everyone up. I like that part. Yes, your grandmother's side. Father's too. Bagpipers, your father's; though there's plenty that'll question whether an ancestor's pipe playing works as a plus or a minus. Your great grandfather Augustus could fill a sack. He'd come out in the evenings over on this side of the harbour, to answer tunes of a second piper on the other. Whole other world, then. No pavement I'll tell you. On calm evenings, with the water like glass, notes entered backyards plain as day. And because you heard nothing else, you picked up tunes just by lying on your back in your bed. You could work out how they were played, ear or no ear. Got the thing on you?"

"Right here."

"Play as we go along. I'll listen to every note."

Rodney played his piece and its melody cut crisp from the reed instrument, altering receipt of spring nature during their walk. But Rodney left off when Frank stopped to admire the view of Smokey from atop Shea's Field, to smell loudly for the ocean. Rodney put his harmonica away altogether when they stepped off the road at the marshy point where spring freshets filled ditches to produce pluvial pools and sucking muck. "I see they didn't quite get this part of the road right." Frank came singly; Rodney skipped ahead and waited. Sparrows warbled in song; rills rushed sprightly into machined ditches, gathered here to press at clogging debris. The two men met none on the road save when a single blue car overtook them. The horn was hit, when it had gained some distance ahead. Frank and Rodney waved at brake lights.

"Everyone knows you're back."

"I've got to learn to accept that, I suppose."

Grace's house had been freshly touched with paint, its eaves and cor-ner boards, trimmed in green. She had a perimeter flowerbed, gnarly lacquered driftwood logs detailing it. Her husband Charles was bent over beyond lush turned-up soil, where he painted his foundation, his back to the road. Speckled grass showed where his brush had flicked. Rodney and Frank were on the gypsum driveway, when he stirred and got off his knees. "My God, my God," he called, brushing cuffs and thighs, touching hands at their fleshy points. He wove his cap and swallowed; set the brush better in a plastic tray then touched his hands once more. He stood fully for them, held his cap by the bill, in a curled hand set akimbo.

"Hi, Frank. How you doing, bai? Gentle frig. Some sight, you are. I'll tell you that right now. They told us you were home."

"Good day, Charlie. Who'd you cut a deal with to keep from looking a day beyond what you were?"

"Ho, that's something to say. I'm older, Frank. And by more than a day, me son. Come on in, fellows. Grace is whipping something together. Pancakes with blueberries she picked out on Smokey and dried in the sun last summer."

"There's not many to say no to an invitation like that, Charlie."

"I know! She spoke of your letters, Frank. She's right in here. I say, Grace! He's here, Grace."

Frank drew down the zipper of his beige spring jacket. He let the others pass into the house and stood till their shoes were off before entering on his own. He heard buzzes, clicks, rolling bars – all from a remote time. He was back there, when he entered the buildings. Grace waited with a hand on a staircase spindle, her eyes behind horn rims, adjusting to the light, her hands twisting apron fabric. She had a full head of grey hair, crow's feet at her temples, sacks under her eyes, sagging jowls; she shook her head. "Look what the cat dragged in, will you? You got a gold tooth, that worth anything?"

"Always good to carry money on you."

She came forward and put her arms around her brother. She spoke into his ear, forgetting where she was, to say painfully: "Christ, oh Christ." She pulled back to study the bashed nose.

"You said you were coming back. Never completely believed it. Although you said it."

"That should only tell you something."

Grace could hold out no longer seeing how unsteady her brother was, seeing on his face a long history of scars and gashes. Tears welled up. Because in this general disorientation she read of his strange cold places, of heartbreak and denial she would never learn. She didn't want to know it. Gone, these years. A life alone. Rambling. Locked up. His hair undone. The nose had been broken, badly left, at least once. Though the shy dark eye, still, when another's were searching. Grace looked away. The back of a flour-caked hand lifted to the bridge of her nose. Charles looked away. Rodney, likewise. Grace sniffed.

"Ah, come on. Don't mind me, all of you. I'm all right."

"Home to stay, Grace," said Frank.

"Are you? Yeah, right."

"Me and Rodney, we're building a house."

"What for! Come in, come in, I'm blinded here in the dark."

"To live in, is what for."

"Come in the kitchen, I say, speak there. The light's better."

They went down the hall as Frank said, "Go on, Rodney. Tell them what else, Rodney." Frank then saw a tidy area where a family sat and ate. Spaciousness and sunlight welcomed him. And the sense came of the hard work there could only have been to accomplish this. There were good straight cupboards, clean counters, two windows over a sink, facing south. Sacrifice, commitment, worth.

"Tell them. What else?"

"A gasoline stand."

"God in heaven! Hear that, Charles?"

"I heard."

"A garage," said Frank. "Proper place to fuel up and get repairs done. The money is in the fixing of the cars."

"It'll be the clear thing, sure," said Charles who wove a hand for Frank to sit at the table head. Frank wove back, deferring, and drew out a side chair.

Places were set. There was hint of maple syrup and Frank spotted the stainless steel dispenser, its broad pouring lip with no trace of drip.

"You spoke of something like that in your letters," said Grace. "I didn't think it'd be here, though. Some awful undertaking, won't it?"

"Give me one thing in this life that isn't, Grace ... I got a small stash, from going around to the schools. That right, Rodney?"

"Schools. Right."

"I had the idea, awhile back."

"A person doesn't ever get over home. Do they, Frank?"

Frank answered with a swipe of his chin, getting his jacket off: it was a swipe of uncertainty.

Using oven gloves, Grace brought her tray. They would use forks to poke from stacks. Grace had them bow their heads, cross themselves. She led in prayer in the way Jessie might have – early on. Squares of butter made circles in the syrup. The dispenser got messy, its metal thumb operation difficult to manage. Grace poured for Frank. Mary Anne came in then. She'd been an infant when Frank left. Or was she even born? He wanted to mention how she was in his arm on that muddy road that day when they said it was Clifford not Wil-

307

liam killed. She didn't have Rodney's looks. No. She had her mother's smile and was careful in speech like the others. In a housecoat, she kept to the counter to make her tea, which she carried away. "School exams. Final year in Baddeck."

She travelled by car with a friend to Baddeck, stayed weeknights. It was an hour and a half there are now, by car. Frank listened to all and was glad to hear it, as well as to share a meal, one with butter. He took another square; butter was one of the few items he counted on these days to help with cravings, the anxieties. He had managed this first stop at Grace's. There was next, the Shore; this stop being the practice for that. He long knew that coming home meant one uncertain reconvening, followed by another. He knew now it was a series that never ends; it was part of the contract: to face loose ends, to then live with them. Butter left off melting.

"We said you were innocent, Frank."

"Grace!" said Charles. "I told you, he might not want to talk. I told you that."

"He's my brother, you."

"Time for that, Grace," said Frank. "Let me come home first."

They had a bird feeder beyond garden doors. A black-throated sparrow sat among its bounty. "Watch," said Rodney, whistling the bird's five curt notes. The creature could only respond – choking up sunflower seeds caught in its throat. In the laughter that followed, Frank choked too, and Charles.

"Rodney!" said Grace. "We're at the table. Smarten up or you'll get your teeth to drink."

Frank put linen to his lips, he wanted to say something of Grace, something in relation to hearing Jessie in Grace's tone. He stayed quiet. His way to play it, even when there was joy.

thirty-two

*F*rank bent at the Crick, as the Sandbar beyond threw high ocean mist. He braced the rake between arm and rib cage, hand clutching for the steel head. He had used a bucksaw on the alders, the smallest he yanked free by their roots. He had torn raspberry free by twisting them around his arm – raspberry and poplar shot runners under the soil, hauling one meant hauling others. Rodney worked ahead of Frank, knocking down bordering trees with a sharp axe, limbing cleanly what he cut. A pick was between the two, used for loosening stones. A good fire burned, one to which both added brush.

Their momentum broke as land opened, as views came in want of appraisal. The men thought they knew their village but angles free of obstructions gave the strong impression that all formerly known had been misrepresented. By a single morning's end, the land had revealed its value. Over the upper side was a visible ocean now and down over the hill was the harbour inlet to Dunphy's Wharf. East was Middleheader's Wharf; beyond, the cannery buildings and abandoned icehouse of the Government Wharf.

The brush fire had burned a foot-deep disc through topsoil. They had burned it that hot. Around its perimeter were smoking branch ends, sharp like the work of beavers possessed of charcoal teeth.

Walking backwards Rodney circled the fire, kicking these bits in, when Frank rose from below.

"What do you say to a cup of tea, then? Bite even?"

Rodney frowned at the heat.

"I was wondering when you might slacken off. I didn't think you ever would."

Rodney removed wax paper from the crab sandwiches his mother had prepared for them. Frank got out the half-moon pastries he'd purchased at the Fairway. The night on clean sheets at Grace's came back to him: the good feeling of lying on them, this he felt still in his back, his groin tightening at the thought. A bent figure appeared on the road, in front of the property, the curling ocean bay his backdrop.

"Who's that, Rodney?"

"Who – you don't know?"

"I know the shoulders; no name's coming."

Since returning Frank didn't trust the names that did come; at the Fairway it was bad. All names seemed ludicrous: how could they be called that? Yes, it was a Scotch, an Irish region, but why that? Many times, the person in question had been somewhat of an intimate during Frank's past. His strategy became sincerity, and patience. And when names got offered he latched onto them, would use them right away. It seemed folks were out to trick him.

"Why you looking at me like that?" called the old man, rising up the path. "Queer-faced like you don't know me from a hole in the wall? Me, Frank – your uncle. The best you got."

"Not the Sheriff? For God sakes, how are you doing, old-timer?"

"I can complain, but I won't." Leo crossed level ground. "But what in the old Joe-frig you got going on up here? Me son, she's clear-cut!"

"Little cleaning up is all, ah... Leo. Will you have a sandwich? They're crab."

"Pass one over, then."

Frank handed him what he had, then broke off a piece of his half-moon. Leo received the half-moon in his other hand. He looked at the sandwich and pastry measuring one weight off against the other.

"Oh, boy, the decisions. I'll start with the pastry then," said Leo. "It's lighter."

"Tea to wash her down?" said Frank.

"Eh?"

"I said, we got tea. You want some of that?"

"Pour us a cup, then."

Rodney flicked his cup dry then from the Thermos poured a dribble of tea over the rim to wash it. "Set it down there," said a chomping Leo using his chin to indicate a point at his feet.

"This is where my great-grandmother's people had their house, when first over from Ireland. The Highland Clearances brought the Scots, but the Woody Shore was taken by the Irish. The Scotchmen liked their patch of land, for farming. They couldn't fish. They learned to fish only after. The very first were the Portuguese. They fished. They had a whaling station on Ingonish Island that burned to the ground, first insurance claim in North America. Lloyd's of London. There's a Portuguese graveyard over at the golf course, on Number Four. Down in a pit at the mouth of the Clyburn – where they wintered. Meagre spot, I always thought. They couldn't have had a big operation, or many bones to lay out. And why in a hole?

"The first census had Doyles on it. That was the group she came from, your great-great-grandmother. That old foundation down there with the cans in it, and the roots you're throwing in – that's the place, washed beach stone, see, mortar, see? They must have got the salt off well; they're still stuck.

"Her name was Molly, but she was gone long before we came. Something struck the whole family toward the early part of last century. They're all buried in the same plot, one decorated with a stone border as if the bones were interred, quarantined. But, I guess they were. It's in the part of the graveyard way down over the hill by the beaver dam. The first of the parish were buried down there, only later did they start climbing the bank. They were saving the space up on the flat for a community that was to grow. They soon realised not so many were dying as first anticipated."

"Not dying? What were they doing?"

"They were dying, just not here. The wars took them. A lot went other places to work. Which is, to live. They married. Died wherever they ended up. Yes. The first priests thought there'd be a sizeable population so they put the first down alongside the beavers. The census of 1864 said 992 inhabitants, the census of 1964 said 996. Grew by four. Go over and see their names next time you're there. You'll be surprised to see how many died in their thirties. Something struck half-dozens, carrying them off to their deaths."

Wiry eyebrows rose and fell. His look stayed on the fire.

"Frank?"

"Right here."

"You weren't here when Adrian passed on. You were his son. We weren't all that close, for brothers, not in the way you expect them to be. Or, that could be a myth like everything else is. When he got infirm I went to see him. He started talking to me right away, too. Couldn't take care of himself in the old place. I know that. I asked your sister Grace, his daughter, to go get him out of it. He was seeing ghosts. She tried, but no, he held on at that place like it was the Taj Mahal. Roof leaking, snow blowing in under the sill. Memories, I guess. I would have gotten out. But this one night, toward the end of a winter that none thought would end, I went and knocked on his door. Which was unusual, to begin – knocking on the door of a family member. The feel of the place wanted it. 'You drinking in there?' I said. 'Not so much', he replied. I kicked open the door and there he was. Sitting in the company of the blackened glass of an oil lantern. But shaved, dressed... like he was off to church! He wore shoes, dress socks. 'I think it's time, Adrian,' I said. 'You got to get the hell out of this. Come live with me since you won't go with anyone else.' He asked why, why he had to go anywhere. 'Because it's not natural here, Adrian! What, with wood bugs and centipedes for company. Keep it up. The last word you'll have will be with one of them.' He sat back in his chair. 'You don't understand,' he said. 'What?' I said, 'That it's your end? I understand.' He wasn't looking at me, 'That I don't mind,' he said.

"I asked what it was he didn't mind. I wanted an answer, I got no satisfactory one. It was difficult to get him to look my way and when he did his eyes were a mile away. I didn't harass him. I promised him I wouldn't. He was reading the Bible, he said. 'Those names we heard a thousand times over. You aren't interested? I am.' I don't think he could read. But then this feeling struck me, as he mentioned Abraham taking his daughters in a cave. The feeling struck that it wasn't me who had things figured out. It was Adrian, him! I always thought I had one up on him – him with the harder go of both lives put together. The raising of his family in straightened circumstances. He had come through this life with sense of purpose. I wanted to be taught a little of what he learned, in his strife, on his own. This way, that; he didn't mind. Because not to mind – tell me a greater blessing! He didn't go in too bad a way, Frank. Not many would understand. I believe you might. Ah, this meal was just the thing. I'm full till four o'clock, my supper."

Wiping the back of his wrist on his mouth, Leo flicked final tea drops into the fire. He wove the cup in long strokes then a wide circle. "Here. Put that on your Thermos. Frank, you look confused. Don't be. You're home now."

"Little tired, Leo."

"What! You with all kinds of life in you yet! Don't be. The rest of us around here see you as something, Frank. The front line of something, no matter what you were through out there. All right then, I'll be here tomorrow, bai's, for another meal. Same time?" He winked at Rodney and then Frank, as they watched him take one unsteady step backward.

"You all right?"

The old fellow had aged to the point where little was left. He was frail, his shoulders bent as if being roped down for many long years. He had eaten half the sandwich, placed its generous crust on a rock, for the birds. Frank had wanted to ask whether his wife lived; he suspected not. Gloria was her name. He suspected his uncle now lived as his father Adrian had. Rodney would tell him later. Frank took what he could of his father from Leo, who hesitated leaving, who waited for confidence.

"You never made it home for the funeral, Frank?"

"I didn't, Leo."

"He asked after you. I never breathed a word of your misfortune. Your sister Grace told him – what she saw fit. You probably never got word till he was gone, what, with you being away winning all those arm-wrastling matches! No one ever beat you, eh, Frank? But your mother's people, they were the lions. They had muscles in their hair. Rock-pickers. And tough work, that. Bending. No end in sight. Your father was not strong, he was tough. I didn't like to tangle with him, though that hardly stopped me on occasion. One night I remember I grabbed him and he put me on my back faster than I-don't-know-what! And me, the elder!

"The people who lived here, the ones who died early, were lions all right. You had to be, to clear land, to plant potatoes and the grand-daddy of them all – row out to Middle Head to get your basket of fish. How they got through the winters back then. God himself holds the key. Greater mystery than the pyramids, that.

"There was a front step on that house, and a back. All nine sons went out to the front first thing on a summer morning. They lounged till the sun crept round and left its shadow. Then they hauled them-selves around to the back step to take light there. The fishermen pull-ing nets near the beach saw them here in the morning, then there, on the back step, when heading home with their catches. They were cold, I guess. Thing is, those fellows, all of them, had strength like you wouldn't believe. And proved it on occasion, which often resulted in trouble. Scars. Ah, you got to throw in some leisure to get the force."

But an angry turn of expression stole over Leo's face. Frank and Rodney looked at each other. Leo swallowed slowly but seemed un-able to control this rash shift in manner. A fit, perhaps? The trotting of a horse came out on the road.

"I can't go anywheres without seeing that."

"Seeing what, who?"

"Enemy number one."

Rodney and Frank had to wait till the horse trotted around the turn and came into the view offered by cut trees. They saw a second old man direct a slatternly beast that drew a carriage, a woman aboard and a fellow younger than Rodney. The old man pulled hard his reins and called a haw. He passed the ends to the young fellow then turned to alight. On his side of the rig he pulled out a long stick to start the hill.

"Dad!" called the woman aboard. "I said – where you going, and what for?"

"To pay my regards, I said, to a legend, is where and what for. Can you wait?"

"You'll be getting all the legend coming to you, answer me like that again," she called in subsidy. He waved at her but did not turn.

"Someone speaking of me? Legend?" called Leo. "I'm right here. You don't need to mount no hill."

The new visitor ignored this, concentrated on making the hill. "You? You're as much legend as this dirt I'm climbing over. You might think you are." The old man tried to hide how the incline winded him as he stepped onto level ground and approached the men at the fire.

"Where's your pitchfork?" said Leo.

"Pitchfork? What do you mean, pitchfork?"

"That's what the devil carries."

"Don't call me the devil. You're the devil."

"I'm God, ready to settle the score between you and me. Or did you forget?"

"How can a person forget? Or get a chance to, when a memory harbouring like yours is here to remind him? You're like an old miser, you, hanging onto to every tidbit. Like the first coins he ever got."

"Just don't go dying. I saw you take that hill."

"I dare say *you* saw me take every hill I ever set foot on."

"Daniel Dunphy?" said Frank. "Captain?"

"The same, Frank bai. I remember you as a boy, Frank. I was friend to your father."

"Yes now, you a friend to anyone," said Leo.

"Look! End that saucy mouth or I'll pick you up and fire you in the water. The ocean there, lake there, harbour there. Take your pick. I come here to see Frank, not you. So clam it up once and for all."

Leo wore a sullen face, and one perfectly oblivious: as if not hearing a prior word and none but himself were present.

"They told us down the Shore you were home, Frank. I was planning to come by. You're clearing land, I see. And, down here."

"Rodney's doing the clearing. I'm hanging around to help where I can. Yes, the aim is to put a little place up."

"Well now. If this just ain't the spot. That's great, Frank. Here, give us your hand."

They shook and the fire crackled. In the harbour, a loon wept. In the fire something loud popped. The men peered past blue and orange flame, past to rising mists and lush mountains, the harbour's far side. But the carriage wavered. The horse raised a hoof. "You've got a good-size blaze here. You can get rid of a lot of stuff when she's real hot. That's my daughter, Doris, her son young Edward aboard. She grew up after you, Frank. She's timid around the horse. Though not around me. I'd better scat. I'm just down along the road here, you fellows need anything, just sing out. I got equipment. Lots I don't use anymore."

They waited a moment: no saucy answer from Leo.

"Thank's, Daniel, for your offer," said Frank. "I'll be by, at least for a visit."

"Better be. Very well then, we'll see yas all later. And this uncle here of yours, Frank. You'd arm-wrastled him early, you'd never got out of Ingonish!"

"Better believe it, mister," said Leo raising biceps extra high, a bony fist clenched. They laughed while old man Dunphy descended the hill with a swagger, waving his own hand in triumph upon reaching his rig, upon inserting his stick below his grandson's feet. Frank glanced at Leo, who had laughed as much as the rest. Perhaps the end of all our days could be staved off with a little humour. Perhaps the two admired each other. Long hate sometimes grows to that.

"You'll be getting people stopping," said Leo, the horse trotting out on the road. "Now that you opened the gates. They didn't pave here yet. There's talk of it. Don't let them interfere, the visitors, keep busy. They'll only stop plaguing you after the roof is on. Some make it their project to delay others, when they see a person trying to get ahead a little. Let the advice come. Hum the 'Four Marys' when it does. Or get Rodney here to break out his harmonica. No – don't do that! It'll prompt a trip to the liquor store that will end in a rip-roaring drunk. But if it does come to that, you call me."

He went on his way. And when on the road, after he looked left and right – a dog appeared from the bushes to begin a trot behind. Leo did not turn to see what haunted him. The dog sniffed what was in sight, travelling in the nervous habit of a runaway.

"Leo's paying as much attention to that dog as he would the man in the moon."

"Could be he doesn't know it's there. The old guy doesn't seem all that with it. Listen. Rodney. I got to go back up the road to the house, lay down for an hour. I'm not used to this stuff the way you are."

"Go get some rest, Frank. I'll carry on."

"I'm only hoping this is not all there is left in a fellow, of a day's work. Till I get back. If you could keep it going. Also, how about not telling anyone where I am."

"No?"

"I like it uninterrupted sometimes. A lot are coming around."

"I won't tell a soul, Frank."

*F*rank went where the others had gone, and with a stick. But out on the road he stumbled, dropping the support of his stick. Rodney tore down the hill. Frank was on his back.

"Cursed stone in the clay. I'm all right, Rodney. I only hope you didn't get legs like these, bai. Drinking, that's what ruint them."

Rodney let Frank go on his own. But, back up on the hill and stepping over the sod bank through the tight spruce, he watched his uncle make the turn. He waited till no footfall came on gravel before returning to work. His hand gripped balsam. He shook his head at the reasonable thought of just going down after the uncle: nope, allow the man his leave. He knew of delicacy, how delicacy, went hand in hand with the rough and tumble. He'd heard about that relationship, all his life.

thirty-three

$\mathcal{F}$rank glimpsed past closing lids, the ceiling of this, the backroom of early life. Old walls bent as feverish falling made him grip a musty cot mattress; at hand sparse furniture washed about. "Anyone there? Could I have a cup of water?" In soaked sheets he concentrated, pinching the covering now, as breeze at the window stirred its worn blanket. In trickling carousels of light, in delirium, he reflected upon past circumstances of even less comfort. In mind's eye he saw too clear the long frosty fall of 1960. He saw his own figure, upright and battered, road-weary, trying hard to reach home to retrieve a little property with which he would winter in Sydney and, once there, win any wolfish brethren he could. In the cups. Intoxicants. Not the matter: piety the matter, during inebriation's swim. The drunk returns but for love.

Frank had come up from Miami where a promoter had stiffed him seven thousand. He had been the year one-arm boxing, long-bar power lifting, Indian arm-wrestling. The promoter took a swing at Frank, who pinned the hustler to the wall and dug from a pocket eighty-five dollars. Frank walked the highway for two days till persuading a northbound driver to let him ride in the back of his candy truck. The trucker swung the door open only in New York City, when Frank said out to squinting sunlight: "Count, I want you to see I didn't touch a solitary chocolate bar. Not that a man wasn't tempted the whole way. Hardest thing I ever done." The driver took Frank's arm to help the celebrity. Frank bedded at a dive in Manhattan's Lower East Side until its owner decided she didn't like the look of him. In Central Park he got in eleven nights before authorities drove him out. It was summer solstice, the twenty-first of June when he set out on foot. He took breaks, but, once begun, he walked home to Cape Breton.

When arriving by way of the old highway into Sydney, he put up at Paul's Hotel till measures of drunken thrashing culminated in his eviction. "These walls are residential walls, not anything else. Guests stay here." Frank spent four nights under a table in Wentworth Park where he wrestled more demons and one in particular others faced: October rain. Folks pointed him out when he'd sit out at any dry hour. But users shunned the trim grasses and falling Chestnut canopy. When on Charlotte Street, he saw Ingonish faces but crossed through traffic to feign contemplation of goods in a shop-window ... lest these fellow northerners spot him.

Hearing whistle through brass, he paused at Sid's Used Furniture where a man of flared nostrils and sloping chest made a trumpet appear toy-size. Frank dipped head in deeper and the man looked up: "Easier to get a note out of the teacher. I know you. Right well I do. You're Frank Curtis from Ingonish. Know every match you fought, you. Here's a tip. Cops got it in their heads you're trouble. Harder, I know, for the bachelor man to keep his nose clean. Foot patrol, working downtown here comes in and asks after you ... yesterday. Hard times have bore down, all right. I see them. We don't get to pass down this road but there's patches where all is upside down."

"How much?"

"Trumpet? Well, hell – this! ...Wants ten bucks, he says."

"There plastic to go with it?"

Frank passed the money as customers stole light from the door, as a mother screwed her child's head away: "Come I said you."

Swallowing pride, being spat upon by rain, he searched vacating streets for any heading north. He couldn't be seen walking up Kelly's Mountain. Not trolling down Cape Smokey. Get in, get out – quick. That's the way. With eight dollars in his pocket he entered a liquor store and bought two pints. The cash-register lady recognised him, though none of the guaranteed weather commentary came. Seated at the park he took in a clearing fall afternoon. He left off fingering trumpet pistons when a uniform approached.

"Just about to move along," said Frank. "Catching my wind here was all."

"Don't mind hearing that, not a bit. Catch it in a different town."

Out on the Esplanade rain fell through the sun. Frank took berth of husky men, stopped, one decked out in denim. "Don't be alarmed, Champ. Saw that back there, too. Don't you worry. We get that wherever we go, us. Gets to be the regular life of a pariah. Friends only, makes the difference. Got a smoke?" The denim's accomplices wore pink rain outfits, one had a neck tattoo and each long hair. Frank nodded no, then followed silvery train tracks, detouring steeply when he spotted harbour water through undergrowth. He surveyed an impartial rained-on west soon, breathed for a land climbing to a wet sun. He ate a lumberjack sandwich, upon less damp stones, twisting off in his teeth the cap of a pint. He saw across the harbour; northeast ... where North Sydney lay.

But proper rain came. He thus followed banks inland for Sydney River, rising past residential plots and sporadic commercial attempts to enter the Pocketbook Bar – in relative control. He warmed up, drank draft in a far corner until a neighbouring table laughed in his direction. The bartender approached. "Got to keep it down, fellows." A girl was with them. Frank did up a jacket button and the bartender winked more than half-kindly.

Outside, he was witness to a hard rain falling, to police across a muddy lot. A searchlight flashed.

"Follow me? Here!" said a halting Frank, indicating his bag.

He went along with bag as cops followed, their window down.

"Exactly right. Got wind of your trouble down in Florida."

"I did nothing I'm not proud of."

"Best to keep silent on that. On all accounts, you."

Sidelights flashed on him, fast in the rain.

*F*rank, breathy, made it through cherry tree tangles which now forced him to wade a black autumn harbour below private property posted, its bitches barking. He took the shore north, always north, crossing a train trestle – to beat out a return, underneath, to wait out rain burst. He broke for hours next through soaked spruce and thorn, dogs crying, men calling. He was faint, his legs wanting long rest now as he stood in his soaking fog outside a landmark he knew: the North Sydney Forum.

But a throng was departing. He heard Jesus, above derision, scoff, taunt, cat calls; a blood hot and high in its people here. Bottles smashed centre lines. This was a melee. He read the marquis: Atlantic Professional Wrestling Championships: October 1–3.

People spotted him and sang out.

"You know that?"

"That what – that? Bum, I see. And, look at the sight of him."

"Not at one time. Bum, he wasn't. Something to be reckoned with."

Frank turned feverishly for the street, ushered himself down a lane but here met with more returning revellers, blood a-boil, laughter and violence ready. Two had shirts off. The pair made a scamper for him when a fight broke out between a black and a white – both standing good ground and coming in hard with fists. Frank backtracked and got in behind the forum, away from electric light. He lay his back against the edifice and huffed. Drops pelted him. He drew his plastic.

A misted-upon stranger smoked at the forum's corner in pre-dawn twilight. He was a Native, younger, cleaner, at his feet his own canvas knapsack of army issue.

"Insanity here," the Native called, but lightly. "That wrestling, last night? All the rage. People take it too serious. Confetti, look. Regions on the periphery, soak up all madness. Sugared coffee ... in the Thermos here."

Frank got to his feet: he hardly wanted to be seen tramping yet. He felt little was left but to approach.

"Well, I'll be. You Frank Curtis? Up against it, are you fellow?"

"Wet, some." Frank had the man's hand, but for assistance.

"That your bag? That's not a trumpet? Bring it all... No? John Sillyboy."

"Off somewhere, John?" said Frank, voice wrested further from cobwebs. Frank spat then excused himself.

"Catching that round-bow for Boston," said Sillyboy. "Look, the bay. She's altogether sick with boats. Going for a year. Harvard, the States. I'm a poet." John Sillyboy had an oversized head, a sharp eye and proper cheek lines. His hair was combed in oil and he smelled partly of deep woods, its welcome parts.

"Write about me."

"Oh, somewhere I have. Home, Frank? That where you're headed?"

"Always I think. Just don't know how to manage this last leg. Closer I get, harder she is to make it."

"Must be a ride, you're pretty well there."

"All kinds of rides."

"Never owned a car myself, else I'd take you, and my boat here. Can't afford to miss our boats, now can we."

"No, we can't."

"We do journey but further so, into our displacement."

"Ah? What's that?"

"Only that not signing up makes a good life a rough life, Frank."

"Who's signing up? Who's signing, for what? For wrestling, that what you're saying!"

"No. No one, being chased off. I'm hoping school empowers me."

"School? How'd you get in? There? That's the one for big shots, ain't it?"

"Well now I wrote them and their board was consolatory. All take a representative few. Hardly matters. The matter is, it is you, here, the same who prompted me. This therefore becomes some meeting this. I know where you're from, Frank. I know because I went there to learn where you're from. My people walked those hills and shores. Summers, they did. They wintered in kinder floods. In Bras d'Or. You threw them off, fair and square. My intention's no different. Fair and square. Just not with my back."

Frank handed the Thermos lid and took proffered cigarette without regard.

"There's after the fair," said Sillyboy. "Luck needed there too I expect."

"Luck is needed before, after, during, any cursed fair! You making fun of me?"

"Take it easy, fellow. Cops on the lookout, for all sorts during this tournament. Blood, last night. I saw a Paddy wagon, I saw cops arrive, by bus. I didn't take a room. Not because of it. Don't like rooms, me. Not when you're a people only got the vote this year. No, you can't trust folks when they're all together like this. Daylight or dark. Best you get that ride north. Mail truck. Transfer even."

"Boat, even."

"Boat? Why not a boat, best way. Going or coming."

"I need something stronger than coffee."

Sillyboy readied lip to speak of the trumpet when the half-clad seducer sang with no pursed blow, no piston pressed.

"Shake your hand, Frank?"

"Ah?"

"Listen. Keep from town proper. Nothing but trouble. And this is a hard state you've stumbled into, I don't mind saying."

"You just do all you can! Hear? Whatever your name is! Hear?"

"Calm down, Frank. I hear loud and clear."

"Well then, good, I said… Show them Yanks all we're worth."

John Sillyboy gave Frank three two-dollar bills… to see the hero wade a return for his own army knapsack, draw flap aside and peer at nothing. Sillyboy walked the ticker-tape streets to the launch terminal where inside he sat abreast thick pane. Forward, he saw his steamer, its generous chain, her Portuguese crew at scaffold adjacent, gloved to scrape barnacle. Sillyboy took out his pen and coiled book to write title and verse of the work some recall as his magnum opus, the final work before his untimely end in a rail mishap. "Strongest Man In Ingonish… And so we dip headlong into trough unbefit, these grub boxes not to know our charm nor wit. Yet, I chance to meet in my twenty-seventh year to all knowing – carved in sweat, valleyed in fear, my brother father, sister dear. Tramp, hobo, spilt saline for all. Ruint! He's ruint! Suffer, now, the hand that claps the neck. Oh, form formless. Stock, shock at unfinished when spirit cries: full, complete! Strength livid in emptiness when two is one, when two do meet. No! Return not, charm, nor wit! Under eaves that soak of haunts now to frighten. To winning forum, formally, broken and broke in twilight flight. I see years fast ravelling to yarn's end and smell well extinguished fires of Fate. Crestfallen, lame, border for insane. Wish me now they lay me down in distant Ingonish. Wish me now they draw me down to nothing, to nothingness… (Upon meeting Frank Curtis, North Sydney Forum, October 2nd, 1960)."

It was evening of the same. Frank sat at a lover's bench where port brimmed two soda tins – then, where port brimmed one. He nursed weighty remains. He heard hack; so dark was it night. A seagull scratched, it scathed. Marine scent broke, marine bell south clanged south. Pitch dark, at the muffled cry, the muffled wail. He was on his feet: the boxer never to box. He was charging, carrying his nursed port to see a woman post-slapped in an alley black, treated with dishrag regard. "Hear now, cut that out!" Frank set down his tin, grabbed the offensive hand which remarkably broke free. He saw an alley eye when he knew his own was to go cold at a strike to his ankles, a two-by-four plank. On the gravel, the even pavement, at mortared brick he clutched and stammered. A barking face, too near his own: "How's that, now? You don't know? No name coming? I know yours, you filthy one-armed bastard! Take a man's sport! Make it mockery!"

Frank was on his knees. He had the offensive throat, even stood with it to crush what windpipe he could. He bit tongue: there now, disregard, to throw you like doffed clothes. And, there, you slink off expertly. There were singing voices: a lot was wrong, scuffs, he heard a trumpet note not quite got when he was bashed with its tempered edged brass. He bled nose, blew, bled eyebrow: tasted ice-floe salt. Blinded but firm he stood his feet.

"Come on, Tommy! Frank Curtis! One of them flat-nosed Mac-Donald pricks are at him!"

Frank spat a molar as he was set upon his bench.

"Hello Bulldog. You don't remember us? What? We drank a glass – your first win? Young Jimmy here broke like the goddamn German blitz just now to rout me out of bed. I only live there. Because it's you, that'll save he's hide."

Frank blinked through blood.

"Here I say, use it, a hanky, she's clean. Your nostril's come open. We followed you that night, remember? Up the street. Ah – he don't know us from a hole in the wall, Jim. Jimmy, I said? Listen and, mark – all out to get your kind, Frank. Stranger are catching it. So you come with us. You never lost favour, not here. You beat those other two. Sent them packing, up at the forum, up the street that night. Owwee, sour. No, no? He don't know us. Jim? Jimmy … don't go far."

Frank wiped his eye and folded the rag.

"So I say come along, Curtis. Rough night. Rough town, this. Now that Sydney politics took over. Steel, coal, backroom palm-warming. Rats roam after the big thrive. We got a bed. Over the shop."

"Leave me be."

"Ah my. Now how can we? Frank? Tell me how?"

"Leave me be. I said so."

The interlopers drew shoulders, as each embraced fully when a man spoke his heart, how words alone finally were to be honoured. As for that MacDonald pair – how they had plagued the soul out of these and so many others over the years. But this is a true sin, this one. They'll get their due. Watch and see they don't. Mark.

Frank sat on the dock, consciousness slow to restore. "Food. Can't keep it down – can't." Sardines, in his pack. He saw lights from the round-bow steamer. What? She not gone? He saw one vessel he re-cogised, in name at least: *Aspy*. She, here? Was she redone? I think so, she was. He stood, perhaps to make for it – when two figures approached, one toting a pipe. There was the dance, the baffling brushing scuff to preface all close-violence. Frank's wrist broke the weapon's falling blow.

He got another throat, no – the same! But, sniff, gun oil. He wheeled, there: its innocent house, just visible. "Leave him go, I said, I got what I got here." Frank had a knee on concrete, released when the other closed in, for ... grapple. Roll. Bang. Four frightening others in tight succession. Maybe five.

Frank was over creosote beam, into hateful sea-salt water. He swam with dark cold success not known in years. For, the *Aspy*? And, was he shot?

He saw the round-bow, the *Olivia* out of Portugal.

At her anchor chain he discovered, bit by bit, he could climb the links. He panicked higher, enough to fall when moon tide eased the ship toward its line, as cop lights dizzily blazed ashore. Steadily, in open prayer, he crossed onto the scrubbing scaffold, to secure himself, draw himself up, working one side then the other. The precipitous gunwale came; he bent gut over harsh steel to find the deck. Cutting squeezes and wriggles took him under lifeboat tarp, from where in the night came rising the sound of a cranky chain. He smelt again the powder at the joint affixing thumb and index. But, he had always smelt powder, here.

Lawyer of the time, Abe Flowers knew Cape Smokey. He knew In-gonish. Attorney Flowers had beach front property in Ingonish. A prominent member of the Highlands Links, his handicap lowering steadily all the time. Flowers knew better yet the caddies who stole his balls, the caddies who had begun to flee the shack at the cheap sight of his arrival. He paid one dollar for four hours in the sun. So, what? Lucky they got that! The Professional called these irreverents out of the spruce and birch, called for their entire expelling. Petty? Certainly not. What in this world is petty when all has great meaning, and all greater consequence? Advocate Flowers lifted not a finger to help Frank Curtis. This was a vicious crime, vainglorious, planned. And, anger? How long can anger last: hours, and: 1 plus 4 bullets? First degree here. Good Samaritans? The Wallace element? They could testify, just not well. How could they when their long hate did much of the trigger easing?

Police found a trumpet. They questioned waterfront residents; a second-hand used-goods store employee, way over in Sydney. There was Sydney's foot patrol. Murder the investigation. All questioned had reservations. "Yes. Did he *ever* look dangerous!" Reservation in consensus heaps in frosty climates at dark winter's approach. This perpetrator only overheated media outfits – weighing now heavily in the slow minds of judicial powers. Frank Curtis? Why, he was at large. The bogeyman, in form, for children, for women: for men. The story made for black ink, for blot – for outright spillage at the fugitive's capture on Christmas Eve in Buffalo, New York.

It was a border crossing, foiled. Curtis had been living his wet months out as a hobo, until one of his own jungle ratted him out over a misplaced canopener. He was taken in fetters before new year bells struck down 1960. In custom-made single manacle he moved, manacle grimly attached to partnered ankle steel. Once lauded for incompleteness here was figure finally vilified for the same. Posters got shredded. Figurines thrown out back-city windows. Once-bestowed, New York City key opened no door. Upper Canada acknowledged no parentage of this adopted East Coast son. Mythology has its rise: it has greater, its fall. Two of New York State's tallest and most gallant marshals led Frank onto the sunny winter terraces of the Buffalo City Courthouse at year's blow-out. Each uniform smiled good teeth when it was the private three, when jocular talk came of "the Sport of Arms" – that particular wrestling once to hold it big. Uniforms fell taciturn when clicking heels came; these of rabid reporters abandoning assigned outdoor nooks with its excellent light, with its decent angles, its brick fore-drop: to capture pics to make careers. One photo did go the distance, supplanting the much-to-do hopeful image of the 35th Yankee president John F. Kennedy (as always, brasher prevails):

"At Large No Longer!" read a 48-font caption, a brutish Frank Curtis staring down a petrified lens. One sub-caption, of many, was to read less magnanimously: "One Bulldog Best Chained!"

"Canada's greatest story to date! Concluded – on U.S. soil!"

The story eased minds. Look, how land, how home too is protected. The dawn of another hurtful American era, one that would see the United States involved in a botched overthrow of a Cuban leader, a president's assassination and before long a protracted Asian tangle, one deeply face-losing. And, to no end, this residual Red Scare to harass minds.

Frank was returned to Canada where he was processed and came to know both height and might, of walls. How mentally sharp, their capping rolling razorblade wire. Dorchester Penitentiary – its boxy bed sheets and cold spoons during seventeen years of privation. Frank wrestled the first night for dawn – drowning his penal pillow. He took on the second, to learn how mute was man – how mean and utter the reprobate.

Now in his cot, in this darkened room, Frank slowly came to grips with this day, this new old reality, free and home. Belief in Good? That it would win out? Yes, except, addendum: Good was a battling force, all on its own.

thirty-four

*O*pen for days, the porch doors and window removed no must; it rather seemed to have deepened it. Boards covered the back windows, still. The house had been built like a warren; no cross breeze swung through. But little of that was of real concern here on the cot at the childhood walls, where the only true rest of life had been got. This alone might have drawn Frank home.

The air stayed chill. Drawing up army surplus blankets, bringing the coarse wool to his shoulders, Frank realised the burgundy bedding had stayed in excellent shape. It was testament to the short distance from long dead youth till now. He waited on his back, keeping as far as possible from the pillowcase mildew. The open window ushered in a cooling air. Eyes closed and the churning thought, the dialogue pieced from mouths long ago but clear as any present. A lifetime waited, with eyes shut, a sanity poorly tuned – all which became remotely known when awake. Specifics welled up when drifting off – or drowning. Specifics never influenced the reason by which one lived day to day. But this guilt, why? And what for? A mind in turmoil is what age manifests for all. A drink before sleep had it fixed. So did opening the eyes.

Frank opened his eyes and, seeing the old backroom, terror vanished. Here the twilight walls and corner-webbed ceilings that had fascinated him in infancy.

He turned for the open backroom door; fever raged. Anyone could waltz in. Anyone was welcome to because to waltz in; it would be just the ticket – a little conversation. He fell off then, fell deeply asleep with damaging thoughts passed, the bridge traversed, his room his protectorate.

$\mathcal{F}$or days he lay in fever. Rodney brought food, helped him outside to the woods and kept his promise not to alert Grace, who had gone to Cheticamp for a religious retreat. Retreat from what, Frank hadasked. One bright afternoon, Rodney working at the Crick property to keep up appearances, Frank did have a visitor to the old homestead. Strangely, his brother stood before the cot. But which? Frank could not focus without the glasses of Adrian's he'd found and been using indoors.

"Well, hell, Christ. That you, Clifford?"

Clifford was mute, standing bedside, tall, hands in pockets, staring. Frank sensed there was much youth in him yet.

"How did you stay that way, Clifford? Clifford, I say!"

"…come out of it, Frank, you're dreaming…"

Frank's pupils constricted. Here was the backroom, the old house. He was being held at his shoulders, by an aging woman.

"Claire?"

He could sense breasts, smell hair.

"You can let go. I say, leave go. You'll choke me yet!"

She settled into the chair Rodney had hauled in from the kitchen. She was indeed older, a big-boned version, with appealing eyes. Her cheeks were sunken and crow's feet walked her temples too. The full lips had abandoned the mouth. Her scented hair was crayon silver. She puffed the wind of the indolent.

"You were out of it, my dear, calling me Clifford. Clifford's in his own cot where he's not set foot from for six months. Don't worry about him. Frank? You listening? This is no place to be, Frank. Here.

You're in a bad way and you'll catch it. I arrived to a big leak pouring onto rusted stove grates till I put a pot under it. It made my heart sick."

"All right."

"It's true. And the pot had a squirrel's nest in it – of toilet paper."

"I said, all right! Any more to say of a man's home?"

"Home? Catacomb, more like. I was stopped at the road for I don't know how long, getting the courage to come down. I was afraid with the place so run down that wild animals might live inside."

"One does ... is trying to."

"Every car North of Smokey passed. I couldn't take the gawking."

"Ahem ... thought you didn't worry about that. Get me up."

Claire once more noted the assortment of medical creams. They had swollen her eyes at their discovery upon entering, and now, a second whelm at the eyes. She helped him. She looked at the ceiling for relief, but that was so ugly she lowered her head and put the back of her wrist to her nose. A fresh roll of toilet paper was alongside a storm lantern set on a card table, she balled a wad of this and honked her nose. A wool blanket hung from galvanised nails above the window. No air could really enter.

"What are you trying to prove?"

"Claire?"

"What? I'm listening."

"Do you think I can say, good to see you?"

"You can. I'd say the same except you're beat to pieces."

"You might ease up on the compliments. None of us here is the beauty we once were. Pass me those glasses, will you? Thank you. No that's not true ... you don't look the worse for wear."

"There's wear. And you laid up like this doesn't lessen it. How old did your face get! It frightened the life out of me first going. And not knowing whether you were lying there among the living or dead."

"So what's the verdict?"

"I thought of my own face. How it must have come just as far. We don't ever see ourselves in this light, do we? As when we get a look at someone returning from a long way off? Clifford sent me. That was a shock. He never spoke of you. But you didn't speak of him. In your letters home."

"In my letters home – to Grace? They public domain now?"

"We've been close, Frank. Me and Grace. Like sisters, you know that. More than."

"A person can't mention everyone when he's composing a line. That would be a lot. I'll mention him now. He still moody as ever? And what's wrong with him he's laid up?"

"You needn't ask. Nerves shot. Liquor. And when he'll swear to this day that liquor is the only thing that ever eased them. They can't see the lie they live. No, he was never one for going out in public. There's the crux. Never realised the importance of it."

"I wouldn't mind knowing that one myself."

"You got some sense, some, to get out and see people, Frank. You did have, anyway. A person must, otherwise none comes to see you when you're down and out and in need of it. A little practised good-will goes a long way. You'll not end up like this – with people wanting to lend a hand, but too afraid to go through with it."

"People are nosy, Claire."

"Only as far as to fit you in somewhere. What do you know? How can you know? All men have that the inwardness about them. Think they're accomplishing something, when they aren't."

"I can see what your life study has been. Inwardness? Wayward-ness, maybe."

"I say, *in*."

"A man is a hermit, Claire."

"A woman is a hermit."

"Not in the spirit of a man."

"And thank be the Lord for that. If it were up to yous, birthdays and Christmas would be done for. Weddings, go first. Wakes, funer-als. All by the wayside and farewell to eating at the table."

"I'm waiting for the negative aspects."

"Clifford mentioned you, right after you left. Then, your name was not spoken in the house again. I couldn't say it was anything in particular. You were just gone. The real trouble didn't seem to be it."

"And what real trouble are you referring to, Claire?"

Claire looked ahead and Frank saw in her eyes the spoil of traps that had caught her and her people.

"Sounds like you coaxed yourself into something?" said Frank.

"A little funeral gets held for the person who departs, who vanishes. Those remaining have to cope."

"Funeral? To account for a person again, is it? Fit you in?"

"Something like that. Here, drink it. Juice. A person needs a project, to bring things to the fore."

"I don't know what you're talking about. Give me a second. Ah... catch my breath. I'm worn out all over again talking to you."

Clicking juncos and zapping black-capped chickadees foraged in the field below the line of spruce. They wouldn't leave the air alone. They'd start young soon; it was time nests were built, time when mates were found and having young the preoccupation.

"This land of yours, Frank, what you had Rodney clear. From daylight till dark, that fellow has worked, but now doesn't know how to proceed. He hasn't got the experience for what you have him doing. He's missing chances, Grace says, fishing with someone. There's work cutting grass on the golf course. Lots to be done on the trails for the national park, the world is timing, in these parts."

"Hear! Don't talk to me of those criminals. National park: I know better now how they came and offered people nickels for their homes, shooed them off land their ancestors settled, whether good agreement was made or not. Willa Lourdes had to crawl on her belly under a chain-link fence to get to her chickens, six months pregnant."

"Work, Frank. They brought work. People need it."

"What they should have brought is fairness, first. Didn't one of their higher-ups on the sly buy land and home near the sea recently, park land, long after this so-called national park was established? Where is the clause for that in the national park act?"

"Ah my. People find their tongues. They go away, to find them. Did you have anything to eat, you?"

"Two cans of sardines, on bread there, I ate. Three or four dough-nuts yesterday evening."

"There's health. Think you can you rise to your feet?"

"Well now...."

"What? Well now... can't end your days here. Or are you home to do just that? Make your peace with God?"

"We never quarrelled, Claire. Not to my knowledge. Did you ever stop to think a man might just be under the weather?"

"What! When they come strong as you? The strongest man North of Smokey."

"Not every man goes the way of Clifford, Claire. Some are tired. Let me. I'll rise."

"First thing is to shave that face."

"Yes ... Jessie. Right quick. There's no hot water."

"Rodney was heating things up, he said, on a woodstove."

"So he told you I was here. Wait till I see him."

"Where would you be, Frank? The Keltic Lodge?"

"No, I wouldn't be there. Another fair-trade property. He broke up some wood, Rodney. I heard him. He hauled up an old potbelly from below the Rock where some kids had a log cabin. He set it out-side, but smoke came in the window to near choke me alive. We put up the blanket here. That's what I thought your hands were, on me, more smoke."

Frank rose. Oh, how he had thickened over the years, his shoul-ders, back, broad like a bear's. The sinewy arm looked like dead weight, muscle mass dropping like sand in nylons. His neck and jaw showed twitching muscle. This made him rakish. And though sitting yet, his hips were wide, as if to have born children. The man was the bloated cast of any boy he had once been. He lifted legs and put feet in leather shoes with buckles, lined at the foot of the bed. He stood, straightening a long back. In a sweep he raised his neck then pulled on a long-sleeved work shirt, plaid, the left sleeve pinned by two heavy safety pins.

"Fever, Claire. I get a good one off and on. Been a while since the dizzy spells."

"How's the arm, Frank?"

"The arm?"

"You know what I mean. I saw the lotions, there. Grace said you never really recovered. That there was always pain. She said the wrastling ruint the other."

"Tweaks. Who of us don't get them? Nothing a little exercise won't loosen. You know what? I feel starved."

"We can set you up, but let's get you out."

Frank stepped for the backroom door and Claire pulled at his shirttail. The weight of the two supported by the panels over the floorbboards became audible.

"What you doing back there, Claire?"

"Holding on, for frig sakes! These foolish stepping boards, the whole place is a regular dungeon. Walk! Slow! Guide me. Oh, I hate the gorge you got to cross. The floor looks ready to give."

"Only because it is."

"Well I don't want to hear about it. I don't want to be down in no cellar, not here."

"Yes. Lord God knows what we'd land on. Dad's play pit. Probably a bottle or two. I'll tell you one thing, you don't loosen up on that shirt and we will! Here. My hand, don't be shy."

In the centre of the kitchen Frank stopped to bounce the floorboards; straining the joists.

"Ha, ha! Swinging bridge at the Clyburn, me son! Hee-hee!"

"Stop, Frank, stop, stop. I'm serious, stop."

Claire slapped the back of his head and they moved. Her laughter came with tears.

*H*e let her hand go in the porch and out on the step, where he touched his forehead in the sun, he said, "Sweet Hallelujah, my head – cured." Claire touched his forehead, for heat. "Sweet Hallelujah, you say. Bald's what I see."

"You start."

Claire took out her cigarette matches and looked to discover what was available to burn. Birds flew from tree cover, swooped at safe moments for seed and building material, preferably bleached animal hair. A junco wore a moustache of it. Sparrows worked the grasses, producing assortments of clicks and flutters.

"Any snakes here?" said Claire. "This tall grass is riding up my dress." Frank's eyes opened wide at this; he felt his appetite cry for something sweet. He went behind the house to urinate, keeping extra, extra careful not to get any on his pants. When he returned he raised an axe by the bit, making a poor job of breaking plywood. The potbelly had rusted grates, but deep ash inside, with embers. Rain had dampened any wood near; larger stuff was unusable. Claire returned. She bent and blew on a blue flame, catching catalogue paper she had tucked in the firebox. She left Frank to tend the fire, going again to the grass.

"Where you off to now? If you're worried about snakes, wait till you see what awaits you there. Come on, Claire. There's hornets."

Frank found a cedar shingle in the porch. He tore a strip of ceiling moulding and hauled down two posters, the topographical map of the Cape Breton Highlands National Park he balled. Breaking the moulding with his foot against an oil barrel, he carried in two trips what he had to burn, stuffing posters through the stove door. He found his shaving bag. The fire smoked like a locomotive, puffed in flame. Claire came with a tin of water from the well.

"How did you know about the well, for God sakes?"

"I grew up here too, mister. I saw where the grass was trampled."

She emptied half the tin and placed it on the grate. Good access to fresh air made fire shoot through the door grates. Yellow flame licked the flue connector.

"That won't heat."

"You got a razor?"

"I got a blade."

"A bare blade?"

"My mirror's inside."

"Well, don't expect me to go back in over that floor."

"That'll take forever to heat up the water. Forget it. I'll use it cold."

Frank soaped his brush and shaved in his unique way.

"Doesn't look too safe, what you're doing."

"What is? I mention the garage?"

"Give me that. You're missing spots. Hold still, what I have is sharp. Ah, rough, like hay, this."

Frank felt a wave of gladness at the thought of how well his garage was going to work, here, on this spot. And he was getting a shave.

"Hope no one sees us."

"They'll have to see through the jungle, Claire. Rodney dig the hole for the house?"

"He did. People are commenting on how big a change it is to see land cleared down there. Many are attempting the hill for a look. I went. I saw the wharves across the way. You'd swear professionals tackled the job."

"Everyone in for a gawk. What? With me not there, is it?"

"You're not what you call a regular, Frank."

"Why? Did things, did I? I didn't do things, too."

"Here, we're done. Take it. We'll go."

"I said I didn't do them, too."

"I heard."

"Go where?"

"To see him, your remaining brother. Clifford."

They walked down the road as cars hit horns and occupants raised hands. They passed the Fairway Market, the Nova Scotia Liquor Commission, the Bank of Nova Scotia – the latter two built opposite and alongside Mary Helen's old property. They walked the unfinished pavement under the sign: Creek Road. New gravel crunched.

Frank soon saw where Rodney had cleared. "Claire? Me son! A whole house is started!" Collected fieldstone, used in a frost wall, followed a perimeter Frank had only suggested. "Ah, my God – you said he was stalled! Yalp! I only told him where I *thought* the place might go and, look! Concrete laid out for a building before a person had a decent chance to rethink it! I wasn't sure, the size, where. What

I wanted. And the old well down over the bank? He's got a trench dug!"

"I didn't want to say anything. He wanted to surprise you."

"He succeeded. Good thing my heart is strong."

"You mean a lot to him, Frank. All the years growing up. He never had a lot of friends."

"You seem to know him, Claire."

"He was around, Frank. They all are. I think it was hard on him with an uncle like you."

"It was hard on me with an uncle like me. Rooted me out of bed... to see this. No. I can't tell you how good it is to see it, Claire. Truth is, foundation and all, one I wouldn't be able to break supposing I wanted to. A fellow got this far, at least, my dear. Coming home. I'm glad."

"You'll get further. Let's move on to the next chapter while you're still up to it."

"Yeah. Let's venture the chronic."

They walked the Woody Shore Road and passed three wharves built a good piece out. Wharves of solid, heavy creosote. Everything was odd in its newness: lands cleared, houses off the main, invigorating views established. Most odd was travelling through it with Claire. Out of a passing yellow station wagon, an open window, their names came hooted.

"Who in the old dying frig was that?" said Frank. Claire shook her head. She gave a big wave and called to the open windows.

"Does it matter? You're home. Wave, bai."

The sun brought powerful glints alongside harbour dories, from painted shingles and screen doors. Spring light trimmed the eyes. Salt came in sniffs; high tide seaweed dried on shore. Iodine shared the air with the rattle of engines. All was seaside preparation, where gulls were vehement over boats whose motors chugged in test runs, or laboured in return with mackerel catches for lobster bait. Kitchen and living room curtains were open. "Slow, Claire. I say. I'm in no hurry. I know you're afraid to be seen with me, but no speed at this age."

And yet Frank grew anxious. Perhaps, speed *was* at this age. A breeze lifted from the head of the harbour. He turned and got startled. He saw the red-roofed lighthouse vigilant. Vigilant like all great watchers, in lasting silence.

thirty-five

*F*rank was ogling. He turned eyes from the screen door, jammed with a wedge of wood while Claire bent to remove her shoes. From the step he could see the play of waves.

"Kids are grown and gone," she said. "Dawn Marie's in North Sydney with three of her own. The other, Christine is married on the North Shore. Four boys. Two working at a hydro plant in Ontario. One married here in Ingonish Centre. The other has that high house across the water you're looking at. He works away. Some kind of teacher for other countries. Just the two of us here now."

Greased black bread pans were on the counter and, beside the oil stove, under the tall green hot water tank whose pipes sweated at soldered joints, was a bulging pink towel of rising bread. In slippers Claire crossed the linoleum to remove the towel and jab dough with three fingers, ring and all. She replaced the cloth and checked the temperature gauge at the stove door. She increased oil from a dial behind then reached past the grates to turn a timer clockwise.

"Leave your shoes on. He's in there. This dough's been setting all this time I was out. I want to get it in the pans. Go on. Leave your shoes on."

Frank stepped into a darkened nook off the kitchen where, positioned under drawn blinds, was a daybed. The foot was tightly tucked in. A pair of tartan slippers were lined up on a round mat. The daybed had a patchwork quilt and clean pillow, wine and tobacco were detectable. Clifford lay up with fingers knitted.

"Dark in here," said Frank. "It's night."

"The way I like it."

"I've come to see you, Clifford. It's Frank."

"Gosh. Hello, Frank. Let me get the light. It's a small bulb."

The chin was cleanly shaven, silver sideburns accessory to the face; a woolly moustache matched, one tapering off to sunken cheeks. Clifford moved to get higher, to become centralised at a headboard. Frank started forward. "No, no. I got it," said Clifford, clearing his throat. He spread his fingers and forked a full head of parted white hair. With lustre yet, yellow cod-hook ends. At the pyjama collar, salt and pepper chest hair rose in sprigs to his throat. It made cotton there appear soft, baby-like. Frank pulled a hard-seat chair out from a wall and set it at a distance. Violin music played, across the yard.

"When they let you out, Frank?" asked Clifford, with dignity. It took Frank a moment to recall the voice. But it came and stayed.

"Better be a joke, that. Two weeks Friday past I got home. I came down with a spell myself and got laid up. We all end in the cot. Napolean did."

"Oh, I'm not down with anything, Frank. Nothing you could put your finger on. I get these bouts that not many know of. You feel all is closing in."

"When doesn't a person feel that?"

"What's that, Frank? Something going on with you, you say?"

"No. My own nerves get bad is all."

"I expect so, all the travelling a fellow like you did."

Clifford coughed and hacked. Frank spotted a tin below the bed. He bent forward, then got out of his chair entirely in order to pass the tin to his brother. Clifford coughed spit and blood.

"Excuse me."

"You can't get up, at all?"

"Well … now. Not so well."

"You haven't been out, she said."

"Just this while. Soon, I'm making tracks."

"Fair weather's the ticket. There's a world of difference between getting a lungful of air and being in a house. The Irish call a man's home, his grave. First thing I do when I wake is get outside, throws a whole new perspective on things. Good to know right away the kind of day it will be. Houses, they tell you nothing."

"I don't know what you're talking about, Frank. But yes, I heard tell of something of it."

On the wall Frank saw a framed photo from the twenties. The subjects were Jessie and Adrian. They wore long coats, stood on Ingonish Beach. The photo was taken over by the Rocks, where Middle Head reached for the sea. Jessie's raven hair was past her shoulders.

"You must have had quite the life, all right, Frank. All that roaming. Seen a thing or two, I bet. Much more than most."

"Too much more. And enough to know that all there is to see is right here. I'll make that my report."

"You will? Then I'll be sure to pass that on then."

Food was being prepared in the next room. Water ran and a lid was set on a pot. Frank saw better, his eyes adjusting. He spotted ebony rosary beads at Clifford's night table. He saw a tiny framed picture of the Virgin Mary. These had to be Claire's. They could be Grace's. Not Clifford's. Adrian had raised hard hearts. Tobacco, the acetone scent of alcohol stayed prominent in the room. His stash? It had to be kept down behind the bed or in the night table drawer. Not as much as an ashtray was out for view.

"You still have your boat at all?"

"My boat? Well, yes, I do in fact. I get a young fellow next-door to scrape her down and stick a coat of paint on her. Come spring usually. Now that the weather is about to turn I must call him over. I was thinking about that very thing before you came. A tarp is hauled over her hull all winter."

Frank wanted to stand. To tell Clifford to come, get out of it. To take a little charge; life was in both of them yet. He was making things hard on Claire. Always had. The selfish prick.

"You know there was a time you couldn't go a day without a trip to the woods?"

"Me? Ho, for a lot of things there was a time, Frank."

Frank drew his lips tight. Yes, he'd seen sights in his travels. He'd seen the holes people are apt to fall into. Holes dug by their occupiers. Holes whose sides simply could not be gripped and crawled out of. Frank's own head for booze and dope made him appreciate what it was to be whelmed. He kept his mouth shut. He had stumbled. Him? He'd slept for years in dank earth. Was he wrong to think he himself had ever crawled out? You just rolled over.

"Can I use it?"

"Can you use what?"

"Your boat."

"My boat? Gosh, you never cared for the water, Frank."

"Only because, there it was, growing up. When there it's not, well, you wouldn't believe how dear it becomes. They tell you I was working on that little strip of Dad's? Down the Crick?"

"They did."

"Well, just below is the loveliest of spots to keep a dory. The bottom that's there falls off like there's no tomorrow. Sandy, all through. It'll hurt nothing. I was thinking young Rodney could go out in the harbour and get us a feed of lobsters. Mackerel are schooling."

"Not for a while, the mackeral aren't, Frank. Rodney even know how to row? I'm doubtful he does. He's never been near the water. He's like you."

"I swam."

"You swam. To swim is another thing altogether."

"Rodney is slick. With all kinds of things. You should see the foundation he erected. He can row a boat, for the love of God – he must know how oars work!"

"Ah, you never know. The weather turning. I myself might take her out for a spin. You get tired of this. Tomorrow I might make a move, you back home and all."

Not once did the brothers make eye contact. Family custom: another of the tacit agreements preserved, this in order to convene. The family spoke. They spoke openly and cordially, just never intimately. All families become this. The brothers never knew a handshake. That is a fact. There was no move to change that now. Little was different, from way back. What was the same, in fact, stood firmer ground. And yet, meeting... they could never go without that. They spoke language endemic to them is why. One no others could learn.

"Suppose you can get up to have a bite? The very least? With a brother returned from long off? I hear Claire out there. Can't disappoint the woman."

"I can do that much. But you go along ahead of me. I don't like another to watch as I rise. I got to put on a decent shirt. Go on now."

Frank waited beyond the doorcasing, his back to the little room; he heard the slow arrival of feet to the floor. He walked to a chair at the table and leaned it outward, his hand gripping its back. "Sit," said Claire. She stayed at the stove when Clifford entered in plaid slippers and a tied robe. The work shirt was under the robe, the pyjama top below that. He began with an angry sweep – "Frank, sit, sit!" Claire cleared a spot for her husband. "Thank you, Claire." She grimaced and nodded at Frank, communicating the patience and obedience all must adhere to now.

Boiled cod was in one stove pot, potatoes cut and fried in white lard in a cast-iron pan. The heated oil, the salt and black pepper were lovely to smell. Claire put a jar of sweet pickled onions on the table: chow. She laid out napkins. The men drank their tea; they crunched crackers with jammed rhubarb. Frank asked where the cod had come from and Clifford wiped his mouth, inhaled, readied for a long answer.

Someone was at the door, just when Claire set the main meal on the table.

"Who's that, now? Rodney, is it? Get in here, you. We were just talking about you."

"Apologise for arriving during a meal. But Frank here disappeared from the old homestead and I thought he was wandering lost in the woods or drowned down at the old well, till someone said they saw him and Claire come this way on foot."

"Drowned down at the old well. Listen to that."

"Sit, Rodney. You're making a person uncomfortable."

Rodney unlaced his work boots. Claire passed him plate and utensils which he carried toward the men. She came to pull in her own chair, for a moment, to experience the goodness of having people at her table. She hoped goodness would stay, goodness of some sort. She knew this one visit had the power to change all. But these old fellows ... each wary of the other, like old red foxes. Nervous at a set table, company around it – a Curtis, ruffian, that! Claire opened the jar of chow. She had never minded ruffians. She enjoyed them.

Frank saw his brother in good light. Good features had hardly abandoned the man; they'd grown sharper. A nose and lip, well preserved, neither discoloured, despite the certain liver abuse. Miraculous, that in itself. Black eyebrow, combed, sideburns trim, moustache full – here was a man who enjoyed his toilette. Frank knew appeal of his own was long gone, not to be salvaged, but rather kicked-in like an old box. He was conscious of his offset strawberry nose, his cancerous lip and lumpy skull. Both men yet shared the keenest eye, with its pencil-lead pupil, the sole feature left to identify them in the anonymous public as brothers.

"Haven't seen you up and around for a while," said Rodney.

Clifford turned.

"You addressing me?"

"You."

"My brother's here. How can I be anywhere but at my table to receive him? Ahem. Especially since he's got his eye on my boat."

"That thing still float?"

"Still float! Listen, hemlock bottom, soaked in the brine. Cross-ribbing hull with brass screws. Still float? One more crack like that, my boy, and you'll be floating."

"Just asking, me son. Don't get all up in arms."

Silence was broken by a raspy laugh, one cured by years of tobacco. Claire was at the stove, dishing up potatoes. She had a lit cigarette going – keeping her back to the men, which she did yet, as an awful wave of joy hit to bring tears to her eyes. The fit made her shoulders jostle in a way they never had. Her neck took the strain. She had to be careful, her false teeth were over the soup pot; she had lost a previous set through the grates. They could go the other way too: get garbled at the back of her throat. Tears splashed onto the backs of her eyewear, dropping now into the hot pan.

"Have a look at that one?" said Clifford, pointing a thumb.

"Can you blame her?" said Frank. "Lazarus. Just out of his bed and first thing, he's going to chuck someone out in the harbour."

"No wonder. Asking a man if his sole possession is of any use."

"That's not how I meant it."

"Calm down, the lot!" said Claire. "Or I'll be the one doing the chucking, out into the harbour."

She had her glasses removed. She used her apron to wipe them. In the middle of the floor, she stood, eyeing Clifford.

"What did I do now?" he said to her.

"I'm just waiting for you to launch into how the thing was built."

"Oh, that," said Clifford. "Ahem. That was quite an ordeal, that."

An account began of how Clifford and William had cut pine up MacKinnon's Interval. Trees two arm-lengths around. In winter, using a cross-cut. They let spring freshets carry the logs down Ingonish River then ripped the logs, wet, up on the shore, up near the clam-flats. When the moon tides came they tied planks to a boat and rowed everything down the harbour. In two weeks he and William had developed shoulders like bulls. Everyone in the community thought they were bloated, sick, before realising it was just muscle.

"It wasn't only you," said Clifford, pointing with tines at Frank.

Frank nodded. Clifford had looked off into space during his recounting – toward the sweating pipes of the hot water tank, or the spindles of the drying rack over the stove. He honed in on Rodney who could not have the greatest number of distractions going on because of a young head. Also, Rodney was the proper medium for the brothers, a way by which the two could sit longer, peaceably, in lighter spirit. Clifford tapped two fingers on the table to illustrate a point, to centre action and restore his own wavering interest. Looking at one of his allocated points of meditation, his latest detail sinking in, he'd raise his voice to shout two-thirds through the tale, revealing details that needed gusto, as impact otherwise amounted to no impact. The ruckus! Anyone passing the door outside would have thought that inside the greatest of fights was being fought. Claire kept the noise of her table clearing to a minimum. She had pumpkin pie, cut and ready on matching plates. Far off, marine engines gurgled, gulls cawed; closer, a stove carburettor hummed. The window was open to encourage fresh air in over the floor. Air climbed the table legs with its reminder of Mayflowers in bloom, the variety that often breaks under spruce in June. Frank waited for the others to finish with the canned milk. He looked at his pie and frosting; a good portion of the visit was done, his dessert fork now set to crust.

"Tearing the old place down," said Frank.

"*You* are?" said Clifford. "I mean. Not alone you aren't."

"Don't know about that yet," said Frank. "Didn't think that far ahead. I will be, I mean. Why? No objections, is there? It's not habitable. The old fellow left it to me to do what I might; that time I spent with him. I find it an eyesore."

"Oh, it is. You did help him a lot."

"Not for a while am I doing anything. Got to get the other place up."

And as simple as that there came the heaviness.

"Best be going. What do you say, Rodney? Show me your work?"

They thanked the two for the meal and Clifford returned to his bed long before they were out of sight of the kitchen window.

*O*ut on the road, Frank said, "Hope I didn't startle the old fellow. He's over sixty now."

"You? You didn't startle him. No, not at all. It's never easy to finish a visit around here."

"Not, is it?"

"No, it's not. You had him up. That's the breaking news of the year." They followed the shore where gulls cried, crows sailed, the sun was shamed by cloud.

thirty-six

To close spring, a martial rain beat tattoo and tried apprehending what it could of a burgeoning nature. It was June twentieth, the summer solstice threshold, yet the white-cap ocean sent in another day of cold fog and mist, of rolling, raking, chilling breakers heard from the house shell where Frank lay. He never expected air so persistently fresh; nor this ready drowsiness, nor a mind cleansed by passing salt mists. He and Rodney had finished the bull work of the house in less than two months. Frank alone was doing the finish work, niggling jobs allowed to take forever. Trim. Light switches. Faceplates.

Sydney contractors worked to complete the garage, installing presently the super-pane glass to comprise most of the wall facing the road. Frank had successfully lobbied his Member of the Legislative Assembly for proper fill to be dropped in the marsh between the Crick and the garage. It had been paved, but got washed out. The grand opening would be late fall, licensing pending, and Rodney would run the enterprise. Frank had his eye on other real estate, the Beach Rock Inn. A suitable landmark situated at the start of the beach and just this side of the Sandbar. White edifice, stately. It was property not three hundred yards from Frank's bungalow and included an adjunct beach business, the Tartan Tavern. The listing read twenty-seven thousand. The properties were behind in taxes. He knew lawyers waited on such opportunities – some did their real estate shopping in the county tax office. Where misfortune lingers, so does opportunity. All Frank's money was gone. The garage had taken the remainder of the savings bonds bought with remuneration the Nova Scotia Government allotted his wrongful imprisonment. The postal bag stashed under the well was long gone. Should the garage prove successful, in the books at least, he could show this to the bank. He hoped to borrow enough to make his bid in late fall, or better, winter, when the region sealed up and the last thought in even the crafty minds of many was securing ownership. He wanted a rainy summer to steer clear prospective investors. The Sydney, and lately the American buck. All beachfront was going. Becoming involved in real estate had never been an intention; yet one project seen through to completion seemed to beg the start of the next. Frank wanted to set an example, to show a community a fellow need only act to have a little success in the world, a fellow from here. Greater motive, however, was the drive to have his remaining days active, very active. It put knives through phantoms.

He would think of no Beach Rock Inn or Tartan Tavern today. He would do his best to get up, make the tea and break eggs into a bowl, to mix in milk and bitten bacon bits, then have toast with butter. Lying abed awake, invites gloom. Yet he hesitated. He let the arriving rain fall its few more drops.

Spells passed quickly. He attributed this fact to his body's soundness, its physical conditioning; moreover a mind engaged in projects, working logistics out in the night. Years of gulped toxins would be purged, possibly for all time forward. Resilience of spirit was a ready feature. That he knew. He had learned it again. His good shoulder gave trouble, the joint pinched. The left side of his neck had lost some mobility. He told none. Rodney knew. Rodney had to know. And in these downpours, now, how the lost arm still ached. Frank no longer woke with the sensation of its hand being intensely itchy, as once was disturbingly the case. He recalled fingering for violin tunes, which was most peculiar: to come this late. He found himself welcoming this oddity. But, again, why at this late stage? A quandary. And yet at this late stage, every day, every one, seemed to grow closer to the first stages, then stage.

In the wood-scented kitchen he looked out the window, the new glass-slider facing west. Black dawn broke the inlet, but on the so-named Creek Road, truck lights shone high beams. It was the garage men, the contractors. Friday. They were driving materials up the road to begin early so they could get away early for the weekend to see their Sydney families. The garage had a roof on it, silencing the advice of passers-by, as astutely predicted. The roof kept materials dry; the contractors being away was no longer worrisome. The concrete service bay, where men would climb below to work under cars, was completed. That had been a good place to hide tools, still is. The shed in which Frank's family had once kept the animals had been useful as early storage. The backhoe used to dig the service bay hole had knocked over the family house with a single nudge of its bucket; the structure offered no resistance. Grace had come to watch the dawn destruction. Clifford hadn't. But Frank had seen Clifford, earlier, at the house two days before its destruction, when Rodney and Frank were beginning to gut the place for any good materials inside and so it could topple better.

Frank had wanted no ostentatious blaze to bring the community buzzing around. He was ashamed at how people flocked toward loss, like moths to a flame. He saw Clifford early that morning, carrying something out from the house in a black plastic bag, something of some length, weight possibly. "Deer antlers, the coat hanger," Clifford called to him. "You remember." Frank did remember what had hung in the porch long ago, but he had not seen it in the house since returning. He questioned Rodney about the part of the backroom wall he didn't remember them removing. "No. Wasn't us. We were picking up the seaweed as we went along." A bedridden Clifford, who courted death, back to life suddenly to remove a part of the wall. If he had jammed the antlers in there, in truth, he was as queer as Adrian was for hiding things. Frank thought no more of it. He was accustomed to mysterious village ways, be it family or other. It wasn't antlers.

The house had sat on the flattest ground available, an area precious for parking and turning. Spilling tractor diesel fuel over the downed structure, the operator burnt the house where she lay buckled and smashed. The rotted floor, the lower sills grim with soggy wood, were slow to consume, permanently dampened by years pent. Grace stood in the swirling dawn alongside son Rodney, both arms folded. Frank shifted restlessly.

"How would Jessie and Adrian react at the sight of their house knocked over, Grace? Flaming orange, smoke spinning, crackling?"

"Probably warm themselves, like us."

Nothing was saved. The dwelling had been held together with every variation of nail going. Variation held true for partition framing materials, moreover, for wallboard, sheathing, insulation. Only the tarpaper was of a consistent make. The tarpaper sent up the best billows, stringent, acrid, whorls of black punch, those characteristic wolf-turns of clawing soot. None was said more on the topic and before long their backs turned to it.

Rodney was off today, returning only Monday. He had struck his tailbone painfully, hitting an existing cyst which became readily infected. In one night the contact point took the shape of a ball-peen hammer-head, giving him horrible pain to sit or to stand. He had gone north to Neil's Harbour, but the doctor there sent him south to North Sydney where they scraped away what they could in day surgery. "Travelling – that was the ordeal," said Rodney. "The car over those bumpy road, over Smokey!" Frank had nodded, neglecting to mention he himself was possessed of the condition, never treated. Although it flared up from time to time, it just had never been exacerbated to the point where it limited a day's activities. Frank chose to forget ailments when he could. "The tails humans once had," he said. "Wanting to grow again on some folks. Might be a family, even a community thing."

"I can believe, community."

"Meanness, Rodney. Grow out of that, if anything," the elder admonished.

A knock at the door gave Frank a start. He walked forward, carrying his clean cast iron pan, feeling its dead weight at his radial bone. He'd been on his way to the stove, fortunately the door was just steps away. Frank pushed door curtains aside and saw a pair of visitors deep below. One a very old man near ready to perish, the other, the parish priest. "What the hell...?"

Frank shoved over the latch bolt. "Let me put this pan down."

The old gentleman wore suspenders under a dress jacket, a necktie tight to a collar that hung contrarily loose from the neck. A silver-headed cane raised him a step: he had got in front of the priest. The priest wore his traditional black, but sported a dark fedora; his tight red curls managing a show, his blue eyes half-alarmed. Both wore dress shoes with inch-high rubbers. Frank had built no porch; the temporary step was available only deep below the door. He realised the value of a porch, putting his hand down for the senior – giving sanctuary, a neutral space to process visits. "Hello Father. Hello, sir. Still in the construction stage here, I'm afraid. Can you get up that all right? Watch it, I took a tumble the other day; nearly kilt myself."

They were wet, they were coming in. Frank attended no Mass, though he had spoken to this priest, Father Reid Donovan, Red Donovan they called him. He was from over Port Hood way. Scotch-Irish as the day is long. The Father liked to carry his evening walk as far as the Sandbar, to rise from the beach below Frank's, to gain a return here by road. They exchanged hello on occasion. Frank's church neglect, the obvious question, never broached. Baptised, assigned Godparents, probably a First Communion in there – the subject did want discovering. Moot reply was appreciated, probably by both: it created a peculiar bond, yet, producing more and more knowing smiles, winks, when eyes chanced to meet.

"Awful early to be popping in on a man, Frank," said the priest in lispy brogue. "I'll say that straight off. I do remember you saying not many were up as early as you – that you follow the sun year round, beating it by an hour."

"I did?"

"You or someone else."

"Hasn't been much of that for a while, Father. Sun."

"Afraid not. No."

"Come in, fellows. Right in off the mat."

Frank spread a leaflet of newsprint for each, on his two available chairs. He lifted three bound pairs of worksocks from the table then instructed the men to draw chairs, to forget their dripping feet. Frank stood poised at his stove, awaited the business of the visit. He recently had hair shaved at the back of his head so he knew he looked attentive. Gave humility. He wanted whatever it was laid out before gauging whether to offer the men tea and eggs. Really, it was an awful early hour. His clock tocked on the bedroom wall.

The old fellow sat mute, though he hardly looked ill at ease. Self-possession was his, something the old really did gain without employment. The fellow had his silver-headed cane at the table. He tapped a ring he wore on the stick.

"I'll make tea," said Frank and the visitors dearly obliged him for this, for its afforded distraction.

"You don't recall this fellow, Frank?"

Frank had had his back to them. He faced the stranger and received, as uncustomary as it was, a long hand set out for him, again – second time. Frank took two steps. The hand was more limp, its bones coming through spotted skin more so than at first. But the old man did not release the grip. Frank looked down as a whisper rose from the chair.

"Henry Connelly ... Doctor."

Lime eyes waited, glanced toward Frank's missing limb.

Frank returned to the warm spot at the new second-hand oil stove hauled in two weeks ago. Now – where had he set the frying pan down? Just moments before? Here; he added a dollop of white lard. Slick oil ran, to pool at the iron side. Frank pushed the pan to the back of the stove. Priest brings doctor. Someone say I was in need?

That's not it. This old fellow? He can't practice. Frank had never been to see a doctor in all his days since. He had such an aversion toward hospitals that he would look the other way when he chanced upon one in a city. He'd cross the road, even. He had been curious about the human body, albeit studying what and when he could of ailments and how they came on. There was the hardcover *Home Remedies and Anatomy* he carried from town to town, a fine possession, that. This Father Donovan? Father Red. He had initiative. He had also dropped, a degree in Frank's estimation. His father was right: Clergy meddled, instigated. In the end.

No, can't can't be... that he has brought him to have a look at me? Because what could this old fellow do; he's ninety if he's a day. Frank went on and on entertaining the ostensible, in this light regard in the moment affecting him – all the while refusing the deeper, malignant connection apparent.

"Feeling fine," he said, dropping tea into a dry pot at the hot end of the stove. He bent and clicked the carburettor, then stood. Water was in the kettle. Canned milk out. Spoons. Sugar. He plugged the kettle cord into the outlet at the counter, one of the many with missing faceplates.

"It's no call, Frank," said the Father. "Doctor Connelly merely wanted to meet you. He's travelled a long way off for it, taking a room at the Keltic Lodge. Since you haven't got a phone in, we couldn't reach you beforehand. He arrived early last evening. His plans are to leave first thing this morning."

The priest paused, "Frank?"

"I hear you."

"He knew me from when I had the parish in Sydney Mines, Frank. Can you look over here? Sorry ... but ... I was to be the go-between. He's the one who operated on you, Frank."

"I know who he is, Father."

With thumb and first finger pinching the knob of the teapot lid, Frank turned to meet the man's eye. He felt strain in his neck and so took his gaze to a countertop – then back to the stove. Beads of water at the teapot base spun outlandishly. They performed ever widening circles till they broke and shyly retreated to cooler surfaces, to exhibit their loss of speed, of form, of grace, wholeness. The excess water had come from the rinsing of the pot, to make it presentable, to make it hygienic. Frank faced the cupboards; he got down cups one-by-one. He took out cinnamon rolls purchased at discount at the Fairway Market; the sweets were seven days old. Rodney had his Toyota car for the large orders. These cinnamon rolls Frank had gone to get, all on his own.

"Frank? I say, Doctor Connelly is a little hard of hearing. Since he's here from a long way off, I wish you would grant him his word. He came alone. I can only suppose his people don't know his where-abouts and that they're worried. We'll make the thing brief. He wants you to himself. I'll step out. You got a woodshed I saw. The Glebe, here since the last century hasn't even the simplest of pens to hold its wood, or coal. I know a little carpentry. I'll stand under the eave, learn how it was built. I have my pipe. I'll see to it he gets right back to town when you two are done."

With white collar in primary view the Father backed out the door. Frank heard a careful stepping down. He listened to feet mar-shal soaked, seeded, raked ground.

"Hungry at all, Doctor?"

"Eh?"

"I said, have you got an appetite? Are you hungry?"

"I'm not angry, no!"

The kettle's electric element had the water gasp then boil. But the old fellow came forward. Frank hurried tea into his visitor's cup. Milk, then sugar. The cup trembled in the doctor's hand transform-ing the custom of accepting hot tea into a dangerous act. Frank felt a whole lot better to see the cup reset on its saucer. And he hoped that was it; that there would be no reach for it again, till cooler. A bag of hand-rolled cigarettes was on the table. Frank pushed them along and the doctor took one. Frank lit this for him too, but raised his hand, no, when the doctor made gesture for the host to do likewise, to ac-company him.

"Years ago. It was rough, I say, the thirties. Hard times all around. I was asked to minister to a boy who'd nicked himself with his gun, crawling up shore rocks. It was some call to get. Dead of winter." The doctor stopped, and with an elaborate grimace sipped his tea. He swallowed little, as the timbre in his voice found itself only in these last phrases: he was eager to get on with it.

"The older you become the heavier early things get. You go around to fix up what you can. I had finished training but it was so cold and bleak where they had me go. I thought it was the end of the world. Nothing stirred. Bare coastline, rock, stark mountain, nub trees and all, for miles. The people! The way they talked, how they crowded their stoves. I imagined groups here as being left from the dawn of Creation. The family was traumatised, all right, and right away authority was given up. The parents were worn through and through. As I was, just getting here. I learned the state of affairs. I learned if we didn't do something we'd lose him, quick. No one was coming. Not down there."

He looked fully at Frank, cornering the face into looking back into his own wasted watery orbs, pluvial and grim.

"I never again saw any take what that boy did. And the trust I was left. This was my first moment as a medical man, yet he offered no resistance the whole night through, immovable as the hardest of soldiers. Nothing to ease it! No alcohol, gin – no time! Snow. Ice. What's that? And in all the calls to all the houses, those eyes, the way they looked up in consent. Any fortitude I would need to call on was in them. And time and time again, in the years to follow, I would need to call on it. I became useful, is what I come to say. Because of that boy, the worse case I faced – the most tragic events thereafter paled. I was prepared for anything thereafter is the point. My life was of value because of what happened here."

He stared out the east slider, his hands clutching his cane top, beginning then a speech for Frank, one changed in texture. Frank started. He sat, was aware the man thought himself alone, that no other was present to eavesdrop upon thoughts coming now.

"Later, afterwards. Winter trip done, I report to the doctor in charge of northern Victoria County. Asking me to his office, home office. Make it at night. Your words. Go through the thing again. I said what I said, I committed it to paper. What more? You doubt my course? Faint pulse, you wrote? I think so, faint. If I said so, then I thought so, faint. Necrosis setting in, capillaries collapsed, you wrote? I think so, collapsed. If I said so, wrote so, then I thought so – collapsed. Kept your front at the fire, kept your back to me, thanked me then see me to the door. I with my gloves on, you bent to my ear. I'm going to file it, but keep it here. This could be the happenstance that makes you a great doctor yet. Why? Out the door. Never to speak again. Not as we had. Not beyond neutral talk of medical cases. I saw him. The most part of my career. The bone between us buried."

The doctor stared at Frank, eyes coming much wide.

"Well, ahem, tea was the best there is. Always was, down here. I'm not much of a smoker. Not as I was."

The doctor had smoked none of the cigarette; rolled too tight, it burned no longer. He touched its end and upset it into the ashtray where its ash lay dashed. He got to his feet using his cane and Frank's support. "Can you tell that Father Red to come? That I'm ready?"

Frank put his head outside the door and saw past a gathered fog rolled in over the priest, the cleric who in dawn mists was ducked under an eave, knocking clean his pipe on a corner board. Poorly sheltered from the weather, in a dawn just begun, he was deeply wet. He came with hand over his fedora, though no full rain fell.

The doctor stood alongside Frank who provided assistance, lowering the gentleman first onto then down the step. There was handshaking here, then the visitors stepped through a pattering shower: the gentle priest at the dear doctor's elbow. "Car's down over the hill. He came to Ingonish by bus. He'll catch it at the Fairway. Where it stops to pick up the outgoing mail."

Frank wove and they were out of sight. He listened to the hidden car drop from a forward to a reverse gear, its braking over a crunching shoulder before stationing itself out on hard dirt. In the early hour it began a respectful cruise, lessening tire impact, motor revving in such a way to avoid needless disturbance. To the Sandbar, up ahead it went, the turning place, the Beach Rock Inn. The car came again when Frank on his feet had abandoned his omelette to crack eggs simply into the pan. He heard gearing, for the turn.

At the kitchen table, before his meal, an act hardly performed since under his parent's roof, and with both living, took place. Frank blessed himself. With experience equally as remote, he put the back of his wrist to his forehead and shook, shoulders rising as he spoke through salt drops, his type of general prayer always carried with him now. He was quick. He took up his fork, purposefully, piercing yolk where more crying fell, dipping a corner of buttered bread, eating his breakfast with ocean breakers bursting broadside on the shore and in his ears – his chest hollow.

Rain struck steadily his roof. Kelp scents entered to wrestle with linoleum and new cupboards, but breakers above all, simply rolling in from the sea. On his feet, he saw them curl, from the window, how they threw spindrift into rain before cutting in tumble, to wash un-satisfied to the shore, unsatisfied because all could not make the full final surge up here to the heart, to recede then. Rattling, rumbling, spilling tumbling spent waves struggled to rake a whole beach free of its stones. To gather in its long arms all the pain of those afoot above.

Frank pushed the curtain back. He plugged in the kettle for more tea, broke two more eggs in the pan. There was work, today. He would concentrate on work, today. Then in days to come. Then in days to come.

thirty-seven

One evening in high summer, Frank was enjoying the curved back of a wooden lawn chair. He smoked a home-rolled cigarette and watched the stillness of the harbour. Breeze from the ocean touched over his property, just enough to keep the flies away before dying at lower heights overhead. No weeping from the loons. Frank thought he might catch a glimpse of the pair floating in the harbour: they were nowhere in sight on the Freshwater Lake. From where the beach breeze rose came steps at a trot. No moose, horse, rather a lone dog. The fellow that had followed Leo. It sniffed a corner of the house. Its wiry leg and a black and white shag coat spoke of the border collie – the breed which shifted direction as the coyote did, flattening in high motion. The paws left the gypsum drive for the soft clay.

"I got grass there, you. Git!" The brash creature paused also in harbour reflection, before coming to sniff the lawn chair arm, its swishing tail brushing Frank's shins.

"Hello, me son, you look half-starved." It dropped to the right and, drawing its jaw shut, watched Frank. It turned its snout to where Frank had spied the inlet and encouraged the patting at the softness behind the ears, shutting its eyes. While stroking the dog, Frank looked down at fresh gouges in his knuckles and the caked Ozonol ointment, the hand awfully tender yet.

"Abandoned, were you? You got the cautious feel of homelessness, fear that comes to call, and to stay." Frank sensed ravenousness in its silence. He had not decided whether to feed it, yet already it looked to have reached the place sought its entire life through and, now here, it was intent on staying. Someone owns it. Ingonish has no strays. Frank tapped the bony head and looked at tangled huckle-buckles, at a red clay mix in the fur. The huckle-buckles needed cutting out.

"Your teeth no good?" Frank stood and there came after him the stare of longing, the subject of many a religious painting. "Going in the house, only. Stay."

Frank came with three Italian sausages that the dog swallowed without the slightest mastication. Using the scissors from his shirt pocket he cut the burrs free. The dog allowed tugs, opening its eyes wide when there came pause in the work. A hind limb looked lame. Frank got dish detergent, a basin of water, and this time four strips of Canadian bacon. "Now you wait before I give it." The creature would have nothing of etiquette, eyeing the man who held back that to ease carnal suffering.

"Shut up, I say, or you'll get none." The dog swallowed the bacon whole. "Ah my. Suppose you'll never leave my door now."

The basin was too shallow. Frank went for an empty riblets bucket down under the sink but when turning saw the dog had entered his house. "That's all right. Salvation through starvation. I know about it. I ate from the garbage, an Arctic Bar once." Frank got it outside and though the water in the bucket was cold, coming from deeper in the well, the dog allowed care. It waited with soaked, pressed ears before pulling back, erect, to shake from head down to tail. Frank used his hand to protect his golf shirt. "By the old dying...! Get out of here! Ah, what you invite!" The dog got on its belly in triple-seeded clay hardly producing grass shoots yet. "All that work! Why don't you scram!" The dog mixed its back in, then lay on its belly, tongue lolling. It shook dirt and water when Frank struck his Zippo flint off his thigh, a smoke in his mouth.

"Plague."

He stood, put his hand against the house corner facing east. In the little time taken to help the animal, the light had altered. A glassy harbour swelled, water peaking in full moon tide. He smacked a fly at the back of his neck. Coughed. Looked toward the road. Apprehension had not left this entire evening. Any minute he expected a car to raise dust coming up the hill. But who would be in it, when it did? One of two parties, certainly. He hoped to God not the plaintiffs, especially after his role as assailant. Should representatives from each arrive, well, the fight of summer begins. His apprehension rose out of a late afternoon incident. A bull had been struck and killed during the rescue of grandchildren. Grace's. Frank did the striking and not with a club.

Three children, a pair of girls and a young boy, were down from Sydney with their mother, Betty. They were playing in Shea's pasture as Frank headed up the road to check on the garage. He noticed right away the trouble, that the kids were in a place they shouldn't have been – a spot where Ranald Burke irresponsibly grazed his Black Angus, Parnell. Ranald Burke didn't own the land. It might have been community pasture, at one time. Burke brazenly let the bull roam the black spruce woods that passed through the lower property of the garage. The animal had got stuck on a sheet of plastic one day behind the garage; four men used twelve-foot, two-by-six planks to coax it off.

It liked the field's lower end. Parnell the bull had a bad hatred on for humans, attacking a national park lifeguard returning from a party one night, opening the man's thigh and prompting an investigation. Most recently, the brute had been seen out on the road charging carloads of tourists. The Royal Canadian Mounted Police showed up at Ranald Burke's, telling him either to fence in his land or keep livestock in the barn. Ranald was as ornery as his bull. And harassed so, sneering, he raised his voice: "Look! No one like you or any other is going to tell me what to do. Especially if they don't come from here, badge or no badge! And that park lifeguard had no business tending the beach anyway!" With the authorities leaving, a rough-looking dog appeared, and Burke felt he had upped them one. "And *stay* off my property!" He made a great public viewing for concerned neighbours on front steps. Mothers directed little heads with peering eyes back into houses.

"Hey – hey!" Frank hollered at the kids. "Clear out, the lot of yas! Here!" The kids were stunned by Frank. The warnings had worked against him. It triggered Parnell, bent in relative peace, drawing, snipping forgotten grasses – the iron head rose high from where it privately chewed the lower field. The bull saw three children moving across its plain.

The kids thought Frank was the owner, an irate farmer shooing them off prohibited land. He looked the part, rushing up the road, winded. What's wrong with him?

"Out, I say! Beat it out of there!"

Petrified children make little progress. These travelled half-assed while Parnell kicked into a brisk trot.

Frank got over the first barbed-wire fence, hopping, tripping on the second. He ran uneven pitch, stumbled on a forgotten foundation, trying to get out far enough to head off the danger. The kids contemplated a rural man terribly upset now, with something definitely wrong, physically – stopping fully, the three cried their eyes out to realise what. Commotion excited the bull whose warmed instincts reacted to disorder simply by the random charging of forms moving through it.

Frank ran with all his might through thigh-clutching grasses, going badly over on the same ankle a second time. The smallest fell; another screamed blue murder – what now! Wasp nest! The bull passed terribly close to the fallen child, lowering its horns and narrowly missing the small of her back, the trot frighteningly cool. Frank saw the beast slow, a cloud of wasps rise over its neck. The bull shook horns, flicked ears at buzzing. It stepped back, snorted, dug in hoofs and with batting scarlet eyes; peered, taking a moment to adjust to this further insult. Vengeful wasps tried in vain to injure hide. Two experimented with eye tissue. Three stung lips, nostril, tongue.

Frank had reached the fray, he wove his arm, "Ya! Ya!"

Answer came quick. A ringed nose snorting bees, leather ears twitching clockwise and counter for their removal – the iron head marshalled a furious frame forward. Frank reacted to the charge in the way he would in the human arena – by hauling off with a haymaker. He struck the beast a barn-door smash, bare fist meeting calcified bone, rock-hard jaw. The bull, expecting nothing so decisive as this, especially from this awkward form giving it so little council its entire life, was staggered.

In the most elongated moment of trauma Frank had ever witnessed, his fist making contact, he saw the broadside expansion of the brute's single eye, its surfacing as if after a deal of time underwater. The strangest of buckling shook Frank back to real time, as the beast attempted to stop. Weight drove it on. The eye had rolled up till all was white, corpulence swayed, front knees sank like the gravitational breaking of a clay bank. And four legs, none recoverable, balance gone and gone miserably. Pressing forward, falling drunkenly, presenting massive chest to the earth, whooshing grass, tearing sod – Parnell's head impacted with smart contact on the hidden crop of field-rock foundation, a history trodden underfoot, passed over for centuries with minimal regard. A twitch. An eye eager for heaven; moan, knell, blink. An eye rolling, but closed in the concurrent final swat of a fly-weary tail.

Frank chanced forward. He slapped a leather ear, painfully pinched a boulder skull. "That hurt?" The eye remained sealed. "Parnell?"

The children, well over the wire enclosures, were back out on level road. The girls regained some wherewithal, enough to plug tears, while the boy had given himself to misery more fully. The trio looked behind, pressingly, indecisively with wet faces. A sister held the hand of the brother whose cries mingled with the breaking buzzes of the disturbed wasps; now within earshot, Frank hollered, "Wait, you three!" He marched through the field, calling for them to stop, to calm down. Halted, paralysed, they waited. "We're going to be killed!" said one girl – trying to keep voice local.

"You won't be kilt," said Frank. "I'll take you back to your mother."

They were ushered terrorised, Frank allowing distance to buffer a measure of settling. He had decided against eye contact: how could they trust him when they didn't know him, and after the harrowing incident? Someone like him must frighten them. Some introduction to a granduncle, all right. He was related; Grace had told him her grandchildren were coming. I won't tell them that. Perhaps, I should. But what are their names? Best I don't know. The three glanced back through their suffering to see how far back he was; but then also to see through the trees, to gain once more any details they could of the scene. Not to mitigate memory – to sear it: that each might tell it better one day.

Grace and Betty waited on the road; prescience for disorder bringing the matrons here to the shoulder.

"He killed a cow! Right in front of us!" bawled the eldest, long arm instructing.

Betty gave Frank a wholly dirty look and with tormented, tempestuous eyes commanding, ushered her brood into the house where she cleaned them with soap and water and told them to gather their toys.

"I didn't kill the frigging thing," said Frank, to Grace at the road. "They were playing out in the middle of Shea's Field when that savage bull of Ranald Burke's made for them. I jumped in, steered it clear!"

"What did you do to scare them so? Their hearts are rent."

"What did I do? Nothing. They're just afraid – of me."

"No, tell me, what did you do?"

"I saved them from being impaled, to begin."

"How?"

"By striking it."

"By what?"

"The bull."

"What did you strike it with?"

"My fist."

"Ah, Frank. Not in front of them!"

Frank rubbed a knuckle, saw shearing to scarlet bone, a tendon that worked a second knuckle presentable. "It fell on its own, is what happened. There was an old foundation. They only thought I murdered it."

"It's dead?!"

"I don't know if it's dead. It wasn't moving."

"Merciful God in heaven, what next?"

Frank said no more on the subject and Grace took him inside to soap his knuckles: they had to pass Betty. She had heads aimed for the car, her eyes replete with parting sentiment. Frank didn't stay, and only on his way home did he calm. He walked past the field. Herald! Proclaim! Dragon slain! Persecuted villagers, no more! But looking down into Shea's Field and seeing where this dragon lay, dropped and hidden, Frank lost his sarcasm. He saw the ancient upright figure of Ranald Burke morphing past grey alders, enter a morass of thorny raspberry bushes, in a hurry. Frank shot erect. He was a soldier, now on leave, determinedly pressing forward with the face of a man troubled by heavy battle and loss – thoughts a thousand miles away from the least bit of knowledge of this field or of any event occurring in it.

"Curtis! You seen my bull?"

Frank was sure he heard the old man call it. And so he turned, irritated by strong sun, by these remote thoughts plaguing him. He looked on, curiosity taking over, innocence.

"What's that?"

He squinted, the sun was in fact behind, but somehow getting in his eyes. No response. Had the old one even spoken? He saw him catch his breath, a hand up on an apple tree. Poor old fellow.

Frank moved on, stopping only at the Fairway to buy an extra box of Joe Louis pastries, a second tin of Export-A. He bought rolling papers and four rolls of toilet tissue. He went straight home then, never to learn how the episode ended, whether the bull ever rose. Whether the old man had even found it?

Frank looked at the dog. "See what happens when you try to do a turn? And every time, too." The dog came to press against his leg; it

365

wanted his foot. "You'll get a foot all right, you don't back up. Back up Stormy. You like that name? How it was on the beach last night, where you crawled up from."

He was patting the dog when eyes trimmed on the inlet, the backdrop a bruised black, the dying light of day. Strokes came. He stood. A vessel. Gliding, pushing through still water. Very well. By water, is it, the besiege?

At the inlet came the frail shoulders of Clifford working dory oars. Claire sat astern, holding with both hands, convening gunwales.

"God help us," whispered Frank.

Oar strokes, tempered by gentility, implied a rower conscious of the sight he must make, coming in now; he would do what he could to extend it. Water trickled in equal measure from the blades and, from bow meeting surface there came cadence till oars dipped once more in smooth burial to propel the craft. Claire wore the most forlorn of faces, hers a world looking to have ended, till sharp contrast became her – till she recognised Frank exit the shadow, pass a wall now shingled. Something at his feet growled, breaking her spell, her look puzzling. Frank bent and slapped a head, hard. It was a dog, pressing close with lowered ears. Claire touched one of Clifford's half-drawn arms and he too turned to see his brother descend the field. Clifford's eyes were shielded by a cap bill, but his bow tie mouth was free to express what it wished … nothing elaborate, a smirk. Quitting the oars Clifford shifted his weight and let momentum and moment carry them to Frank's property. Salt trickle eased from raised oar tips, a set of closing faucets restricting flow. Clifford grinned at the cleared land; it was half worth the trip. The mutt followed Frank to water's edge as the boat resisted mooring, edging, waiting above a drop-off.

"Got yourself a friend, I see," said Clifford.

"He'll not be one for long, he doesn't shut up growling. Forgot what they were like. I was sitting out in the lawn chair when he waltzes up from the sand. As if returning to its eternal home."

"Maybe it is."

"I saw him," said Claire. "Over around the graveyard. No one could catch hold of him. He was down around the beach too. Eating from Park garbage cans."

"I think he got struck by a car, his hind leg is lame."

"That's a pretty black and white coat he's got. Can you wade out, Frank?"

"Yes, look out now! I'm going to wade out into cold water!"

"Get on that rock there. I'll swing her around. There's a rod and a reel aboard. We wanted to commandeer you. To improve our luck."

"It's nearly dark, me son."

"Ah, dark! What did dark ever matter, pair like us? You grew up here, me son. I think you did. The moon's not up, but she's full to-night. And there's light in one of those August buggers enough to read by. We'll watch it trace the furrows on the forehead of Smokey. You were right about the mackerel and their eyes. They're schooling in the harbour, now. Late Summer. I got tired of looking out at them the last few days, seeing the surface shimmer. I was thinking about you wanting to go in the boat."

"In the boat? That was a long while back, Clifford. But very well. He come along?"

"If he will. Of course."

"Ah, no – don't bring him aboard," said Claire. "He's got to stink to high heaven!"

"Just washed him, Claire. With half a bottle of liquid detergent."

Frank got a foot soaked lifting Stormy into the dory, the other foot sliding under the boat, bringing the dog back down on him in the water. "Bai, I'm telling you!" Frank hooked the dog at the ribs, upset it over the gunwale. Stepping over rope it settled beside Claire then shook. "Ah – don't I hate when they do that – stop, you! And doesn't stink, eh? No, by God – not at all."

"Go on. He's a regular bouquet of roses."

Clifford drew on the right oar before involving the left when the bow was righted. He moved them toward the inlet, drawing evenly over her hull's drag. Frank saw a brother waxen in the light of night.

With lips over-coloured and wrists bony, in the shoulders there lived determination.

"Ranald Burke found that big bull of his dead today, Frank. Parnell he called it. Stone cold on its back. Shea's Field. Someone killed it, they say. The old fellow daren't go to the Mounties. Not too well liked there. He rounded up eight men from the head of the harbour to lift it onto a flatbed one of them has, before driving it up the road. He had Edward Williams from the Sandbar take a hacksaw to it."

Frank stared at the harbour, spread into view. He saw the pitch east sea and by drawing eyes over Smokey saw to the clam flats at the head of the harbour where above was the faint glimmer of red west. He listened as loons were wont to weep.

"Should be some racket up there tonight," said Clifford.

"Up where?" said Frank.

"Up on the hill there, what with a butchered bull. Someone bringing home a half an onion is cause for that crew to kick her into high gear. Any moment we'll hear one of them haul out the pipes, I figure. That's another reason I wanted to come out. They might actually sound good from the harbour, guaranteed distance and all."

"What happened to the cow?"

"Bull, Frank – hear that, Claire? Frank wants to know what happened to the cow. You tell him."

"Someone clubbed it to death. Didn't they? Isn't that what they're saying? The jaw was broken on the wrong side it fell. Wasn't it?" Clifford looked squarely at his youngest brother during the telling, but established only vague eye contact. Frank laughed, shook his head.

"Yeah, you laugh, Frank," said Clifford. "No. Word is no one knows what happened to it. It was old. Seizure, most probably took it. Ah me, ah my. He'll report it. Old Burke! I know he will. Imagine the delight of the cops to see that clan coming. You were up that way this afternoon? Frank?"

"To have a look at the garage. See how she's coming along – How? I go up every afternoon."

"No reason. I'll just row."

It was the calm hour and words unwelcome. The moon split the ocean – a golden trestle with a hop of the Sandbar to come and meet them in their boat. Bagpipes trilled, drones bled. But a new player seemed to take them up, as all kinds of fast tunes came well played. But fast tunes just as soon ceased. Night wanted nothing of them and whoever played realised it: for there came the single most pensive plaint.

"Hear that, the mournful one?" said Clifford. "Must be called, 'My Days Will Be Lonely With My Bull Departed.' Well – he won't be home tonight! Ow-oo!" Clifford called for the echo.

Reply came – not his.

The dory slid into the perfected blackened reflection of the harbour's north striding peak. Mackerel were plentiful below, fishing minnow by moonlight. Clifford demonstrated the jigging technique, his line decorated with four hooks. He caught, hauled and slapped fish to the floor, freeing with ease, snagged bodies in smashing thuds. Curled spines left taut line, flapping, settling, slipping over ribbing. The dog sniffed, then turned its snout from this gathering of bending life. It scrunched between Claire and Frank to steal some of the stern seat, pulling its tail up, tucking it behind. Claire, using rod and reel, helped Frank free his jigged fish. Success made the group laugh and laughter made the dog howl: to the pipes, the bobbing boat, the full moon. Festivity filled the harbour whereas its Woody Shore houses stayed mute, giving the impression here none lived. When the moon reached Smokey's broad zenith Clifford rowed ashore. He had Frank shine the light where bottom rose and they saw past phosphorescence, through to seaweed, to mussel-covered rocks. Clifford said to look out for lobsters, they'd be purple black. He elaborated on how they could be flicked ashore with an oar blade. Claire spotted one, on sandy bottom, but Clifford was unable to manoeuvre the blade properly to bring the delicacy in. His vocal fear was that he would upset them, that they'd all have to swim for it. "Worse for me!" he said. "I'll have to crawl on someone's back!" The dog sat in discomfort. Its dignity increased nearer shore.

"Nice out here, Frank. What?"

"It is nice, all right."

"Good chapter, even, in life."

"It's decent, Clifford."

Nearing Frank's house Stormy leapt overboard. Splashing, it swam to get its four feet on bottom rising unseen. Rodney's car was at the house. Frank kept his eye on it, getting out, wiping his slimy hand again on his thigh. He saw Grace descend the field. She nodded to the troupe. To Claire. The four spoke in whispers, as if night would concede only this. Grace's visit was to tell Frank that the bull was dead, that she would not tell a soul; she naturally said nothing at present. Frank had hardly forgotten. His pained hand reminded him throughout the expedition. Clifford gave mackerel to his sister. Frank took six. They bid good night and the couple rowed off.

At the bathroom mirror, Frank took off his shirt. "Grace, come see where that horn clipped me, will you? It look that bad at all? I can't see. I can see part."

"A mark from an animal always is bad, Frank. Yes, it broke the surface. You'll get some scar out of that."

"There's a worry."

"You have something to put on it?"

"I'll get some salve on it."

"It's purple, ugly as sin. Go to Neils Harbour in the morning. Let a doctor have a look. Rodney'll take you."

"No doctor. I'll answer no questions."

"Rodney will drive you and, also... Frank?"

"Also Frank what?"

"I been meaning to ask you about money. Money possibly owed. Put your shirt on."

"Money possibly owed who for what?"

"There could be some sort of back-pay. I was figuring it out with Charles. You got a proper address now. You didn't always, I mean."

"Owed for what?"

"The government's got programs."

"Unemployment?"

"Disability."

"Grace. I was always able to do something, Grace. Give them money so they don't get ahead. But keep giving it."

"What?"

"Programs, Grace. Unless you're laid up in such a way you can't walk, stay away from assistance. Any sort, or programs. Do it alone. That's what life is. An arse paid for sitting ruins a person inside a month. I wouldn't take something, supposing there is something! I wouldn't!"

"All right, Frank. Don't get all bent out of shape."

"Also, don't be talking to Charles about me behind my back. It's the thing I noticed foremost since coming back here."

"What?"

"This crutch of gossip. As if this alone allows for survival. Let it, and it will, too."

"You were the one saying he was interested in the Beach Rock."

"Not anymore, I'm not. As of this minute. A person with any sense chews what's on his plate – except that dog. I never seen anything so hungry as that. I know you want to help, Grace. You always did."

"I tried."

Frank snapped the last button of his red plaid shirt and stood in the kitchen. Grace was at the door. "I don't want to keep the car out late. I won't press you again on things."

Outside in the moonlight, they faced the sea.

"Hardly need the headlights."

But, Grace didn't hear; she was gone ahead, opening the car door. Frank came alongside.

"Think I could get my licence someday, ah, Grace? Be a sight, wouldn't it."

"No, it wouldn't be. Sure you can. I got mine. You don't like cars."

"Wouldn't mind a licence all the same. Have the getaway ready."

"You don't really feel that way, do you Frank?"

"Faulty memory brings a person back. No. I don't feel that way, Grace."

Grace employed her gears and rolled off. Frank stayed at the corner of the house to survey lost mountains in a settling night. The moon was in its permanent, host form. Breeze, a wind change, lifted his shirttail. No longer came the bagpipes, only the buzz of an outdoor bulb with a hundred millers attacking thin glass. Frank would go in the morning to apologise for the bull ... when Ranald Burke would be sick from liquor? Might be better to wait. Steer clear of that crew. If he didn't go and confess by supper, he wouldn't go at all. That's how it worked. He fell asleep thinking of no bull, no scars, no government assistance. A gust of fresh air eased up a curtain sheer; a visitor tightened bedding. "I said down, and I mean, down!" Bitter a moment, rueing giving the animal a name, Frank slept twenty minutes till up she came. At one waking he thought of the nights it must have spent damp under beach crag, solitary and fearful.

"Come up, then. I know all you know." With a big sigh the creature at last drifted free. Both did, the heavy sleep of the stumbling just.

thirty-eight

In the adjacent aisle of the Fairway, Rodney listened to a pair of biddies hush to obscure sentences: "...I'm not saying his coming back was wrong. He helps they say, out here and there, does no one any real harm ... there's a rarity."

"Why do you think it is he came back at all? He was a terrible drunkard I know."

"I know too. He couldn't get away from what was always here."

"What? What was always here?"

"You don't know? Well ... my sister Barb used to go to card games that old Mary Helen used to hold. Years ago, it was now – she's long gone – he was fond of someone there. I will tell you that much. They'd meet. They would."

"Who?"

"Oh, talk of it is all. I don't like to say who. He was supposed to court someone's wife, his brother's, who was overseas fighting. The two took it beyond courting. There was an identity mix-up. Word came that one brother died, when it turned out he didn't. And, the one supposed dead, the proper husband, came home. Well, there was hell to pay. A bed to sanctify. Had to clear out, on the double."

"That where he lost the arm, overseas?"

"Who?"

"Who? Who we're talking about, who!"

"He wasn't overseas! Not that I know of. No, all this was before. He travelled in some circus outfit, away, did time in jail but you know that. Awful for the liquor is right, I heard. For the women too. Say he was equipped. Land sakes, can you believe it? You see him come up the road and he looks like hell on earth. He must have come home with money."

"I'll say. Have that house built straight off."

"And the garage. Don't forget that."

"I didn't forget."

Rodney stared at a package of raisins. He had not come in for raisins, he'd come in for white icing sugar: the opening of the garage was Friday, his mother was baking a chocolate cake; she bought wax candles in the likeness of steel-belted tires. Rodney carried the icing to the counter but waited in line behind the biddies, who were silent now. One had a lengthened arm, the fingers gripped the wire handle of a bucket of riblets. Rodney prayed the strain would give her arthritis. They knew him, knew he had been there – it was why they hushed, had broken off at first, but their deafness and age gave them volume. Rodney kept an eye on their skull wraps; he coughed and sniffed in long, loud draughts. They looked left and right as if in a backroom of their own homes where none stood to observe them. The one with the riblets set the bucket down: it had come her turn to pay.

"I heard what you said, back there, the two of you, now," spoke Rodney with courage, as they were leaving the store. They employed the pretence of daft old age to appear not to hear him. He saw their faces in the good light of the door. He witnessed their shame. The counter girl tucked her chin in.

Rodney returned to a windless day, and to the few cars of the parking lot. Walking to his own he saw Daniel Dunphy lift dust in arrival with the black Cadillac the old man and his wife drove late afternoons. The wife, a stark French woman with the lifeless grey hair of the mad, sat mute, stared like a monolith. Her door opened and Rodney nodded. She brought a mothball scent. Daniel rolled down his window and put his elbow out. He dropped his hand happily on warm black contours of metal.

"You fellows open Friday? I saw your sign. I think it's grand, a place like that. It will be the best thing ever to hit this community. They're paving the North Shore. No time at all, watch and see how people will be flocking for fuel – but fuel to get out! Many will start going into Sydney more and more to buy goods. The Fairway here will find it tough to hang on. She might crumble. People need their outing. And if they don't take it from time to time, watch and see a world cave in."

"I know a case or two to testify to that."

"Frank buy you that car?"

"Me son! How does everybody know things so quick? Yes, he bought it."

"Finest kind of man you'll meet, Frank Curtis, always was. I could have beat him at the arm-wrastling racket. When I was younger. I just didn't want to show him up is all, lessen his chances. I gave breaks. You tell him that Rodney, will you? What I said."

"I will, Danny."

Rodney unnecessarily let his Toyota wagon warm before backing out onto the road: no sign of the genteel ladies. He pulled away and drove the marsh before turning for the Woody Shore, his carburettor sticking. He gave it gas, inched up the volume on his eight-track player. The season was breaking, all right. Hints were in the thickening light, an air with tang, this sullen south breeze arriving at doors to make folks realise how lonely it has been cannot compare with what is to come.

Rodney slowed right down to let the steering wheel find its own will in the potholes. The gossiping women in the Fairway tormented him. He aligned their information to his mother's allusions, coming over the years when the topic of Frank's bachelorism rose. She had got his letters. William was the uncle, dying in the war. He hadn't married. Had he? Clifford married Claire.

Rodney did notice the explicit tact in exchange between Uncle Frank and Aunt Claire. The formality. Frank employed the same with Clifford, when the gaunt uncle had showed at the garage for a gab. Clifford, the recluse. But what had made him so? Did there need to be a reason? No, there did not. But this not stepping away from the house, for decades, really; and the whole of last winter, confined to his bed; those reports, hardly to rouse, of his imminent death. The man had life yet. He was not done, but making more and more tiny showings in public. Out to protect his stake in something. And all since Frank got back, too. But Frank has that effect. People did see him at the fore of something ... those with hearts half-decent. Frank's generation were all odd. They shared some far-reaching sorrow, one Rodney could never put his finger on. Sure, there was the accident. The ice. Ah, but none of this was his business and he chose not to make it so. And yet, he did hope no trap was being sprung, for his family, for him. Life had always felt that. Might always.

Parking adjacent the garage he paused to stare up at the tall glass. It could take a head off if it broke. Frank had become nervous to see these windows in place, with the many cars soon to pull in – some, for brake work! Vandalism crossed both their minds. Too late now. They would have to wait and see. Rodney got out on crunched gravel. The Sydney men were installing the custom-built counter newly arrived by transport truck. A sixteen-foot counter, to service eat-in custom-ers. The contractors were removing its Arborite top to get it in the doorway when Frank arrived on foot. He stood alongside Rodney. "Study what they're doing. Assembly is important. And you being in charge, from here on in."

"In charge?"

"I told you that, I need to be free. And you're far better with peo-ple than I could ever hope to be. I do want to mention one thing...."

"Go ahead?"

"Refuse no meal to any arriving strapped."

"What kind of business practice is that? More AA talk, is it?"

"You know I never went for that."

"I know, Frank."

"I mean poor luck. If a person is really up against it and can't pay, why not give them a break? An empty belly is no slight consideration, although few in this part of the world know it. None."

"No, that's true. But bums never get here. That's a city feature."

"Well, what's going to be in the cars will be a whole lot of city feature. Other features will follow. Refuse all you want, those that don't show the respect due a person opening his tables to the public. You'll get them. Throw them out quick as you look at them – the first sign of loudness, ignorance. This is your spot they're entering, remember. First off, is when you got to establish what kind of place it will be."

"I'll remember, Frank. Why didn't you get in the car back there? I saw you coming up the road. I wove, braked. You wouldn't get in?"

"Yeah, and I saw the clip you were going, heard your music. No, this vehicle here needs all the leg transport he can get. You got to keep moving when the bones get a couple of years on them. Keep on, then remember each day to keep on."

"You ain't so old, me son. Old Danny Dunphy figures he could have taken you. He told me."

"They all could have, Rodney."

"The black and white dog likes the grass speckled in paint. No one come for him yet?"

"He's a *she*. A she that won't leave a person be. I'm half the time tripping over her, every room I set foot into. She's always right there at my feet. Hearts break for their masters, this breed. Or for anyone that shows them a bite of food, I should say."

"But she likes you though, too. You can see it. Stormy, that what you call her? She looks the picture of the RCA dog."

"I gave up on Stormy. Millie's her new name, after the first dog we ever had. I paid no attention to whether it was boy or girl first few days, then I saw her squat to take a leak. The dog we had growing up at the old house was affectionate like this. William got the name out of a picture book my grandmother had, about a little dog over in Brazil called Mililica. It hung around the stables, barking its head off at horses who paid her no mind. A woman vet came for visits from the city and brought the dog watermelon, which she shook in her jaws like a big rodent."

"There. Counter's in. Perfect fit, looks to be. They'll be done here today and I can't wait – the responsibility! It'll be good to be alone, to think. I'm first going to finish the painting. And with that done, we're pretty well set to open the doors."

"Nothing I can do?"

"Don't think so. Got her under control. And you just said you were out of it."

"The public end."

"No. Stay and talk though. How's the shoulder today?"

"Barometer. Must be in for some wet weather. Your arse ever act up again?"

"It wasn't my arse, bai! My tailbone."

"What's the tailbone if it's not the top of the arse? Coccyx is what it's called."

"There's a useful word. It's better. I feel it the odd time."

"Don't worry about feeling it. I knew it would be the case. Treatment: no cure. My own once bothered me from time to time. Runs in the family I think. I got this tea tree oil from Australia I'll give you. It tackles inflammation of any sort. You're supposed to mix it with water, I never do."

"You mentioned that stuff. I think you said you drank it."

"Bai, how good is your mind! But I've been thinking about that. Chronic? I don't think so. It was teaching yourself not to be a pig. I would have liked to try teaching myself that."

"What are you talking about, drinking?"

"And other things."

Rodney strapped on his painting overalls and adjusted his cap. His moustache was shaved – the brush had caught it two days prior and he didn't want to put gasoline near his mouth to get the paint off. It was time for a change, he said. He did feel bare, baby-faced. They said he looked a proper Curtis now. He felt insecure about the comment. He used a flat head screwdriver to pry the lid from the paint can. With a piece of wood trim, he stirred.

"Mix that well," said Frank. "You should use a clean, flat stick. Store-bought, if at all possible."

"Frank. I know. I was painting from this only an hour ago."

Rodney carried the tin by its wire handle and chose a safe spot in the grass to set it down. He flicked diluted thinner from his brush, dipped and continued with the foundation, its concrete curing a couple months now. He took care when reaching the windows, deciding to come back later with a smaller brush for trim. At the very glass, he would use masking tape and newspaper, to make a good job of it. He had a razor blade for any smudges on the pane.

"You keep at this, you'll finish the bigger part today."

"That's the plan."

Millie watched the work. Her mouth shut, ears rose. A silent crow shifted in a tree.

"Been in love, Frank, ever?"

"Hundred times, a thousand. Why? Who's asking?"

"Right here. Me."

"Not like you, springing a question like that on a man."

"Springing? You wouldn't hesitate to ask me."

"The world's laid out for you yet."

"It is for you."

Rodney dipped the brush and stirred, deep. He took the wire of the tin in his hand, crouching less now, feeling his thighs. He kept strokes in the same direction. Frank had not answered him and the bad air would not dissipate. The bad air confirmed a couple of things in Rodney: that he was in want of maturing, that what people said in grocery stores did matter.

"I was thinking of asking Peggy Roper to the dance, is why," said Rodney."

"Oh. You mentioned her before. The Protestant from North Bay."

"That's right."

"There was a time you'd be strung up for buzzing around that hive. It can only be good to get in with a Protestant, though. One only six miles north. Less guilt, to start off. And they have that whole other day. Sunday. They live theirs, not die off in it like the Cro-Magnon. Yes. Whole other day of the week, you get in with her. Live one-seventh longer. Going to ask her?"

"Hard. Small community and all. Frig it up and the whole town knows."

"How are you going to frig it up? And what town? No one inter-acts much with North Bay folks, do they? I didn't think they did. Per-fect testing ground for courting, far as I can see. Mess up there, come back here. Get it right. You won't mess it up. Invite her to our grand slam opening. It won't look as though you're bending over backwards, then. Bit by bit's how I'd play it."

"That right?"

"If she's nice at all, you got a chance."

"She's nice."

"Invite her. Don't prolong it. Tomorrow springs its paws on you like a starve-gutted lion. And you might be wanting to get along in that department. Listen, you're all right here. I'm taking off. Clifford wants to take his boat out for a spin before hauling it up for winter. Last trip he says. First, I think. In the bay. He wants me along, for fall fishing, as he calls it. There's supposed to be nice cod out there with the air temperature below the water's. We'll be gone the evening. Long as there's light. Watch from here. I'll make sure we wave from the Gut, have him raise the oars. Millie – get away from that grease! She ain't hearing me … you can't rename things. I say Millie! Stormy! Come on, dog. We're heading back down the road."

Rodney reviewed his progress. All that could be done from the ground was done: time for the ladder. He shook his head gripping the ladder, but as he tried, still could not shake the bad feeling of ask-ing Frank his personal business. He blamed the biddies, cursed their drawing him into their private torments. He had gotten close to his uncle these past months; the two had talked on every subject going, to the point where each was comfortable and each was good company. Joked a lot. Ah, he told himself, better to forget it. Better sometimes not to open the ears, too. The mouth, a given. Rodney set the ladder at a suitable distance from the corner facing the sea: he jarred sides to determine stability. Frank will understand. One thing about Frank is the way he sees facets, finds in each some shimmer. He knows I'm not the malicious type. And, he corrected me on being negative. Too bad he coudn't correct others. Not malicious, no. He has to know that by now – though unconvinced I stand here. Convinced only that I wounded him: a man who has always needed precisely that.

Gripping the highest rung, Rodney surveyed Shea's Field and followed over the lower field's jammed spruce to the grey harbour. He saw the Gut being smacked by glory-filled waves; it whitened one moment east, icy green this moment west. He peered for the Red Bank adjacent Smokey's pink colossal crop. He skimmed the bay north then, to Middle Head, to its precipitous peninsular rock. To the rendez-vous of gun and arm. His mother spoke of it, his father spoke of it. It was lore before he was born. Rodney noted the distance, he raised his chin at it, and coughed at it with full eyes – from there, reversal of the bay, into stark winter sea, climbing beach, black stumble here. Rodney took in all. The walk one frozen night, over a sea now buoyant but chilling, over less tender land now, one abandoned by summer.

The Keltic Lodge took back his eye, cock-proud on the promontory. Tourists were gone for the year. He saw beyond the peninsula, North Bay. She's there. The whole of Ingonish Island, then. He aimed eyes for Europe ultimately: then, the robin shell of heaven, but always back to its mysterious marine floor. Rodney would not mind to go out on the ocean with his uncles. If he could finish he could catch them, and he would try. But one more stepped rung and a chill at the nape scattered desire. Wind lifted coolly in shadow here. There was much painting and there was the returning point, what Frank had mentioned: no Curtis is of the sea. Forget blood: desire was an empty vessel.

thirty-nine

The sun had wandered Smokey's ridge to its early evening post. From there it threw visceral glints of half-appeal onto the aging year's waters. Squinting, Frank turned his head to watch his brother resume rowing. The coal of his cigarette fell onto his sweater and, swearing, he brushed what he could overboard before laying the arm to rest on his knee. Above his brother's left shoulder was the far autumn maple, the hearty damp deciduous, earliest turned, a red proud leaf waiting for all others to make their move. Mountains squatted like hunters who for centuries waited to prove none watched quite the way they did.

"What's the big idea of that huge Jesus log you got perched up there on the bow? Can't be making rowing any easier."

"It isn't. I told you. Claire. She's been after me all summer, to get her a good piece of driftwood. Her flower garden. Ahem. They all have flower gardens now. Late, but I got it. She had it in her head that only driftwood would set hers right off. They varnish them. I spotted it on the Sandbar and took advantage of some young fellows nearby to help me load it aboard."

"You couldn't get it on the return? I could have helped you load it in."

"Ah, we aren't coming back that way, Frank. And we'll have fish."

"Fish."

Clifford hacked from his lungs, coughed material he spat over the side. He kept both oar grips in his right while using the back of his left to wipe his mouth. A swell lifted the bow and rode wood planking to where Frank sat astern and past.

"That didn't feel natural."

"Might have been a whale pushing its tail underneath. I've seen them swim in twenty feet of water. They go anywhere that fishing is good."

"Like the rest of us."

"I hate the bastards."

"What, whales? Why, for heaven's sake, when half the world is in love with them?"

"Half. Me, the Japanese, and Norway represent the other."

"I think it was a rogue wave, myself. You get them out here every so often too, right?"

"What?"

"Rogue waves."

"I don't know what you're talking about, Frank."

"You see the sky last night? That red horsetail cloud? I thought that meant weather's on its way. There's been no weather all day to speak of, only calm. Ah, damn it all."

"What?"

"I forgot to get you to raise your oars coming through the Gut. I promised Rodney we'd signal so he could see."

"Where is he?"

"Up above, painting the outside of the garage."

"This hour? Bai, you're driving him. Why didn't you bring him along?"

"I asked him, he's got a girl on his mind. He wanted to get the work over with. But, hear – it's darker earlier these nights so let's get this fish you're talking about and pull the hell for back. I didn't tie the dog. Just threw a rock when she tried to follow. She'll be down on the beach wailing like the Banshees, we aren't home by dark."

"By dark? We'll have a greased frying pan looking for its second batch, by dark."

"I know. Remember, we're not as young as we once were."

"You aren't maybe. I am – now I am. I'm strong as a horse."

"Yes. A horse employed in a coal mine. I saw what you retched up back there."

The men waited in waters below Red Bank. They looked high to see the ledge where the bald eagle had its perch. A white head surveyed marine flats for shadows. Two cormorants burst the bay then, wings brushing just over surface at high clip gained.

"Those birds die blind."

"What? No."

"Cormorants? Yes they do. They strike the water in high dives, you've seen them. They go down and turn for their fish, grab it on the way back up. Try this trick, that many times over the years, see what happens to you. Their lids and eye tissue get worn raw."

"I imagine so, plunging into salt water."

"When they get old and can no longer fish, they starve."

"Fine images to dwell on. Got any more?"

"Hardly a board game out here. Come on then, drop your line or whatever it is we do out here. I don't suppose you learned they have motors now."

"What – and miss the excellent exercise! This is how our ancestors did it."

"Yes, I know, and were laid up with ruint backs at twenty-seven, standing bent with canes, at the Pearly Gates by thirty."

"They spend half the time working on their engines. Lawrence Hawley...."

"I remember Lawrence. What about him?"

"Him and his brother Allan got a little money when their father passed on."

"Right."

"Well, this Lawrence goes straight out with his share and buys a new boat engine. Allan, always fond of music, bought an organ with his. Well, the two fished lobster in separate boats and Allan's engine quit one day so he had to wait for a tow. His brother Lawrence comes along and Allan hollers: 'Give us a tow!' Lawrence hollers back: 'Go put in your organ'!"

*A*nother surge. A mile off Red Bank. In middle of South Bay, the men with spools let out, keeping deep line taut at the second joints of fingers.

"Frank?"

"Yes, dear."

"We grew up in Third World conditions Frank. You don't know that."

"No we didn't."

"No?"

"I've been there.... It's warm."

Clifford looked with a wide grin.

"Where were you?"

"Rio De Janeiro. Fought a goldminer from Minas Gerais, big black fellow name of Gliberto Meirelles Da Souza Villa Lobos. House of wolves. They had to stop the match, because of his ear."

"His ear?"

"Blood vessel burst."

"Christ. No one ever beat you. Eh? Frank?"

Frank looked. Clifford lifted with the boat.

"You know, in a single good night out here," said Clifford. "You can catch enough to get you through the winter. There's just Claire and me now. And there's just you. With any luck at all our meagre circumstances can be taken care of. For a while, they can."

Lines tugged.

Clifford grabbed the oars, he knocked his knees and yanked line. Frank recoiled, almost as quickly, the square design of his spool allowing it. Frank used unique elongated twists of the tackle, knees keeping tension at the gunwale. Clifford bashed five fish free from his hooks and helped Frank with his. Seven fleshy white-bellies with applauding tails and arched spines were on the dory floor and for the men, talk ended. It was a mackerel school, the work had to be quick: the distinct moment which had always returned men to ocean water, was here. The two drew heavily from below, each a pair: weighted.

"By God! Cod! The fish with not flesh, but meat!"

The heavier fish, especially after breaking surface, had to be eased up the gunwale. The gaff waited near – as too easily good fish are lost in this jarring transfer to air weight.

"That damn log you got aboard – toss it over ...

"I will, fish now."

Cod leapt and kicked under foot, settled the moment they came in contact with the comrade bellies and backs of the captured. The men cared nothing for the faring of fish on the floor. They cared nothing for their drift in the North Atlantic, nor for weather change. Concern aimed at Fortune, chanced upon, just how efficiently each could use body, mind, soul and equipment to exploit it. Fish thumped.

Frank hooked a meaty salmon, "Ho!"

"Ho, is right!"

Fatness and iridescence impressed both while ensemble they worked it aboard with the gaff and line. It had been hooked on the way up each man figured, as its brotherhood did not normally swim the depth of the cod. But then, a powerful jolt, followed by the livid gasp of foul air rushing as if from a mineshaft expiring at sea. The men turned to see the slick black back of a minke slither back into the waves.

"Jesus, Joseph, the size of that!

"The closeness of that!"

"Submarine, I think! Big lout is out here fishing, same as us. It's only a pilot whale, the biggest of the porpoise. Still, that bulbous prick will drive the school off yet."

"And us! He comes that close again!"

"Don't talk like that, Frank. His back was arched, he was going deep. Those things can travel twenty miles in an hour, they want to.

He was going low, that one, where the fish must be. Drop lines low. We'll try for what he knows."

A grey seal raised its head to investigate the men in their little cork on so much sea. It snorted appraisal between its six-inch whiskers.

"Enemy number two," said Clifford. "Harbour seal. They don't go low, but he's chowing down. Must be two schools, a lower and a higher. Keep yours up. I'll run mine deep."

Rain sprinkled. Surface roll. Foghorn moaning, and the smell of a wider marine damp entering from far off. Out of habit each man looked to the flash of the lighthouse at the harbour entrance. Cod were no more. Purple rain cloud bunched in the dying light of evening.

"You're eager to get back in, I know you are. Thing is, there's luck out here tonight. The likes of which won't come again to the unlikely pair of us tackling it. That I know. It's dirty. But no real weather can happen here in the bay. The fish strike because it's dirty. You were right. Weather's not far off. Everything below is feeding to top up. I say we stay and find where that school went. We'll keep ahead of it, the weather, you'll see, then head right in, she gets too bad, I promise. But you say the word now and we'll pull for shore. Summer rain, yet, this. That never hurt a soul."

Frank looked through misty eyes. He tasted a drop of sea on his lip. They had no raingear; they had no grub. Not a Thermos of tea. But the near air was hardly what you could call cold; they could snack on the fish if it came right down to it. Frank peered at innocuous chop; benign rushing whitecaps filled his ear, as in tumble, each died over slate waves. That a good sign? Slate waves? Toward the bow, the housing where fishermen kept their little jars of holy water blessed directly by the priest had its hatch lifting. Frank saw in against ribbing, but just barely, the bottle's neck, its white cap.

"All right. You must know what you're doing. You can row through it, though? And I want you to tell me, if you can. So, can you?"

"This? I can, because she's blowing ashore. The worse that can happen is we're driven landward to strike the beach. I can row, no worry there. We'll just sit atop it and let her drive us in while we gather fish."

Clifford sent his oars deep, to right the boat, to break for where he figured the school had gone. He had marked as best he could where the seal had popped its head before dipping. Frank had lost bearing, as the cliffs of Middle Head now wore a veiling mist which settled only deeper and deeper. He too had eyed the seal. He kept aware.

They drifted seaward as magnificent precipitous banks of Smokey opened at the parts not shrouded by burnt-tobacco clouds to show the rain-worn seabird ledges.

Thighs pressed gunwale, lines dropped. The fever of the gambler ran in hot blood. In Clifford's, burningly. He had lost much time being laid up. And for what, he felt? For nothing. His heart was all regret, a hard, hard state, but one broken up like dandelion spores out here. He had forgotten the sea, the healer that it was. If he could make this one run, tonight – if he could turn this trip into the most excellent of catches, one of spoils returned: then his mind would be free. He'd last the coming winter, knowing what waited. Grey hair stuck to a square lumpy head to make him no more beautiful a man than Frank. He knew. Bent ear tips drained rainwater and spray.

"Far enough, Clifford. Stop I say."

"Little further, Frank. Look, she's passing. Years ago all they ever did was this. Come out in these boats, in this stuff. They'd go all the way to Middle Head, beyond! Some of them. Far as Ingonish Island."

"We're not going to Ingonish Island."

Frank searched Middle Head. The last knuckle of the promontory digit was open to view; it bent inward. They were out, out this far. But the rain, the mist, the fog – all perspective shifted when the eye shut, even if to blink out weather. Clifford hacked over the side and wiped his mouth on the back of a rowing forearm. Swell raised the two, set them down into points to erase sight of land. Flaws of rain broke to usher forward a wall-in of fog, to take for good their dearly-beloved private landmarks. Wind rose, tormented, but high above: and indecisively. Knowing not whether to blow or to hold. The tender feel of the south was in it. The cutting sound of the south was in it.

"There's our luck."

"What, luck?"

"Wind change. She's coming around south to drive us ashore. Even better. And not into the beach either, but back toward the Gut. Where we want to be. We got nothing to worry about, me son. And when we get in close the wind won't have any real power because of the bay's layout. Middle Head one side, Smokey the other. A cradle to all. Southerlies are dashed by the topography of the Highlands. This fog, though. Ever seen the likes? Hear how the voice goes? I'm lowering it because the feel is like that of a vault. Watch your step."

They waited with lines sunk, drifted in the company of hissing whitecaps. The wind did not descend but rather strengthened, higher, completing its shift there. And, as Clifford had predicted: the swell did drive them on, to what seemed shoreward. The wind died. All airs calmed. A feature of the tropical storm, each knew, that long-travelled prankster bent on pursuing with romantic delight this continent's innocent northern height.

More slate-grey barrelled against the boat, salt-laden, thick, as if one could tread upon it and not get sole wet. The sky glimpsed them, revealing a horrid black thunderhead wadded like excessive packaging, and – as even monsters have some appeal – it dropped lacy pink lining below it. The weather front did look to be passing. And, as could be written, they were safely under it.

"You never found anyone, Frank?"

Frank nodded no at the second goddamn coming of this goddamn subject today. What was going on here? Ill timing? Coincidence? Court heralds to preface change? What change? Where is the change, the sign? None. No sign. Just these waves – these bunching threes. Ride them out. Clifford left off on the topic as quickly as he raised it and, unlike Rodney, would not return to it. He touched his oars for balance, leaving neatly spooled nylon at his feet, briefly looking expectant over his shoulder as if about to be called from there.

"No, Clifford. Never did."

"Claire was my only. And that's, ever. Even when overseas I took no other woman to my bed. I didn't see cause to. Plenty were, taking the girls back, doing what they could with them. Me son! It was an epidemic! Rage. That can't have changed, I don't expect. I told the soldiers in the outfit I was taking girls back, to peacify them. You were friends, you two, I knew that. She told me that herself. I felt bad about William. I did Frank. On occasion, long after. When the weather would turn just so. On a certain day to make everyone feel good. Or some little luck you weren't expecting chanced to come out of the blue. Or even, Claire, if she had some particular success with her flowers – I thought of him, first. Thoughts came that stole any good to come afterward. You top up with guilt. With early things gone unanswered. You got to snap to, when they happen – solve what comes right away before moving on. That's the part never told, when young. I changed tags. Do you hear? I made him change with me. That's why the mix-up, why when I got home they thought I was Will. I felt I laid the finger of fate on the poor bastard. What struck him was meant for me. As God is my witness. To this day, I can't help but feel that."

"Why did you change tags?"

"A jam. I asked if he would help me out. Didn't work. They caught me and presented me an honourable discharge. Canadian Army, lenient, foolish, I don't know what. I do know it's easy to look innocent. I never told a soul about that. If I ever did, I knew it would be you, first. That shell that struck him was the shell meant for me. Last time I ever laid eyes on him he was leaving, Private Clifford Curtis."

"Nothing here. We got plenty. Let's head back in."

"There was of course the day you went with the gun too. I knew you'd take it. I knew very well. I prayed for it. What I didn't tell you was, I knew the safety was faulty."

"Dark now, Clifford. It'll be night before we know it – it is night."

"Never said anything then either. I made it faulty. I did that."

"Jesus Christ Clifford – I cocked it! I climbed the rocks! I was out there! Me! Me! Take us the fuck ashore."

"I will. I am. It was never about the rifle. It never was that."

"Ashore."

"It was before that, long before. The day I came home from the woods and you played the music. You remember. You had an aptitude like none ever even knew to exist. Heart. I heard it. All heard it. That tore me apart worst of all."

There came then what might have been the far off crippling cry of a tormented beast. Neither man spoke. Foghorns, they played tricks, didn't they? The men had been looking at their load of fish when, as one brother followed the other's eyes upward for a fresh hint in the weather system, there came the profound surge. Clifford rose twelve inches above his bench to fall miserably back into the scaly near corpses behind him. His legs stayed put on the bench, pasty and frail from alcoholism, whitened bony sparsely-haired shins at cotton cuffs above boot tops.

"Jesus in heaven, I'm covered. What struck us?"

"You tell me!"

"Let me get up. Not our whale. Tell me it wasn't that. Help me up. Here, grab hold."

"Here. Was it him, or not? A whale doesn't do that. Do they?"

"I think he meant to spill us in the sea. Like he was connecting us with the cod."

"I never heard of that possibility."

"Anything's possible out here, me son – nature. I know one thing, my back is ruint."

"Pull for shore, Clifford. I've had enough of this foolishness. No one in this boat is any fisherman. There's nothing more to catch. Food's at the Fairway, if a person goes hungry."

"Ashore we go, then."

"You figure he saw the cod aboard? That he may have been going for that?"

"Christ, Frank. Some thought to put in a fellow's head."

"You put it into mine!"

The tail of the mammal broke, slapping fresh brine onto the men. Clifford held the oars tight so as not to lose either. He pshawed with a full mouth. He dipped oars low, yanked hard with eyes closed to establish some stability.

"The gaff, Frank! The gaff! Jab that foul fucker in the eye, he turns again! Smell the breath? I could. Stinks in a way you don't soon forget. The gaff, I say – take it!"

"The gaff? What's the gaff going to do, Clifford? Bent hook, into a head like that?"

"A lot a bent hook into the head can do! Be something to have in your hands at least! Ah, look. Cursed log ... shifted. All fish spilt to one side, ah. And we're tipping, bai! Hold still, least little bit will capsize us. Get to that side, Frank, on the double!"

"Jesus Christ, I told you we shouldn't have taken it aboard! But did you listen? No, you didn't. And we should have gone in before this, too! You and your precious winter fish."

"Relax, me son, relax. We're okay, stay calm we are."

They looked to see water all around. Water blackened by heavy night falling and heavy air closing ten yards at a blink. The minke had broken portside. While feeding, it had mustered curiosity of the vessel. It left its footprint, the moments-long lapse in a stirred ocean, a swollen sea puddle at re-entry. Its breaking sent water inside, and now a bad list caused by the repositioned log, encouraged sea spills to babble aboard. Dribbles became pitchers-full when the larger waves of three struck.

"She's coming in! Bailer, Frank, bailer! You got it there? You find it? Did you? I had it in here last night. That half-Javex container?"

"Do I got it? I've only been using it since we left shore!"

"Here. I'm taking off my boot, using that."

"First thing we got to do is to throw the fish back in, Clifford. And let's dump that Jesus log before we touch anything else."

"No, Frank. Touch that and we're in, for sure, the way she's hung up. Stay where you are. Keep weight here, to the other side. We'll upset if we even go near it. Why, why, why, why, why – do I give consent to that woman? Just tell me. Concentrate now – ease the water out."

They bailed and bailed but the work was slow. They kept an intimate eye on the sea. The grey seal popped its head, rolled back in luxury, its sudden emergence taking on that of a large human head rising, chin pointing astern on a lovely backward sea puddle. But reclining, with all the buoyancy in the world now; the creature made itself out to be the picture of ease. Frank saw the salmon. It arched, balanced upright, swished a slow then flicking tail as it righted and swam over the other fish, hopped the gunwale hurdle to plink itself whole into the sea. It swam gently while brushing off this distasteful experience, sink freed as it was again, into an eternity of the proper medium.

The men knew they had to lighten the load, fast. Bailing restored nothing. They had to remove fish – plus bail, and never jar the boat with either. They took turns releasing one cod at a time, over the side, keeping what shifting weight they could, opposite the driftwood. But such fish-catching practice wanted deft mastering, as lush seawater just kept entering and larger waves replenished easily that tossed.

The men bailed while light died wholly from day. Squall rain snarled at white-capping pitch, wind rose over waves. In the tension, the two spoke nothing of the little success, presently – of the little boat riding a little better, fewer fish inside, the heavy stupid vessel, ridden of cod. Some of the fish set back in would snap back to life, but later. None showed the vigour of the salmon. The simplest of trails formed thus in the water, obliquely downward went swimmers no longer swimmers. Neither man was conscious that by their efforts to improve the boat's stalwart value they created also this underwater demarcation which continued for some distance off. The trail at points varied in depth but more or less waited arced and ready to be consumed.

The minke – as the half-life cod – patiently sank, its brain programmed for half-sleep. This was its delicate feature. It knew not fitful sleep, only half-sleep. Respiration could never be guaranteed by a brain wholly switched off. No. And with full departure of consciousness – could not a lung collapse in the iron depths the mammal fell? Muscle must always be taut, ready, therefore. But that school back there, it had been plentiful. And the aftertaste of the sea's bounty? Its sudden disappearance always returns the hunger – another eternal drawback. Appetite cannot dull in a stomach never sated. In some gain is much loss: as in any air-breathing creature.

The whale dropped dreamily. It was ready with brine spitballs, circling techniques, sonar, scythe tail – high and low, these wonderful abilities. But nothing more – except this? This mysterious, broken line. This trail. What is it? Teasing. Morsels. Morsels. Investigate.

One eye of the mammal reckoned the blood trail and relayed to its brain the message of circumnavigation, now, to meet it. The mammal could feed rising, a manoeuvre managed with total ease – an oblique surge, mouth ajar. Intelligence was sufficient to gobble a rising line of fish, keep steady plane, and lose none in the track.

The marine equine pressed on. And that scavenging seal was always near, lest we forget. Near in cases like this. Moreover, the resumption of air. Yes. Retreat to pressure lessened. Always the air. Sinking, resting, mating, feeding, blow and, to blow, to free the hole that brought inward these precious gases.

forty

𝓔ach man was long slumped in the rain when Clifford freed the last fish. The boat gave no sudden righted aspect, heavy with water and a maladjusted log. Yet they took relief from any inch granted from the sea. Frank had the Javex bailer in his hand, the gaff handle jammed under his armpit. In a soaked sock foot stationed on its heel, Clifford nodded for Frank to regard the thickening shadow, the swelling water's approach. Each gripped gunwale when the mystery rose and took up the whelmed boat. But the gravity, the calm, the mid-air. Horrors visit the human such: fearful calm prefacing the fall, stability facing down the end, the ten thousand brain rehearsals for such a drop during the normal course of the normal life. Dreams: the waking subconscious. But how new again, to know what it is to be thrown and dashed below a gurgling sea, immersed in a frigid black inkwell. Under it all.

Frank kicked with the strength of a man facing his mortality, writhed with no idea where surface lay. In puppetry he swung his arm where water pushed heaviest. He retreated for the precious break then, but too early he gasped a lung of salt.

Gagging, kicking to get higher, salt permitting it, he got out of the sea enough to spell the arm's toil. Twisting, he saw frightful night firmly arrived, encompassing rain that liberally bashed a cold sea. The boat, beautifully intact, had righted itself to sit bolstered, free of all cargo and plainly, far-off driven, to where its streamlined design bucked on a wild night through a carnival of slosh. The lightened hull rose so preciously above a single wave, next, superior ribbing visible, hull as if cork planked – then hot on its way it disappeared from sight. Frank spun in his water, wits mercifully slow to alarm.

"Clifford!"

Black sky. Towered, twisting wind. Lashed slats of rain. Forgotten bouy clanging. Foghorn, tolling, beacon flashing. Ingonish Island? Gut? Sandbar, there? Adrenaline petitioned Frank, it wanted chest higher, higher, more kicking, to see and be out of this, to establish bottom. Frank turned an ear for breakers of the beach then spotted in the direction the boat had travelled a raised arm fall out of sight.

Forward he threw his own arm lustfully at tempest and pool.

He scrambled to grab his brother, to take jawbone and throat.

"Get above!"

"I never...." Seawater spoiled both mouths. Frank knew the *never* – the *never* and the what of the never. The boast had come one thousand times, materialising at last into an honourable badge his brother wore. Its ironic play – proclaim deficiency and you'll never deal with it because the world knew it. The dry world. Come, come to the sea! Come again as a man wholly safe on the slim material dividing him and the medium to end him. Speak contradiction, act contradiction – it is where the human excels: in the courting of the situation up to the day when situation ends him. Live. Endure. See it become law.

Frank grappled preciously with a struggling jacket, got his hand under Clifford's neck and dug to cradle the throat, head; keep chin aloft and in the locked crevice of an arm. Clifford thrust to extricate himself from this horror, hating hotly his back to a sea floor, hating hotly this full access to black ceaseless sky.

"Don't fight me! We're in the water! So don't!"

Night threw storm currents to shift the men which way it would. Frank overpowered his brother. But laid up so long, feline fight remained in Clifford. Frank kicked to propel the two, sinking the duo when slowing. These drops, lurches and quick disturbance sent Clifford into concerted adrenaline tumults and the two dropped to below waves to know desperation there. How quick the body, how quick the spirit alights in final battle with a tossed sea. Yet Frank got them above. "For the last ... pah! Clifford! Let up I say, let me do it, all!" Clifford could not answer, not as he wished, not in the execrable answer called for – submitting to these tactics unbearable for a respiring throat with legs and arms knowing support no more. Submission ... all right, all right – till right, here, and this new fight. Ah, grapple, to exasperate both. Sooner die than be held – a choking Clifford wanted to inform his protectorate, and pleadingly, inform just this. Communication, manifest only through imposing will.

Frank twisted for bearing, kicked always to keep both their heads up, when Clifford, splayed over his front, burst backward to stove his skull into Frank's mouth. Frank spat blood, touched a salt tongue to salt teeth.

"You got the worst of that!" Frank said, and listened for breakers, blew mucus, brine and blood. He twisted helter when he saw a slow rising.... Driftwood. Not more than thirty feet.

With post reserve, the clean strength left to animals at violent death, Frank scissor-kicked and bobbed a reverse. He closed in, but soon on nothing, with these poor mechanics, this cargo. He knew he could get them there. Clifford still fought.

"No, no, no – not now – leave off, leave off, I say! I'm trying for the log!"

Aware of no log, aware of a swimming brother's fresh vigour, Clifford interpreted it as their last moment. He willed to show life left. Frank lost grip. Exhausted, but knowing respite with freed arm he soon punched the black pitching currents, patted for his brother, slapped for him, then went under.

Miserably ... there, a grasp, the ineffectual clutch at a sleeve button, then waist. Clifford clawed, but downward. Frank kicked a long leg for him. He clawed at nothing, taking him in the last ditch of manoeuvres, scissoring him in his legs, swimming up with arm breaking.

Frank's head was gouged by a knot of the log he was attempting to reach.

Letting go, circling, reaching, he yanked Clifford by a handful of hair, the log a counterweight. He got a face out of the sea.

"Breathe! Take in air! Take it!"

Clifford had no life to take it. He coughed, took one long, long gasp before teeth got washed with salt. Frank had to come around, speak to his brother's face. "Hold the wood." Frank draped his brother's arm over the log, squeezing the hand as he ducked, surfacing opposite while hollering for his brother's continual securing – just that!

The log between them: a fistful of jacket collar, snug shirts at the nape, Frank held. Encouraged by salt, the log suspended them. The rest brought by routine arrived to upright postures, stopped in embattled water, when a gushing whitecap insulted both faces, reminding each just how each stood in the sea. Frank slipped in his hold, taking jacket collar merely.

"Final time – mouth above water! You have to speak Clifford. I can't see you!"

"Here, pah...."

"Here. Hold, on your own. There's nothing to be sorry about. Just work with me. Keep your head above. Swimming is that. I'll hold you all I can."

They used small mouths in the frigid Atlantic, sister to the frigid Arctic.

"Extend the feet. Paddle like a bike. That's all the work you got to do." Frank wanted to be didactic here about many things but, exhausted, he fell off into whisper he himself couldn't hear. He had told Clifford to hang on. Did he? Had he explained that he, Frank, needed an adjustment of grip; that his arm dug into knots so horribly that circulation was cut off from the artery.

"Frank?"

"Right here, Clifford."

"Frank, your dog."

"I heard. Shut up about that now. You hang on. The wind will take us ashore. That right? It will?"

"I'm holding on."

"Right? You said? That it will take everything ashore? You said."

"My legs want from this log. I can't. It isn't keeping me up. I swallowed water."

"We both did."

"I'm holding."

"Hold, and I'll hold you."

The men drifted as there came an improving time-sense and wind-sense direction. Rain backed up to charge in gale force from the northeast while a coal-mired black proctored a world of snapping, roiling seawater. The two witnessed spindrift hurry over waves they rode; they waited through farther-off assaults that marked them and came for them. Frank did not speak of the strain caused by the grip, nor ask for his brother to use his own strength to make himself upright. Clifford was mastered by his paralysing fear of the sea, a fear too grand in him to know any option held. So Frank spoke over the log to ask if kicking was going on – that it was important to kick, to keep the circulation going. It hadn't seemed frosty, but this is frost! So kick with the legs! Any assistance got them further. Clifford acted when prompted, fell off with instruction mute. Clifford had not stopped ingesting bits of brine; it was deep in his lungs and trapped in his stomach. Frank swore at the mechanical counting of these moments he held his burden on the log; the abhorred regression, shook his head, implored himself not to get caught up in counting. Concentrate. But the rushing formation of peaks, this drop off into black bowls, rise, ride off, arch, fall, sweep. Waves came as perfect pendulum strokes, gurgle from whitecaps as ticking second-hands. Beyond, was the passage of time. Not here. Well yes, here.

At some point in the night, losing himself to thirty seconds of sleep, Frank forgot his grip and woke to his arm digging deep to catch his slipping brother. Knot splinters tore. But he got him, yanked and took firm hold again, again of the ratty chaffing rags. But holding Clifford became Frank's method to stay above. He called out for Clifford. He kicked and got higher, looked across for the head but waves insulted his face, filled a deeply plugged ear, stung blinded eyes. The irregularities in the log pressed dearly at his rib cage. He could find no smooth spot. Skin tore to abuse flesh. The log and all its irregularities wanted nothing more of this, his bearing, or the other's. "Clifford. Have I still got you? Clifford? Am I holding something there? You're too light!"

Night. Sea. Aching frigid deliberation.

forty-one

While search boats chopped through a wild night's wane, it was not till grey dawn that they spotted the dory. It beat the base rock of Smokey's Red Bank as though pleading for entrance to the cliff kingdom. At first light, along the wide beach, past rotting debris washed in from tempestuous hours, past messes of slung seaweed, searchers spotted them. The whining of a dog led them here, a bitch that had spent the night on the sand watching sloshing forms wash from waves. She'd lain alongside the two in whimpers through dropping tide, its heart broken. She barked like an old man lost of speech to see searchers rush the sand, before becoming again the homeless dog who knew fear, mistrust and how to preserve silence. She kept wholly aloof when the party closed in. This morning was the start of the cold ones. The first frost had descended during the night. Folks had brought in pumpkins.

Nearby was a driftwood log, newly in with tide and harsh breakers, burrowing itself into rinsing sand. It had shorn red plaid embedded in knotholes; each searcher figured promptly: that this was the vehicle to carry the men who breathed yet, despite sallow death masks. Faces, a smoky grey, sand-covered, puffed. Flesh at hands bound or curled, white like the underside of so many fish. The searchers looked at one another without nod nor blink. At last one knelt and spoke roughly into an ear:

"Got to let go, Frank. Of the collar. We can't get you apart."

They pulled on the fingers, welcomed the ease that came, a general loosening that also relaxed the restricted airway of the one with the thinner legs, prompting his sigh, cough. The searchers decided to make transport in blankets they had. One searcher per corner, two riding abreast with ropes drawn under their loads. Those carrying Frank could not help but study the rigid right hand, as heels dug sand: the hand was cramped as if in pose for the sculptor, or, sculpture.

One searcher ran ahead to the Tartan Tavern, the beach saloon, property of the Beach Rock Inn. "We got them. They're living." A cheer erupted, to fall into sniff, throat clearing, whisper, drift into silence as the community came out to see for themselves in lurking dawn light. An unseen gull whooped for the state of the men survived at sea. Another dropped a mussel from on high, to crack breakfast. Two upright human figures choked, one retched onto sopping kelp.

The successful searchers bustled, carried the men up the tavern steps and to its backroom billiard tables where families had waited the night through, where pinball machines lit dim corners. The beverage room's billiard balls were scooped up, dropped in corner pockets and came rattling through their passages to clicking stops as the brothers were laid supine and made comfortable.

Frank's fingers had not come apart. As if special-purpose shipbuilding spikes, they stayed bent like catches. None dared attempting a straightening. None wished to view much else. Blankets were thrown over.

Father Red Donovan and old Leo Curtis stood in iron silence with stiff backs to pinball machines; they'd seen it all now. Daniel Dunphy, his daughter and grandson stood opposite the far billiard table, a corner pocket. Daniel's son Edward had arrived grandly from Margaree during the night to help in the search; he was out on the water, the other side of Middle Head where he'd been checking waters to Ingonish Island. Someone radioed. All boats now knew.

Doctor Joel Roberts arrived from Neil's Harbour Hospital to walk a trench coat over saloon floors. Straightaway his presence cut the grass-fire whisper. Shoulders pressed back, belts adjusted – the man needed to work! Doctor Roberts checked pulses and tongues, lifted eyelids and thumbed the switch of a silver light. He got help to turn the survivors and, while each was supported, traced fingers over spines and, with hands, went in tube-fashion down limbs till satisfaction came of no irregularities indicative of broken bones. Looking to Father Donovan, he spoke: "Can you get them carried to their respective homes? Their families are to keep tight watch. Both are severely dehydrated. They've taken in a thimble or two of seawater, I'd say. Also, dry clothes." He grimaced, but professionally, as his mind reserved right to hold its prognosis of advanced pneumonia. "Home, bed. Packets of fruit salts – but diluted. Have them lie still. Monitored till I get back this evening. Or this afternoon. There will be aching muscles from dehydration. It will feel in each as if everything is long broken."

The doctor leaned to learn the men were carried in blankets.

"No! The Park! Wardens have stretchers. You might have called them! I mean, jumpings – jarring them in blankets like that could have damaged spines! We don't know what happened out there! Lean on each other, the Park, in future. A community. Be that from here forward. I've seen too much of the contrary." He lowered a raised arm and got into his car for his return north, explaining a baby was coming, from a small woman. "Telephone Neil's Harbour if untoward symptoms develop. I'm not far. And don't be afraid to, either."

Father Red grimaced, half nodded in the prejudice of his own culpability. He unconsciously shook his head, blinked yes's and no's.

Grace went with Frank in Rodney's car. The new house was closest, Frank's things were there. Three searchers followed in a second automobile to get him into the house. Millie scrambled, tail tight, into Rodney's car before the door closed, she sat on a front mat where she lacked the room to turn her head. She knew she had as much right and power as the rest.

In the days that followed, fevers of dehydration wrangled survivors, but straining muscles sharply worsened in Frank. Overall rigidity prohibited his sitting up. Clifford progressed, proving to possess the more resilient body; perhaps fewer were the battles fought over the years. It came as irony, for some. As for Frank, who knew his battles? All did, but all didn't too. When Clifford could get to his feet he had Claire take him to Frank. A family member was stationed there round the clock. The doctor had made a visit two days after the event and in a more concerted state reported thoroughly for a crowded kitchen nook:

"Frank Curtis never recovered from the removal of his arm. There's been inflammation at the site. Since boyhood. A condition that could only have dogged him his entire life. The accident with the anchor permanently damaged the bad shoulder, making it impossible for it ever to heal. I try, but cannot conceive the constant suffering there must have been in the innumerable twinges of arthritis, incessant searing rheumatisms, tendons awry. Salves were how Frank treated himself. Ointments. Oils. Topical remedy. That was this man's approach.

"The good arm has a frozen shoulder. I don't know how long. He received breakage in two ribs while on the sea – which I admit to missing when checking them on the billiard table. There's a new scar on the ribcage, his sister accounted for that. Broken ribs are hard to confirm. Beyond an X-ray. Breakage must have come from smashing waves as the two gripped the log that night. There's a hole bore into Frank's side from the driftwood. One that didn't bleed, oddly, not as it should have. Salt. And when they hit the rollers of shore, impact was plenty there, no doubt, to cause rib breakage. I can't put any other guess on it. A body that fought too long. This fever is merely the final staving off of internal organs in too poor a state for too long. Battling ineffectively, I'll say. No, I'll say a job of recovery too large. Outstripped. Shallow pulse, low brain response to light at the pupils. I'm bound by duty to report that Frank has advanced pneumonia. Both lungs topped with fluid."

From beyond the bedroom, a collective shudder.

"You'll have to brace yourselves. He's going. The strength of the younger man is long past. Though he is, I will state, every bit the fighter they told me he was. And that was told not here, but away."

*F*rank broke through the cloud of unconsciousness at the coming of the following night, when his sister Grace sat at his right – not caring at all for his blueness nor his laboured breathing. The gargle and suck. There was a pan for sputum. She stood to show herself bedside, hands clasped.

"Grace?"

Frank reached fingers, but shallowly, for hands. Grace didn't take the prompt.

"Here, Frank."

"Grace?"

"Speak, Frank."

"Your hands. On your way to receive the host? You can't give me your hand? Closer, Grace."

She lay soft knuckles on her brother's forehead.

"Closer, Grace."

"I'm here, Frank. What?"

"Get that dog off the foot of the bed, he's jammed the blankets that tight I can't rest."

"Jesus, Mary and Joseph – here you, get down! Ah, Frank, don't mind us. We thought you might have wanted her there. Get down, I said and – out the door!"

"Not out. In, Grace. Leave her in. Are you listening to me?"

"I'm always listening."

"I was glad to see things work out for you. You were the happiest."

"I can't hear this. Please."

"Young Rodney here? That him out there knocking around?"

"Arranging a chair for you, one you might sit in."

"Here I am Frank."

"Rodney."

"Right here."

"Daylight still?"

"Just, Uncle Frank."

"Could you get me water?"

"I'll get you water."

"No. Listen. The leaves have it covered. Just follow to the source. The spring there never dries no matter the summer, or fall."

Rodney looked at his mother whose lips tightened and she raised a shoulder. She didn't know what the hell he was talking about – the old house? Perhaps Rodney should go.

"Rodney?"

"Yes, Frank."

"Take care of that garage. You did the work. Stay the gentleman for that North Bay girl."

"I will. Uncle Frank."

"That's good, bai. You go now." But Rodney came forward to Frank and squeezed his hand. He saw the green knuckle-tattoos, the thin copper bracelets. Rodney stepped back and stared down the bed, drawing on the sleeve of his fall jacket. He tightened the bill of his hat in his hands, sniffed, clicked fingers for Millie when in the kitchen, where he touched his eyes and put on the hat.

"Frank," said Grace. "Can Father Donovan come in? He's been here these past three nights."

"Doesn't he have a home of his own to go to? Ah, Grace, I never went for that. Makes it harder. Never had the attention."

"No one will press you."

"None did. Too much. Bring him in."

The slim priest with the red curls appeared at Frank's right. He wore black beads weighted by a silver crucifix. The smell of incense fell from this particular black suit he had not worn in public. Frank had seen the collar, the black shirts, the regular jackets.

"I miss our hellos from the beach," said Father Donovan.

Frank stared, "I miss no beach, Father."

"No."

Glint entered Father Donovan's eyes, as onto the forehead he placed an open, warm, soft-skinned hand, a hand possibly never to know physical work, yet powerful, thick.

"I fought hands like yours."

"I know you fought them."

The priest produced a delicate bottle, dabbed oil onto his thumb and touched Frank's closing eyelids then the lips. The priest made a sign of the cross onto the forehead but not with oil: with ash he carried in a metal case, a vessel perfect for carrying sweets.

"Frank? Have you made your peace with God, Frank?"

"I don't remember us quarrelling, Father."

Father Donovan looked at Grace to give her a weighty nod, a smile, one to suspend all in the room from the suffering of the past days. Father Donovan said a rosary and at its end asked if there were any in particular Frank wished to see.

"It was good to see you."

"I wanted to know you better."

"Anything to come had to come for me, Father."

"As it does for all. But a man through what you have – no stronger conviction. Anything outside is powerless in the face of that."

"My sister-in-law. Claire, Father? Is she…"

"All the family, Frank, yes."

"Her then. Just her. And give us a moment?"

Claire stood at bedside in the posture of Grace, the posture of the women North of Smokey, brave in lives asked to come through, slight, listing, gracious and attendant.

"Hello Frank."

"Claire?"

"Right here."

"I know you are – you were. I wanted to tell you that, Claire."

She pressed against the bed, bent close as she could. But he spoke so utterly lowly. He asked that she raise her voice though she had replied no word, yet. She knew she had to speak. She took his hand, weighty, swollen, and grey. She covered it in hers.

"You don't think you can pull through, at all, Frank?"

"I was trying to, but now that priest went and put ashes on my head. Claire?"

She squeezed the palm and he closed his eyes to feel its warmth. He sank so softly and deeply; did not mind letting go. A gurgle came now with his every breath.

"Claire? Clifford got in? He got back?"

"Don't speak of it. He got back all right. We mentioned so."

"We made the best of it."

"Who Frank? Who did?" But Claire broke, uncontrollably. Frank became lucid the moment of it, still entirely able to know pain.

"Those for me? Don't now, I wish you wouldn't. I wish they were my own, what I could have shed. I did. And for you. Go now. He here? After that, no one. Goodbye now, Claire, I'll let you go."

Frank in the next instant opened his eyes to see his lone brother standing above, dressed in good dry clothes, handsome.

"Change from what I last saw. Bring your chair."

"I can't hear you, Frank. What is it?"

Frank swallowed and whispered. Clifford brought the chair closer to the right. He sat, leaned; he had prepared himself.

"I saw what you carried from the house."

"I know you saw."

"I thought they would have destroyed it."

"No, Frank. It wasn't that. They wouldn't have destroyed it."

But Frank could say no more as a fit of gasping struck. A mean sucking. Clifford touched his pillow, but sat again as it subsided. Frank motioned for his hand to be taken and Clifford did this to experience the hand come off the bed, a little, in his, with his, elbow almost propping. Clifford allowed it. Frank's crossed his waxen nicotine thumb past Clifford's.

"I wondered."

"What Frank? What did you wonder? Is that what you said?" Clifford had drawn very close. Breath was on his cheek.

"Which would win."

Clifford saw the eyes shut and, from a long way off, there came a touch against his palm, a force comprised of memory in the departing of the living. Clifford felt for its strength, as the sweet small surge unlike any he knew travelled sadly its course from willing spirit to willing flesh. Clifford put up his own tiny fight in the hands, but could only feel the beautiful foreign force ebb from his brother's palm. He looked at the face to see, there, if the force would linger. To see there its end. He gripped the hand when the vessel emptied its final drop, when the chest welled, a final breath and, light departed. His brother was gone. Heart broken, Clifford watched the face in its moment of the soul vanished. He had to let go of the hand — to stand, to walk, to face the others yet could do nothing as truth seized him: that, between boyhood and this moment, there existed all but emptiness beyond this meeting, of their hands, this touch held now and forever without force and, approaching cold.

forty-two

The funeral was a Thursday morning. At graveside, Rodney had to break from mourners to capture the howling dog and get it into the car. It was a sickening sound. The animal had arrived over lawns to disrupt the service. Rodney caught her after a long chase ending only in a subduing down over the hill near the beaver pond, the site of the oldest graves. The dog had gnawed its rope tether and travelled the Beach Crossing from the Crick. She had jogged Ingonish Beach but panted up the Keltic Road to come down golf fairways and particularly the slope of Number Sixteen, easing into the churchyard where Frank lay prepared for ground alongside Jessie and Adrian.

Rodney waited for breath at the beaver pond where he saw crisp red in maple over the weathered wood of the beaver lodge. He viewed a crisp yellow start in the birch, making white bark all the whiter, smoother. Poplar and beech hung out canopy green.

Ascending, holding the dog by her new studded collar, Rodney felt a land breeze pass over the headstones. It rose to raise hair out of his eyes. He saw at a distance a community gathered graveside, but whispering wind turned him again to view the red maple, from here to view it among all the green of the lawns. As leaders, the maples waltzed their leaves, down over the hill in the soft fall light, where a colourful ripple ran the pond.

*A*mong the pallbearers were Daniel Dunphy and his son Edward Dunphy. Leo Curtis stood with the pair, but opposite, when time came to bear the casket. Leading had been Charles and Rodney, in suits. A former employee of the first Fairway, Victor Shea gripped a side handle. He wore a leather tie. Father Red Donovan doused with the aspergillum the holy water whose drops rode graveyard airs. Father Donovan stepped away with grim altar boys then, initiating community dispersal.

But Clifford surprised the dispersal. He had an informed hearse driver approach with key for the casket, whereupon Clifford carried from his car a sack to graveside. The driver opened the casket top. Clifford removed his object and spoke, but was barely audible: "...no, no gun. But something to take." Those very close saw what it was. Others would later learn it was an instrument a hobo might cast aside for its workmanship. With composure Clifford placed the object on Frank's left, side down. And Rodney, who took the necessary step to handle the shoulders of the uncle overcome, saw upon casket closing, the tiniest of strands, now leaving view, strands caught in an f-hole. Seaweed.

*O*ut in the open air the family stood back for the men ready with short-handled shovels, out over thighs, crunching soil with their now stepping boots. A backhoe and operator waited in the wings, the operator smoking, unlaced workboot over a tire tread. Hat removed. The smell of turned dirt, then the sight of its brown tints, a shovel sliding deftly or, far worse, coming up solid on rock spoiled any family composure. There came contagious shudder, the final mass weeping of general release.

The shovels made short work. Rodney tried his mother's elbow, to start her away when she had called for stoppage to the shovelling:

"I said no large stones! You heard me!" She called this twice, and touched Rodney's face with a glove when they were secure under young birch. She looked in him in the eye.

"You knew. How could you not?" He would not answer this, as to what he might know, but prompted her instead to come with him. She said no to it and for him to go on. Rodney waited in the car for his mother and father, Charles, Millie adjusted on a front floor mat.

Driving home was a silent affair, a far cry from the swooping rides in this wagon through a community, ballast against his rock and roll favourings, an eight-track stereo ablaze and its mesmerising equaliser lights pulsing. Grace wanted to hear a tape she'd bought: it was in the car; she'd forgot to play it on the way over. It was music people played at funerals. "We're fine without." But Rodney at last did insert the tape, keeping it low, the wheels of tape most audible.

That night, Rodney went by Frank's home and stood in the kitchen. He looked at his uncle's things to experience an immediate sadness at seeing what a man leaves. And, if possessions stood in good order, as were his, it made their observance a heavier affair. The moment stayed, and would stay: having great impact upon the slightest possessions elected from here on in. That owned, is that viewed. Rodney saw Frank's teapot was clean. Inside the spout tip, wiped. Mud was washed from rubber boot soles size eleven, their rubber brand-stamps clearly legible. No knife was in the fork section of the silverware tray, no fork in the knife. Rodney had not come here for this. He had come for the troublesome dog. She had run away again and he was certain she'd come back to where she'd been given a home. Then he saw in the closet of the bedroom, a rum bottle, a clean tumbler. The silent bottle was three-quarters full, its seal neatly peeled off the cap.

Rodney stood at the house corner, his smokes in the car. He listened for the cricket to chirp away again – but summer's long past, how can you hope to find your mate? No call answered you, yet, ache bled in song. I said, the year's done for you. So, go. Snows fall now. That'll sort you into silence. Rodney, an index and thumb in his mouth, whistled shrill and long.

He got into his car and eased past the first click of his ignition, lights lighting the dash. He drew on the outside beams, sat to study the gypsum drive, then the back of the house. He rolled down the window to call, but the plague did not come. Bite was in the air. He rolled up the glass and started his engine, reversing with clutch pressed and brakes pumped. Tires took grip.

He drove the dips of the Crick past the new Woody Shore sign. He drove to the Liquor Store junction where he signalled right at the buckshot Stop sign. He moved out onto the Cabot Trail and crept past the Royal Canadian Mounted Police Station, climbing the hill at MacEvoy's General Store, twisting right past the Stone Building at road's centre. At the Cape Breton Highland's National Park entrance he came under the blinking yellow hazard, the park toll booth. He dimmed lights for a car at the Keltic Lodge crossroads, but left them dim, as this stretch had its own streetlights. Eyes adjusted further in more good light at Ingonish Beach Campgrounds. But he braked the worn corner of his pedal coming down the Church Hill, where he signalled, braked centrally this time, steering abruptly onto generous gravel of the graveyard parking shoulder. Saint Peter's Church. He cut wheels, jiggled the shift, yanked the emergency brake and stepped off the clutch. He reached in the dash for his bottle then drew up his door handle.

Getting out, he stood with chin high, to breathe. He peered up the broad fairway of Number Fifteen, searching its darkness for local anglers who found their night crawlers by flashlight here on summer nights. He looked for the Glebe and saw lights firmly extinguished. He studied the neighbouring priest residence where a single light burned, an upstairs bulb lighting a page, a ribbon. How did they spend their nights now that it grew bleak with the coming cold? A clergy, not from here? Neither shore-travelled nor woods-wary, where only there is left behind the mounting sin. He opened his trunk, got out a mallet and straining sack.

Over mown church lawn he passed under the magnificence of the north steeple. He turned at one point to see his wagon illuminated by streetlight, a yellow orange. Buzz and click came from highway bulb and shade, where most shine caught a bushy apple tree, whose depths were a black ground filled with fallen black apples.

He stayed off graves, traversed foots and heads till he came to the yard's freshest. Here he found his played-out friend. She raised her head: to this kind other that smelled as the former.

"I wish we could, but we can't just dig them up and just give them air. Here, you." The animal would not stand. It could not. Forepaws were so awfully sore and bleeding. This was not an aged dog but one with vigour. Paws and nails were excellent tools but hardly adequate to accomplish the job they wished.

Rodney sat with the dog to look at her excavation, the rocks she had tried to skirt, visible in the dark. He patted the beast but his eyes travelled for the beaver pond where a trout skipped or a frog jumped. His eyes roamed marine warning lights of Ingonish Island then, its whale-shaped mass framed lower by falling off land and higher, by stars. He remembered the lighthouse of that island, how it stood shapely at its high end, south, her hump, her breathing hole. It once waited for night and fog there, but no beacon swung around to flash now: none saw. Fixed had replaced rotating. Lighthouses had reached redundancy. No more their men to man them, their women to woman the men that manned them.

Stars ran for the water tonight, down to a horizon free of dust. Such clear sky can only have bearing on weather to come. What the old fellows knew. Rodney stood to uncap his bottle. He poured dribbles, of spring water.

"Didn't make it in time. Got torn to pieces. You made it in time."

He remembered the single letter he'd found among his mother's personal items, when she had asked him to help look for his uncle's birth certificate. A clipping from the thirties he touched, one of an arm-wrestling match held at North Sydney Forum. A letter was attached in a hand he didn't know, addressed to a Cheticamp Glebe. He'd heard of it, the Glebe, where they briefed those who might possess a calling. He compared dates, one outstripping the other ... by months. It was a desperate letter, from a dear desperate friend in trouble – knowing not which brother.

Hearing the spillage, the dog stirred. She limped to get in close. Rodney collected drops in his hand for her. An owl hooted and trees shook in the breeze when the mallet fell, hammering into the ground the contents of the sack. A wooden cross, freshly white – name and year newly black. Some headstones arrive months, even years later. Starting away, he stopped and knelt with the dog to stare at the fixture, in the illumination derived from the road. He touched the carpenter's pencil in his shirt pocket, stood and went forward. Yes. He could easily call the monument men, but.... On haunches, he gripped the right wing, his left hand tenderly but also firmly at its back. To the cross he made an amendment, one that read:

Strongest Man
North of Smokey